The Su

"You blush," Joshua Raven said to Lianna as she clutched her dress to her to shield her nakedness.

"I have gone from a sheltered life to the life of a dockside strumpet!" she replied, her anger flaring.

"Strumpet? No, Lianna. Strumpet is not a word for you. Never," he said, as his strong, tanned arms reached for her, slipping around her waist.

"Let me free!" she cried struggling. "Have you not inflicted sufficient pain?"

His voice was deep, a rumbling lion's purr. "Pain? No, love, I'll give you pleasure. You're a pleasure-kitten, a woman whose body is made for love."

Her pulse quickened . . . and her protests became soft whimpers of surrender . . . until she was aflame, consumed by a force more powerful than she. . . .

FLAMES OF PASSION

☐ **LOVE BETRAYED by Patricia Rice.** Beautiful Christina MacTavish was an innocent when she first encountered Damien Drayton, the "Yankee Earl." But Damien, who had come from revolutionary America to claim his legacy in an England he hated, wanted her only as his mistress. Her innocence crumbled under his desire as she realized that to surrender to his passion was treason ... but to refuse it was impossible. ...
(400232—$3.95)

☐ **LOVE'S REDEMPTION by Kathleen Fraser.** Surrendering to love's sweetest sin, beautiful, red-haired Hilary Pembroke blazed with feverish desire in the forbidden embrace of the handsome, rugged Virginian she had resisted for so long. She was ready to risk her very soul for an ecstasy that was sure to damn her ... or to deliver her to the sweet salvation of love. ...
(140400—$3.95)

☐ **SATIN AND SILVER by Jane Archer.** At the poker table, Shenandoah was known for her icy composure ... but now she was aflame with longing for a man who was leading her into certain danger. Rogue would stake anything on his desire for this precious lady gambler ... and dare everything to possess her forever. ...
(141121—$3.95)

☐ **UNDER THE WILD MOON by Diane Carey.** Katie was Will Scarlet's prisoner, yet she moaned with pleasure as his gentle touch made her forget that he was one of Robin Hood's bandits. For although he had taken her by force, he was keeping her, now, by love. Tonight a deep primeval rhythm would unite them so that no sword, no prince, could part them—now or forever. ...
(141547—$3.95)

☐ **PASSION'S FORTUNE by Leslie O'Grady.** Beautiful and talented Tiffany designer Savannah Webb had everything she wanted except Martin Ash, the irresistibly handsome Englishman she had adored since she was a child—until he return to awaken the tormented longings of the woman he was born to love, and to take Savannah to the heights of ecstasy. ...
(142225—$3.95)

Prices slightly higher in Canada

Tides
of Passion

Sara Orwig

AN ONYX BOOK

NEW AMERICAN LIBRARY

PUBLISHER'S NOTE

This book is a work of fiction. Names, characters, places, and incidents either are the product of the author's imagination or are used fictitiously, and any resemblance to actual persons, living or dead, events, or locales is entirely coincidental.

Onyx is a trademark of New American Library.

To Ann and David Brown,
with love and thanks for being there
when we've had a crisis

1

Sussex, England
1804

Josh

Sunlight glinted on the smooth, silvery surface of a pond beside a grassy meadow in the county of Sussex. On a nearby sloping hill the drooping green branches of oaks cast short shadows in the bright midday sun. Hoofbeats broke the stillness of the countryside as two boys on horseback approached. A bay was in the lead, its long stride steadily widening the gap between the two mounts.

A brown-haired lad leaned over his horse's neck, his fists clutched in the mane while the stallion's hooves tore little bits of earth with his pounding stride. They raced toward the stream at the bottom of the hill and the bay, without breaking his stride, jumped over the stream and rushed across the meadow to leap a hedgerow.

Glancing over his shoulder at his younger brother, Joshua Cathmoor Brougher Raven laughed and shook the brown hair away from his face. They reached a lane, cut across it, and raced up another hill before finally halting at its summit. Walking the horse, Josh patted its sleek, arching neck while his eleven-year-old brother, Phillip, caught up. "You win again!" Phillip said with resignation.

"That's because Mordren's the fastest horse at Cathmoor Manor!"

"If Father ever discovers it, you'll never ride him again," Phillip said quietly.

"He won't. I'm careful," Josh answered as he dropped to the ground. While both boys were clad in identical brown leather breeches and white shirts, they bore little family resemblance. Fifteen-year-old Josh was beginning to fill out and achieve the height of a man. He was far taller than his thin younger brother. Josh had a straight nose and unruly dark hair that held a wave, while Phillip's nose was slightly upturned and his pale brown locks hung straight. The only similarity between them was their green eyes, though Josh's were more thickly lashed.

The horse snorted, dropping his head to pull at a tuft of grass. Josh moved ahead, momentarily listening to the soft whistle of the wind over the hilltop, then stood quietly surveying his world. In the distance sunlight brightened the Sussex oak timbers that framed the flint-filled walls of Cathmoor Manor. Gazing over the trees and hilltops to the valley below, his eyes narrowed, and he raised his hand to block the bright sunlight. Below him, a man moved furtively, crouching close to the ground as he worked with a silver tool that glistened in the light. Josh shook his head.

"There's Sheldon poaching again—risking his life for a few rabbits."

"Why does Father have to be so hard on him?" Phillip asked.

"You know why!" Josh snapped.

Phillip moved to Josh's side and looked down. "I overheard Foster tell one of the maids that Father is trying to drive Drusilla Chance from the village, and according to him, Sheldon befriends Drusilla. If Father catches Sheldon again, he'll have him sent to prison. But I still don't understand why he hates them so."

"Because, little brother, Drusilla Chance has borne two children, a baby girl and a small son, and they have the same father as we. 'Bastardy' is the word for it," Josh said bitterly, revealing what he had learned about the Chances only a month earlier.

"Dog's teeth! We have a brother and sister?"

"No. Our father won't acknowledge them. He wants them out of his sight."

"Is Sheldon acting as father to them?"

"Probably, and it must enrage our father."

"Who are the children?"

"Fletcher and Roxanna Chance. They're babes yet."

Josh started to turn away, when he heard another sound and paused, his eyes narrowing. "I hear horses."

Phillip gripped Josh's arm. "Look over there. It's a hunting party."

Josh followed Phillip's pointing hand, spotting the group of horsemen. Servants, his father, and two of his father's friends quickly disappeared beneath thick trees in a glen. He felt an icy chill run down his spine. "They're coming this way. They'll find Sheldon."

As Josh flung himself on the horse, Phillip spun around and grabbed his brother's leg.

"What are you going to do?"

"Warn Sheldon."

"You can't! You know Father will beat you. He was furious last time you protected a poacher."

"I can't let Sheldon go to prison."

"Josh, don't go."

"Get away from here, Phillip. Ride for home, where they won't see you."

His brother began to cry, tugging at his boot. "Don't! You'll just get another beating! Don't go!"

Josh wheeled the horse away and raced down the hill, his eyes fixed on the thick stand of trees where his father would have to ride if he were to discover Sheldon. He heard the bark of a dog and knew that within moments they would catch the scent.

While a rabbit screeched and flopped in the trap, Sheldon's head came up and he stood up, looking at Josh riding toward him, his head whipping around in the direction of the dog's bark.

"Run, Sheldon! Father comes!"

Snatching up a dead rabbit, the man paused for an instant, then ran into the woods, leaving one rabbit caught in the trap. Josh jumped off his horse, whacked its flank soundly so it ran ahead and disappeared in a copse of trees to his right. He glanced across the field to his left just as the first dog loped into sight.

Opening the bloody trap, Josh watched the rabbit thrash in agony. He picked up a rock and killed it, knowing the hare was maimed beyond saving. Josh looked at the red

smeared on his hands and wiped them on the grass. When
the first baying hound reached him he snapped a command. "Down!"

The dog halted its gait, then edged forward slowly.
Josh's heart thudded as men rode into view. For an instant
as he viewed his father's broad shoulders and the large
stallion that carried his father's bulk so easily, Josh wanted
to find his horse and try to outride his father. He squared
his shoulders instead and raised his chin while his heart
pounded with fright.

William Brougher Raven, Duke of Cathmoor, reined his
black horse. As Josh looked up into the angry hazel eyes
of his father, the other horses swirled to a stop and the
dogs ran in circles, sniffing the ground.

"So what have we here?" Lord Raven asked, his dark
brows drawing together above the bridge of his prominent
nose. He was larger than most men, and the thickness of
his arms and his strong hands were intimidating. A streak
of fear shot through Josh as the duke's gaze scanned the
woods behind Josh, then returned to glare at his son.

"Who's been poaching on my land?" the duke asked.

Josh shrugged. "I just came over the hill."

Josh saw his father's riding crop swish downward and
he flinched, turning his face. It caught him on the cheek
and temple in a stinging blow that made him gasp. He
wanted to throw up his hands to protect himself, yet he
didn't. He clenched his fists, feeling rage ignite within.

"Don't lie to me to protect some thieving rabble who
should be flogged and sent to prison!"

"Yes, sir."

"Who was it?"

"I didn't see anyone. A rabbit was caught and injured; I
killed it to put it out of its misery."

"And whose hat is that?" his father asked coldly.

Josh turned, and following the line of his father's riding
crop, he saw Sheldon's battered old hat lying on the
ground. For an instant Josh was tempted to admit whose
hat it was, but he thought of his father's two bastard babies
and the plight of their mother. Taking a deep breath, he

answered in a shaky voice, "I don't know, sir. No one was here when I came," he lied, bracing for another blow.

His father's jaw squared as he flicked the reins. The horse pranced forward a few steps and turned so that the duke's back faced the other men. He leaned down, and his whispered voice was a hiss. "You'll continue to defy me at every turn!"

Josh stared at him in silence. His father's stern features hardened, and he pulled sharply on the reins. The horse moved back while Lord Westerly glowered at Josh coldly. Josh knew the men his father associated with had reputations for cruelty that matched his father's, a fact Josh accepted in the certainty that no decent man could long stomach Lord Raven's ways.

"Who was poaching?"

"I didn't see anyone, sir. I heard the rabbit in the trap—"

"Who was poaching?"

"I don't know, sir," Josh answered, knowing a flogging was coming. Lord Raven motioned to one of his men. "Set the trap and leave the rabbit carcass as bait."

"Yes, your grace," the man answered, and hurried to do as he was instructed. Lord Raven's attention returned to Josh.

"You were only interested in the rabbit?"

"Yes, sir."

"Then you may tell me whom you protect or you may reach down and take the rabbit out of the trap. You're so deeply concerned with the rabbit, you may keep him."

Josh's blood ran cold, and he stared at his father with disbelief and horror. He heard one of the men gasp, and Lord Westerly swore.

"Damn, Raven, you'll cut off your son's hand! He could bleed to death!"

"No, I won't," the duke said calmly, his gaze never leaving Josh. "I'll learn the name of the poacher now. Even my defiant son has enough sense not to want to go through life with one hand. A poacher is hardly worth a hand," he said, staring at Josh. "All he has to do is tell me the poacher's name. Now, who the devil was it?"

Sara Orwig

"You'll have him imprisoned, sir," Josh replied evenly, though he felt gripped by fear.

"That I will if he deserves it. His punishment is for me to decide. Tell me his name!"

Suddenly Josh looked around wildly, desperate to escape the punishment he knew was coming, yet determined to defy the cruelty of his father. In one swift movement he yanked up a stout stick, thrust it into the jaws of the iron trap as he snatched the rabbit away. The teeth of the trap snapped, closing on the thickness of wood, catching Josh's fifth finger as he screamed in pain and fright and tried to yank his hand away.

"Damn!" his father yelled. "Open the trap."

The groomsman's face was ashen as he tugged the jaws apart. Josh held his bleeding hand open as he faced his father, who had come down off his horse. "Get his hand bandaged!" Lord Raven ordered. He looked at Josh as a servant rushed to cut a strip of cloth from a banner folded in the saddlebag. The duke moved closer, his face tinged purple with rage. "Let me see your hand."

Josh looked down at his bloody hands and maimed finger. He met the duke's angry gaze.

"You defy me at every turn!" He slapped Josh, almost knocking him to the ground, with a crack that broke the silence.

"Tonight you'll be punished for your defiance and you *will* tell me the name of the poacher." He turned. "Dickson, take him home and have his hand bound."

"Yes, your grace." The groomsman rode forward and swung Josh up on the back of his horse. Josh felt waves of pain come from his finger, but he was more aware of what lay ahead—a flogging when his father's fury was goaded to the limit. Lord Raven would beat him senseless and beyond. Josh shuddered, and turned to look back at the group of men, who hadn't moved.

An hour later he was in his room experiencing a pain far greater than anything physical as he faced his brother.

"You might have cut off your hand!" Phillip cried.

"He knew what I might do!" Josh snapped as he bent

down and pulled on high-top boots. "He knew and he didn't care."

"You know he didn't expect you to thrust your hand into the trap! He's probably furious that you defied him—especially in front of his friends."

"So be it," Josh said curtly, tucking leather breeches into his boot tops.

"It'll be the talk of the village that he caused his son to reach into a set trap. And it'll only make him angrier that you did!"

"He gave me damned little choice. I won't take another beating from him."

"Take me with you. You can't leave me alone with him."

"I can't take you!" Josh straightened up and faced his younger brother. "Can't you see, Phillip—I may not be able to take care of myself even though I'm tall for my age. I can lie and say I'm eighteen and maybe someone will believe me and give me work, but you can't. You're small and you're only eleven. Once I find work, I'll come back for you."

"Promise me, Josh!"

"I promise, and you know I keep my promises."

"I don't want you to go." Phillip wiped his eyes with the back of his hand.

"Do you want me flogged to unconsciousness tonight?"

Phillip shuddered as he wiped more tears away. "No. Why is he so cruel? It's as if he hates us."

Josh fastened the laces at the neck of his white chambray shirt, then pulled on a brown coat. "You know he sees our mother in us. He'll always hate her for running away and will blame us."

"You don't know she ran away. No one knows what happened to her."

Josh paused a moment, then dropped five guineas in his pocket. "She ran away—that you can be sure of, no matter what they say. He's a cruel man, and her parents arranged the marriage."

"Old Betsy says he wasn't as cruel before."

"Cruel enough. A tiger doesn't change his claws. I'm taking Mordren."

"You are? That will make Father more enraged than ever."

"Mordren is my horse." Josh's voice softened. "Stay out of the duke's way. Go to bed now and tell them you have a fever and do just as he says. If he asks you who poached, tell him. Sheldon's had time to get far from here." Josh pulled on his coat and picked up a hat. He turned to stare at his brother. Phillip's eyes were wide, his thin body hunched as he sat on the edge of a narrow bed. Swiftly Josh crossed the room and hugged him tightly.

"Take care, Phillip," he said grimly. He hated to leave Phillip behind. "Do as he says. I promise to come back."

"You have to, Josh," Phillip said, his eyes filling with tears.

Taking the small bundle of food Phillip had brought to him from the kitchen, Josh turned away, pulling the hat on his head as he quickly went downstairs, wiping angrily at his burning eyes. He prayed Phillip did just as he had advised. Pausing at the back door, he surveyed the grounds, and seeing that his father was nowhere near, he crossed to the stables.

In another quarter of an hour he rode away from Cathmoor Manor. At a bend in the lane he tugged on the reins and slowed Mordren to a walk, then turned in the saddle to look back over his shoulder. The gray slabs of Horsham stone that formed the roof of the manor could be seen above the treetops. "I'll come back, Phillip. I'll come back," he said aloud. As he urged the horse to a gallop again, dust rose in puffs behind him.

The next morning Josh sedately walked Mordren. Having breakfasted on hard bread, dried beef, and a crumbling slice of rumcake, he was still hungry but afraid to eat more, since he needed to make the food last until he was nearer to Portsmouth.

The lane cut through groves of beech and oak trees whose thick green branches loomed overhead. He heard hoofbeats approaching and sat straighter in the saddle, staring ahead intently.

Three men rode into view, and Josh presumed they were local men, for they were dressed in plain breeches and coats like the villagers who lived near Cathmoor Manor.

"Hallo, laddie," one said, and Josh noticed the pistol he wore at his side. Josh grew wary as he saw the other two were armed with knives.

"Good morning," he answered, trying to make his voice as deep as possible.

"You ride a fine horse there."

"Yes. My friend and I have a long trek."

"Friend? Looks as if there is only one of you," one of the men said as Josh approached them. He gazed coolly back, urging Mordren forward. The three men stopped, blocking the road, although they sat with smiles on their faces.

"My friend is behind me. Only a short distance," Josh said casually.

"Want to sell your horse? Or trade for mine—a few coins thrown in?"

"Sorry." Josh began to edge Mordren toward the right side of the road. He judged his chances and knew he had none if the ruffian drew the gun. "I'm rather partial to my horse, and his lordship would be angered if I sold him."

"Who is 'his lordship'?" one of them asked.

"My father, the Duke of Devon," Josh lied, hoping to make them fearful of reprisals without revealing his true identity.

"A duke's son alone on a country lane?" one of them said, and laughed. "Doesn't his lordship fear you'll be set upon by footpads?"

They spread farther apart but still blocked his way. Josh's mind raced as he studied the men. His only chance would be to keep the one from drawing his pistol.

"Shouldn't your companion be appearing by now?" one of the men asked.

"He's coming." Josh felt a rising sense of panic.

"A guinea and my horse for yours," one of them said.

"Of course not!" Josh snapped, suddenly urging Mordren to run. The horse obeyed immediately, and Josh barreled toward the man with the gun, striking him as he passed.

Josh had wanted to get the gun or knock the man off his horse. He did neither, and raced past, hearing them yell.

Before Mordren could break away, two of the men appeared alongside Josh. One grasped the reins while the other jumped Josh, shoving him from the saddle. He fell, knocking the breath from his lungs, tumbling with the ruffian.

Josh sprang to his feet, but another man jumped him from behind, and they went down. A foot kicked his ribs, and something hit the side of his head in a resounding blow.

"Get the horse!"

"No!" Josh bellowed, lunging to his feet to hit a man. Pain exploded in his hand as he struck the man, and the ruffian's fist hit Josh in the stomach. He doubled over, all breath gone from his lungs, and then another blow on the back of his head knocked him down onto the road.

"Thankee for the horse," a man said, slamming a booted heel onto Josh's injured hand.

He screamed in pain as blackness engulfed him.

When he finally stirred, pain tortured him from a hundred different places as he tried to sit up. "Mordren!" he cried, remembering.

He looked around at the empty lane, but only heard a bird's whistle in the distance. "Mordren!" he whispered, and hot tears stung his eyes. He loved two things in the world, his brother, Phillip, and his horse, Mordren. His side hurt with each breath, his head throbbed, and his hand felt as it had when the jaws of the trap had clamped shut. He stared at the bloody bandage and stood up, brushing dirt off his clothes. His parcel of food was gone, but the guineas were still intact! He found his hat and began to walk, hunger gnawing at his insides.

Josh hadn't walked an hour when he heard hoofbeats. He stiffened and looked for a place to hide, running across the lane, but his foot struck a rock and he went sprawling to the ground once again.

" 'Morning, there," came a cheerful voice.

He rolled over to look up at a man who sat astride a speckled horse. The man's blond hair was a mass of curls framing his face, and a smile hovered on a wide mouth beneath a bulbous nose.

" 'Morning," Josh said warily, getting to his feet.

"You look as if you had the worst of a bad fight."

"I did. Three men stole my horse."

"Ah, friend. This lane's no place for the unwary. I never travel without LePlum."

Josh looked around for another. "Who's LePlum?"

The man laughed heartily and produced a stout stick with a head crudely carved on one end. "My silent friend, Oak LePlum."

Josh grinned. "I should have had my own LePlum. They stole one of the finest horses on earth."

"Gone now, he is, my friend. I'm Terrence McGilly."

"Mr. McGilly, I'm Josh Raven," he said swiftly.

The man dropped to his feet and offered his hand. Josh started to shake, remembered his injury, and reached out with his left hand.

"Where are you bound, friend?"

"To Portsmouth to look for work."

"You're young."

Josh tried to stand straighter, projecting his voice deeper as he lied, "I'm eighteen."

"And I'm twenty-three. Come along. I go to Portsmouth, and my Ned may not be prime horseflesh, but he is stout. He'll carry two as easily as one. Climb aboard."

"Thank you," Josh said, feeling a surge of gratitude.

Within the hour he learned that Terrence McGilly was going to Portsmouth in order to avoid working in a coal mine. He had no more place to stay than Josh, and his steady good cheer improved Josh's spirits. They rode into Portsmouth the next day, and Josh could not resist staring at the sights and sounds around him.

Duke Raven had never taken either son to the city. They had visited neighboring castles on rare occasions, gone to hunt, traveled to the local villages, but that had been the extent of Josh's journeying until now. He could only stare at the fine buildings, the cobbled streets, the elegant carriages, and at vendors hawking their wares. He had told

McGilly about the duke, and as they rode along a busy
Portsmouth street, McGilly shook his head.

"Aye, 'tis bad. He may send men to search for you."

"I don't think he will," Josh said, instinctively feeling
that his father would never want to see him again. "I don't
think he'll want me back. I expect he'll disinherit me."

McGilly looked at him sharply, his gaze drifting down
to Josh's injured finger. "A father who would do that to
his son—I suppose you're right. My own father was a
kindly man, but he died in the mine when I was eight
years old." He smiled. "We'll find work and a place to
stay."

The next week Josh worked alongside McGilly as they
cleaned fish brought into the docks and sold in the market
nearby. At night they found a room and took turns sleeping on the narrow bed while the other took a pallet on the
floor. On Friday night after McGilly washed, he looked at
Josh. "My young friend, I'll be going to a pub."

"Fine," Josh said eagerly.

"Without you," he added. "You're too young. You're
not really eighteen, are you, Josh?"

"No, I'm fifteen. But it took you a while to find out
that I'm not. Let me come with you."

"I intend to have some fun. Tonight you stay home, and
I'll see you later."

"Terrence . . ."

"Look, it's been a long time since I've been with a
lady. Tonight, I go out alone."

"Take me along to the pub. Then I can come home."

"Sorry, friend. This night you're on your own, and
you're safer right here," Terrence said, and left, closing
the door quietly behind him.

Josh sighed, sat down, and stared at the narrow room.
He felt restless and caged. The odor of fish filled the air
from their unwashed clothing. Standing, he looked out the
frosty pane at ships moored at anchor, their spars dark
lines against a gray night sky. In the distance he saw a ship
sailing away from Portsmouth, the big white sails unfurled, and he felt his blood stir. During the past two

weeks he had seen his first sight of the sea and tall ships, and they were a thrilling sight.

Breaking into his thoughts, a woman's laughter drifted up from the street below. Josh turned abruptly and pulled on his jacket, pocketing the key to the room, a guinea, and the shillings he had been paid at the end of the day.

He found a pub along the docks only a short distance from his room. It was smoky and noisy and he moved to the bar to order a drink, making his voice as deep as possible. A barmaid glanced at him, her black eyes assessing him. When she leaned down, Josh saw that the low-cut neckline of her gown couldn't quite contain all of her ripe, creamy flesh. He felt hot and couldn't stop staring at her. She caught him looking, and gazed at him boldly as she sauntered over to place a glass of ale in front of him.

"Thank you," he said, tossing down a coin. "You work here until late?"

"Late enough," she said with a smile, and turned away.

Someone shouldered against him, and he heard a deep voice say, "What the hell are you doing here?"

He turned to look at McGilly, who smiled broadly, swaying slightly as he stared at him. "Thought I told you to stay inside the room."

"I got lonesome," Josh answered solemnly, and McGilly laughed.

"As long as you're here . . . But don't say I didn't try to keep you out of mischief."

"Indeed, you did."

"Don't want to be a lad's downfall," McGilly muttered thickly.

"Terrence, you're barely older than I am!"

"Experience. I'm old with experience. You should be in your room."

"With our fishy clothes for companions."

Laughing, McGilly took his arm and led him through the crowd to a table where a woman in a red satin dress smiled at him. Her black hair was piled high on her head, and Josh felt his pulse quicken as he looked into her black eyes.

"Meet my young friend Josh. Josh, this here's Abigail."

"*Young* friend, Mr. McGilly? He's a babe," she said with a frown.

Josh pulled out a guinea. "Let me buy the drinks, Terrence."

Suddenly Abigail smiled at him. "How nice. Josh, wasn't it? Maybe I have a friend who would like to meet you."

She winked at Terrence, who sat down beside her, sliding his hand over her knee. "Remember, my friend's mighty young," he reminded her.

"Young and generous," she murmured, smiling at McGilly.

Hours later, Josh leaned on McGilly as they tried to weave their way back toward their room. They sang, their deep voices rising lustily, and men ignored them as they passed the lighted windows of dockside pubs. Numbed by ale, they could no more smell the tangy odor of fish and brackish seawater than they could hear the gentle slap of waves against the pilings.

"I owe you a lot, Terrence," Josh said thickly.

"Aye, friend. Now you're a bit older."

"Dorinda was beautiful. Dorinda Lucinda," he said, and laughed. "That's what she said her name was, Dorinda Lucinda."

"Methinks you don't have it quite right, friend." Terrence began to sing lustily. " 'Oh, the whiskers of the cat are long, the ale that bubbles in the tank is—' "

Suddenly three men stepped out of the shadows and blocked their path. "Here's a fine pair, friend," one of them said. " 'Evening. We'd like to talk."

"Can't talk," Terrence said. "Can't talk tonight."

"Want to work? Good work?"

"At this time of night?" Josh said, astounded that three men would seek him out in the dead of night to offer him a job. He stared at them, watching them spin. Everything around him seemed to revolve, and he wondered whether there were three or six men before him.

"Outta our way," Terrence said gruffly, and pushed one of them, adding to Josh's amazement. Why was Terrence getting in such a huff? Terrence, who was always all smiles?

"We've got work for you. Two able-bodied men such as the likes of you would like good pay, wouldn't you?"

"Get away," Terrence snapped, pulling LePlum from beneath his coat. Suddenly he lunged at one, pushing him down. "Run, Josh! Run!"

Josh's rubbery legs couldn't function as a man moved toward him. And then Josh saw the weapon in the man's hand, a short, ugly stick. Terrence flailed LePlum through the air, swinging for all he was worth. He struck a man on the side of the head. The man yelled and fell to his knees; then Josh couldn't watch, as he had to defend himself.

He swung his arms, but he felt weak and his head spun, making him dizzy.

"You dumb oaf." He heard a throaty growl, and then, too late, he saw the knotted fist. He tried to duck, but it connected against his jaw, sending him reeling. His head struck the cobblestones and he passed out.

He stirred and groaned, trying to sit up. His arms and legs felt like leaden weights.

"Get up here," someone called.

Josh shook his head and peered through the murky darkness. Timbers creaked and the floor beneath him moved. His head pounded and he couldn't think. For a moment he remembered Rector Brodkin's threat of a dark Hades and he wondered if he had awakened in another world. He turned and stared at Terrence, who sat rubbing his neck.

"Where are we?"

"You're a sailor now, lad," Terrence said with resignation. "I told you to stay in the room."

"What are you talking about?"

"We're at sea. No doubt we go above to meet the captain and sign on."

Josh looked around at the dim interior below decks. It was crowded with men, some looking as dazed as he felt. Ropes as thick as his thigh lay coiled to one side, and barrels were chained to the deck several yards away. It was dark and damp, filled with the odor of salt water, damp wood, and unwashed men. "They can't just knock someone over—"

"They can and they do," Terrence said. "His majesty's navy does it. Many a ship's captain does it to get his crew. Make the best of it. We'll get to see the world. We'll get paid. It has to be better than a coal mine."

"But—"

"There's nothing you can do, Josh," Terrence said gently. "Do as the captain says and you'll get along. The captain is king of his ship, and you have to do as he says. And pray he's not too cruel or unjust."

Josh felt dazed as he realized he had fled one tyrant to be bound to another. He had no more control than before—perhaps less.

"They can't!" he snapped, starting to rise. "I won't do—"

"Josh!" Terrence pulled him back down roughly. "Hush, man! You have to do as the captain orders for the length of the voyage. If you don't, the floggings you received at home will seem mild."

"Move along!" someone ordered from above.

Josh clamped his jaw closed and stood up, moving ahead silently. While his emotions seethed, helpless rage began to kindle. He was herded abovedecks with the other men. Cool fresh air hit him in the face as he stepped out onto the deck and paused, having never been at sea. Overhead, white sails were unfurled as wind filled them and the ship plunged through the water. Moonlight shone brightly, and his breath left him as he stared in wonder at the billowing sails, the whitecaps of waves, and the glint of a fish as it jumped from the water.

"Move ahead," someone snapped and poked his shoulder. He followed the line of men and stood beside Terrence and strangers, but his attention was taken by the rigging and sails of the ship. He inhaled deeply and the rebellious stirrings he had felt belowdecks vanished. He looked back at the dark shadow of land and felt excitement surge through his veins. He was at sea! Suddenly, intoxicating possibilities loomed before him. Foreign cities, places he had never seen, freedom . . . He felt like throwing his head back and laughing.

He loved the ship! Whether the captain was a tyrant or not, Josh loved the wooden deck beneath his feet and the freedom he knew would be his at sea. He looked back again at land; he didn't have a farthing to his name. No home, not a shilling—and he made a silent vow that he would someday be surrounded by as much as he had lost, by lands and home and family. And this time he gave vent to his feelings, throwing back his head and letting his laughter boom.

2

La Coruña, Spain
1814

Quita

Warm sunshine beat down on the white walls and tile rooftops of La Coruña on the Spanish coast. Along one dusty street, the houses dwindled in size to huts with chickens and pigs in the yards bordered by trees. A slender sixteen-year-old girl moved toward the shed at the back of a house, her bare feet as brown as the dust beneath them. Her long black hair enveloped Quita Bencaria as she walked, and with each step her simple brown cotton skirt swished noiselessly against her legs.

A man on a grey mare rode slowly in the lane behind the shed as Quita approached. The white cotton pants and shirt that Juan Lopez wore contrasted sharply with his dark skin. His feet were as bare and his hair as black as Quita's. Catching sight of her, he grinned, revealing white teeth. He dismounted, and called, "Quita!"

Flashing him a teasing smile, she ducked into the shed to gather eggs, but her mind wasn't on chickens. Unaware of the stifling temperature inside the shed, she was oblivious of all but the heat rising within her. As she gathered eggs into a basket, she glanced up when a long shadow darkened the doorway and slanted over the straw-covered floor.

"Don't run from me!" Juan said, looking worried. "I looked for you last night, but you didn't come out to meet me. We need to talk, Quita."

She picked up two more eggs, glancing furtively at him, her pulse accelerating at a brief glimpse of his broad chest, his white shirt revealing smooth chocolate-colored skin. She looked at his handsome solemn features and drew her hand across her brow.

"Mama kept me busy. She hovers near me every minute," she answered.

"Where is she now?"

Quita shrugged, smiling at him and speaking softly. "I don't know, Juan." Suddenly she wondered if he was worried because she hadn't met him the night before. "No doubt Mama is down the road chasing Manuel, or talking to a neighbor." She took a deep breath, knowing it made her breasts thrust provocatively against the thin cotton. Juan's gaze lowered as he approached her, his frown fading. Two years older than Quita, Juan had been the first man to kiss her. Quita liked the pleasure his touch brought as well as the power it gave her.

He ran his finger along her jaw, then down her slender throat, causing her pulse to race faster as she stared deeply into his black eyes.

"Meet me tonight," he said softly. "There'll be a new moon, and the night will be dark. We'll ride down by the river."

"Mama will catch me," she said, caressing his arm lightly with her fingertips.

"No, she won't. She'll think you're sleeping. I'll whistle for you at midnight. Be sure to listen," he said, and took the basket of eggs away from her.

"Perhaps," she said nervously, her heart pounding. "Who knows what Mama will do? What if Maria is not asleep?" she asked, barely hearing her own desperate whisper.

"You can slip away from your sleeping sisters." He glanced at the open door and pulled Quita into a corner of the shed. "I dream of you, *querida*. I cannot stop thinking of you."

"Juan, not now, not here . . ."

"Shh," he whispered, his mouth lowering to take hers. The moment their lips entwined, her resistance melted. She tilted her head upward as his strong arm tightened around her waist, crushing her to his hardness. His arousal inflamed her, and she leaned back slightly in order to run her hands over his muscled chest. His hand caressed her throat, sliding down to push away the coarse cotton and fondle her upthrusting breasts. She gasped with mounting desire, her hips pressed against him, and he groaned. His mouth slid to the hollow of her throat, and he buried his face in her flowing hair. "Quita, I must have you. I love you . . ."

"Juan, Juan . . ."

His hand lifted her skirt, caressing her smooth, shapely thigh, and she moaned in ecstasy as she wrapped her arms around his broad shoulders, clinging to him in wild abandon.

"Tonight," he whispered.

"Quita!" a strident voice shrieked.

Quita gasped and jumped away, turning to face her mother as she pulled her blouse over her breasts.

"You filthy . . ." Señora Bencaria shook her fist at Juan, who rushed past her through the open door. She snatched up a broom to swing at him, hitting him across his back as Quita cried out.

"Mama! Stop!"

"You rutting goat! You lout! Go work elsewhere and ravage another, but leave my daughter alone, son of a dog!"

Juan escaped from the shed and rode swiftly down the lane, while Quita snatched up her basket of eggs.

Her mother blocked the doorway to the shed, shaking her fist at Quita. "You're a wench! How dare you bring shame on the name Bencaria!"

Quita lifted her chin. "I love Juan."

Her mother caught her hair in her fist and jerked until Quita cried out. "Has he possessed you?"

"No!" Quita burned with embarrassment, and her head hurt where her mother gripped it tightly.

"Are you a virgin? I demand the truth!"

"Yes!"

"You're trash, Quita! Trash, do you hear?" She released her, and, sobbing, Quita ran to the house. She was aware of neighbors staring at her. Señora Quesa held her baby on her hip as she stared at Quita.

Quita put the eggs away and went to her bed to sit down and cry. In seconds her mother was in the doorway.

"You bring shame on your family."

"All he did was kiss me!"

"Because I stopped you. I saw his hand on your leg, your dress half torn off. I won't have it, Quita! He will not marry you."

"He will! He loves me and I love him."

"Bah! He's a young man feeling the blood surge in his veins. He'll get you with child before deserting you!"

"No! Juan would never do that!"

"You stay away from him! Your father told me you've grown up. He told me what I should do with you, and I could not do it, but now I will."

"What's that, Mama?" Quita said, suddenly puzzled by the turn in the conversation.

"Shut up and get to work. You have clothes to wash and yarn to spin."

Shrugging aside her curiosity and convincing herself that her mother's words meant nothing, Quita went to work. The thick adobe walls shut out the heat; the cool earthen floor was packed hard from years of wear. She gathered up all the clothing and began the wash. Since there were ten children in the family, the chores were endless. She glanced at her mother as she fed Manuel, spooning the thick porridge into his mouth, dabbing at it as it dribbled down his fat baby chin. Her mother seemed old beyond her years—her body was shapeless, her hair dull. Uneven black strands hung onto her shoulders, and her faded cotton dress was pulled taut over her large belly. Quita felt revulsion rise in her throat—she could hope for little more if she weren't careful. Yet Juan—Juan was an imposing man with a father who owned two acres of land. Juan dreamed of traveling, of leaving La Coruña to seek his fortune—and he had once talked of taking her with him. He was a man above other men, the strongest she knew. He could beat Garcia in a fight as no one else in La Coruña could!

Her spirits lifted slightly, and she was determined to slip out at night and meet Juan—if he returned. She smiled, her heart beating faster as she imagined riding with Juan astride his horse down by the river at night. She yearned for him to hold her in his arms at night and dreamed of stolen kisses. She looked down at the wash and searched until she found her red dress. It would highlight her flawless body, and she would wash her hair at the fountain so that it would glisten in the moonlight.

Humming beneath her breath, she left the house to go to the large fountain in the center of town, where women washed clothes. Hours later, she turned in the dusty path to the front door and saw her father sitting on the porch, his burro tethered to the fence beneath the shade of an olive tree. A fine black carriage also stood in the lane. "*Buenos días*," Quita said in greeting.

He nodded, his white straw hat bobbing as he motioned for her to go inside.

Her curiosity aroused, Quita entered the crowded main room of their house, and a strange man rose from a chair. Startled because visitors were infrequent, she felt suddenly uncomfortable. He was dressed in a fine suit of gray cloth and he was lighter than the citizens of La Coruña. Three of her sisters and her brother Pepe stood watchfully in the doorway to the kitchen, staring at her with their round black eyes while Manuel continued to play with a trinket. With Florinda asleep on her shoulder, Señora Bencaria smiled, and Quita's heart began to beat in fear. Something must be wrong for them all to be staring at her. Something had happened, and she wondered what, realizing they had been awaiting her arrival.

"This is Señor Larkin, Quita. This is our daughter Quita Bencaria. Quita, Señor Larkin is in the employ of a fine Englishman, Señor Melton."

Quita's puzzlement deepened, and she wondered why the Englishman was a guest in her home. Her mother continued to explain, and Quita recognized a note of satisfaction in her voice. "Señor Melton needs a maid. We have learned of this through Aunt Amparo, who contacted Señor Larkin."

Quita's blood began to run cold as it dawned on her what lay ahead. Resignation and relief were evident in her mother's expression. Beside her a shadow appeared, as her father joined them, standing quietly by the door.

"You're grown now, Quita," Señora Bencaria ventured. "This is a good position and will teach you much. You will go to England to be Señor Melton's maid."

"To England!"

"You will return in a year, and perhaps you will find a suitable position in Spain."

She could hardly believe her ears as she stared at her mother. "No, Mama! I beg you, no!"

"Quita!" Señor Bencaria snapped while Señor Larkin frowned.

"If the girl doesn't want to come—"

"Of course she does. It's simply a surprise," her mother explained smoothly. "If you'll excuse my daughter and me for a moment, we shall talk."

"Of course," said Señor Larkin, and left the house to stand outside.

"Please," Quita gasped, "don't send me away."

"You're a difficult girl, and this position will be good for you. The pay is generous; they will supply everything you need, and you'll return in a year."

"No, please! I won't go!"

"You have no choice," her father said.

Quita began to cry. "Please . . ."

"Your things are tied in a bundle, ready for you," Señora Bencaria said. "Señor Larkin said they will furnish you with new clothes—Señor Melton is a wealthy man."

"You would send your own daughter away?!" Quita gasped, gripping her mother's arm. She looked into Señora Bencaria's black eyes, only to come up against firm resolution—there would be one less mouth to feed, and her mother wouldn't have to worry about her virtue.

"They want a willing worker," her father said quietly.

"You won't let me stay?" Quita persisted. "Juan—he will—"

"He has announced that he will marry Omayra Gomez," Señor Bencaria said in a flat voice.

Quita stared at him in disbelief. "It cannot be!"

"Arturo told me this afternoon. It is the truth—Juan

intended to tell you himself. He told me of the dowry the couple will receive, and how Omayra's father needs a strong hand on the farm. I do not lie to you, but Juan will come if you must hear it from him.''

Quita stared at her father, feeling as if someone were grinding her into the dust bit by bit. Knowing her father never lied, Quita now understood why Juan had insisted on speaking with her later that night.

''I will go,'' she agreed, seeing no escape but to yield to their wishes. She would not stay and watch Juan marry Omayra.

Her mother stepped forward to hug her; then her father took her arm. ''The Englishman will take you in the carriage to the ship where your new employer is waiting. You will sail for England today.''

''Here are your things,'' her mother said, handing her a small bundle. Quita looked around at her younger brothers sitting on the dirt floor, her shocked sisters who leaned against the wobbly, crudely built wooden table covered with crumbs and corn. Suddenly the girls ran toward her for a final hug. Squeezing them, she bid farewell and swiftly left her home, blinking in the bright sunshine.

Down the lane, she saw a solitary figure astride a horse. Juan watched her, turning away as she came outside. Fighting back tears, she was determined not to cry over the man who had deceived her, kissing her passionately when he knew he was betrothed to another. Each breath hurt as she walked across the dusty yard to climb into the carriage, her chin raised as high as she could manage. She didn't look back, but stared ahead, unseeing, too numb to cry.

Within the hour she was presented to Señor Melton, a cold, blue-eyed Englishman who barely gave her a glance, having heard her qualifications from his valet. ''You're willing to journey to England?'' he asked in fluent Spanish.

''*Sí*, Señor Melton.''

''It's Mr. Melton. You must learn to speak English. It is said that you know a smattering of English from your aunt, who worked for an Englishwoman.''

''Yes, sir. I know a little English.''

"Very well. Your family agrees that you may go with us. Mr. Larkin will tell you your duties and go over the employment with you."

"Yes, sir," she said, and curtsied before she left the room to wait in an anteroom with a woman and man who were also being hired. The man was called in next and the woman glanced at Quita. "You look ill. Are you all right?"

"*Sí.*"

"I'm Conchita," the older woman said. "Do you speak English?"

"A little."

"I will teach you, if you like."

"Thank you."

"They say England is beautiful, and Squire Melton is a farmer."

Quita nodded, her attention drifting back to Juan, attempting to shut out his laughing black eyes and, in his stead, to picture an English farm.

3

Wiltshire, England
1815

Lianna and Edwin

Lianna Melton slid out of her saddle and sank down onto the green, grassy bank of a stream, relaxing in the cool shade of a beech tree. The musical gurgling of the stream was interrupted by the snorting of Edwin Stafford's horse as he tethered it. Edwin's gaze swept the glen, well-hidden by trees and undergrowth, and he felt a surge of satisfaction. He and Lianna were well out of sight of his father, who was working at the stable, and Lianna's father wasn't yet home from Spain.

Edwin dropped down beside her, folding his long, booted legs beneath him.

Gazing at each other, they laughed simultaneously. "I win again," he said triumphantly, searching her wide blue eyes, yearning to thrust his hands into the disheveled tresses of raven hair, and feeling a familiar stir of desire.

"And you have never claimed the prize, Edwin, in all the years you have been besting me in races. How very foolish!" she teased.

Her eyes sparkled, and he could detect the faint scent of rosewater on her creamy skin. His gaze swept over her swiftly, taking in her slender body and waist that looked as if he could span it with his hands, crowned by the lush promise of the curve of her breasts. He knew what a sheltered life she led; her father seldom let her off the farm, and just as seldom allowed visitors. Edwin was certain that she had never been kissed. His gaze lowered to her lips, and he could barely restrain himself from reaching out to crush her in his arms. She was beautiful, and reminded him of all that he was denied in the world.

"Perhaps today I'll claim that prize," he said softly.

Her brows arched, and she looked at him quizzically. "What will you claim? We didn't wager."

She was a child inside a woman's body, ripe and ready for the first man to awaken her. He reached out to tilt her face upward to his own. He saw the sudden flicker in her eyes, knowing that with his touch he had crossed an invisible boundary that had separated them all through childhood, the division between landed gentry and servant.

Her eyes widened as she looked up at him, inspiring a flash of heat in his loins. He wanted to tumble her in the grass and take her, but he knew she was as forbidden to him as royalty. Being a stablehand, he wasn't allowed to think of her on equal terms.

He leaned closer, his pulse pounding as she gazed at him in innocence. Lowering his head, he pressed his lips to hers, fighting the urge to thrust his tongue into her mouth.

Her lashes came down and for an instant she allowed the innocent kiss, before abruptly pulling away. "Edwin!"

He clenched his fists, admonishing himself for lack of control. "Sorry, Lianna. I couldn't resist. You're so beautiful."

Pink stained her cheeks. "Edwin, really!"

She breathed deeply, causing the riding habit to hug her rounded curves. His gaze swept over her again, and he threw caution to the wind, leaning forward to kiss her lightly again. "I think I've wanted to do that for years," he whispered.

"For years?" Lianna's eyes widened in surprise. Behind them twigs snapped, and Edwin straightened, turning swiftly in alarm. He relaxed as he recognized the long narrow face and sandy hair of his friend Byron Cleve, another groom. Byron said cheerfully, "There you are, Miss Melton! Your father's carriage has been spotted approaching the manor."

"Papa's home!" she said, and stood up, brushing the twigs off her blue velvet skirt, but gazing at Edwin with an expression filled with unspoken questions.

Silently Edwin damned Byron for the interruption, though he knew it was just as well. He shouldn't have kissed Lianna, because he knew how vulnerable she was, but his blood had pounded with desire. Edwin untied the horses and lifted her into the saddle. She paused before she mounted, her blue eyes sparkling as she said, "I can't wait to show Papa the jumps I can take on Midnight."

"Lianna, don't expect too much," Edwin prompted gently.

Her features clouded as her smile vanished. She blinked as if to dispel gathering tears. "I know, but I always hope he'll care."

She mounted quickly and urged the horse forward. More slowly, Edwin climbed into his saddle and turned toward home as Byron rode beside him.

"Damn you for your interruptions," Edwin said calmly.

"You prefer to get caught by Squire Melton? You risked your neck—but was it worth it?"

When Edwin looked around sharply, Byron grinned. "I saw you kiss her. Squire Melton would send you and your father packing if he knew."

"He won't ever know, and it was only the first time."

"Lots of good it'll do you. You can't get any closer than you did today." Edwin stiffened, hating to hear the truth. Byron glanced at him sharply. "You let your station in life eat at you."

"I won't live like my father—I'll have riches."

"You must be daft. How can you possibly help yourself by kissing the lady of the manor? Even if she were in love with you, Squire would send you away, or worse. Those books you read won't change your fortune, either."

"No, but they'll help me speak like a gentleman instead of a lackey."

"Look at Squire Melton—he never has the attention or friendship of the noblemen in the county, something you know full well he wants."

"The man doesn't know how to be a friend to anything

except a gold coin," Edwin said bitterly, and urged his horse into a canter. Resentment built inside him when he thought of how simple life was for Lianna because she was born into wealth. Edwin had decided he would one day be rich regardless of how he attained his wealth. If only he could wed Lianna! The man who became her husband would possess the land, ships, and riches that she stood to inherit. There would also be a sizable dowry for the man who bedded her legally. He ground his teeth together, knowing that his chances of marriage to Lianna were as likely as the sun falling from the sky.

When he slowed and Byron caught up again, Byron persisted, "You might as well cast your eye on your own level—there be a few in the kitchen who would be more fun to tumble than that Miss Melton."

"Watch your tongue, Byron!"

"Ah, your hide is thin. She's most likely as cold as her stone father."

"No, she's not."

Byron shrugged his thin shoulders, his hazel eyes assessing his friend's reactions. "Perhaps not, but cold or warm, he'll marry her off where it best suits his pocket. You can count on it."

"You're right about that," Edwin agreed angrily. He lashed his horse in frustration, urging him forward, wanting to beat Byron back to the stables, attempting to burn off his anger in a race.

Lianna dismounted and handed the reins to a servant before rushing upstairs. Edwin's words echoed in her mind; over and over she heard his whispered voice: "*I've wanted to do that for years.*"

Her heart raced as she remembered his lips pressed to hers, his deep gray eyes that darkened like storm clouds.

"Edwin!" She spoke his name softly, stepping into her room and closing the door behind her. Her cheeks were pink, and she felt a warm glow when she imagined his kiss. She touched her lips, recalling the sensations she had felt.

Her heart seemed to blossom and open, wanting love

more than anything. She stared into space, seeing only
Edwin, wondering how he truly felt about her. Her pleasant reverie came to an end, however, when a cold realization hit her—her father would never approve! At the thought
of her stern father, despair engulfed her. Even if he knew
that she and Edwin loved each other beyond measure, her
father would never consent to their union. He had informed her long ago that he would arrange her marriage to
a suitable man, and she knew she had no choice in the
matter. She shook her head, refusing to worry about marriage now. Edwin's kiss was exciting.

"Edwin! My dear Edwin . . ." Smiling with happiness,
she brushed her hair, looking in the glass at the black hair
she had inherited from her Spanish mother and the blue
eyes from her English father. English and Spanish. It was an
odd combination that she rarely thought about, knowing
that her father had met her mother during his long-ago
travels in Spain and persuaded her family to let him wed
her and bring her to England. Josefina Anastacio had been
married briefly before, though her husband had been killed
a month after the wedding. If her marriage to Charles
Melton had not been the second one, Josefina's family
wouldn't have allowed her to wed an Englishman.

Lianna had learned about her parents from a servant,
Doria, who had been in her mother's employ, coming with
her to England from Spain. Dimly she recalled the soft
voice of her Spanish mother, who had died three years
after Lianna's birth. Now, thirteen years later, Lianna had
only a blurred memory of warmth and love, of a lilting
voice and soft hands, a recollection that had become so
familiar through the years. Lianna wondered if it were a
memory or a dream.

Humming as she brushed her hair, Lianna thought about
how long her father had been away this trip. An aunt, the
last Spanish relative in La Coruña, had died, and he had
gone to settle the estate and claim his inheritance. Lianna
looked out the upstairs window and saw the column of
dust rising along the lane. Racing down the stairs, she
hurried outside. While she stood awaiting him, servants
lined up inside the hall to greet the master upon his return.

Finally two dusty carriages lurched to a halt. The driver climbed down to hold open the door, and her father stepped out, pushing a tall beaver hat down on his balding head. His blue eyes swept over Lianna as he strode up the stone stairs, his features stern above a full, bushy brown beard.

"Papa!" She ran forward to meet him, stopping abruptly when she heard his harsh tone.

"Lianna, you forgot to curtsy."

"Oh, Papa, I'm so glad—" She said as she curtsied, her words ending abruptly as he interrupted her.

"I've had a weary journey. We'll talk later." He stepped into the house without a smile.

Hurting inside, telling herself she shouldn't have expected anything different, Lianna felt a lump in her throat, but in the long months of his absence, in the empty house with only servants for companions, she had imagined a different homecoming. Hot tears stung her eyes and she chided herself for hoping he would be different this time. She glanced at the unfamiliar servants standing beside the second carriage. One was a girl Lianna guessed to be near her own age. Wide brown eyes stared briefly and midnight hair fell in a cloud across her shoulders. She nodded, smiling, and Lianna smiled in return, then turned to go inside.

In the wide front hall, her father took off his hat and cape. Lianna stared at him—hungry for companionship, news about his travels to Spain, and, most of all, his love.

He nodded to the servants, pausing in front of Hastings, the majordomo. "In addition to two horses, one of which is for my daughter, I have brought three new servants from Spain. See to their quarters and duties."

"Yes, sir."

Lianna felt stunned, listening to the words "one for my daughter." He *did* care! In spite of his inability to communicate with her, he had brought her a gift! She wiped her eyes hastily and hurried to the bottom of the stairs. "Papa! Which horse is mine?"

"The black gelding."

"Thank you! Oh, thank you!"

He turned away to climb the stairs, and she smiled

broadly, rushing outside to see her horse. Within the hour she had it saddled, prancing in a circle before Edwin in the riding ring beside the stable. As the horse trotted and kicked up puffs of dust, Edwin stood in the center, hands on his hips.

"Papa brought me this horse from La Coruña, so I shall name him Coruña!"

" 'Tis good you dropped the 'La.' And 'tis a ridiculous name for a horse!" Edwin said gruffly.

"Aren't you the grouch suddenly! Are you jealous of my gift, Edwin?" she teased, sure that this was an impossibility.

"No!" Startling her, he turned away abruptly, and she thought she might have hurt his feelings. She dismounted swiftly, leading the horse to where Edwin had stopped beside the high wooden fence.

"Edwin, I was teasing. It never occurred to me that it might be true—you can ride every horse in the stable."

"I'm not jealous of your damned horse!" he snapped, clenching his fists and turning to face her.

"What is it?" she asked, shocked at the unbridled anger in his eyes.

"I'm jealous of the man who will someday seek your hand in marriage, of the man who will someday court you and kiss you!" His words poured out in a violent stream.

The world spun with his answer, and she reached out to grip the fence, clinging to it as her heart thudded. "You love me, Edwin?" she whispered, rendered dizzy by his answer.

His blue eyes were possessed, and his voice harsh as he said, "You are everything in the world I want—I dream about you."

Shocked beyond words to hear him declare his feelings and speak so frankly, she was stunned. Edwin loved her. For the first time since the death of her mother, she felt as if someone cared about her existence. "I love you as well!" she gasped excitedly.

He groaned and kicked the dirt with the toe of his boot. "You say that to me and make me want to pull you into my arms, and I can't do a thing! I can't touch you. I shouldn't say to you what I feel. You mustn't say you love me. You have no idea what it means. Damn!''

"Oh, Edwin!" She placed her hand on his arm lightly, thinking this was the happiest day of her life. Love. After all the lonely years, the empty days of solitude, now she had found love with a man she had known since childhood. "There must be some way."

He gave a cynical laugh that she couldn't comprehend. "You're a child, Lianna. A lovely child."

His words stung because she thought of herself as an adult. "That's unkind! I'll be seventeen and out of the schoolroom at the end of the year."

"You're too young to know what your heart wants. You're too young to make your own choices, and if your father learns what I've said to you, I'll lose my job here and, most likely, my father will lose his as well."

"I won't breathe a word."

"Oh, damn," he said in a quiet voice filled with frustration.

"Edwin!" his father called from the east stable door, and Edwin's head snapped up. "If Miss Melton is finished riding, unsaddle her horse."

"Yes, sir," Edwin called.

"I must change for dinner," Lianna said. Her cheeks became hot, and she was aware of Edwin in a manner she had never been previously. "Will you ride with me in the morning?"

"Yes, of course."

"Don't frown, please." She smiled at him, her heart beating faster. "This is a wonderful day. You've said you love me, and Papa has brought me a beautiful horse from Spain." She gazed up at Edwin shyly and said, "In the morning we'll race, and I'll beat you, Edwin."

His frown vanished, and his gray eyes darkened. "This time we'll wager," he added in husky tones that made her warm. She remembered his kiss, and heat flooded her cheeks. In embarrassment she turned away, hurrying toward the house with her thoughts in a turmoil.

Her father was a hard man and he would hate for Edwin to touch her. She burned with embarrassment, remembering Edwin's kiss, thinking of his words. Edwin loved her! He truly loved her. Smiling, she walked faster. The beautiful black horse must mean her father loved her also, in spite of his cold ways.

Trying to please her father, she wore her best blue silk dress to dinner. "I named the horse Coruña."

"He came from Madrid."

"Oh, I supposed you had brought him from La Coruña, where Aunt Maria lived. He's beautiful, and I intend to ride first thing in the morning."

"The Spanish estate has been settled, and as the only surviving heir of your mother, we have received a sizable sum of money in addition to the Spanish house. I found two outlets for our woolens in Spain—which should be highly profitable because our ships won't have to sail all the way to the New World. At sea, English ships prey on Spanish ships, and Spanish ships on English occasionally. In Spain, however, there is peace, and due to our family ties, and my travels there, I'm able to deal with the Spaniards. And deal I will."

"Melissa Hardeston will be eighteen soon, and her father is giving—"

"Lianna, don't tire me with a discourse about each and every schoolgirl in the county. I am weary and have had a long day."

"Yes, sir."

Gradually she realized little had changed, and as they ate in painful silence, she gave up mentioning any topic at all, knowing quiet would please him the most. Mercifully, the meal was soon over, and she expected to be dismissed for the night. Instead, he turned to her. "Lianna, we must talk. Come to the library."

Surprised, she moved ahead of him, crossing the hall to the library, where he closed the doors and motioned toward a chair.

"Won't you sit down? I had a good trip to Spain," he said.

"The house was so empty when you were away," she said, thinking how much she had longed for his return.

He moved his chair closer to the rosewood writing desk

and brought out a chest. Lianna knew it held gold. She had watched her father count his coins endless times. She thought occasionally that this activity was his only real pleasure in life.

"Look at these—you know each coin represents ten more I have in the bank. I've put twenty new ones in the chest today. There'll soon be more. Someday this will all be yours, Lianna."

"Yes, Papa." She began to get a feeling of dread, wondering why he was talking to her about the future.

"I've worked hard to build this farm and to make my ships profitable. Now, with Wellington's defeat of Boney in Spain and the Congress of Vienna meeting to restore the rightful rulers to their thrones, trade should improve. Particularly with Spain."

"Yes, sir," she answered perfunctorily, thinking of the numerous times he had told her how he had built up their fortunes both on the farm and in trade. While he talked about King Ferdinand, her attention drifted to the library books that she loved to read. The library was her favorite room in the house after her own, and she felt a warmth there that was absent elsewhere in the manor. Her attention shifted as his conversation moved to her.

"You are becoming a woman now. I wed your mother when she was eighteen."

She nodded, suddenly feeling a sweep of hopeful expectation that perhaps he planned a party to introduce her into society. She leaned forward eagerly.

He shifted in his chair, slammed the lid on the chest, and turned the lock. "You've led a sheltered life, Lianna. You've grown up on the farm; you know nothing of the world. But you've had good teachers and you've learned the things a woman should learn."

"And a few more besides," she quipped lightheartedly. For the first time in years her father was giving her his attention after dinner, and he had brought her a gift today. She smiled as she said, "I can take Midnight over the jumps. I hope you'll watch tomorrow. Maybe we could ride—"

"Jumps are unseemly," he said sharply, then shrugged. "But if it gives you pleasure, it's harmless enough."

She felt stung, then slightly mollified by his last statement.

Her father leaned back in his chair, his blue eyes focusing on a point just above her head.

"Your grandfather built up this farm, and I inherited it. I'm not a farmer at heart and I turned to trade at an early age, but I've kept the farm growing and producing. None of the noblemen who are our neighbors acknowledge us."

The bitter tone in his voice was familiar to Lianna. She had known for years her father was angry over his inability to mix with the titled men who owned surrounding land. "Papa, there are nice people who aren't titled. My best friend, Melissa, and her parents the Hardestons—"

"Live in another county. You'll be out of the schoolroom soon and old enough to wed. Yet you won't be acceptable to the sons of the titled noblemen of the county."

"Father, there are sons of men like yourself. Squire Landretson has a son, and Squire Cranston. Another county is not another country!"

"Counties don't matter. You deserve a titled husband and you won't find one in this county or any other English county. We have more wealth than the Earl of Pennington! Perhaps even as much as the Duke of Cathmoor, yet he won't so much as nod when he passes."

"I don't care about titles," she said softly, thinking of Edwin. "I want a man who loves me."

"You're young, and this love which you speak of is a girlish notion. Be that as it may, it is time you were wed. I have made arrangements for your marriage, and it is to a titled man."

Stunned, she stared at him, uncertain whether or not she had heard correctly.

"Marry?" She couldn't absorb what he had said, and her senses reeled.

"You'll finish your studies by the end of this year. I've arranged a very good marriage, Lianna, very good! My heirs will be titled."

"Papa, I can't!" She thought of Edwin and it was on the tip of her tongue to blurt out that she loved another.

"Who is this man I'm to wed?" she asked, her voice a desperate whisper.

"I've given a handsome dowry, including the house in Spain I inherited. In return, he's given magnificent wedding gifts. Early next year you're to sail for Spain and there you'll marry the Count of Marcheno, a Spanish nobleman and a man of enormous wealth and power."

Lianna couldn't breathe or move. She felt as if her whole body had turned to ice, and the roaring in her ears drowned out her father's words. Gasping for breath, she saw him frown and come toward her with a glass of water from a pitcher on a nearby table. He gave it to her and then turned away, looking beyond her as if his mind were very far away.

She sipped the water and set the glass down on a table, fearful that she might let it fall from her cold, stuff fingers. "I can't marry a Spaniard. Papa, I'm in love with another, an Englishman."

At her words he whirled around and strode to her quickly, hovering imposingly over her. "You are what?" he snapped, the words pelting her in a tone she was unaccustomed to hearing. His face paled and he scowled fiercely at her.

"I love another," she said with fear, having never seen her father's wrath vented on her.

"For Lord's sake, who?"

She remembered Edwin's words that he might lose his job if her father learned of his love. "He doesn't know that I love him," she said, for the first time untruthful in her dealings with her father.

Her father let out his breath and straightened his shoulders. "Who is this man you love?" he said in calmer tones.

Her cheeks burned with embarrassment. "Edwin Stafford."

"My stableboy?" he asked incredulously.

"We've known each other since we were children, Papa. Edwin is kind and good, and I *know* him."

He rubbed his hands together as he said, "You're a child, Lianna. I've sheltered you from the world, and you're shut away here. Stableboys are the only men near your age whom you come in contact with. I suppose it's only natural you would be taken with a familiar face, but that is childish nonsense, absolute foolishness! I've no doubt that if Edwin knew, he would be embarrassed beyond belief. He knows I would never allow you to wed a stablehand—I promise you that. You are only sixteen. I could have him imprisoned were he even to touch you. You know that, don't you?''

"Papa, I want to marry for love."

"Love would be brief with a stablehand!"

"But you've always said I'll inherit."

"That you will, but no stableboy will inherit a farthing of mine. Don't try to persuade the young man to run away with you. He is two years older than you and should have more sense, but he's led almost as sheltered a life as you. You're two babes—he is still a boy. Understand fully, Lianna, you'll not inherit if you don't obey my wishes."

"Yes, sir," she whispered.

"Enough of this prattle! The matter is settled and you are only feeling a young girl's qualms, which are doubly strong because you have been so sheltered. Your life has been as cloistered as if you had lived in a convent." His voice lightened and he walked away. "You'll like Spain once you are there, and you'll have a marriage better than any you could make in England."

"I don't care!" she cried out, for the first time in her life protesting her father's demands. She couldn't control the words that came pouring out in spite of his forbidding frown. "How can you do this? I don't know the Spanish count! I could never live in Spain."

"Lianna! That's enough! I have your best interests at heart and someday you'll thank me. The count sent the black gelding to you as a gift."

She felt a tight constriction around her heart and saw the faint hope that her father cared for her dashed to pieces.

"I know the news of this marriage is a shock, but you must be aware that you are approaching marriageable age."

Lianna barely heard his words. She saw that her father had made a good marriage—for his purse. He would be rid of a daughter who had been little more than a nuisance to him. She hurt badly as she gazed blankly at him. "How old is this man?"

Squire Melton pocketed something from the top of his desk and crossed the room to stand before her. "He's forty-one, and has been wed twice. His first wife died in childbirth during their tenth year of marriage. She had never been able to bear him children. The second wife died in a riding accident five years later. He requires an heir. Hold out your hand."

She did as he asked and he slipped a ring on her finger. "Another gift from the count. Look at the size of that ruby, Lianna!"

She looked down at a golden serpent entwined on her finger—the serpent's eye consisted of a large ruby and its golden fangs were bared. "That is the Marcheno crest—the striking serpent. There are other gifts. I've had them sent to your room."

"Don't do this to me, Papa. Please, don't!" she pleaded.

"You're young. You will thank me eventually."

"I don't want to marry a Spanish count! Why doesn't he wed one of the Spanish women if he is such a good prospect?" Hot tears stung her eyes, and she wiped them away, attempting to maintain her dignity.

Squire Melton shrugged, moving to his desk to be seated behind it. "Spanish courting customs are archaic, very formal, and too slow to allow a hasty courtship—far too slow for a man of the count's years and a man who has been twice married. He doesn't want to court the Spanish misses who are thrown at him, because it would be so long before they could wed. Also, I told him how lovely you are."

"You sold me!"

"Lianna!" He thundered her name, slamming the desktop.

"Please don't make me marry him!" She sobbed uncontrollably.

"I expect an apology," he snapped.

She raised her head, seeing his blurred image through her tears. "I apologize, and I beg you not to make me do this."

"You've had a shock. It will seem better as the days pass. He is a fine man."

"And you will sell our woolens to him," she accused bitterly.

"To his merchants," her father answered with satisfaction. "The count speaks English, but he seemed relieved when I told him you spoke Spanish fluently. Your mother taught you Spanish, and Doria continued to speak it to you—one more thing in your favor. I told him I would send one maid to Spain with you, perhaps two. Doria will go."

"I beseech you—I don't want to wed. I love Edwin. Only Edwin."

He scowled and his voice became louder. "Lianna, make no mistake. If you do something foolish, I'll have Edwin Stafford sent to Newgate Prison. You have no say in the matter because you're too young. I'm your guardian, and my word is law."

"Am I to have no say in the matter that will change my life forever?" she asked as she sobbed openly now, unable to stem the flow of tears.

"I've heard enough. You don't have the faintest idea what you want. You're an innocent young lass shut away from the world. This is a marriage beyond my wildest hopes for you, and a year from now you will be glad. The man is handsome, rich as Croesus—"

"I don't care! I want someone who will love me! I don't want to marry a forty-one-year-old Spanish nobleman! I want to wed an Englishman and be loved—"

He tugged the bell-pull as she sobbed. When the door opened, he gave instructions to the impassive butler. "Summon Doria to take her mistress to bed."

As soon as the door had closed, he said, "Lianna, look at me."

She raised her tear-streaked face and wiped her eyes to see her father lean across his desk, frowning at her. "You will wed this man. Make no mistake. The plans are set, the arrangements are made, and I will send you to Spain next winter and you will do just as I wish. Do I make myself clear?"

"Yes, Papa," she said through stiff, swollen lips. She hurt all over and she fought the fresh wave of sobs that threatened.

"You are not to be alone with Edwin Stafford again."

His pronouncement sounded like a death knell. It was the blow upon blows to her heart, and her lungs seemed to quit functioning. "No!" she cried. "Please, the last months before I leave, don't deny me Edwin's presence!" she pleaded, horrified that she might not be able to spend the last bit of time seeing him. "He's the best friend I have!"

"You're not to ride with him. You're not to be alone with him. I want that understood."

She put her head in her hands and sobbed, barely hearing a light rap at the door as Doria entered.

"Miss Melton must be seen to bed, Doria."

"Yes, sir."

"And stay with her. She's distraught."

"Yes, sir."

Lianna moved woodenly through the house and up the stairs. She wiped away tears, and long into the night she lay staring into the darkness, hoping within the coming months' time she could persuade her father to change his mind.

By midnight the servants knew of Squire Melton's orders and Edwin Stafford snatched up a bottle of rum before flinging himself on a horse to ride across the meadow alone, the wind rushing through his hair. He finally returned, halting on the lane leading to the manor as he tipped the bottle and finished it. He stared at the darkened house, imagining Lianna was asleep in her bed, knowing she was now betrothed to a Spanish nobleman.

"I wondered if you had ridden off to slit your throat."

Edwin spun in the saddle and looked at Byron seated astride a mare a few yards away.

"I didn't hear you approach."

"I'm surprised you can hear at all, your head's so sloshed with rum."

"Go to the devil!"

"Ahh, Edwin. I heard the news. She's to be wed to a don."

"Damn! I hate them all!"

"It was inevitable. Like the moon above, she's beyond our reach and always has been. There are other lovely women, Edwin."

"Lovely—and poor. Look at this, Byron. The man who becomes her husband will possess every horse, every cow, the land, the house, the carriages—and someday his wealth, his damnable wealth!" Edwin felt as if he were on fire, and he shook his clenched fist at the darkened house.

The moonlight gave his sandy hair a silvery sheen. Byron moved closer, frowning. "I say, I thought you'd be mourning the loss of Miss Melton. Do you love her or her possessions?"

Edwin jerked the reins impatiently, causing his horse to prance in a circle. "If it were not for our lowly station in life, I could make her love me. I could make her want to wed me. All this would be mine!"

"By damn, you love her wealth!" Byron's long jaw dropped as he stared at Edwin.

"She's ripe for love. She's innocent as a spring flower and starved for love, ready for the first man who treats her decently. If only . . . Dammit to hell!"

Byron laughed. "I pitied you so! You don't love her— you love what she owns! Little good it'll do you either way."

"I feel so close to having it all, having her and what she owns, because she loves me. If she could just follow the dictates of her heart, she would be mine and I would be good to her."

Byron laughed again. "How I worried about your poor broken heart. You aren't besotted with her lovely blue eyes, you are besotted with greed."

"I care for Lianna. After all, we've known each other all our lives. But I won't grow up to live the life my father has!"

Byron frowned again, his voice sobering. "Your father's a good man."

"Yes, and an incredibly poor man. He works from

dawn to dusk with no time for fun. He doesn't know the meaning of the word. He's never danced, and owns only simple, rough workclothes. He's never been to London or off the soil of England. Not me, Byron. I intend to do better.''

Byron wheeled his horse sharply. ''Then you'd better get started. You're eighteen years old now, and a man.''

4

Lianna slept poorly that night, and rose early to ride. Her fingers were cold and she needed Doria's help in pulling on the green velvet riding habit. She dressed silently. And her maid's features and graying curls gave her a stern look beneath her starched white cap.

As soon as she was dressed, Lianna breakfasted and meandered about for an hour before the lessons with her tutor began. Her father was nowhere in sight and for once Lianna was relieved to avoid his presence.

Feeling tears rise, she hurried to the stables, where she found Midnight, instead of the new black gelding, saddled and ready. Byron stood near the horse's head, stroking his neck.

" 'Morning, Miss Melton."

"Good morning, Byron. Where's Edwin?"

His hazel eyes narrowing, Byron glanced about furtively and whispered, "He left a message for you—he's ridden ahead and you're to join him."

"Thank you, Byron," she said as he helped her to mount. Hooking her knee over the pommel, she adjusted her riding habit and held the reins firmly as she rode away from the stable.

Gray clouds floated by overhead and the cold wind caused her to shiver. Glancing over her shoulder at the dark, latticed windowpanes of the house, Lianna wondered what her father was doing. She turned back, searching the woods ahead for some sign of Edwin.

She followed the twisting path through the woods, across a meadow, and into a grove where oaks grew in abundance. She spotted a horse and urged hers forward. Edwin stood beside a stream. Dressed in leather breeches and a leather vest with his white shirt open at the throat, he looked like the most handsome man she had ever seen. When she approached she saw his eyes were as stormy as the clouds above.

She reined the horse. "You know what's to happen to me," she said quietly, feeling worse than ever when she saw anger and pity in Edwin's expression.

With one swift movement he lifted her down and crushed her to him, loosening his hold only when she began to sob.

"I don't want to wed a Spaniard! I won't live in Spain—I would die first!"

"Don't say such a thing, dammit!"

She pressed her wet cheek against his leather vest, her tears dampening his white shirt while he stroked her head until she quieted.

He tilted her chin up and lowered his lips to kiss her. Lianna closed her eyes, feeling the gentle pressure of his lips. Suddenly Edwin groaned and spun away from her, slamming his fist against his palm.

"Damn! I shouldn't be talking to you, let alone kissing you. Your father had a talk with mine last night."

She stared in disbelief at his broad shoulders as Edwin continued, a scowl on his face. "He summoned my father last night to tell him that you proclaimed your love for me."

"He didn't!" Lianna gasped, her cheeks burning with embarrassment.

"He also made it clear that I'm not to be alone with you if we want to continue our employment."

"Oh, Edwin, he ordered *me* not to ride or be alone with you!" She ran to him, holding his large, roughened hands tightly in her small ones. "I'm sorry I caused you trouble, but I had to tell him about us. I love you! I will not wed the Spaniard."

Edwin's jaw worked angrily as he spewed forth the unpleasant truth. "Your father said you are not yet of age, and should we try to run away, he will have me put in prison. If you marry against his wishes, he'll disinherit you. Do you realize what that means, Lianna—you won't get a shilling!''

"What difference does it make?!''

"Those who throw away their wealth have never known poverty,'' he snapped. He spun away from her, his rage defeating him, leaving weariness in its wake. "It would make a difference,'' he explained, subdued. "Hard labor would wreak havoc upon your beauty.''

"I would give it all up to forget this dreadful marriage. Papa has never loved me, Edwin. The horse was a gift from the Spaniard.''

"I realize that, Lianna.''

She looked into the eyes of the man she wanted to marry. "Edwin,'' she whispered softly, longingly.

"If he were to catch me with you now, I would lose my position.''

The truth of his words took her breath away. She wanted so badly to touch Edwin, to reside in the haven of his strong arms.

His burning anger was evident in his frustrated expression. "I should ride away from here right now.''

"But I love you, Edwin,'' she said, feeling the tension between them. He moved toward her, closing the distance between them, and her heart began to pound loudly in her ears as he reached for her.

"Lianna, I can't turn my back on you! The thought of you marrying that Spaniard makes me feel as if someone is thrusting a dagger through me!'' His arms slipped around her, pulling her closer.

She swayed toward him, wanting his lips to touch hers more than she had ever wanted anything in her life. Suddenly a crackling of sticks and brush caused them to spring apart, Lianna's blood running cold with fear until she saw Byron ride into view.

"Edwin, your father follows close behind me. He searches for you both to make sure you're not together,'' Byron said.

"Wait here, Lianna. Byron and I will ride away.''

Edwin leaned closer to her. "We'll talk again. Tomorrow morning?"

"Yes, of course."

As they entered the stable Edwin jumped off his horse and began to remove the saddle. "I'll have this all put away before Father returns. I don't know how to thank you for the warning."

"You had best take care," said Byron. "Lianna looks as pale as a ghost today. What a jolt for her to learn that she's to go to Spain. It is said that her intended is forty-one years old!"

"Dammit to hell, do you have to mention it with every breath!"

"Sorry. Didn't think you'd be quite so put out."

"I'm sorry, Byron. It's just that it eats my nerves raw to think of what lies ahead for Lianna. I'd take a chance and elope if I thought her father wouldn't actually disinherit her."

Byron stopped grooming the horse, placing his hands on his hips and shaking his head. "You disgust me—you're just like the squire! All you can think about is *his* damned gold!"

"A fine life we'd have if she's disinherited. But if he would soften . . ."

"Soften? His heart is made of iron. If hell threatened, he wouldn't change his mind."

"You're probably right, though I'm sorely tempted."

Byron grinned. "With her falling into your arms when you snap your fingers, I would suspect temptation! But you had better cool your ardor elsewhere or they'll have you in Newgate. If you deflower her, you'll ruin the marriage offer, and the squire will surely have your neck."

"I still wonder if he wouldn't change his mind," Edwin thought aloud. "I would consider waiting a year or two."

"You would have to wait an eternity, meanwhile he would hunt you down and have you imprisoned. She's too young for your plans."

"You're right," Edwin sighed, rubbing the back of his neck.

"Why don't you direct your attentions to the new maid, Quita Bencaria. Her eyes are already following you."

"She's just a maid—as poor as I am."

Byron grinned and poked Edwin in the side. "I think she's as innocent as her mistress."

Edwin laughed. "She won't be for long—not if you can charm her into a tumble."

"She says she's heard about this Spanish count. Supposedly he's as rich as Croesus—and handsome, as well."

"Shut your damned mouth about the man!"

"Here comes your father."

Edwin picked up a pail of water and headed inside the stable.

The next morning, to her dismay, Lianna found Squire Melton waiting to ride with her. Their lack of conversation convinced her that he was doing it to keep her separated from Edwin. Her lessons began to last longer in the day; the sewing and fittings started for her trousseau; and she began to feel a sense of panic as the days passed without seeing Edwin.

A determination to be with him grew within her, and one evening after dinner when she and Quita were laying out her riding habit for the next morning, Lianna approached the new maid.

"Where are you from, Quita?"

"From?"

"Your home." Lianna changed to Spanish. "Where is your home?"

"La Coruña."

"Were you happy to come to England?"

Quita paused, her dark eyes momentarily meeting Lianna's gaze, and she shrugged. "I was not given a choice—my parents sent me."

"I don't want to go to Spain. Did you know I'm to go to Madrid to be married?"

"Sí, to the count of Marcheno. What a grand match."

"To me it's ghastly! I don't love him and don't want to wed him. I already love someone here in England."

Quita's brows arched. "I am sorry to hear that," she

said with genuine sadness in her voice. "It is terrible to love sometimes."

Lianna looked up abruptly. "You loved someone in Spain," she said softly, perceiving Quita differently.

"Yes," Quita whispered, her brow furrowing. She carefully smoothed the green velvet coat, giving it all her attention.

"Did your parents send you to England to separate you from the man you love?"

Quita shook her head. "No. He married someone else because the families arranged it. My family is poor, and her family was able to give his father a generous dowry."

"Quita, I'm so sorry. I understand, since I must leave the man I love as well because of money." Lianna felt drawn to Quita. "Tell me about the man you loved."

Quita gazed into space, beyond Lianna. "I no longer think of him. He is gone from my life," she said practically, shocking Lianna, who felt she would never, even for a day, fail to dream of Edwin.

"I'm so sorry. Do you ever miss your family?"

"No, I don't miss them, because I know they wanted to send me away. There were so many of us, to feed. None of this would have happened if we had been wealthy. I would have had a different kind of life with Juan." She looked around the room. "This is what I want. I don't want to go back to Spain when you wed the Count of Marcheno."

"My father plans to send you back with me?" Lianna asked in surprise. She hadn't asked her father about any of the arrangements, since she didn't want to think about what lay ahead.

"*Sí*. Doria and I are to return with you."

"But you don't want to go back?"

Quita's dark skin flushed and she said quickly, "I shouldn't have told you. I do not want to lose my position here for the present. When the dressmaker returns to London to get the lace for your wedding dress, I will accompany her. While I'm there, I'll seek another position," Quita said with determination.

Lianna suddenly reached out and took Quita's hands in her own. "I hope you find what you want."

"Thank you. You're very kind, and will like Spain better than you think. I hear the Count of Marcheno is a handsome man."

"I don't give a fig if he is or not! I'll never love him. Never!" Her thoughts went back to the worries at hand and she studied Quita again. "You confided in me about your prospects in London—now I have a request."

"*Sí?*" Quita tilted her head to one side, staring quizzically at her mistress.

"Would you take a note to Edwin Stafford from me?"

"*Sí,*" Quita said quietly.

Relieved, Lianna hurried to get the note she had written earlier that day. "Here it is. Don't let anyone see you give it to him if you can help it. Thank you, Quita," she added.

Quita thrust the note beneath the white apron into the pocket of her coarse linen uniform. "I will go now."

"Good. Wait for him if he has a message in return."

Quita was boldly curious. "Do you love Edwin Stafford?"

Lianna nodded and blushed at Quita's frown. "He's just a stablehand."

"I don't care."

"You would care if you knew what it meant. Your father would never allow such a love."

"My father can't stop what my heart feels."

"You haven't even met the Count of Marcheno—perhaps he is a wonderful man. A stablehand can give you nothing."

"Nothing except love," Lianna whispered softly, her thoughts with Edwin. "And I'd rather have love than all the riches on earth."

"You don't know what you say. Without riches, you have nothing."

"Oh, Quita, that's not true! I know you'll love another one day, and it will be better than before."

"You and I have both grown up knowing little of the world. My world is poverty and yours is wealth, but . . ."

"This isn't wealth, Quita! Melissa Hardeston has three times the dresses I have and a grander home by far."

"Nevertheless, it is wealth to me. It is the finest house I

have ever seen. When you go to Spain, you will begin to learn about the world. Edwin Stafford will become a childhood infatuation when you meet the count and see his castle.''

''No, I will never forget Edwin!'' Lianna said, feeling a tightness in her chest. ''I've known Edwin all my life. We have ridden together since childhood, discovering secret places on the farm; he's taught me to take my horse over the jumps and I've lent him my books to read.''

''These are the things of childhood—you'll become a woman when you wed.''

''No, I won't. I'm sorry you were hurt, Quita, but you are beautiful and will find another.''

Quita smiled knowingly.

''Take the note and be careful,'' Lianna urged her.

''I will. Who would risk the wrath of the squire?'' Quita answered, and left to do her mistress's bidding.

She returned an hour later with an answer, and Lianna had Edwin's promise to meet her by the stream in the early dawn.

With her heart pounding in defiance of her father, Lianna descended the stairs carefully the next morning, listening for any sounds, startled by every creak of the boards beneath her feet. Once outside, she knew she was in full view of her father's rooms, and that he was an early riser. She prayed he would not discover her absence and begin pursuit.

It seemed like an eternity before she mounted and was riding beneath the protective cover of trees. She halted momentarily to glance back at her home. The thatched roof and whitewashed walls with the dark oak beams were awash in the early-morning pink sun. A thin wisp of smoke curled from a chimney and she knew the servants were stirring. Before long her father would discover that she was gone.

Abruptly she whirled the horse around and urged him along the winding lane, taking no pleasure from the tiny wrens in the branches or the silvery sparkle of dew on leaves or the crisp stillness of early day.

"Lianna."

She turned so swiftly that she almost fell from her
saddle. Edwin rode from the shadows between the trees
and stopped in front of her. "We don't have long together," he said solemnly. "They intend to keep us apart."

She stared at the stormy slate of his eyes, and wanted to
fling herself into his arms.

"We need to be away from the path."

She followed where he led, branches scraping at her
arms and legs, ducking her head to protect her face.
Finally he halted, dismounted gracefully, and pulled her
from her horse. As his arms wrapped around her, he kissed
her, pressing his lips to hers. "Lianna, I've been thinking
about us. Will you run away from here and marry me?"

5

Lianna's heart was filled with joy, and tears of happiness stung her eyes. "Yes Edwin! I *will* marry you."

He caressed the smooth skin of her cheeks with his hands. "I've thought about it constantly since your father announced his intentions. He will disinherit you, and if he finds us, I'll go to prison."

"I don't care about the money—we will go where he won't find us," she cried eagerly, her spirits soaring. "Oh, Edwin, you make me so happy! Tonight can't arrive too soon."

"No!"

His forceful refusal prevented her from standing on tiptoe to kiss him. He frowned, smoothing a tendril of hair away from her temple. "I've given the matter much thought. My father takes most of my wages for my family, and I have little money available. It would not be practical to go until you're on your way to Spain."

"But, Edwin, that's still months away!" she protested.

"It's for the best, Lianna. I can save my wages between now and then, and give my father some excuse. Your father may give you money to take to Spain, and you'll have new traveling clothes. We—"

A dog barked, causing Edwin to look up sharply, his eyes narrowing suspiciously. "We can talk later. Find out exactly when you leave for Madrid."

"How can we escape with my father traveling beside me in his carriage?"

"During the night you'll stop at inns. Since I'll probably be driving your carriage, we will have easy access to the horses. We'll take three—one for each of us, and one for your belongings.

"It will be too late to hunt us down and transport you to Spain without the count learning that you have run away with another man. He will refuse to marry you then."

"You're right," she agreed, realizing the wisdom of Edwin's plan. It would end her chances of a Spanish wedding forever.

"Is this what you really want, Lianna? We will be risking everything. The years during which we must hide until you come of age will be lean."

She looked into his intense expression and whispered, "I want you with all my heart! You're the dearest person in the world—but I couldn't be the cause of your going to prison. I would die if that happened!"

"Make no mistake—your father means what he says. In his fury he'd send me to prison."

She frowned, biting her lip as she studied him, suddenly fearful she might be wrecking his life.

"Surely we can find someplace where he can't find us."

"I think we should ride to northern England, perhaps Scotland. If necessary, I can work in a mine. It will mean doing without the nicer things in life for several years."

"If I have you, I will have everything I need."

His gray eyes seemed to devour her, and she wanted his arms around her, holding her tightly. Closing her eyes, she tilted her head to receive his kiss. When Edwin's lips opened hers and his tongue touched her lips lightly, Lianna's eyes flew open in shock. Startled, she was experiencing strange sensations, becoming aware of how little she knew about men or what to expect from the marriage bed. Blushing furiously, she smoothed his ruffled collar. "Edwin, I've been sheltered and know nothing of men—what do you expect of me?"

He chuckled softly and tilted her burning face upward, amusement twinkling in his eyes.

"Don't worry. I'll teach you, and it'll be the most

pleasant moment of your life." He looked beyond her, and his smile faded as quickly as it had appeared. "We must separate before your father discovers your absence. Send your notes by Quita—we can trust her. For the time being, we won't take chances on being caught together."

She threw her arms around his neck spontaneously and kissed him on the mouth. "I love you. You've made me the happiest of women."

He stared at her solemnly. "I hope you will continue to say that when we live in poverty. Lianna, if your father disinherits you . . ."

"I don't care!"

"I do," he said quietly. "I know what it means and you don't. Our love might wither away."

"Please don't say that! I don't need elaborate clothing or several horses."

"When the time comes, you must promise me that you'll do everything in your power to reconcile the differences between yourself and your father."

"Yes, I will," she said, knowing she would promise Edwin anything he asked of her.

"I'll go now," he said in a deep throaty voice. He crushed her to him, giving her one last kiss, then climbed up on his horse. "You had better return to the house."

She smiled, feeling as if everything in the world had been set to right. "I'll ride, and he'll find me alone."

Hurrying away from her, Edwin turned his horse and plunged through the trees. Lianna placed the palm of her hand against her heart, feeling like laughing and shouting for joy. All her life she had longed for someone to love her. Ever since her mother had died, Lianna had witnessed her father's love for material goods; there had been no true love—until Edwin.

As she rode along the fenced pasture, she spotted Edwin's horse grazing. Her father came to meet her, and she squared her shoulders, assuming a stern expression—she knew she mustn't look too happy.

"Lianna, where have you been?" Squire Melton asked angrily, his cravat tied carelessly beneath his narrow chin.

"Riding. I left early this morning."

"I expect you to be accompanied by me on all future outings—I thought I had made myself clear."

"Yes, sir. It's just that I'm accustomed to riding alone."

He moved alongside her. "Since you've had your ride, we'll forgo my riding with you now," he said, turning back toward the stables.

After a moment, acting as casual as possible, she asked, "When do I leave for Spain? You mentioned that the date was near the first of the year."

"February 16, to be exact. We'll ride to Bournemouth and take a ship to La Coruña. The count's carriage will meet us there, and we'll be escorted to Madrid. By that time, I'll have another shipment of woolens ready to sell at La Coruña."

Nothing he could say would hurt her now, Lianna thought, basking in the reassuring certainty of Edwin's love. She smiled, anticipating February and marriage to the man who loved her.

6

1815

Beneath crystal chandeliers that reflected the flickering candlelight, dancers swirled around a ballroom in London. Josh Raven stood on the sidelines watching couples sway to the waltz that had become so popular in England only a few years earlier. "Would you like to leave now?" someone asked from behind him.

Josh turned, amused by William Craine's red hair, which was pulled neatly behind his head, though a stray tendril here and there escaped, curling around his freckled face. His brown eyes reflected friendly concern, and Josh smiled. "No. An occasional dance partner is fine with me. No need to spoil your fun."

"I don't know why—"

Josh's smile faded instantly, and he felt a brief flare of anger. "I know why," he said belligerently, trying to curb his feelings. "Nothing's changed from the last time I was here—my father has done his work well. I'm a pariah in my own country, unwelcome in the best circles, all because of my pirating—which has added to the coffers of the kingdom. My lack of formal schooling, in addition to my disinheritance, renders me heartily unwelcome in the eyes of the young ladies and their guardians here. At least it doesn't matter a whit to the men I befriend."

William smiled. "No. We like you for who you are, and I count you as one of my best friends."

"I appreciate it," Josh said quietly.

"Have you met Alissa Bradington?"

"No."

"She is someone you should meet. Come along."

Josh followed his friend and was introduced to a slender, dark-eyed brunette in a blue silk dress who surprised him by not only dancing the next three dances with him but also accepting his offer to go riding in the park the following afternoon. From that point on, it seemed as if there were more young ladies who were willing to dance with him, and his spirits lifted.

The next day he whistled under his breath as he rode along St. James. It was a foggy London day with a nip in the air, but his spirits were high. He was in England for the first time in over a year and it felt good to be home.

Dressed in his best fawn-colored breeches and a brown coat, he drew rein in front of the two-story stone Bradington house. A solemn-faced butler in gold-and-wine livery opened the door. "Yes, sir?"

"Will you tell Miss Bradington that Mr. Joshua Raven is here."

"One moment, sir."

He waited in the spacious entrance for only a few minutes. "This way, sir."

Josh entered a long hall with a gleaming wooden floor. Remembering Miss Bradington's deep brown eyes and the merry ring of her laughter from the previous evening, he smiled. His glance took in the potted palms, the winding staircase, the oil paintings of family members. Following the butler, Josh only heard the sound of his booted feet hit the polished oak floor.

The library was open and the butler stepped inside. "Mr. Raven, your lordship."

Josh felt as if he had had cold water thrown in his face. As he entered the room, the butler left and closed the door behind him. Josh faced a black-haired portly man dressed in gray breeches and a navy coat as he rose from a sofa. "We met last night, I believe," Lord Bradington began, offering his hand.

As soon as Josh had shaken hands, Lord Bradington offered him a seat. "May I help you?" he asked with a frosty smile.

Josh felt like swearing and laughing at himself at the same time for being such a fool as to think Alissa Bradington would be allowed to ride with him.

"Your daughter and I have a riding engagement."

"Ah, yes. I'm sorry. She's not free to ride unaccompanied by her parents. Indeed, Mr. Raven, she's not free to ride with you anytime. You are not welcome in our home."

Josh's anger was tempered yet again by his ability to laugh at his own foibles. He threw up his hands in mock regret and rose to his feet. "Very well, your lordship. Give her my regrets. I hope she understands why we won't ride."

"She does," Lord Bradington replied coldly.

"I wouldn't want her to think I never appeared."

"She knows you're here now, but she will not be able to see you," Lord Bradington concluded.

"If you'll excuse me, I'll be leaving now."

Lord Bradington rubbed his jaw, regarding Josh curiously. "May I ask why you're taking this bit of news like a gentleman?"

Josh shrugged. "You've been honest with me. I haven't been shown the door with some flimsy excuse. I should return your forthright attitude, wouldn't you say?"

"Well, I'm sorry, but this has to be."

"It is only a ride in the park."

"To a young girl, a brief ride in the park can change the longings of her heart. I can't take the risk with your, er, background."

"Good day to you, sir. At least you had the courage to be honest as you turned me away because of my dark past."

The earl flushed, his skin darkening to scarlet, and Josh felt a surge of satisfaction that he had dealt a blow in return. Once outside, he sighed, held his head high, and climbed onto his horse. Three blocks away he saw William cantering toward him.

"I came as quickly as I could. I learned Lord Bradington wouldn't permit Alissa to ride with you."

"So you came with great speed?" Josh asked in amusement. "What did you expect of me?"

"I was afraid . . . of what you might do."

Josh laughed. "I wouldn't call out her father for refusing to allow her to see me. He was frank enough to tell me why instead of merely slamming the door in my face as is usual. Damn," he said quietly. "My past has wrapped around me like a cloak I cannot shed, and I'm seen only beneath its cover."

"Sorry. I've put your name up again at the club. Someday we'll break down the barrier."

"You and your damnable club!" Josh's anger vanished. "Ah, William, don't risk your own reputation with a ne'er-do-well."

"I'm safe," William said dryly. "With my father's wealth, my bachelor status—I'm at the head of the lists."

"Aye, that you are. While I'm a bloodthirsty pirate who's been disinherited, and not fit for anyone's daughter."

"That isn't completely accurate. Jenny and Kate are waiting for a picnic."

"Barmaids and strumpets—perhaps a deserving fate for me."

William turned in the saddle and laughed. "What sweet innocent would you spend your time with if she weren't in the social circle?"

"I don't know one, otherwise I would be willing to spend my time with her. Social distinction and money are not what matters—it is the sweetness that I hunger for, William. A woman to bear me sons. Besides, rich or poor, if the lady is a sweet innocent, her parents don't want the likes of me around."

"My poor exile in his own land. I'll trade you a few sweet innocents for one lusty trollop!"

"You jest, but sometimes the jest wears thin."

"You flaunt it in their faces with golden earrings and your hair longer than fashion."

"The earrings I wear to please the natives of a village in Bahia, and they amuse me. The woman I seek won't mind whether or not I wear earrings."

"Your father really is a cold bastard!"

Josh laughed bitterly. "That he is, and as cruel as he is cold—he'll never forgive me for taking Phillip."

"He has no heirs now. Someday maybe he'll soften and change his mind. My father says old age changes one's views."

Josh laughed. "I don't think of your father as being in his dotage!" He sobered and added, "I don't think my father will ever change. We were always at sword points with each other, for I'm as stubborn and strong-willed as he, although I hate to claim one quality from him! He was glad to be rid of me, but Phillip was a different matter. Phillip wouldn't defy him purposely, for he had a more gentle nature," Josh said, his eyes no longer seeing the London street, but remembering when he and Phillip were on board the *Venture*, his first ship. By the time Josh was twenty, he and Terrence had gotten their own ship. When the ship docked at Portsmouth, Josh had ridden home at his first opportunity to get Phillip.

They had slipped away from Cathmoor Manor in the darkness of night and had ridden as swiftly as possible for the port. The ship had been unloading cargo and was then readied to sail. Josh knew that the danger of their father finding Phillip was growing. Two days before it was time to sail, he was working up on the rigging in a cloying fog when out of the swirling mist his father appeared.

Josh had scampered down the lines, calling to Phillip to get below, and informing Terrence of his father's whereabouts. Moving to the head of the gangplank, Josh faced his father for the first time since he had run away from home.

Lord Cathmoor looked little changed except that the lines in his face were more pronounced—he was not quite as awesomely large as Josh had remembered. For an instant emotions tore at him—anger, resentment, and the dread fear that his father had always been able to stir.

"Get out of my way!" the duke ordered, standing at the foot of the gangplank with two men beside him.

"This is my ship," Josh said firmly.

"Phillip is not of age, and I'm his father. You have no right to refuse me."

"You cannot be sure that Phillip is here, and I'll not allow you to set foot on my ship." He heard a sound beside him and glanced about to see Terrence appear with a pistol in his hand.

"Very well. If that's the way it has to be, I'll get a constable to force you to hand over Phillip." His father took a step up the gangplank and shook his fist at Josh. "I promise you—if you hide him from me, I'll disinherit you both. Neither of you will ever again be welcome in the house of any decent person in London. Society will be closed to you both forever!"

"I don't give a damn what you do," Josh said.

"You will. And I have the influence to do it. You're young and headstrong now, but loneliness will wear thin. I'll make outcasts of you both."

"You're a cruel man, and I disclaim my ties to you! Phillip never could understand why you hated us so," Josh said, feeling his temper flare and trying to keep from shouting at his father.

The duke glared at him. "I have one son, and I don't hate him. You're so like—"

He snapped off the words, and Josh finished, saying, "—like my mother. The first one to flee your cruelty."

"Damn you!" He climbed the gangplank, and Josh stiffened for a fight.

"Get off the plank," Terrence ordered, and leveled his pistol at the duke.

Lord Raven glared at Terrence, then arched his eyebrows as he looked back at Josh. "So now you have a bodyguard. You're a pirate—like the beggars of London. I'll make you regret the day you ever crossed me." He turned and strode down the plank, his black cape whipped by his abrupt movements. In seconds he was in his carriage and lost in the mists.

"We sail now, laddies," Terrence said quietly.

"We're not ready. We have calking—"

"It's seaworthy enough for now—he'll be back."

"Thank you for stepping forward."

"Glad to help out, Josh. I've seen your scars," Terrence said in a quiet voice.

Phillip emerged from a hatchway, his sandy hair tousled. "Can he forcefully search the ship to retrieve me?"

"Indeed, he can. We're sailing soon, so step lively. Get up here and watch how it's done."

"Aye, that I will!"

They had sailed within the hour, and Josh felt relief grow as the English shore receded in the distance, because he knew his father never made idle threats. It was a year before they returned to England, and when they did, they let Phillip off at a port in Wales, picking him up when they commenced the next journey, because he was still not of age.

"Thinking?"

The voice broke into Josh's reverie and he looked at William with mild surprise, so absorbed was he in another world. "Yes. My mind was years away. Sorry. I was remembering when I took Phillip, how the duke threatened to do just this—make me a social outcast. I gave little heed to his warning at the time."

William laughed. "If you had known full well this would happen, would it have changed what you did that day? Would you have returned Phillip to him?"

"Of course not." Josh frowned and brushed his fingers through the horse's thick mane. "If I had, though, he would be alive . . ."

"You can't take the blame for a seabattle with the Spanish!" protested William.

"No, but he would have grown up at home and would probably have married. Phillip was frightened of our father, but he got along with him as well as anyone could."

"You can't torment yourself with what might have been."

"No, I suppose not. The duke has gotten his revenge. His threat has been carried out, and I am a social outcast."

"Only with parents of marriageable ladies and a small group of men to whom you wouldn't give the time of day."

Josh laughed. "You're right!" They rode in silence down the long street, and after several blocks Josh said, "William, last time I was here, there was a man named Miranda who talked of the fate of the Chileans. They were ruled tyrannically by the mother country and Miranda was enlisting Englishmen to help in the fight."

"Yes, to voyage to the ends of the earth. It's their battle, not ours. The Congress of Vienna is just getting the Continent back in order after Napoleon. Who would want to get involved in more war? I have no quarrel with Sp . . . I'm sorry. I forgot for a moment."

"That's all right. My quarrel isn't with all Spaniards, merely the man who owns a fleet, and his sailors. It was the Count of Marcheno who murdered Phillip and Terrence—and too many other fine men from our ship."

"I thought fighting was part of sea life."

"That it is, but torture isn't. I despise Marcheno. Terrence was like a brother to me. We had been together since the time I left home."

They rode in silence another block before Josh said, "There will be Englishmen fighting to liberate these people in Chile from Spanish rule."

"Yes. There's an organization here to give aid. Quite a few prominent men have pledged their help." William twisted in the saddle to stare at Josh. "Don't tell me you're going to contribute the spoils of the last voyage?"

"I'll do even better than that," Josh replied softly. "I'm sick to death of being turned away from every decent family in London."

"Oh, come now, I don't—"

Josh laughed. "Every decent family with a marriageable daughter! 'Pon my soul, I'm sorry, William. I didn't mean you! It's the exclusive clubs, the other places I want open to me, as they are to my father," he said, and his voice became harsh as a muscle worked in his jaw. "Where does this Laturo Lodge, the organization of Englishmen for Chilean liberty, meet?"

"We're about two blocks away from their headquarters, and they meet Wednesday night."

"That's where I'll be Wednesday night."

"You jest!"

"No. If I fight alongside Englishmen in a cause they believe in, will they slam their doors in my face when I come home?"

William stared at him a moment, then threw back his head to laugh. "You'll sail around the world, risk your skin—it would be simpler to settle down to a respectable occupation and earn their trust.''

"Aye, and have a long white beard if I succeeded. How can I earn the same here?"

They stared at each other, and William sobered. "I suppose you're right, but I'm not sure that when you return, you'll think it was worth the price you paid."

7

Wiltshire, England
January 1816

Sunlight streamed through the latticed windowpanes in the library of the quiet manor. Lianna sat with her legs folded under her in a window seat, her pink muslin dress billowing over pillows and woodwork. She was sewing trim on a thin batiste nightdress she planned to wear when she was married to Edwin. Her heart ached for him; it had been over a month since they had been alone together. Her father kept her busy and watched her more closely now, but she contacted him through notes carried by Quita. Lianna knew, therefore, that Edwin was now in London and would be home in three more days.

Having finished her schooling, Lianna was packed and ready to leave for Spain a month early. There were still dresses being made, morning calls to make, and a farewell party given by Melissa Hardeston's family. Lianna knew from Edwin's most recent note that he had been sent to London along with another groomsman to receive goods from one of her father's ships. Since her father had fallen off his horse the previous week and broken his foot, he could not travel to London.

Unfolding Edwin's latest note, Lianna reread it for the tenth time in two days.

Time draws nearer. I go to London on a brief errand. Return on January 16, only one month before we go. We'll meet when I get back. E.

She folded it and tucked it beneath her chemise, keeping it near her heart. A light rap on the door made her look up from her sewing. Doria stood there, her face as solemn as ever. "Squire Melton requests you to come to his room."

"Papa wants to see me? Of course." Lianna left her sewing on the windowseat and hurried to greet her father. The squire sat at his desk with his bandaged foot propped on a stool.

"Good morning, Papa. How's your foot today?"

"Better. Your spirits improve as time draws near to leave for Spain."

She sat down on a straight-backed wooden chair.

"I have made arrangements for Doria to live with you in Spain. She is originally from there and more than willing to return." He rubbed the bridge of his nose. "Lianna, I have sent word to Marcheno about my foot. It aches and gives me trouble and I regret to tell you that I can't make the long journey."

Lianna received the news with mixed emotions. Her father wouldn't have been present at her marriage to Edwin and now his absence from the journey would make it easier for her to escape. Yet she suspected her father was glad for the excuse, because he cared little about spending time with her, and that saddened her.

"I'm sorry, Papa, but I understand and I do want your foot to heal properly."

He studied her. "Your departure date has been moved up. You leave for Portsmouth and the ship to Spain tomorrow morning, January 14."

Stunned, she clenched her fists in her lap. "A month early!"

"Yes. Everything is ready."

"I'm not ready!" she protested, appalled at the change of plans.

"Come now, you're as ready as you will ever be. Your trunks are packed—some are already loaded on the carriages."

Lianna suddenly realized that her father had planned for her to leave on January 14 all along because he had suspected she might try to run away with Edwin.

"Papa, you can't send me away so soon—I can't possibly say good-bye to all my friends by tomorrow."

"You'll leave at sunrise, Lianna. It will do you no good to defy me. And remember that you're a young girl and youth is impetuous. Don't try to send anyone to London to tell Edwin Stafford. I've told the staff that if any man leaves here to talk to Edwin, he'll no longer be in my employ."

She stared at her father in disbelief. He had thought of everything; there was no longer any reason to lie about why she didn't want to leave so quickly. "I've known Edwin all my life. The least you can do is let me say good-bye."

"No. I've talked to both Edwin and his father. Should you defy my wishes, I'll disinherit you. You'll be penniless. John Stafford is a good man and he's promised to put you aboard *La Joya* for Spain, and I know he will."

"And you'll pay him extra to do so," she said bitterly.

"I'll excuse that remark because you're distraught."

"Papa, I beg you to reconsider this dreadful marriage!" she cried, feeling desperate. "I love Edwin Stafford."

"I want it understood, Lianna," Squire Melton said sternly, "if you should try to run away on the trip to Portsmouth and find Edwin to wed against my wishes, I'll have him sent to Newgate Prison. Nor will you escape my wrath. Do you understand?"

She looked down at her cold fingers clasped together. "Please Father, let me wed the man of my choice."

"The arrangements are set and in only a few months you'll feel entirely differently. Now, if you don't mind, my foot pains me."

In a blur of tears she ran to her room and threw herself across the bed to cry. But within minutes Doria informed Lianna that the dressmaker was waiting to finish whatever garments she could, and Lianna was kept busy for the next five hours. She suspected her father had planned that too.

Unable to sleep, that night Lianna sat in the windowseat gazing over the treetops, trying to will Edwin back from London.

*   *   *

The tall masts of sailing ships pointed skyward at the wharf in Portsmouth. Their spars were darkly outlined against the early-evening sky as the last rays of sunshine spilled across the gray water in a shimmering red glow.

Josh Raven walked down the gangplank of a sleek frigate, his long legs crossing the dock while wind blew his black hair away from his face. He was accompanied by a shorter man with light hair across the crowded, busy dock.

"Tomorrow, instruct Simms to paint a new name on the ship. She'll become *El Feroz*—ready to deceive the Spanish and accomplish my mission."

Fletcher Chance squinted, looking at Josh. "Anger can eat your insides out—I should know."

The retort that rose swiftly to Josh's lips was forgotten as a girl swirled to a halt in front of him, her hands on her hips. Dark hair fell over her shoulders and her black eyes gazed in open admiration at first one man, then the other. Her coarse woolen shawl was tattered, the hem of her skirt was covered in mud, and a smudge of dirt was on her cheek, but none of it hid her lusty earthiness.

"Two fine gentlemen out for a stroll." Her gaze came to rest on Josh. "A tall one you are. Have a lady waiting?"

Josh was amused by her boldness and smiled. His gaze lowered to the knot of her shawl. Beneath it, he spied the string that tied her blouse over an ample bosom. He laughed softly. "Maybe I do—now."

"I'll go on ahead," Fletcher Chance said dryly, moving past the girl.

"I'll be along," Josh answered without taking his eyes from the dark ones watching him. While sailors and workmen walked around them, Josh asked, "What's your name?"

"Tillie. It's Matilda."

"Tillie, want a drink at the pub?"

Her smile widened. "Yes, sir."

He slipped his arm around her waist and was dismayed at the heavy, musky scent that assailed him. He wished that Tillie had touched water recently. For an instant he was tempted to haul her on board ship for a bath, but the notion passed.

"What a strong one you are!" she said as her hand rested on his arm. "A ship's captain?"

"How'd you guess?" He wasn't sure he wanted to hear her answer, too aware that she had known many a sailor and more than a few captains. Her reply was lost as a carriage careened around a corner and bumped a cart loaded with fish, sending a silvery cascade beneath the carriage wheels.

The driver fought to gain control while the horses lunged toward the edge of the dock. Josh sprinted after them as the horses reached the edge. He caught the bridle of one and struggled to bring it under control while the driver leapt to the ground to calm the other.

A couple emerged when the horse quieted. "Damn," the man swore. "Thought we were headed into the sea!" While the man talked, the woman clinging to his arm gazed into Josh's eyes, then looked demurely away.

"See if anyone was hurt, John," she said in a soft, lilting voice.

"William, see to the man with the cart," the man instructed his driver; then he stepped forward, extending his hand to Josh. "Thank you, sir, my wife and I are indebted to you." He reached into his coat and produced three gold pieces.

"There's no need of that," Josh said with a smile.

The man eyed Josh's finely tailored black coat and breeches, his white shirt, and replaced the gold pieces in his pocket. "Thank you." He turned to help his wife into the carriage and she glanced once more at Josh, smiling briefly. Her features were delicate and a faint trace of roses assailed his nostrils. Josh was reminded of the world that had been denied him and looked down at the dirt-smeared face of Tillie. Feeling a tinge of revulsion, he reached into his pockets and gave Tillie two gold coins. Her fingers instantly closed over them and she laughed.

"Thankee, luv."

"Have a good time, Tillie. I just remembered some business."

Her smile vanished. "You're going?"

"Yes. Take the coins." He brushed her cheek with his hand and turned to walk away.

Tillie looked at the gold coins, then at the broad-shouldered man striding away from her. He passed a sailor who was headed her way. Tucking the coins into her blouse, she smiled and walked forward.

Josh strode back to the ship, pausing a moment on deck to survey his surroundings, thinking the sea was the only satisfying thing in life. He inhaled the sea air tainted by salt water and fish. He would soon be under way on a mission he hoped would accomplish more than one purpose.

Josh climbed down the ladder to his cabin and poured a dash of brandy in a glass. He peeled off his coat and sat down, looking at a ring he held in his palm. It was a coiled golden serpent ready to strike with fangs bared and an eye made of a deep red ruby. He rolled the ring in his palm with his thumb. Marcheno's cousin was the governor of Chile, a despot whom Englishmen hoped to help over-throw. The Marchenos had murdered Phillip and he wanted revenge as well as a chance to earn the respect of his countrymen. He tossed the ring in the air and caught it in his closed palm, turning his hand to look at his deformed finger. His father still caused him trouble. Every exclusive club in London was closed to him, every home with a young daughter refused him. That would change in time. This was his chance. He dropped the ring into a sea trunk beside his chair and slammed the lid shut, remembering William's words: *"I'm not sure, when you come back, that you'll think it worth the price you paid."*

Along the road to Portsmouth, jagged lightning rent the sky, casting a silvery brilliance across the weathered brown oak walls of an English inn. Two black coaches were reflected through the driving rain. The gloom of the night was no greater than the despondency experienced by Lianna as she emerged from the doorway of the first coach.

Wrapped in a voluminous dark woolen cape, she placed her cold fingers in the outstretched hand of Byron Cleve while he held the door open. This was the moment to speak; she might not get another chance to carry out her plan.

Before stepping down, she leaned forward, her eyes level with his as she whispered, "Wait for me near the stable door at midnight."

"Miss Melton—"

"Please, I must go inside," she said while her heart pounded with fear and with a growing determination to rule her own fate. She dashed ahead, followed by her slender young maid.

Inside the inn, Lianna flung the black hood of her cape away from her face, ignoring the rivulets of water which fell into small puddles on the floor's polished planks.

A great fire roared, sending warmth into a room filled with the odors of rum and succulent roast fowl. Across the spacious common room men sat in a semicircle intent on playing their game as they slid coins along a long trestle table.

With a haughty lift of her chin Lianna ignored their stares. She was embarrassed by the strangers' glances and eager to reach the privacy of a room. Grasping the maid's slender wrist, Lianna whispered urgently, "Quita, I want you to stay with me. I won't spend tonight with Doria watching over me. I shall inform the innkeeper—"

She was interrupted by the shrill call of her name. "Miss Melton!"

With a regal turn, Lianna hardened her voice. Trying to hide her qualms, her tone a pitch deeper than the older woman's, she said, "Doria, tonight you'll have other quarters; Quita will remain with me."

The wrinkles deepened in the older servant's brow. "Miss Melton, when we left London, your father imparted strict instructions."

"Quita will share my room." Hiding her fright, Lianna drew herself up, raising her chin. In order for her to escape, she needed to be free of Doria's watchful eyes.

During the sleeplessness of her last nights at home, Lianna had determined to choose her own fate. There was no longer time to worry. She had to act.

The elderly woman murmured a disapproving acquiescence and Lianna turned away before Doria glimpsed her relief. Motioning to Quita, she followed the innkeeper up a narrow flight of stairs to their room.

After dinner, in the confines of a comfortable room where a fire blazed on the hearth, Lianna paced the floor while Quita shifted the cloaks to dry in front of the fire. The odor of damp wool mingled with the aroma of burning coals. Lianna noticed neither as she bent her head over the paper before her and dipped the quill in ink to write:

My dearest Edwin,
    Papa has managed to keep us apart, but I will not willingly marry the Count of Marcheno. I intend to run away tonight, and later, when Papa no longer can threaten you with Newgate Prison, I'll send you word as to where I am. Wait for me, please.

All my love,
Lianna.

As she finished sealing the letter, she paused to look at the slender girl kneeling in front of the fire. "Quita, how many more nights are there before we reach Portsmouth?"

"Two," the maid replied softly.

Lianna moved to the window. She had put behind her the despondency over her father's callous treatment, but she still ached when she thought of Edwin arriving home to find her gone.

"I hope we don't sail during a rainstorm. I fear the sea," Quita said, interrupting her thoughts.

"Once I am on *La Joya*, sailing for Spain, there will be no turning back, nothing to deliver me from this dreadful union. I won't do it," Lianna said, frightened of running away, yet determined to escape the unwanted marriage.

Without replying, the maid smoothed the folds of her mistress's black cape. Lianna strolled to the window and watched as lightning flashed, illuminating the muddy yard of the inn where glistening silver puddles dotted the brown earth. Thunder rumbled, shaking the panes and adding to the tension Lianna felt. She glanced at the ormolu clock—midnight approached.

Tracing her finger down the cold window glass, she let her gaze rest on the wide ring on her hand, the golden serpent wound around her slender finger. She hated the count's ring and all it represented, yet she had promised her father she would wear it. The serpent ready to strike gave credence to the rumors she had heard from Conchita about the count's cruelty. "Quita, do you really plan to leave our employ at Portsmouth and sail for the New World, for the Spanish colonies?"

"Sí," Quita answered.

Temporarily Lianna forgot her own concern and gazed curiously at Quita's raven-black hair, as dark as her own. Quita's deep brown eyes contrasted with Lianna's blue ones. Her maid's features were symmetrical, conveying a sultry beauty in her full lips and thick hair. "So you *did* acquire other employment when you were in London. You're to sail on a ship destined for the New World?"

The girl shrugged. "A person in London, a Mr. Summers, in the employ of Captain Joshua Raven, searched for a suitable female, one who can speak both English and Spanish fluently."

Lianna's lips tightened bitterly at the thought that a serving girl was free to do with her life as she wanted, while her mistress had no say in her own fate. Clenching her fists, Lianna said, "Quita, I intend to run away."

"*Por qué*? And where will you go?" Dark eyes widened as her brow furrowed.

"I don't know. I have no relatives to run to, but I've made up my mind," Lianna answered grimly; then her voice wavered. "This is my last hope! I must do something before we sail for Spain!"

"Your father will find you," Quita stated flatly. "The Count of Marcheno is one of the wealthiest men in all Spain."

"I don't care a fig for that! When my father returned, bringing you, Conchita, and Alfonso from Spain, Conchita told me clearly what kind of man Marcheno is—deceitful and dreadfully cruel. She has lived in Madrid and had a relative imprisoned by the count."

"Conchita may have exaggerated."

"I'm afraid she didn't. I don't want such a marriage!" Lianna crossed the room impatiently. "You must help me, Quita. Give me my cloak and say nothing. Allow me as much time as possible."

Biting her lip, Quita whispered, "Your father is a hard man. If he discovers I have helped you escape—"

"Nonsense, Quita! In spite of the discovery of my absence, it will be a simple matter for you to reach Portsmouth on time. I shall make Byron promise to see that you do."

"Byron Cleve, *señorita?*"

Lianna nodded, fully aware of how Quita's dark eyes had followed their young servant during the journey. She had seen Quita openly flirting with him on several occasions, but had been too worried about her own affairs to pay much attention. "When is your ship to sail?"

"I am to be in Portsmouth by late afternoon day after tomorrow."

"You see!" Lianna swirled the heavy woolen cape around her shoulders. "No one will miss me until morning. Byron can see that you're transported to Portsmouth. You'll be quite safe from my father's wrath."

Brown eyes peered intently into blue ones; then Quita said, "You'll need money."

"I have some. I can get some kind of employment. Most anything would be preferable to this marriage! And then someday I can marry—" She snapped her mouth closed without saying Edwin's name.

"You have no knowledge, Señorita Melton, of what it is like to be poor or alone."

"Hush, Quita! My mind is set on this." Fastening the cape securely beneath her chin, she raised the hood over her head before gathering her reticule and gloves. "I must flee now. Tomorrow Doria will be continually at my side and tomorrow night she might insist on staying with me. If I wait until I'm in Spain to escape, I'll be a foreigner in a strange land."

"Your Spanish is like a native's."

"Nonetheless, it would be difficult, and I couldn't let Edwin know where to find me."

"Your father will follow every step Edwin takes until he finds you."

"I'll be careful. This is my last opportunity and I plan to be far away by the light of morning." She faced her maid; they were the same height, but Quita bore the deep olive skin of many natives of sunny Spain, while Lianna's heritage of Castilian and English forebears was displayed in a skin of creamy whiteness. "Pray, Quita, that I'm not discovered."

"*Vaya con Dios*," Quita said solemnly.

Stepping into the hall, Lianna rushed for the stairs, her ears straining to hear if anyone stirred. The inn was dark; the customers had departed. Outside, the rain was now little more than fine mist, though it blew cold and wet against Lianna's cheeks. She drew the hood closer about her face, catching up her skirts as she waded through puddles to the stable.

"Byron! Byron!" she whispered urgently, waiting for his deep voice. Shifting nervously in the darkness, she called, "Byron!"

Wind whistled around the corner; disappointment and fear chilled Lianna more than the mist. Drops sprayed against her ankles, causing her to abandon the wait, to reach impatiently for the door. It opened swiftly and a man emerged.

Gasping in surprise, Lianna stepped back as lightning flashed. Relief surged in her upon seeing the familiar face, the locks of pale brown hair clubbed behind his neck. "Byron! At last!"

"Why are you here?" he whispered.

"I'm running away. Help me get a horse, please. I won't marry the Count of Marcheno!"

"What'll you do? Where can you go?"

"I won't tell you. Then you can truthfully tell Papa you don't know, but I'll ride far away, and later I'll send word to Edwin. Will you give him this note without fail?"

She held out the folded note, and Byron whisked it out of sight. "Yes," he said, but his voice was grim. "You can't get far. Your father will be enraged and he'll spare no expense to find you and bring you back quickly."

"I'll have an early start before he learns what happened."

"Miss Melton, brigands haunt the roads. It isn't safe for you to go alone." He shuffled his feet as if he were torn by a dilemma.

"Don't worry. I'll be very careful. Now, please fetch me a horse."

He hesitated and rubbed his hands on his coarse leather breeches. "If Squire learns I furnished the horse for you, I'll lose my job."

"Then just stand aside and warn me if someone comes. I'll get my own horse."

"You can't!" He looked over her head at the inn. "John Stafford will be back in minutes. He's talking with the innkeeper about a hole in the roof over our quarters. If you run away, your father will leave no stone unturned until he finds you."

"Byron, watch for John Stafford or hide me until he has gone to sleep!" She grasped his cold hand in hers.

His voice was tight with agony. "Your father would send Bow Street Runners. He would have me imprisoned if I helped you."

Realizing he spoke the truth, and having no desire to cause Byron misfortune, she said, "Move out of my way. I can ride like a man, without a saddle."

He stared at her and finally answered, "Wait here where it's dark. I won't take long." He reached for the door and emerged within minutes with a saddled horse. He helped Lianna up. "Take care," he said.

She reached down to squeeze his hand, saying good-bye to another from her childhood. "Give Edwin my letter, and farewell, Byron."

As she straightened, a figure emerged from the inn. Lightning flashed, revealing everything as clearly as the noonday sun.

"Miss Melton!" the man gasped, rushing toward them, his black boots splattering mud as he raised a musket and blocked her path.

Lianna swayed; for one brief second her eyes closed in defeat before she faced John Stafford. "See 'ere, now. What's this?" he asked.

The wail of the wind was the only answer. Words failed
Lianna as she knew her attempt to run away was foiled
before she had escaped the yard of the inn. "John, I beg
you to turn your back and forget you saw me. You taught
me to ride; you've watched me grow up. Don't send me to
this marriage. I love only one, your son Edwin."

"Ye both are still children. Foolish dreams cannot help
in the realities of life. I've given my word to yer father,
Miss Melton. I'll shoot the horse if ye try to ride past
me."

"Very well," she said stiffly, defeat crushing her. "But
don't blame Byron. I ordered him to get the horse."

"Yes, miss. Now, ye best return to the inn. Yer father
left strict instructions with me."

"Very well," she murmured, understanding full well
the futility of any further attempt to escape. She dismounted and handed the reins to Byron, who whispered,
"Sorry, Miss Melton."

Byron doubled his fists as he watched her go. He had
heard in detail from Conchita, the older Spanish maid,
what kind of man her father had sold her to. Whether
Edwin loved her or her possessions, he would be good to
her.

"Let her go," John Stafford said, moving to stand
beside him. "Ye cannot help the lass. Don't do anything
foolish because of my son. Edwin has not learned that he
must live the kind of life fate has handed him."

"Her father's a flint-hearted bastard!" Byron said quietly.

"Aye, that he is. And he would hunt ye down and have
ye hauled to Newgate if ye helped her and cost him a
farthing. Let her go. Ye cannot do otherwise. Come along,
Byron. The innkeeper said to get our things. There's a dry
room in the attic." John Stafford went inside while Byron
stood peering into the empty, rainy night, his fist doubled
around the paper in his hand. Suddenly he threw himself
into the saddle and turned the horse into the road northward toward London.

Unaware of Byron Cleve riding the horse away from the
inn, Lianna scurried inside. Hot tears coursed down her
cheeks as she rushed past Quita into her room.

* * *

In a dockside London tavern mens' voices rose in laughter and conversation, and the smell of ale—tainted with the ever-present odor of fish—permeated the rooms. Coins clinked and the door swung shut behind a customer, letting a blast of cold, rainy air into the warm room. Six men sat at a round wooden table, its surface scarred by knives from customers through the years. A large man with broad shoulders and fingers as fat as sausages talked to a golden-haired man.

Edwin Stafford leaned forward in his chair, oblivious of the noisy crowd in the inn. His attention only wandered from the subject at hand when a pretty serving girl leaned over the table and brushed his shoulder with her breast. His concentration was otherwise focused on the scarred, grizzled giant of a man seated across from him.

"Aye, matey, the sea is the place to make your fortune, and pirating is the way to do it."

"And the crown will sanction it?" Edwin asked, swiftly grasping the possibilities.

"Aye, sanction and bless you if you return a share home. And occasionally we prey on ships that aren't sanctioned—pirate ships like our own. I have a ship, mate, and . . ." He paused while the serving girl returned with a tankard of ale. Her dark eyes sparkled as she set it before him and glanced boldly at Edwin.

Edwin grinned and held up a coin. "Another mulled rum," he said.

"Yes, Mr. Stafford," she said, flashing a full smile. As she left, one of the men watched her, then looked at Edwin. "Seems Nan's favor is yours now."

Edwin grinned as his gaze returned to Captain Turner. "You were telling me you have your own ship."

"Aye, and treasure buried in spots o'er all the earth."

"I'm a groomsman for Squire Melton. How hard is it to sign on a ship?"

The men laughed. "They scour the streets of London looking for men to sail—some captains do. I have no trouble finding the right men," Captain Turner said firmly.

At that moment Nan returned to lean over Edwin, her

soft breasts pressing against his arm. He raised his arm to slip it around her waist and give her a squeeze. She looked down at him laughingly and he winked again. "Thank you, Nan," he said as he reached up to tuck a coin in the low neckline of her gingham dress. His knuckles brushed warm flesh as he tucked the coin away, and the men's laughter drowned out Nan's giggle. "I'll see you later?" he asked.

She nodded and turned to go. Edwin's hand slipped across her rounded buttocks, feeling the firm, warm flesh beneath the dark gingham. "I don't want to stay on a farm," he said to the men, his mind working swiftly over opportunities he had dreamed about.

"You can sign on with me, mate," Captain Turner said. "You'll earn a living wage—more than a groomsman. Plus, you'll have a share of the spoils."

Edwin's pulse jumped as he realized the possibilities. "Thanks for the offer." He thought about Lianna waiting for him to run away with her. If he didn't return and leave with her, she would be sent to Spain and out of his grasp forever.

"How soon do you sail?"

"Not for another two weeks. We're having some repairs done to the *Adrian*, my ship."

Edwin nodded as he calculated two weeks' time. It was a month before Lianna was to leave for Spain. If they ran away, could he hide her somewhere and get back to London in time to sail?

"I planned to marry soon and have to—"

The men's burst of laughter stopped his words.

"Wed! Damn, the man's daft," Captain Turner boomed.

"He'll wed between times he beds our Nan!" one of the men said, and slapped the table.

Captain Turner leaned forward. "Don't tie yourself to some country lass. The world is full of women to take your breath—"

"And to take a few other things," one of the men said with a leer, making everyone laugh.

"Stay free, man! Gold and women are yours. Leave the country lasses to the farm."

"She's not a country lass," Edwin said abruptly.

"Oh no! Of course she isn't," Captain Turner said with laughter. "And our Nan here is a lady to the queen!"

"She's not," Edwin said flatly. "She's highborn and wealthy."

The men laughed, except the captain, who stared at Edwin. "And her father allows this marriage?" he asked.

"No, sir. We would run away."

"You're asking for more trouble than you'll find at sea," Captain Turner said, and took a long drink of ale, some of it spilling down his shirt front. He wiped at it and slammed the tankard down on the table. "Are you with us or not?"

Edwin looked into impassive black eyes and felt the race of excitement. Here was his chance. He would hide Lianna somewhere, manage some way. For an instant the thought troubled him that she might be left without funds if he sailed in two weeks. She had said she was willing to go with him no matter how poor he was, and he knew she would keep her word. He nodded his head, feeling to the soles of his feet that his life was changing on this one word as he said yes.

The men slapped him on the back and raised their tankards to him. He picked up his flagon of rum and clinked it against theirs. "In two weeks I'll return to London to sail on the *Adrian*."

He drank as Captain Turner lowered his ale. "This trip, my friend, we sail south, where the warm winds blow to islands where we can get indigo dye and hemp, and we'll cross paths with Spanish ships and Dutch, both fair game."

As he listened, Edwin leaned back in his chair, stretching his long legs beneath the table. As his gaze swept the room, he saw a man standing inside the door, and he felt a shock of recognition. "Byron!" he said softly.

"I see a friend. Perhaps you'll have two new hands to sail. Excuse me." Edwin stood up and walked toward the door while Byron spotted him and waited.

Edwin thrust out his hand to clasp the other. "You've come at a good time! I have something to tell you."

"It better wait until I tell you my news."

"Nonsense! Come meet your future employer. I have found a—"

"Lianna's on her way to Spain," Byron blurted.

8

Edwin felt as if the world had suddenly disappeared around him. "What did you say?" he asked, blankly staring at Byron.

"I've ridden as hard as I could—and probably lost my job in doing so."

"Come sit down. I'll get us drinks." Edwin saw an empty table in the corner. He motioned Nan over as he led the way to the table.

Edwin ordered two ales and fish and chips for Byron. As soon as Nan was gone Edwin snapped, "What happened?"

"Lianna's on her way to Portsmouth. Her ship, *La Joya*, sails Friday."

"She can't be! It's a month early." His thoughts swirled and he remembered teasing Lianna about getting ready early. She had replied that her father was as eager as she, aiding her in every way. "Damn the squire!" Rage buffeted Edwin as he slammed his fist on the table. "He deliberately sent me to London to get me away from Lianna and he lied to us about the sailing date!"

"He's hired two men to ride with them, one on each carriage, and they carry pistols." Byron reached into his boot and withdrew the rumpled note. "She said to give you this, but it was before she tried to run away. Your father drew his musket and stopped her."

"My father?" Another shock struck Edwin, that his peaceful mild father would draw a weapon on Lianna.

"You know he had orders from the squire."

"You'll lose your job. You'll never be able to hide the fact that you left them and came to London."

"I do honest work. There are other counties and other jobs."

"Thank you, Byron," Edwin said quietly, his mind beginning to function. Nan brought the ale, took Edwin's coins, and left. "Where is Lianna now?" When Byron had first spoken, Edwin had assumed she was already at sea.

"On the road to Portsmouth."

"Oh, damn his soul. The squire knew! All along, he planned this! I should have suspected; the squire's not a fool. He's a cold-eyed, greedy man who is iron-willed and shrewd. Does he ride in the same carriage with her, or in his own?"

"He didn't go. Claimed his broken foot prevented the trip."

"He doesn't want to return to Spain. He can stay here and see to his affairs instead of taking more time in another costly trip." Edwin drank the ale swiftly, his mind racing. Lianna was still traveling to Portsmouth . . . there still might be time . . .

"She tried to run away, saying she would get word to you where to find her. She and Quita travel together. She put Doria in the second carriage soon after we left the manor."

They sat in silence while Byron ate swiftly. Edwin drank his ale, looking across the crowded room at Captain Turner.

"Byron, listen to me. I have found a way to have more than a simple groomsman's life. See the large man in the black hat over there?"

Byron turned. "Ugly one, he is!"

"He's a ship's captain, a pirate. I intend to sign on and sail with him."

Byron choked on a bite. "Damn! You're daft! It's dangerous. You don't know how to use a sword; they'd cut you down in the first pitched battle."

"No. I can learn just as they learned. They weren't born with cutlasses in their fists. And I can use a pistol with ease."

"That you can! You can shoot the blossom off a daisy at fifty paces. But you know nothing of the sea."

"I can learn. They sail in two weeks. Come with me."

Byron's head snapped up, his hazel eyes narrowing. "I can't sail. I know horses and stables and the land, and I don't want to risk my neck sailing on a bit of wood on a great sea of water! I don't dream of wealth as you do."

"All right. You can ride back to the manor in my place with the tools we purchased for the squire. Let me take your horse and ride for Portsmouth. If I ride hard and have luck, I might get there before Lianna sails."

"That's why I came to London. The horse isn't fresh, but it's a good one. Miss Melton plans to sail on a ship called *La Joya*. Quita Bencaria is going to work in another employ and she sails on *El Feroz*."

"Who goes with Lianna to Spain?"

"Doria."

"That harridan! Squire knows she'll watch over Lianna closely. As soon as you eat, I'll show you where we stay, and you can ride home with the others."

"Give me one more minute," Byron said, gulping down the food. In another few minutes he stood up. "Let's go."

In half an hour Edwin left the lights of London behind. Anger surged through his veins as he rode to Portsmouth, determined to arrive before Lianna sailed. He would be the one to go to sea. Two weeks from now he would leave England while Lianna awaited his return.

The next morning the two carriages pulled away from the inn with their wheels splashing in the muddy lane. A chill wind whipped through the cracks in the doors as Lianna rode in silence, staring at the cold January countryside. The drizzle continued, with droplets gathering and running in rivulets across the glass, giving the brown landscape a sullied appearance and intensifying the gloom she felt in her soul.

"Señorita Melton, once you're in Spain, it will not be as evil as you fear," Quita offered gently.

"I cannot bear to wed the man." Lianna shivered.

"They say the Count of Marcheno is handsome and powerful. He has a fleet of ships, a magnificent castle—"

"Castle! That means nothing!" she snapped. She could not tell her servant of the dreams of a lonely girlhood, the longing to someday find love with someone who cared for her deeply, who wanted her love in return.

Instead, she merely said, "I would forgo it gladly to be free of this marriage. I have heard of the tortures and murders by his orders. They say the count has a dungeon filled with prisoners."

"It may be true." Quita sighed. "But I suspect half the young girls in Madrid would eagerly trade places with you."

"Not if they knew Marcheno!"

"Oh, but they would!" Quita answered solemnly, her dark eyes as round and long-lashed as Lianna's.

Lianna straightened in her seat to stare at the maid intently. "Quita, whom will you be working for on this ship?"

Quita shrugged, her dark eyes glancing away. "Captain Raven."

"But you didn't make the arrangements with the captain, did you?" Lianna vaguely recalled their conversation of the night before.

"No, I have never seen Captain Raven."

As if discovering a rope at hand while she drowned, Lianna let her mind race over possibilities. Steadying herself in the seat of the rocking carriage, she leaned forward to grasp Quita's hand tightly. "Exchange places with me," she said suddenly.

Quita gaped as if her mistress had taken leave of her senses. Lianna pleaded, "Exchange places with me if this Spanish marriage is not odious to you. Become Lianna Melton, marry the Count of Marcheno, and allow me to become Quita Bencaria and serve Captain Raven on this voyage to the Spanish colonies."

Before the maid could protest, Lianna went on in a rush. "The count has never seen me. My Spanish relatives are all dead. Doria is the only person to sail with me and I can manage to lose her before we sail. If you're clever, Marcheno will never know the difference."

"*Madre de Dios,* no!"

Lianna went on eagerly, her thoughts racing on the means of escape. "His servants are to meet me when I land at La Coruña. Quita, board *La Joya* and sail in my place if you think the marriage bearable. You will have all the wealth and luxury you ever dreamed about."

"An impossibility! Your father's servants guard you well."

Lianna sank back in her seat. "There must be a way to eliminate interference. If you're willing, I'll let no one stand in my way."

The carriage lumbered roughly over the rutted road, but both passengers were oblivious of the ride. After a lengthy silence Lianna straightened. "Her sleeping potions! Doria carries sleeping potions to take each night. The next time we stop to change horses, I'll slip them into her tea. Once she is asleep, we'll leave her behind!"

"You can't!" Quita protested.

Lianna nodded her head in determination. "Yes, indeed, I can. I'll see to it. Consider Doria eliminated from the situation."

"Your father will have me imprisoned."

"My father let eighteen years elapse between trips to Spain. I think he used his broken foot as an excuse to get out of a journey he didn't want to make. I don't think you will have to concern yourself with the appearance of my father. The Count of Marcheno wants a young, beautiful bride to give him the male heir his first two wives never provided. After you have been wed, even if he learns the truth, you should be able to make him happy."

"It's impossible! If the count learned the truth, he would have me not only imprisoned but also tortured for such folly!"

"Marcheno will never know!" Lianna replied emphatically. "How can he? He hasn't seen me. No one in Spain has seen me." Lianna's voice became breathless with emotion.

"But your eyes are blue," Quita said. "If you have been described to him, he'll take one look at me and know the truth."

"My eyes may not have been mentioned, but even if they have, you can convince him he has remembered incorrectly, Quita! That's a small matter." Leaning forward, she fastened her blue gaze intently on the maid. "Do you object because you don't want to marry Marcheno?"

When Quita remained silent, Lianna pressed further. "If you were absolutely convinced you'd never be discovered in the falsehood, would you do it then? Would you wed Marcheno?"

"Madre de Dios!" she whispered, her brown eyes widening. "Me, Quita Bencaria, a countess!" Feverishly she added, *"Sí,* Señorita Melton. I have come from nothing. There was little food, we washed out clothes by hand in the fountain, and I helped Mama care for the babies . . ." For an instant her dark eyes gleamed; the look disappeared as swiftly as it had come. "Madness, truly! *Es muy* imposible!"

Lianna grasped Quita's slender wrist tightly. "No! The only obstacle is Doria and we can deal with her within a few hours. Unless . . ." She paused while Quita's eyes raised questioningly. "What is the employment you undertake? Will there be anyone aboard ship who will know you?"

A pained, almost guilty expression crossed Quita's face, then disappeared. "No." Lowering her dark lashes, she twisted her fingers together in her lap. "There would be no person to know." Quita continued hesitantly, speaking so softly that the creak and rumble of the coach all but drowned out her words, and Lianna had to lean forward to hear. "The only person who would recognize me is Mr. Summers in London."

"What are your duties?"

Quita raised her head, a cold hardness darkening her eyes, and Lianna was momentarily taken aback. In a forceful voice, Quita asked, "How badly do you want to escape this marriage, *señorita?"*

"I would do anything!" Lianna squeezed the maid's wrist. "Nothing on earth could be as vile as marriage to this Spaniard. And if I sail with an Englishman, we'll return—and I'll have a chance to wed Edwin!"

Brown eyes looked at her impassively. "Edwin Stafford won't know of our deception. He may wed another."

"I can post him a letter at the next inn. He will keep our secret."

"When your father dies, you will inherit wealth. This you will lose if you give up your identity and sail far from England."

Lianna gazed out the carriage window at the bleak dead grass, the wet tree limbs etched darkly against a gray sky. "All my life, wealth has been the most important consideration. My grandfather accumulated it by his labor, my father has increased it greatly, but all that money still hasn't enabled him to gain acceptance from the noble families whose friendship he desires so highly." She turned to look at Quita. "Wealth does not matter one jot to me. Please say yes."

"You will have to be a servant with a master—Captain Raven—whom you'll have to obey. He is a privateer."

Lianna considered the revelation. "That amounts to being a licensed pirate. The kingdom will support his piracy." She straightened and shrugged. "If Captain Raven proves dreadful, Quita, I shall run away. You weren't afraid to take a chance by casting your lot with this Captain Raven, so neither am I. It is the only opportunity I'll have of someday marrying Edwin."

Quita studied her intently. "I don't think you'll want to serve him in the manner I've promised."

The words had been barely spoken when Lianna broke in hastily. "I'll accept any position! Think, girl, you can be mistress of Marcheno's houses, of his castle! You can wear his rubies and emeralds. Your children will be nobility! Never again will you have to wait on someone other than the count."

Quita's eyes glittered as she whispered, "We will be caught and punished."

Lianna's spirits soared as she sensed the maid wavering. She pressed her advantage. "You'll have servants, a life of ease, Quita. Your children will be titled. You will have anything your heart desires."

Quita's face paled. Her pink tongue flicked nervously across her lips.

"Quita, if you don't object to the Count of Marcheno, how can you hesitate?"

"And what if, *señorita*, you change your feelings on the matter? Perhaps you won't like your new position in life."

"There will be little I can do, eh?" She lifted her hand and the ruby serpent's eye glinted dully. "I swear, Quita, by all that is holy, I will never under any conditions attempt to reveal your identity to Marcheno." Watching breathlessly, Lianna felt a nagging impatience at the terrible slowness of the girl. What was causing the difficulty? Why was Quita so afraid? Lianna's desperation made it difficult for her to tolerate the maid's hesitation. "Quita, think! A countess . . ."

"*Sí*," Quita interrupted in the smallest of whispers.

Lianna's heart beat fiercely. "Thank God! I pray you have all you desire, and I thank you will all my heart!"

Quita fingered her skirt, her voice barely audible. "Perhaps a fortnight from now you will feel differently. You know nothing except a life of ease and wealth."

"Never! I will never regret the decision, and you won't know if I should!"

A sly glint came to Quita's eyes. "*Sí*, that is true."

"Consider it done." Lianna felt as if she had been granted a reprieve from the guillotine. Elation filled her as she settled back into the corner.

"Now, the only obstacle in our plan is Doria. When we stop at the next inn, we must see to it that she takes the sleeping potion."

It proved to be as simple as Lianna expected. Doria unwittingly drank tea laced with the potion. Lianna's nervousness mounted until they were once again in the coach, pulling away from the inn, leaving a sleeping Doria behind.

A blast of wind whipped against the coach, causing the leather over the windows to shake. Quita leaned down to pull a fur lap robe across her mistress's knees, then another across her own. Lumbering in deep ruts, the coach gained speed. Lianna raised the leather flap, peeping out the window at the half-timbered inn. Mist shrouded the steeply pitched roof and twin chimneys. Inside, sleeping with the soundness of the drugged, lay Doria. Sitting stiffly, her fingers clutching the fur lap robe, Lianna watched the inn until they rounded a bend and it was out of sight. Jubilantly she looked at Quita.

"Now we shall succeed," she said as she unfastened her cloak. "Quita, quickly, change garments. Whatever you do, guard against discovery by the coachmen and lackeys. They are armed, and John Stafford promised my father he would see me safely aboard *La Joya*."

Struggling with the heavy clothing in the chilly confines of the coach, they worked quickly until Lianna's full lips curved in a smile of satisfaction. Dressed in the maid's simple black cotton and rough woolen cloak, she gazed at Quita in the black cape, the pink batiste skirt peeping out where the folds of the cape fell open.

"Thank goodness we have the same color hair. We can pull the bonnets low to hide our eyes. Here, pull this gauze down over your bonnet." Lianna adjusted black gauze across the arching brim of her poke bonnet. "Our black hair will aid in the deception." She looked down at the serpent ring and withdrew it from her finger. "Put this on, Quita. The striking serpent is the Marcheno crest."

With each minute Lianna's excitement mounted. She would be the first to depart from the coach, since their plan was to deposit Quita at the wharf to board *El Feroz*.

When they reached the busy docks, the coach threaded slowly toward its destination. The mist had abated; gray clouds scudded low across the sky, yet their gloominess could not spoil Lianna's enthusiasm as she gazed out the window at the tall masts, the webs of rigging. Along the wharf people milled about, with barbers trimming hair, mates moving to and fro, calling orders. Stevedores heaved crates of cargo, exotic bundles from faraway lands, while vendors hawked their wares.

Dampness cloyed the air; shouts, the creak of wheels, and the thud of cargo lowering to the dock sounded clearly. The smell of fish, baking bread, and the salty sea mingled with odors of damp wood and leather rigging. As the coach rolled to a standstill, Lianna turned to grasp Quita's hand. Lianna's pulse raced as swiftly as the clouds. "*Gracias,* Quita. And I pray you find what you desire."

Lowering her gaze, Quita murmured, "God forgive me, forgive me . . ."

Lianna stepped out of the carriage.

Speaking over his shoulder, John Stafford lifted down Quita's portmanteau. " 'Ere now, be quick, lass. Yon ship will sail before ye be aboard her. We're running a mite behind schedule." He shouldered her portmanteau.

Hurrying ahead of him, keeping her face turned away so that the gauze veil tied under her chin hid her face from his view, Lianna approached the frigate. She stared at the ship which would give her freedom; the long row of black cannon on the gun deck was a grim reminder that danger might lie ahead. The lion figurehead appeared ready to spring. The red ensign hoisted at the gaff proclaimed loyalty to the kingdom. The sleek lines, the activity of seamen aboard her, the prospect that the ship would give her a new life, caused Lianna to deem *El Feroz* a beautiful sight, and her breath left her lungs as she looked up at the tall sails. Men crawled about above, untying lines, readying the ship to leave, and Lianna thought it one of the most exciting moments of her life. Her blood pounded swiftly.

They mounted the gangplank, where John Stafford placed the portmanteau on a gleaming deck. "Quita, I wish you well."

Lianna merely curtsied. "*Gracias, señor.* Farewell."

John turned and his long stride carried him down the gangplank. Her heart thudded as she looked across the docks at the land of England, knowing it might be a long time before she saw it again. Wind tugged at her veil as she lifted it to see a rider on a horse rush into view between two buildings. Her heart thudded as she saw his familiar shoulders and golden hair. Edwin!

She rushed forward to grip the rail as he rode straight for her carriage. She waved frantically, trying to catch his attention. He waved back, but continued toward her carriage.

She dared not cry out because John Stafford was within hearing distance. John yelled at Edwin as he jumped from his horse and disappeared into the carriage.

Lianna couldn't breathe. She ran down the gangplank in desperation as John Stafford sprinted toward the carriage.

Before he could reach it, the man on the seat leapt to the ground and raised his pistol.

Lianna stopped in her tracks, her hand flying to her mouth in horror as the man yanked open the door of the carriage and pointed his pistol inside. Edwin climbed out, and the man slammed the door as John Stafford reached them.

"Yer a damn fool, Edwin!" John Stafford yelled so loudly that his voice carried across the wharf. Swinging his clenched fist, he knocked his son to the ground.

Edwin rubbed his chin and stood up, but his gaze looked beyond his father to Lianna, who could hear his voice. "I'll tell Quita good-bye and join you."

"Aye, ye will, riding with a pistol in your side! Hurry it up."

The man with the pistol turned to watch Edwin while John Stafford climbed into the driver's seat.

With each step Edwin took, Lianna's pulse pounded faster. To be so close, yet so impossibly far from marriage to the man she loved, seemed to tear her in two.

He paused in front of her. "Quita told me. I can do nothing to stop you because if I do, the guard your father hired to prevent our running away together will most likely shoot me. Dammit, you can't go on a ship with only men!"

"I'll just be a serving girl. I'm sure the captain needs someone who can speak Spanish because he sails to the New World. If we talk much longer, your father will suspect something."

"Can you slip off the ship after we're out of sight?"

"I can try, but they look ready to sail."

His gaze swept the ship while wind caught his blond locks and tugged them away from his face. She ached to reach out and grasp his hands, to press herself against his reassuring solidness. "What can we do?" she whispered.

"I've agreed to sail on a ship leaving London soon. If we have to, we'll wait until I return. Or if I can find you, I will. Quita goes in your place?"

"Yes."

"And Doria?"

"I slipped some sleeping potion into her tea at the last stop."

"Ah, Lianna! What a cruel fate, yet you'll be free. If I kiss you, my father will suspect what has happened."

"But they won't suspect if I kiss you," she said, and flung her arms around him. "Don't touch me, just stand and let me kiss you." She pressed her lips to his, then stepped back.

"Get off the ship, Lianna. Get off and meet me at the first inn on the road to London. It's the Coachman's Inn."

"And if we sail in the next hour?"

"Then you'll have to sail, and we'll find each other if I have to go to the ends of the earth! Lianna, promise me you'll wait."

"I'll wait, Edwin. It is far more likely that you won't."

"I'll wait." His skin flushed a burning red while he clenched his fists. "Damn!" he whispered.

She felt trapped, caught by forces beyond her control. She wanted to remain in England, to go with Edwin. They were hopelessly caught in circumstances beyond their control, and she couldn't bear it.

He turned away, squaring his shoulders as he walked back and mounted his horse beneath his father's watchful eyes. Lianna returned up the gangplank and stopped at the rail to see her father's carriages still waiting while John Stafford talked to his son. She could no longer hear them, but John kept shaking his head. One of her father's men stood with his pistol tucked into his waistband while he watched her. She wondered if he suspected her true identity, and she moved back a step.

To her horror, as she watched John and Edwin talk, sailors raised the gangplank. She wanted to cry out, to tell them to wait for only another quarter-hour until her father's carriages had moved out of sight.

Behind and high above Lianna, a man shouted, "Heave up anchor to get under way. Set all topsails."

She turned to gaze upward. Clinging to the footropes on the afterside of the mast was a tall, broad-shouldered man with a mane of burnished brown hair. The laces of his white shirt were open on a chest bronzed by months in the

sun and his narrow hips were encased in black breeches.
He looked at Lianna and a grin flashed on his face.

Close at hand, a tall flaxen-haired seaman dressed in a
striped red shirt and baggy trousers answered the command, "Aye, aye, sir." In turn, he raised a speaking
trumpet to call, "Yardmen, lay aloft; loose topsails."

At the call, seamen scrambled to unfasten the furled
sail. As white sails began to pop and fill with wind,
winches creaked.

The ship began to move beneath Lianna's feet, and as
she looked at Edwin only yards away, she began to sail
away from him! Feeling as if her heart were splitting apart,
she clung to the rail while warm tears streaked her cheeks.

The gap of murky, swirling gray water widened. Across
it, Edwin turned his horse to follow her father's carriage.
He turned in the saddle to look back at her.

On impulse, aware that her life had changed irrevocably, Lianna raised her hand to wave. "Good-bye, Edwin, love. I promise I'll wait for you," she whispered.

As Edwin rode slowly away, she felt as if her heart were
going with him. And in that moment, starved for the least
shred of love, desperate in her new circumstances, Lianna
vowed to get back to him no matter how long or how
difficult it would be.

She watched until Edwin and the carriages were far
down the dock and the ship streamed out toward sea. Her
tears were whipped away by the wind, and her burning
throat began to return to normal. "I'll be back, Edwin,"
she whispered one more time. Gradually she became aware
of what was going on around her. She was sailing now,
and nothing could be done to stop it.

The agonizing yearning and hurt stirred by Edwin's
parting began to change to curiosity. Lianna accepted her
fate and began to take in the feel of the wind, the tang of
salt water, and the awareness that she had escaped the
dread Spanish marriage. She was free and beginning an
adventure.

She stood at the rail watching the buildings and houses
of Portsmouth dwindle into a dark line. Edwin could no
longer be seen. She shivered as a fierce wind struck her,

and she looked above at the sparkling white sails, the wide
horizon. Her future was uncertain, but promising.

The man on the footropes climbed down with a lithe
masculine grace that adapted to the constant movement of
the ship, his muscular legs flexing with coordinated strength
as he called, "Get the wench below, Fletcher."

"Aye, sir," the seaman beside her replied softly, and
passed the speaking tube to a second man. "This way,"
he said, lifting her portmanteau to lead her toward the
hatchway.

Swiftly she caught up her skirts to follow the man
below.

Edwin twisted in his saddle to watch Lianna walk back
up the gangplank. He knew he could not stare at her too
long without arousing his father's suspicions. As John
Stafford talked about the foolishness of his son's actions,
Edwin saw the gangplank lift. *El Feroz* was sailing!

He felt as if someone had plunged a knife into his heart.
Now there would be no way for Lianna to get off the ship.
His anger grew as he looked at his father, who had reined
behind the carriage as it moved away, watching Edwin
with a furrowed brow.

He had no choice but to move on with the carriage. There
was still the hope of her returning to him someday, since
she hadn't sailed to Spain and a wedding, but Edwin still
cursed the circumstances of his birth that separated him
from Lianna and the life-style he craved. His thoughts seethed
and he vowed to himself that somehow he *would* rise
above his station and lead a life only he would command.

"Yer a young fool, Edwin. She's not for the likes of us,
and ye only make yerself miserable."

Edwin couldn't answer for fear his anger would erupt
and he would disclose his full intentions. His father rode at
his side, and he couldn't so much as turn in the saddle to
watch what was happening with *El Feroz*.

They slowed in front of a two-masted brigantine, *La
Joya,* its men getting set to sail. Quita emerged from the
carriage, and Edwin dismounted swiftly. "I want to see
Lianna on board ship and tell her good-bye."

Before his father could answer, Edwin climbed down while lackeys began to unfasten the trunks and carry them aboard ship.

Quita's dark eyes met his gaze briefly; then her head lowered as she took his arm and he escorted her aboard *La Joya*, where they met the captain.

"Sir, may I tell her farewell?" Edwin asked.

"Of course, lad. Miss Melton, we were sorry to learn your father would be unable to sail, but we're happy to have you join us. We'll show you to your cabin when you are ready." Captain Lackly looked at the men unloading her trunks. "Where are the servants who are traveling with you?"

"There are none, sir. My maid became ill during the journey."

"You travel alone?" he asked with a frown.

"Yes, sir."

"That's highly unusual, but I'll see to your welfare. When you're ready to go below, just signal. Good day, sir." He walked away, and Edwin pulled her a few steps farther away from the gangplank, where they could talk without interference.

He fought an urge to lock his fingers around Quita's throat as frustration welled up inside him. "I told Lianna farewell, and they've sailed. She can't get off the ship now."

"She begged me to change with her."

"This is madness! How can you trick the Spaniard?"

"He doesn't know what she looks like."

"Where does *El Feroz* sail?"

"To the New World—to Santiago, Chile."

The words were foreign to Edwin and he repeated them softly. "Why?"

"I don't know."

"What were your duties to be?" He stared at her, putting his hands on her upper arms without thinking while he held his breath.

"I was to be maid for the captain."

"That's irregular as hell. What *were* your duties?"

"To serve him."

"How?" he snapped, his fingers tightening.

"You are hurting me! Your father will know . . ."

"Tell me, Quita." He watched her as emotions played over her features, and his worst fears were confirmed without her saying a word.

When she spoke, it was a whisper. "I was to be his mistress."

Edwin's head reeled as he thought of Lianna's innocence being taken by a rough sea captain. "Damn you," he said.

"Unhand me! She wanted to exchange places, no matter what! She said anything would be preferable to the marriage! I tried to talk her out of it!"

"Did you tell her she would be his mistress?"

There was a moment's hesitation and then she whispered, *"Si,"* and he knew she was lying. His fingers tightened on her arms again, and it took all his control to keep from striking her.

"You lying wench!" He stared at her as her wide black eyes peered at him through the heavy veil, and suddenly he laughed, a mirthless chuckle as the irony of what had happened struck him. "You kept her from the marriage and that at least gives me a chance to get Lianna back and lead the life I desire. You and I are alike, Quita. You too, want riches."

While she stared at him in silence, Edwin relaxed his grip and rubbed his hands on her arms. "I can't blame you. You have a chance for something that never would have come your way otherwise."

"I warned her she might not like servitude . . ."

"I wish you luck. I'd have done the same if I had had the chance. 'Tis hell to be poor."

Her black eyes widened. "You are unhappy because you love Señorita Melton."

"I'm unhappy because I'm poor. Luck to you, Quita!" He kissed her cheek and strode down the gangplank. He turned to wave to Quita; then his gaze shifted to *El Feroz,* sailing out of the harbor.

"Lianna . . ." he whispered, clenching his fists, as he imagined Lianna's innocence taken from her. She could not know what she had done with her life. He threw himself into the saddle and turned for home, determined to pack his belongings and another week's wages and then return to sail with Captain Turner.

"Santiago," he said aloud. He would have to get into the squire's library and find it on a globe.

When Lianna lifted the bonnet and heavy gauze veil away from her face, the mate sighed in admiration.

"Saints be!" His gray eyes raked over her in a manner which caused Lianna to blush. He grumbled in a low breath, "Josh will be pleased this time." He raised his voice. "Stay inside. Been aboard ship before?"

"This is my first voyage," Lianna replied softly.

His brows raised. "You talk like a lady but look like a temptress from the sea." He shook his head in a disapproving manner. "We've lost Josh for most of this voyage."

"You call him Josh?" she asked in surprise.

One corner of his mouth lifted in a sardonic manner. "We're relatives by blood."

"Oh, I see." She looked closer at his rugged face. "Is he your father?"

Her question brought a laugh that softened his features, but his voice remained cynical. "No. I'm Fletcher Chance, his bastard brother. We shared the same father."

"Oh, I'm sorry!" Lianna blushed once again.

"Women and high seas don't mix well," he said abruptly. "Stay inside." He crossed to a large wardrobe secured to the bulkhead. Opening it, he revealed a row of dazzling dresses in a rainbow of colors. "These are yours."

Startled, Lianna gazed at them in surprise. "And where is my cabin?"

"You'll have to ask the captain," he said dryly, and left.

Lianna tossed her bonnet on a desk and surveyed her surroundings with joy. She noted with pleasure the heavy oak timbers in the bulkheads, the polished deck and curving glass panes over a wide bunk. Near the bunk a washstand was fastened to the bulkhead. It contained a lavender porcelain enamel bowl and pitcher of water. Captain Raven lived in comfort. As she explored the cabin, she envisioned a man like Thomas Hardeston, Melissa's father. He had thick white hair and a pleasant smile and his library was always as neatly arranged as Captain Raven's cabin. It was easy for Lianna to envision another Thomas Hardeston as captain of *El Feroz*. She picked up a pillow. Stitched in fine linen was a lion's head similar to the ship's figurehead, and she noticed the same snarling emblem was also engraved on the bookcases. Nearby was a wide desk and chair, and a circular dining table and four chairs. Even the smallest items bore the lion's head, and she wondered about this man who put his stamp so permanently on his possessions.

Along one side of the cabin was a row of hooks, several holding men's clothing. She crossed to the wardrobe, touching fancy dresses that were beautiful as well as costly. She withdrew a pale blue silk, impressed by the fine stitching. Her wardrobe, while adequate, would be no match for these gowns. Her father's funds could afford the same quality, but he was far too frugal to indulge her. Smoothing the material of the black dress that had belonged to Quita, Lianna smiled—the poor captain must not know how to shop for a maid.

Unable to resist the temptation to see how she would look in one of the dazzling creations, Lianna unfastened the maid's dress, letting it fall until it billowed around her long slender legs and settled on the floor around her ankles. Since she had not exchanged underclothes with Quita, her soft cambric shift clung to her creamy full breasts and slender hips. She stepped into the blue silk dress with its scoop neck of white lace embroidered in dainty seed pearls. While slightly large at her tiny waist, it fit elsewhere, revealing the soft rise of her breasts.

Lianna swirled in a circle, enjoying the cool material swishing against her legs. Never had she worn such a creation; her father would have considered it the utmost frivolity. She could imagine his sandy brows drawing together in a frown at the sight of it.

She stepped in front of an oval mirror and was shocked at the expanse of ivory skin the dress revealed. She had commenced upon a new adventure, so she would wear it and be daring! She laughed, reveling in her independence.

Smiling, she withdrew the pins in her hair. She found a brush in her portmanteau and pulled it through silky midnight locks, humming as she watched the hair spring from the bristles and drift softly down again. With a deft movement she caught up strands on either side of her head, looping and pinning the locks high to let the remaining tresses hang down the back of her neck.

When she was finished, she tossed Quita's black dress into the wardrobe and closed the door. A spirit of eager anticipation filled her and for the first time in months she was free of the dread prospect of marriage to the Spanish count. When this voyage ended, she might even have earned enough in Captain Raven's employ to sail home to Edwin. Lianna realized, however, that she had already made one mistake by telling the mate that this was her first voyage. If she were truly Quita Bencaria, it would be her second voyage. She made a mental note to be more careful in the future, although little would it matter if the truth were to be discovered. What difference could it make who served the captain?

She paused beside a bookcase to peer at titles in French, Spanish, and English, then walked idly to the desk. It held a small brass telescope, ink and quill, and a leather-bound ledger. Opening the ledger, she read a sweeping scrawl. "Today we ran south. This latitude, which is 43° 30′ . . ." Lianna closed the book. A faint smell of tobacco mingled with the cabin's odor of damp wood and masculine scents; all were new to her.

Crossing to the bunk, she sank down and looked out to sea. As they sailed, there was a gentle rocking of the ship, an endless creak of timbers. Concerned with her problems when she had boarded, Lianna had given little thought to the Spanish name, *El Feroz,* and the British seamen, as well as the Union Jack fluttering in the breeze, but now she wondered. Why would an English ship have a Spanish name and sail to the New World? What mission was Captain Raven on that he needed a Spanish- and English-speaking serving girl?

She remembered Quita telling her that Captain Raven had his country's permission to plunder Spanish ships, and guessed the name was a deception. She realized she had exchanged her allegiance from one ruthless man to another.

Without ceremony the door opened. Startled, Lianna looked up as a man filled the doorway. He halted and smiled.

It was the same man who had been on the footropes high above her when she had boarded. She looked into his sea-green eyes and felt as if she had fallen overboard, tumbling fathoms below the surface, where she could not get her breath, drowning as green engulfed her and closed over her head.

While her heart thudded, she forced her gaze from a look that ensnared with the tenacity of seaweed tendrils. She looked at a thick mane of lustrous brown hair, its stray short locks curling above a wide forehead. Skirting the devilish green eyes, she let her gaze lower to his prominent cheekbones. His strong face fit the body beneath it. His broad shoulders tapered to narrow hips and lean legs. She looked upward.

He stood lounging against the door while smiling at her, and once again her attention was captured by green eyes. The flash of white teeth and the creases in his cheeks invaded her very soul. She smiled in return.

Suddenly all of Lianna's self-assured relief vanished. As she viewed her new employer, she felt a rising panic. With a mocking glint lighting his eyes, he gazed at her with disturbing boldness, a daring look that alternately heated and chilled her. An icy premonition of disaster shook Lianna.

9

The prolonged moment grew tense and Lianna's mouth became dry, her fingers cold. She was sure he mocked her, and although her heart raced, she carefully rose to her feet and curtsied. *"Buenos días, señor. Cómo está usted?"* She asked in perfect Spanish.

"Muy bien, graçias." His voice was a drawling baritone that soothed her with velvety warmth. Never had she heard a male voice take ordinary words and by mere tone change them to a sensuous, whispery caress. Heat diffused into her bloodstream as he asked, *"Prefiere hablar español?"*

Dazed, she shook her head. "No, I prefer my . . ." She almost said "native tongue" but caught herself in time, replying in English, ". . . second language, to which I have grown quite accustomed." Her words came out in a breathless whisper, and she wondered how he could so effortlessly tangle her thought processes.

"Very well, we shall speak English." His gaze drifted down with an audacity that made Lianna quiver. She felt as if invisible fingers had reached out to divest her of the silk dress. Slowly, carefully, his eyes lowered, then raised, pausing heart-stopping seconds on the full rise of her breasts above the soft white lace at the neckline of her dress. His deliberate study made her draw in her breath and caused her breasts to strain against the fabric, sending a heated flush to her cheeks.

Josh felt his pulse quicken. Mr. Summer had selected

well. The girl was lovely, with alabaster skin, a waist which was temptingly narrow, yet breasts lush and full. Her wide blue eyes held a look of innocence that beguiled him—or did he see innocence because he wanted it so badly? he wondered, amused at himself. He leisurely closed the door behind him and crossed the cabin. "Mr. Summer succeeded beyond all my expectations. He informed me of your beauty, but he didn't adequately convey the extent of it."

His voice was husky, buffeting Lianna's senses like a warm evening wind. Lianna's cheeks grew warmer. Her pulse became erratic and she took a step backward. As her legs bumped the bunk, she grew angry at her own foolishness. One would think she had never seen a man! She raised her chin and stood quietly, yet her heart thumped louder than the groaning of the timbers. Captain Joshua Raven was not like other men. He dominated the cabin, diminishing it. For a fleeting second she wondered at the phenomenon—his broad shoulders were overwhelming, his height was greater than most men's, but she realized it was neither height nor width that lent him power. The man's entire manner demanded attention. Even while standing still, he would rule his surroundings. He was born to command as surely as the sun would rise each morning.

She couldn't look into his eyes any longer so she looked down at her dress. "The wardrobe you have for me is magnificent."

"I see it is slightly large around the waist."

Lianna was surprised he noticed. "I shall be able to correct that with needle and thread. The dresses are beautiful."

"Quita. What a lovely name."

Again she felt the rush of liquid warmth as his husky voice spoke to her. He reached out to touch her chin, and she wished he would not stand so close, for the moment his warm thumb and finger caught her jaw, raising it gently, she felt as if lightning had streaked from the heavens through the cabin, through his flesh to hers.

His fine skin was burnished to the color of teak from days in the sun. Thick lashes, long and dark, framed his eyes above a thin nose which had a slight crook in the bone. Raven was the name of a wild bird, but the symbol of a lion was far more fitting. He looked wild enough to be a pirate with golden earrings and a scar along his jaw. A curious mixture of fear and attraction tugged at Lianna's senses.

A rap at the door broke the silence, and a steward entered. He placed dishes on the round table while the captain moved away to wash his hands. She was rooted to the desk, unable to move or think. She looked at the figure bent over the washstand, willing her eyes to avoid drifting down his back. When the steward had closed the door, she asked Captain Raven, "What will my duties be, sir?"

He turned, drying his hands, his dark brows narrowed. "I thought Mr. Summer made that quite clear."

"Oh, of course," Lianna added hastily. "I merely meant . . . at this moment, what would you like me to do?"

The frown vanished instantly. He waved a hand. "Join me while I dine, of course." He dropped the cloth on the stand.

It was her turn to frown. Never had she known a maid to dine with an employer. It was highly irregular. But perhaps life at sea was irregular—she had no way of knowing. "I think that improper, sir. After all, I was hired to serve you."

His smile appeared, the creases deepening in his cheeks, a merry twinkle flashing in his eyes. She wondered how many more battles had been yielded to that smile than to the cannon on the gun deck.

"Quita, I think it unnecessary to concern ourselves with propriety." His fingers rested lightly on her arm as he led her to a chair. "Please be seated."

With a fleeting glance at him, she sat down. Lighting a taper, he reached up to a lantern which swung from a hook overboard. His slim hip was so close, inches from her, and she was suddenly fascinated by his narrow waist, the tight black breeches which confined the fine white shirt, a sharp hipbone which thrust against the material. How could powerful shoulders taper to such narrow hips? Blushing, she looked at the covered dishes on the table. He lighted the lantern and then the candles on the table before sitting down to pour red wine from a decanter into pewter flagons. He uncovered dishes of a strange new meat, hot biscuits, steaming potatoes, and fat green peas. She noticed that a white scar crossed the back of his right hand; the small finger on his left hand was mangled, the tip missing, and she wondered about the battles he had fought.

Acutely aware of his hands moving over the table, serving her plate, touching first one dish, then another, aware of his green-gold eyes, of his arrogant features, she wondered if she could get down a bite of food. Perhaps the reason for her discomfort was the fact that it was the first time in her life she had dined alone with a man other than her father.

Carefully Captain Raven sliced through pink meat to cut a piece and place it on her pewter plate. Steam curled in a dancing spiral from the dish, but her appetite was gone. He lifted a flagon and raised it in a toast. "To our voyage, a good sea, and a memorable, successful adventure!"

When Lianna raised her drink, she looked into his eyes and became ensnared as if held by bonds. He reached across the remaining space to clink his flagon against hers, their fingers brushing lightly. Never taking his gaze from hers, he raised his drink. Spellbound, she looked at him as he sipped.

"Quita." He looked at her flagon, and she raised it to her lips hastily, to feel the wine warm her insides as it went down.

"How delicious this looks, sir," Lianna remarked, more concerned with the man across from her than the food before her, in spite of the fact that she had eaten little the past few days.

"Enjoy it well—the fare will change rapidly as we get farther along on the voyage."

She bit into the meat and chewed. "It's delicious, but I don't recognize what I'm eating."

"Perhaps you'd rather not know."

She paused, saw the twinkle in his eyes, and relaxed somewhat as she laughed. "Some monster of the deep?"

"A very delectable monster from the depths of the sea."

"Served up by Poseidon to a ship's captain!" she answered lightly.

Captain Raven looked up in surprise. "A serving maid who knows Poseidon?"

"Not in the flesh."

Josh laughed with pleasure that increased when her cheeks turned pink. The wench could blush! Her red lips curved and his breath caught at the sight of her smile. It was a smile to coax Poseidon from the deep! Momentarily he forgot all else. Her soft laugh was melodic, an enchanted sound that held magic to melt a man's heart. He lowered his voice and said, "How nice your laughter is."

"Thank you."

"So you like to read," he said, thinking she looked so very young and wishing he had asked Mr. Summers more about her. "What else do you like, I wonder?"

"I love to ride, and if I have a chance, to race." Beneath his gaze Lianna felt giddy and lighthearted.

"Race? I regret we're on board ship. But I'll remember that when we reach land. We will race—and we will wager on it."

"And I shall win," she teased, beginning to enjoy herself and the challenge she saw in his eyes.

He laughed. "You're sure of yourself when you're months away from the event!"

"I will feel the same then. I've ridden since I was a child."

"And now you're a woman," he drawled softly, making her tingle and grow warm. "I think I owe Mr. Summer a bonus."

"Thank you, captain. And what monster do we consume?"

"Squid."

"Poor monster, but it is tasty."

"Where are you from?"

She debated how to answer, finally asking, "Sir, did Mr. Summer relate many details to you?"

"No, I know little about you, except that you agreed to this voyage."

"I was born in Madrid," she replied, exhaling a silent sigh of relief. "This past year I have resided in England in the employ of Charles Melton.'' To change the subject from herself, she asked, "Why does this ship bear the Union Jack and a Spanish name?"

Josh shrugged a broad shoulder, a casual lift and fall that pulled his white linen shirt tightly across his broad chest. Continual effort was necessary for her to avoid looking from the dark tufts of hair revealed at the open neck of his shirt. "It will be under a Spanish flag soon. When it becomes necessary for my purpose, *El Feroz* will have allegiance to Spain," he said dryly.

His explanation made little sense to her. Sipping her wine, she persisted, asking, "Why do you, a Briton, sail for the New World? You just said you would be allied to Spain."

"Only to deceive them. I intend to aid in a revolution. When the time comes, I shall fight with the patriots against the Spanish."

As if the cold north wind had blown down across the barren sea into the cabin to chill its occupants, Lianna shivered. "You'll fight the Spanish!"

"Quita . . ." His quiet voice was filled with curiosity. "Mr. Summer went over the details with you, yet I have the notion that you are receiving one shock after another."

"No!" she protested, all the while keeping her gaze averted. She drank more of the heady wine. It would be an impossible task to face his damnable searching stare and not reveal the truth. Finally she raised her head to meet his steady regard. She tried to speak calmly. "Mr. Summer didn't make clear your reasons for traveling to the New World."

"Have you heard of a land called Chile?"

"It has belonged to Spain for centuries."

"Ah, you know about it!" He sounded pleased and went on to explain, "Two years ago a junta was formed and Chileans struggled for independence, but failed, and Spain dominates again. The Spaniards have plundered and conquered and enslaved. They rule with greed, draining the land of its wealth. And in particular, the governor is a cruel man, from what I've been told." As he spoke, he stared beyond her as if looking into a great distance. His voice lowered, an angry note filling it. The man must hate the Spanish!

While she pondered this, her eyes, as if drawn irresistibly, drifted down the long legs angled toward her, studiously avoiding the pull of material low between his hipbones. A hot blush consumed her as she looked at the tight breeches that clung to his narrow hips, to legs that were muscled and powerful. Suddenly she realized he was silent.

Alarmed, she glanced up to meet a mocking gleam. Her blush became a raging fire, burning her cheeks, bringing a half-smile to his lips.

"You blush, Quita!" His husky voice played further havoc on her nerves. He sounded surprised, delighted that she could blush.

Hastily she said, "You were saying, sir?"

One corner of his mouth lifted a fraction, as if taunting her, but to her relief, he continued. "In London, I met Francisco Miranda, a man who is a great believer in human rights. He is concerned with tyranny in the New World. Miranda led a group to liberate Venezuela, but the Spanish governors learned of this movement and were able to combat it successfully." The lazy smile vanished as his thoughts drifted back to his subject. Fascinated, she watched the transformation, the rise of anger that was unmistakable. "That will not happen a second time."

What had the Spanish done to Captain Raven to cause him to fight in such a faraway cause? He must know she was Spanish. Quita Bencaria could only be a Spanish name.

Pouring more wine into both flagons, he said, "There is a man in Chile, Bernardo O'Higgins, who is gathering forces to fight."

"I recall reading that O'Higgins was governor of Chile."

"That was Bernardo's father you read about. Quita, you're one delight after another!"

His praise embarrassed her. Remembering their conversation, she prompted, "O'Higgins?"

"Bernardo was educated in Europe and he believes firmly in freedom from the Spanish throne. While he was in Europe, a man named Carrera led a group in an attempt to overthrow the Spanish, to set up a dictatorship.''

"Did they succeed?"

He shook his head. Flickering candlelight, an orange glow from the swaying lantern, danced over his features, casting burnished highlights on his prominent cheekbones, his firm jawline. Deep golden glints showed in the brown waves of his thick hair, and she watched him intently.

He answered gruffly, "No. Spain quickly sent a large army to combat the rebels. Bernardo had joined Carrera. When the Spanish army arrived, Carrera, Bernardo, and a force of two thousand met them in Rancagua. From a church tower Bernardo watched as the Spanish routed Carrera and his men. O'Higgins fled with the others, breaking through the Spanish lines to retreat over the Andes.''

"You're an Englishman. Why is this your concern?"

His eyes leveled like cannon ready to fire; she drew her breath. She hoped she never had to face him in anger. "I want revenge. I want what should be mine."

The words were said quietly, yet they chilled her, and she wondered if his hatred was for all Spaniards. "You know I'm Spanish.''

A fleeting smile raised one corner of his mouth. "Ah, my quarrel is with one particular noble Spanish family and one particular noble Englishman,'' he said so bitterly that she was afraid to pursue the conversation. "You're loyal to the English. That was an absolute requirement. Mr. Summers did not misjudge, did he, little Quita?"

She felt as if her life hung in the balance. How softly, without passion, he asked, but she felt the blade beneath the words, and realized this was a man who could be as hard as the timbers beneath her feet. Ignoring her own heritage, thinking only of the Count of Marcheno, she raised her chin to reply, "My allegiance is to England."

She met his eyes unflinchingly.

When his dark lashes dropped, she knew he had found satisfaction in her answer. She wondered how long she could deceive him about her identity, for he seemed to be able to discern every thought in her mind. "This O'Higgins hopes to try again?'' she asked, trying to steer the conversation back to something more impersonal, because his direct stares and questions made her nervous.

''Indeed, he does. After the patriots' defeat, Spain installed the present governor, Francisco Marcheno.''

''Marcheno!'' she gasped. Instantly his full attention fastened on her.

''The name means something to you?''

Her thoughts were spinning wildly, searching for a suitable explanation, because she realized she had just made a mistake. ''There may be many Marchenos in Spain. There is a Spanish nobleman, the Count of Marcheno . . .''

The flush that crept up his cheeks was a warning to her. Carefully, as if stepping through a bog, searching for firm footing with each stride, she said, ''The count has inflicted cruelty on my family. I was startled at the name, but the man I speak of resides in Madrid.''

''Aye, that he does. They are cousins. Close enough.'' He leaned across the table and again she felt as if he had drawn a dagger. ''Little Quita, your family will be revenged for whatever wrongs Marcheno has committed.''

The words fell like a death knell. Once, on a journey when she was a child, her father had driven past Newgate Prison, and she had looked out the carriage window as a man had been hanged. Immediately her father had dropped the leather over the window to hide the view, but she remembered the terrible sight, the body falling. For nights afterward she slept fitfully, with dreadful dreams. The vision returned now.

Captain Raven's voice lowered. ''The other Marcheno, Francisco, rules with a fist of iron. He is a tyrant whose cruelty is legend throughout the land of Chile.''

''Where is O'Higgins now?''

''When they fled, Jose de San Martín, who liberated Argentina, gave the patriots refuge.'' He studied her solemnly. ''I shall be in contact with them, and when the time comes, I'll fight with them.''

Through lowered lashes she gazed at him, longing to ask more questions. Why his anger? What had Francisco Marcheno done to Captain Raven? Did his hatred confirm

her fears of the Count of Marcheno? Was he as cruel as
she had been told? And who was the Englishman he hated?

"Will the voyage be dangerous?"

A lazy smile drifted over his features. "We have talked
sufficiently long of somber events."

Frightened he might launch into more questions about
her, Lianna asked, "When did you begin to sail?"

"When I was fifteen."

"Fifteen!" she repeated, startled by his reply. She ran
her fingers across her brow; the cabin had grown uncomfortably warm and the ship's movement had become more
noticeable to her.

"Aye, many lads turn to seafaring early in life. Their
families have ships, they are runaways, they are impressed—
one reason or another."

Curious as to which of the reasons had caused him to
turn to the sea, she studied him.

"I was a runaway and I was impressed."

His answer to her unasked question startled her. "How
did you know I wondered about it?"

He leaned forward to trail his forefinger along her jaw.
"Big blue eyes reveal a great deal," he said in a husky
rasp that trailed its own touch across her nerves. With his
words, his warm wine-filled breath assailed her, his eyes
seemed to draw her very soul to him. Heat flooded her
cheeks and she lowered her lashes lest he discern the
disturbing effect he had on her. He had been a runaway—
the same as she. Momentarily she felt a bond and wished
circumstances had been different so that she could tell
him.

When she raised her head, the whole cabin spun, re-
volving slowly, and she gripped the table. Too late, Lianna
regretted the amount of wine she had consumed. Never
before had she partaken of a drink stronger than ratafia.
She struggled to focus on Captain Raven, to hear what he
was saying.

"Do you feel ill?"

Did he look amused—or was that her imagination? "I
am quite fine, thank you," she whispered.

"More wine?" Josh asked, knowing full well she had

had too much already. She was so lovely, it took his breath. She was educated, something he hungered for—a woman he could actually talk to about world affairs, about his life. Her wide blue eyes looked as if she had never known a man in her life, and he shut his mind to the realization that she had.

"No!" she blurted to his offer of more wine, another blush making her cheeks enticingly pink. As he stood, she looked up at him. "Am I to remove the dishes?"

"No, Quita, love." This time there was no question of laughter in his eyes. The word "love" floated through Lianna with a dim shock, a note of warning which registered dully in her wine-befuddled mind. He moved around the table and reached down to help her to her feet.

With an effort she stood, swaying dizzily. Firm fingers closed gently around her arm, and he turned her to face him.

"It must be the sea," she said, pressing her fingers to her temple.

"Did the voyage to England disturb you?"

"What? Oh, no." For a moment she almost asked what he meant. She felt compelled to add more to her answer and invented from her imagination. "It was stormy and cold, but I wasn't bothered by it."

Captain Raven stood facing her, and she could see a blue vein throbbing steadily in his neck. She watched each beat as he talked. His voice was low, weaving through her senses like strands of woolen yarn.

"Mr. Summer said you fled Spain because of an unhappy love."

"Aye," she replied, listening to her voice as if it came from a great distance. "He wed another."

"Then a great fool he was," Captain Raven murmured. His breath, carrying a hint of wine, brushed her temple with the softness of a dove's wingtip. His fingers drifted higher to her bare shoulders. One hand rested on her shoulder, his thumb drawing small circles over her collarbone, sending golden rivulets of heat cascading down her limbs. Never had a man touched her in such a manner, yet she didn't want him to stop.

Lianna felt as if she had split into two persons; one stood observing, drinking in the sweet wine-filled breath that wafted lightly over her skin, relishing each tiny stroke of callused fingertips, while a counterpart tried to protest, to step back, to stop the insidious fires kindling within her, to tell Captain Raven that his improper attention must cease. Each part warred silently with the other while she closed her eyes and tipped her head back. The room became a furnace, a whirling pit of suffocating heat as scarlet fires raced along her veins, their flames ignited by gentle fingers.

His fingers slipped along her slender neck. Sensuous tugs, gentle and languid, pulled a pin from her hair, then another and another.

She should protest. If only the cabin would stop spinning! She couldn't think, couldn't speak.

"Quita, how lovely you are," he whispered huskily. She quivered as the baritone voice wrapped around her, closing her into its own tempting warmth.

A coil of black tresses tumbled over her shoulder. His fingers continued withdrawing pins. Lianna felt trapped by a will greater than her own. "Sir, the cabin . . . it spins. I am unsteady."

He laughed softly. A strong arm banded her waist. "I shan't allow you to fall."

His head lowered. She guessed what he intended, knew she should stop him. Raising her hands, she pushed against a chest as unyielding as the bulkhead. She turned her face and his lips grazed her cheek, leaving a flaming trail. His fingers held her chin, forcing her to face him.

Firmly, lips like velvet pressed against hers, and she felt the pressure to open her lips. She resisted, trying to summon her wits, yet his hands were everywhere, and feelings she had never known engulfed her, and somewhere deep in her heart she realized she had a more violent reaction to this man's kisses than she'd had to Edwin's.

He raised his head, studying her so intently, yet she couldn't think or reason why he would look at her in such a manner. She wondered what thoughts ran through his mind, but she couldn't ask.

"You play the game damned well," Josh said, seeing a puzzled frown on her face. If he hadn't paid Renfrow Summers such a tidy sum for a wench, he would swear he held an innocent who had never been kissed!

"Sir, please . . ." She opened her eyes as if it were with a great effort, and Josh felt something tug at his heart. He had never gotten involved with the women in his life. They were hard and experienced, sometimes widowed and wealthy in ports away from England, but he yearned for something else and he didn't want to get entangled with this wench who looked so beguiling that his senses felt drugged, yet how sweet she was!

He told himself he was an addled fool and perhaps he'd had too much wine, but deep down, he knew what he felt wasn't caused by wine. He looked at her mouth and heard the quick intake of her breath, watched her tongue flick out to touch her lips, then her mouth closed. He lowered his head. She did play the game damnably well! And he would give himself over to it. He brushed his lips over hers, teasing, coaxing her to open her lips.

His tongue touched the corner of her mouth, and he had to fight the urge to crush her tightly in his arms. He heard his voice as if from a distance and realized he had groaned. He wanted her so badly he hurt, yet he wouldn't rush her. Not this time. Game or not, he felt as if he were holding someone precious and fragile despite a sensuality that flickered to life with the slightest of his touches. He knew he was being a fool, but for this night he would amuse her because it was what he wanted, and she held a breathtaking promise for him.

His hand drifted to her breast, feeling the soft fullness, the taut nipple as he sought her lips more urgently. She gasped and his tongue slid deep into her mouth. He felt her tremble and his arms tightened while he kissed her now as he had wanted to all evening long.

He watched her with half-closed eyes but he saw that her eyes opened and her body stiffened as he kissed her more deeply. She seemed so innocent, yet he knew she couldn't be! Still, she seemed not to know what to expect or do. He bent over her, pressing her to his long length, relishing her softness while he continued to kiss her passionately. Her eyelids dropped, the thick lashes a fringe above her pink cheeks, and she clung to him, her hips moving against him for the first time. This woman was special—so very special, he thought as he kissed her wildly.

Her eyes closed, and in the darkness his tongue's moist strokes were transformed into brilliant hues of color in her mind. Her heart thudded, while flames seemed to burn in her blood. Beneath her fingers she felt an expanse of muscled hardness—and Captain Raven's own rapid heartbeat.

His kisses wreaked more havoc than wine, she thought, consumed by a tempest that stormed her senses. Each kiss drew her down into a whirlpool of new sensations. His arm around her waist tightened, drawing her closer.

His lips left hers momentarily, and she was bereft, befuddled by the onslaught of passion. He caught her earlobe between his teeth, nibbling so gently, yet the sensation made her gasp.

Releasing her lobe, he whispered, "Put your arms around me, Quita."

Protest! Stop the man! An inner voice raged at her, but it was so dim, a faint cry overwhelmed by her desire for him.

Again, "Put your arms around my neck. I want to feel your softness against me."

She couldn't deny the delicious sensations she had only dreamt about, nor would she stop herself from feeling them. She longed to fling caution away, to close her eyes and let strong hands and a hungry mouth work their incredible sorcery. Slowly she slipped her hands up his smooth cotton shirt and spread her fingers across his broad, hard shoulders, exploring the firm muscles tentatively. Then she twined her arms around his neck. A steel band tightened around her waist, crushing her to his chest, molding her slender form to his.

She should move away, yet how could anything feel so marvelous? Her thoughts spun like dried winter leaves tossed in a blustery north wind. He should not kiss her throat. She hoped he would never stop.

His hand touched the fastenings of her dress. She closed

her fingers around a hard, bony wrist and tugged, a useless protest.

The blue dress billowed to the floor in a silken whisper, floating around her ankles, leaving Lianna clad only in her shift. Cold air enveloped her, making her draw closer to his warmth. How good his body felt! Never had she clung to a man, let her fingers wind through silken curls, touch hard, solid muscles that made her tremble. With an effort she raised her lashes while he stepped back to view her.

Dark lashes shadowed his cheeks as he looked down at her slender feet, then raised his eyes slowly over her long pale legs to her hips, higher to the lush fullness of her heaving breasts, to her fever-inflamed face. The amber flecks darkened and she saw his purpose. He wanted her and he intended to have her.

As the realization penetrated wine-fogged reason, she drew back. "You must stop!"

"Little Quita, you're a delight! So responsive, yet there's a shyness, almost as if—" He broke off abruptly, a lazy smile flitting over his features. "Now, come here, love."

His smile widened, an indolent assertion. He reached out to place his fingers lightly on her throat, his thumb idly tracing the outline of her lips. When he touched her, tiny flickers of fire dazzled her, making her lips hunger for his kiss. He moved closer, leaned down, and his mouth replaced his thumb. Without haste, his lips parted hers, his tongue became a demand.

He kissed her relentlessly, weaving a spell of rapture through her body. Like spilling rays of the sun his fingertips grazed her bare shoulder, her breast, and then her smooth belly.

Her gasp was smothered by his kiss. A tautness filled her; an exquisite agony made her hips twist, seeking his hard frame.

"Ah, how sweet you smell," he murmured against her arching neck. He pressed closer and prodded the softness between her thighs.

Her eyes opened to look down at his lowered head, the thick waves of brown with glints of russet in their softness. Her fingers touched the inviting strands while his lips discovered the rosy tip of her trembling breast and her shift fell to her feet.

He lifted her swiftly and lowered her to the bunk. Naked, trembling, she was pink and ivory-fleshed, her breasts soft and round. The spinning in her head continued as she watched him peel off his white shirt and cast it aside.

The bronzed body before her took her breath away and made her burn with embarrassment, momentarily protesting. He moved to the bed. His chest muscles rippled, coiling like tight springs in a tanned masculine body that was honed to perfection, and she couldn't look away from him. A thick fur of black curls narrowed and then tapered to a dark line across his flat stomach. Candlelight flickered over his skin, a damp sheen giving glistening highlights on the curve of hard muscles.

She dropped her lashes, burning in an agony of need, and she moaned softly while her head reeled.

"What a passionate kitten you are!" he murmured, laughing softly. "You're out of my dreams . . . how I've wanted you!"

And then his hands were everywhere, stroking, exploring with arrogant leisure, moving over her intimately, seeking to set her aflame. The cabin spun, and she was overpowered by sensation.

"Ah, Quita, you're perfection!" He shifted above her, and with deliberation he parted her legs and lowered his weight.

Pain sent a rapier sharpness through her. Her eyes flew wide as a glimmer of reality penetrated her passion-heavy mind. "No!" she gasped.

"You are virginal?" Josh exclaimed, pausing to stare at her in wonder. He saw the answer in her eyes, and realized her innocence had not been feigned. His body's clamorings were too strong to wait or stop, so he moved slowly.

"Yes, I am!" she gasped, trying to escape his weight and the pain. "You're hurting me . . ."

His mouth covered hers, and his hands began to move insistently until her hips began to move against his.

When he couldn't wait longer, he thrust his maleness

deeply into her warmth, invading her softness, taking her, and Lianna felt torn asunder as pain racked her. A cry was muffled by one of his kisses. Then slowly he moved, filling her, and as he took her, she knew his possession of her would last for eternity. Part of her body, heart, and soul would forever belong to Captain Joshua Raven.

As the pain slowly gave way to growing sensuality and need, she moved beneath him. A sense of urgency ultimately clasped her loins, making her writhe and whimper, impaled by his hardness. His body carried her beyond the brink of reason and reality and when a shuddering release broke over her, he cried her name softly. His weight lowered, warm and heavy onto her.

He shifted, pulling her close as he lay beside her, fitting her to his warmth, stroking her hair, murmuring to her while he kissed her forehead. Through her blurred senses, at his continual languid caresses and low, tender words of endearment, Lianna felt loved and cherished. She timidly stroked his broad shoulders, feeling happy despite the realization that something was terribly amiss. But she refused to let discord intrude on the precious moment.

The big, hard body that cradled her against its warmth was fulfillment. She ached; the sharp pain had become a dull throb. The cabin swam if she opened her eyes, so she closed them to a merciful darkness while she fitted closer to Josh's broad chest. Her ear lay against his heart, her cheek on his heated, damp flesh. His big hand stroked her long hair.

"Ah, love, how perfect you are. Quita, we shall deal well together, you and I. You are so much more than I expected . . . so beautiful . . . both shy and passionate . . ." He turned to kiss her brow.

With her eyes closed she clung to his strong shoulder while she inhaled the scent of his skin. Her fingers toyed with a curl on his chest. The candles were extinguished, the lantern's light gone. In place of their golden glow, silvery moonbeams fell through the small panes of glass, bathing the bed in their candescence, giving a silver luster to a male body that looked like a marble statue of Adonis.

Only, Lianna knew so well, the body was not cold marble, but taut, hot, demanding flesh.

Her skin still burned from his fingers, from his mouth; exquisite tingles sparked along her nerves as she thought of the past hour. Or had it been hours? Forever? When had she not known Joshua Raven? She laughed softly.

His fingers caught her chin and tilting her face upward he met her eyes with his.

"Little Quita, why the laugh?"

She trailed her finger across his firm jaw. "It is not Quita, sir."

"Eh? What, if not Quita?"

"Lianna."

"Lianna? Quita Lianna Becaria? Go to sleep, sweet one." His arm pulled her to his length. "Your brain will clear with the dawn."

Dimly she thought of Quita, sailing on another ship toward Spain, toward a husband who was cruel and wealthy. And Edwin, Edwin journeying home in her father's coach, sleeping at the inn while she sailed away in the arms of Joshua Raven. Why couldn't it be Edwin who held her instead of this arrogant stranger who merely lusted after her flesh? Edwin, who had cared for her truly . . . "Edwin," she breathed.

She felt the muscles tense beneath her before she realized she had spoken the name aloud. Too late, Captain Raven looked down at her. His broad, powerful shoulders loomed over her, his hips pressing her into the bed. Moonbeams splashed across the bulge of his muscles, the thick tangled locks of his brown hair. Josh's broad hand drifted lightly to her throat, lying still over the lifebeat of her pulse.

"Love, it is Josh. Joshua Raven."

His tone of voice brought a howling blizzard of ice and snow into the cabin. With a lion's head engraved on everything in the cabin, now he wanted his stamp on her soul. Her head ached and swam, yet she instinctively sensed the danger, the contained fury in his low voice. "Say my name, love."

"Joshua," she said sweetly, and reached up to stroke

his head. She locked her fingers in his thick hair and smiled, holding her breath.

His deep voice sent its own strong fingers over her waiting nerves. "You were a virgin. That's good, because otherwise I would teach you the foul consequences of calling me by a former lover's name. I do not want to be called another man's name, Quita," he said with quiet force, and she knew he had a particularly violent distaste for such a mistake.

"Josh . . ." she repeated gently.

"Ah." He let out his breath with satisfaction and sank down again to draw her to his side. One muscled leg lay across hers as his arm circled her waist to hold her. "Sleep, love. You have earned your rest."

It was the last conscious thing Lianna knew; wine took its final toll and oblivion closed over her boneless limbs.

The next morning, the first thing Lianna saw was the smooth planking overhead. Disoriented, she stared at the polished oak boards. She should be peering up at the plastered white ceiling of her room. And with that thought came the memory of last night. She was not alone. A warm body was fitted against hers. The bed moved, rocking gently, rising and falling in a steady rhythm.

The creaking and groaning of timbers made a continual noise, mingling with a dim slap of waves against the hull. Light streamed through panes of glass, spilling over the bunk. Her body ached, hurting in places that she hadn't known existed; her head throbbed. She looked down at her bare breasts, and below them, a muscled brown arm sprinkled with short dark hairs clasped her waist.

A sudden disbelief at what had transpired overwhelmed her. She sat up violently, turned and stared at the man stretched beside her.

Long dark lashes lightly touched his face. One arm was flung over his head and his bare chest rose and fell with steady breathing. The white sheet fell about her hips and lay across his loins, shaping his male body with a clarity that made her cheeks burn.

Memories made her reel, almost collapse with shame.

Just as quickly, shame was replaced by an all-consuming, savage fury at the manner in which she had been used.

Then the captain's long lashes fluttered open and his eyes gazed at her.

"Love," he murmured, and stretched forth his arms, reaching for her. This stranger, a man she had known less than a day, the man who had plied her with wine and taken her virginity . . . he lay with smug pleasure, reaching for her lazily, as if she were a strumpet.

"Love!" Lianna spat the word and leapt from the bunk. Flinging her dark hair behind her head, she backed away from him and, for the first time in her life gave full vent to fury.

He raised himself up on one elbow and returned her stare. His gaze swept over her in a consuming, appreciative glance, then drifted down like his fingers in a soft caress, lingering on her breasts.

She felt the reaction of her body to his appraisal without understanding it or wanting it. Peaks grew taut, in need of his hands. The response heightened her anger, and she looked around wildly, spying a bread knife on the desk, where it had been tossed carelessly the night before.

Without thinking of the consequences, in an emotional surge of hurt and rage, Lianna clasped it and lunged forward.

10

With a startled glance Josh Raven scrambled out of the way and caught her arm in a clamp which closed around her slender wrist like iron. His anger surfaced as he jumped to his feet, dropping the covers on the floor. Their bodies met in a struggle which was over in an instant, for Josh crushed Lianna to him, tightening his hold on her wrist. With a cry, she let the knife clatter to the deck. As Josh kicked it aside, she sank her teeth into his bare shoulder.

"Damn!" he exploded in a rage, flinging her across the bunk. "You bit me, you baggage!"

With a shriek she twisted and reached again for him. What possessed the woman? he wondered, catching her easily and pinning her to the bed. Now she tried to bite his hand.

Deftly he released her wrist, wrapping his fingers in her long hair, tugging it until she gasped and stilled. Josh fought to control his fury. He was tempted to backhand her as he clenched his fist more tightly in her hair. "What the hell has gotten into you?"

She kicked at him. "Let me free!"

"Damn, woman!" He would put an end to this! Kneeling on the bunk, he caught her around the waist and pulled her up against him. With his hand still locked in her hair, he kept her face unmovable. Hot with anger, he demanded, "What the hell is all this? Explain quickly, before I take the cat to your lovely bare skin."

"You beast!" she cried. "How could you do such a cruel act? You filled me with wine and violated me—"

"Violated!" he interrupted with an explosive sound. Suddenly the ridiculousness of her accusation struck him. He threw back his head, and deep-throated laughter rang in the cabin. "Violated! Love, I paid dearly for you."

He looked down at her cheeks, rosy from anger, and into her wide blue eyes filled with terror. He frowned. Whatever trick she was up to, the expression on her face was clearly fear. And in spite of her fury, she was so lovely. More lovely than any other woman he had known.

His voice softened, lowering to a husky tone. "You were worth the sum I paid. Damn, if you weren't! I shall be willing to pay more than the agreed sum. You lied to Summers about your virginity." A smile tugged at the corner of his mouth. "Why the lie, little Quita? You would have earned far more with the truth."

Lianna's face flushed. "I don't have a farthing of yours! I had no notion of what lay ahead." She snapped, "Release me! You're hurting my head with your grip."

"No tricks now," he said, watching her warily. His fingers slipped out of her hair, but his arm still held her pinned to his chest.

Lianna gasped for breath as she looked at him. The long hair on the back of his neck curled slightly above his shoulders, falling free from the strip of leather that had fastened it earlier. Her soft breasts were crushed against his chest. His skin had a faint salty odor, a teasing male scent that tickled her senses. Attempting to free herself, she squirmed in his arms. Her breasts scraped his chest and something flamed in her loins, an ache that she could not control. Suddenly she was too aware of his flesh against hers, his arm around her, their bare skin and his muscular body.

Her heartbeat became erratic. Memories rose like a hot, nectared tide, surging over her, battering her senses as she looked into his eyes. His head lowered, his mouth found hers, and he tasted her slowly, curious about her reaction.

She turned and felt an agony low in her body. The dull pain from the night before lingered and brought with it a return of anger, and she pushed away, tearing her lips from his. "I had no knowledge of any agreement for you to . . . to do what you did . . ."

Inches away, his eyes pierced her with their emerald hardness. "I know not what game you are about, but fail it will. You are getting dangerously close to a thrashing," he snapped, but he watched her closely. Renfrow Summers was a reliable man; he wouldn't have taken the girl against her will—her actions yesterday decried that.

"You monster! Have you not done enough?" she said, and there was a tremble in her voice that tugged at his heart. "I'm not Quita Bencaria. This is a dreadful mistake."

Josh Raven caught her chin. "What the hell are you talking about?"

"I'm not Quita Bencaria. She was my maid, and I exchanged places with her in order to escape an arranged marriage."

"You're lying, wench!" Anger rose in him again. No mistress would trade places with a servant. His shoulder stung from the bite and he wondered what trick this girl attempted. He had already promised her more money because of her virginity. "I want the truth," he said quietly, attempting to hold his anger in check.

"Why should I lie now?" she cried. "Look what you've done! I'm Lianna Melton. My father is a squire. I was on a journey to Spain, where I was to wed a Spanish nobleman, the Count of Marcheno."

"Marcheno!" The word was like a blow. She had to be lying through her teeth—yet every time he looked into her blue eyes, he felt a tightness in his heart. He shook his head, as if to free himself from a spell. "If you're English," he said, trying to hide his fury, "why would you wed a Spaniard?"

"My father made the arrangements," she said breathlessly. Her lashes dropped to veil her eyes, and he could barely hear her answer. "It was quite profitable for him."

There was no mistaking the pain in her voice. He lifted her chin and noticed that her lashes were wet with tears even as her eyes remained closed. He felt another jolt in

his heart. Her words conjured up many memories. *My
father* . . . He could clearly picture his father's livid face
as he laid lashes with vigor. Suddenly he felt a bond with
the woman in his arms.

At the same moment sympathy touched him, his mind
warned him that she could be tricking him. He hadn't
survived years at sea by trusting strangers. "Look at me,"
he commanded.

Her dark lashes, sparkling with tears, raised, and wide
blue eyes watched him. The guileless look in her eyes, that
delicate beauty made him want to cradle her against his
chest. He was tempted to brush her lips with his, to tell her
there was no need to fear him.

Torn between conflicting emotions, Josh relaxed his
grasp. She reached down to gather the sheet to her chin. It
fell lightly between them, partially covering him as well as
her. A smile tugged at his mouth over her modesty. Was
she acting? Could she be a Spanish spy? His blood ran
cold at the thought, and his mind raced over events since
she had boarded his ship.

"I think you're lying," he stated flatly, yet hating the
cruelty he inflicted when she flinched.

"No! I'm Lianna Melton."

"I saw the fond farewell on the wharf. That man was a
servant. The master's daughter wouldn't be in love with a
servant. You're Quita Bencaria, and I grow weary of this
foolishness!"

"No! I'm telling you the truth." She looked down. "I
grew up with the man you saw. His father has worked for
my father since we were babes."

"His name?"

"Edwin Stafford."

It was the name she had said when she had lain in his
arms. "How much does this man mean to you?"

"I love him!" She nearly yelled the words.

Something sharp twisted his insides and for a moment
he felt a flare of sardonic amusement. Why should be
care? He had known many women. Why did this one seem
to have a hold on his heart?

Lianna drew a deep breath and he watched the rise of

her soft breasts beneath the sheet. Shining midnight locks of hair fell over her pale shoulders. "I love him." Her words angered him, even though he knew it was unreasonable.

"You have taken my body; you can't take my heart."

"Damn you, wench," he said, and she shivered, yet she faced him unflinchingly. Tension grew between them, yet Josh could see the fear in her eyes. He felt a strong urge to comfort her, to try to banish that look of a frightened fawn, despite her declaration.

Leaning forward, he placed his lips on hers and pulled her close as he tasted her sweetness, brushing her mouth lightly until she trembled in his arms. He wanted to stroke away all her pain and worries. Was he being a fool? Succumbing to big blue eyes and a skill in treachery?

Her breath was sweet, intoxicating to his senses. Her words—*I love him*—made him burn. His mouth settled firmly, his tongue thrust between her lips, and he kissed her as if to kiss away all thought of Edwin Stafford. He felt the tremor that rippled through her and became convinced that she was telling the truth. A lovely Englishwoman, educated, brave, young—and so very passionate. Something protective stirred within him at the same time his body flamed with desire for more of her. He had to know the truth!

His mouth became her captor; he tried to drive all else into oblivion while his insatiable tongue searched and stroked, playing on her senses. When she stirred against him, moaning softly, he released her abruptly. Startled, she raised her black lashes slowly. She looked dazed, befuddled by passion, and he felt a flare of satisfaction.

"Quita or Lianna?" he asked. "The truth now."

"It is Lianna Melton," she whispered breathlessly. "I asked my maid to change places with me. Quita is now aboard *La Joya*, sailing for Spain. She told me of her employment, but you, sir, presuming me to be a mere serving girl, have taken the foulest advantage."

Emotions conflicted: triumph, passion, and pity. How well he understood her plight. His own past rose like a specter and he brushed a long lock of dark hair away from her cheek.

"I took no advantage of you," he said quietly while his mind struggled with decisions. He could turn the ship back and take her home to England. It would cost him days and money, but they weren't impossibly far yet. "It was your maid who took advantage. She made full arrangements with Mr. Summers to become my mistress for this voyage."

"Mistress!" Her eyes seemed to widen endlessly, and he felt compassion for her innocence. And he knew he wouldn't turn the ship back. He touched her cheek lightly with a longing that went to his soul.

"Aye," he returned firmly. "I paid handsomely for a wench able to speak Spanish."

"Which I cannot do!"

He laughed softly, feeling another tug at his heart. "It's too late for such a lie. I recall your greeting yesterday."

"I won't speak Spanish," she protested. "You must return me to England! Allow me my freedom."

The words danced between them and he was torn with conflict. He wanted to pull her into his arms and kiss her until she burned with passion as she had in the night. He knew her body would betray her, and he could claim victory easily, but he was beginning to want more. This lovely blue-eyed woman might be worth the effort to win her heart. He remembered Tillie, the girl on the dock, and how weary he had grown of casual intimacies.

"I've sealed my part of the bargain. When you exchanged with your maid, it was your own folly. I won't turn back now," he said, not wanting to look too closely at his motives.

Lianna paled. "You can't mean this!"

"Shh, Lianna. I will give you time."

"Time?" She sounded so outraged, he had to struggle for patience. Didn't she realize he could do as he pleased with her, that he owned her for the voyage?

"Haven't you done enough?" she gasped. "You've forced yourself on me—for that alone you should respect my wishes."

"I recall little force last night." He didn't try to hide the mocking tone in his voice.

Lianna turned crimson. As he watched her, his blood pounded. Her lips were red from his kiss, and the angrier she became, the more difficult it was for him to resist wrapping his arms around her and stopping her protests. There was a fire to her that dazzled him. He remembered the sparkle last night in her laughter, the eagerness of her hands touching him, and he wanted her to desire him that way again.

Josh lazily ran his forefinger along her bare arm. He heard the soft intake of her breath and knew he stirred a response. His voice became a husky timbre as he said, "I recall these arms wrapped around my neck."

"You scoundrel!" she breathed, leaning back away from him. "They shall never be that way again!" Her eyes flashed with fire, yet the tip of her pink tongue ran across her lower lip and her breasts heaved as if she had to gulp air to breathe.

"Never?" The word was a crimson gauntlet flung into the wind between them, hovering with a glittering brilliance. He whispered, "We shall see how long 'never' is."

"Don't touch me! Can't you understand? I intended only my husband to touch me."

"Only a kiss, Lianna," he said softly. "I promise." He leaned forward, unable to understand his own foolishness, wondering if he would keep such a promise—or if he could. "How old are you?"

"Seventeen." Her cheeks flushed, and she asked shyly, "How old are you?"

"Twenty-seven. You should have guessed the arrangement of your maid. Why else would a captain take a troublesome wench along on a voyage?"

"As a serving girl. To demand more is loathsome!"

Laughter rumbled in his throat. "Last night, Lianna, you thought I was far from loathsome."

"I was filled with wine, and you're a devil to remind me. I won't willingly let you touch me again." The moment she said the words, she bit her lip, and he wondered if she had the slightest idea how tempting she looked.

Unable to resist, feeling the tight ache in his loins, he reached for her. Instantly she drew back against the mound of pillows, a protest rising. "No!"

He paid no heed, holding her steadfastly.

"Will you stoop to force?" she cried.

His pulse raced as swiftly as hers, and his voice dropped to a husky tone. "I told you—only a kiss."

"I'll have none of your tricks! I'm not filled with wine!" she gasped.

"Shortly, that will be of no significance to either of us," he said softly.

With a wild scramble, without thinking that there was no place to escape, she struggled to get off the bunk, out of his reach. In an easy, lithe movement, one arm circled her waist to pull her down while Josh's other hand locked both wrists together and pinned them above her head, stretching them high and holding them to the pillows as he leaned down to touch her lips.

How sweet, and what promise was given! Suddenly he burned with desire. He trailed kisses across her lips, her throat, as he whispered, "I want you, Lianna Melton. I want you to willingly wrap your arms around my neck as you did last night, to tell me you love me."

"I never will!" she whispered, sounding dazed.

He sat up to look into blue eyes that would be forever in his memory. "I would wager my life that you will someday!"

He leaned down, his mouth covered hers, and he kissed her deeply until he felt her hips shift. He released her wrists, and her hands came to lie against his chest, but she didn't push.

A commotion sounded outside the cabin. A gruff voice called loudly, "Captain! Sails sighted!"

Josh swore under his breath, straightening to answer. "Aye. I'll be there." He smiled at her, stroking her cheek lightly before he rose. As he turned his back, he heard her gasp and knew she was shocked, as others had been before her, over the scars crisscrossing his back. Without a word he snatched up discarded breeches, pulling them on. As he slipped into a shirt, she stood up and wrapped the sheet around her.

When she raised her chin defiantly, he felt another surge of admiration mingle with a hungry need for her. The sheet molded her slender form, and her tangled black hair was a cloud across her shoulders.

He smiled and touched her chin. "We have a long, long voyage."

Emotions played clearly in her features, her blue eyes held first fear and then fury, and suddenly she raised her hand to strike him.

He caught her wrist. Amused, he laughed softly, then with deliberation turned her palm up to kiss her soft flesh, to trace a moist tongue over sensitive nerves.

She jerked violently to free her hand, but he held it while he gazed into her eyes, then placed his hands on either side of her face to hold her. He kissed her deeply until he felt her soften against him.

When he pulled away, Lianna opened her eyes to meet his mocking gaze. They both knew he had won. Another second and she would have clung to him.

Smiling, he left and closed the door behind him.

Lianna stood still for a full minute. All the events of the past hours rushed in on her, his words, his threats, his kisses. Her world had changed too swiftly to grasp the events with logic.

She was caught in a turmoil of emotions: rage, longing, uncertainty, and fright. She rubbed her hand where he had kissed her, realizing how unthinkable it would have been, only days ago, to strike a man. Captain Raven had pushed her beyond the layers of well-mannered social customs. He had taken her virginity . . . Questions swarmed in her mind like angry bees. Would Edwin still love her and want her? And a nagging thought she didn't want to acknowledge surfaced—why had Josh Raven's kisses stirred her more than Edwin Stafford's? Her thoughts drifted to Josh, and the image of his strong body flitted to mind, making her burn with embarrassment, yet her pulse speeded at the same time.

His back had been laced with scars. She frowned as she thought of the fine white lines etched in his tanned flesh. She had not discovered them in the night, unaware when her fingers had played over them. What had happened to him?

If she had not changed places with Quita, she would be on her way to Spain and marriage to a man who might be far worse than Captain Raven. But then, what would become of her when Josh Raven tired of her? She remembered his husky voice saying, "I'll give you time . . ."

Time? Time to become accustomed to his presence? Time to accept the idea that she was bought and paid for? Never! Deep green eyes with gold flecks danced before her; her lips tingled as she recalled exactly how his mouth had moved on hers. Blushing, she remembered last night, and a heated warmth flowed into her.

In agitation she swept up and down the cabin, attempting to forget the night, to forget how she had responded to Josh's kisses.

Her mind worked feverishly over her dilemma. Would he cast her aside in a foreign port? Leave her penniless? If she escaped, could she return to England and persuade Edwin to . . . what? And would Edwin still want her?

Her head throbbed, and she walked over to the desk and opened the drawers. The second drawer held a long, sheathed stiletto.

She turned it in her hand; the silver hilt was cold against her palm; then she dropped it back into the drawer. At the moment she felt she could have cheerfully sunk it into Captain Raven.

Outside, in a light mist, Josh reached the poop deck and took the spyglass from Fletcher's hands. "Spanish bark in distress, sir."

"Spanish!" Josh peered at the foundering ship that had a broken mast and was listing to port.

"Run up the flag of Spain. Prepare to launch longboats. We'll welcome them aboard."

"Aye, sir," Fletcher answered promptly, but Josh saw the question in his eyes.

"The Spaniards may be useful," he said softly. "I want them to think we're fellow countrymen. Give orders to speak only Spanish. The men will know what to do."

"Aye, sir." With an almost imperceptible nod, the first mate gave the orders.

As *El Feroz* changed course to reach the sinking ship, Josh watched, but his mind was belowdeck. Lianna. The name was lovely. Could he keep the promise he'd made to her? Give her time. He laughed softly. Had the days at sea addled his brain? She was so young, yet she'd had the spunk to defy her father and run away. Just as he had so many years ago. His jaw tightened and he stared at the distant ship, now looming closer.

He could sink the Spanish ship and every last man aboard her, but if he took them on board, returned them to their not-too-distant homeland, he might gain some knowledge from them that would aid his Chilean venture. While he watched men move frantically about the bark, he could hear Lianna's laughter, remember how her blue eyes danced when they talked during dinner. She was the kind of woman he could so seldom meet—damn, she was the woman of his dreams! He shook his head and laughed softly at himself. He should have taken Tillie and cooled his ardor; perhaps then he could view his new passenger with logic.

"Sir, did you say something?"

"No, Fletcher, except that my Spanish serving girl is not what I expected."

Fletcher looked through the glass at the bark. "She's a beauty."

Josh lowered his voice. "Aye. She is also an English gentlewoman. Her father is a merchant."

Fletcher's head whipped around, and Josh nodded. "She ran away from home."

"How in the sweet hell did she get here?"

"She exchanged places with her maid, Quita Bencaria, not guessing what kind of service little Quita had pledged."

Fletcher glanced at the hatchway and looked curiously at Josh.

"She stays with us," Josh answered the question he saw in Fletcher's eyes.

"And will we have the constable after us when we put into an English port?"

"I don't know, but she stays." Josh raised the glass to his eye to look at the sinking vessel, closing the subject.

Below, Lianna washed and dressed in the severe black dress, brushing her long hair up to fasten it in a bun on top of her head. At the sound of a knock, she paused, then called out to enter. A steward came in.

" 'Morning, ma'am," he said, removing the dishes from the night before.

"Good morning," she answered stiffly, barely able to speak. Her cheeks flamed in the realization that all men on board knew she was the captain's mistress.

"I'll have your breakfast in a minute," he said, and retreated, returning shortly with a tray of steaming dishes.

When the steward left, Lianna sat down gingerly to a breakfast of ham, biscuits, and oatmeal. From abovedeck, shouts could be heard, mingling with the sound of running feet. She rose to step to the window, but could see nothing except endless water, which had grown rougher since early morning. Gray clouds hid the sun, darkening the day ominously. Wrapping a shawl around her shoulders, she opened the door cautiously; no one was in sight. She climbed to the deck, then paused beside the galley funnel, standing out of the way of the milling men. Cold air made her shiver, and she folded her arms across her chest.

Seamen rushed to and fro; Captain Raven's voice barked commands. In the choppy water, another ship was floundering. Broken and splintered masts thrust jaggedly into a gray sky. A burly crewman rushed past, noticed Lianna, and halted. His gaze swept over her, his eyes burning insolently. "Holy saints!" he breathed.

Before she could say anything, Captain Raven appeared. His green eyes flashed as he took in the sight of both of them. "Reef sails," he commanded curtly.

"Aye, captain," the man answered, and hurried to obey. "Get below," the captain ordered.

Although Lianna had been on the verge of returning to

the cabin, a perverse anger at his command caused her to raise her chin defiantly. What was there between them that made her want to defy him at every turn? "No, Captain Raven."

He had turned, her presence already forgotten, with his gaze in the direction of the sinking ship. At her response, his head whipped around and his eyes glittered, but he said nothing, and turned again, to disappear toward the bow of the ship. Lianna felt a small measure of satisfaction that she had annoyed him. Yet, had she? Could she really dent Joshua Raven's armor? In her heart, she knew the answer.

Her attention returned to the sinking ship. Breakers curled and licked against its hull like greedy tongues lapping at a morsel which would soon be swallowed. The roll and pitch of the ailing vessel became violent. Cutters were lowered; men climbed down footropes, dropping into the small craft.

While a longboat pushed off from the sinking ship, men ran to and fro on the deck. The yardarms tilted crazily with the broken masts and spars were black lines sharply etched against the sky. Suddenly Lianna realized how trapped she was on *El Feroz*. If it went down, so would she. Holding the rail, she peered at sails draped in tatters, tangled around the broken masts. The mizzenmast dropped lower as the ship sank and the bowsprit raised skyward. She traveled with a privateer who was sanctioned to commit piracy by his own country. How soon would she have to endure a pitched battle, to hope that Captain Raven came out the victor and was not sunk at the bottom of the ocean? What an exchange she had made with Quita!

A longboat was launched from *El Feroz* to rescue the crew of the sinking ship. Lianna saw the yellow-and-red Spanish flag flutter above. Spanish seamen would not refuse rescue by Englishmen. What trickery was Josh up to now?

Waves swamped the afterdecks of the Spanish bark. With a froth of bubbles, gray water closed over the splintered masts and the vessel vanished. Bits and pieces of wood bobbed to the surface. Men swam and floated, calling to the crews of the longboats. As Lianna gazed at the rescue procedure, Captain Raven reappeared.

"I ordered you to get below."

"To hell with you, captain!" She had unthinkingly used language she had heard Edwin and other men at home employ, and realized she was changing day by day.

His brows raised, but his mouth twitched in a manner which looked as if he were attempting to suppress his laughter. He stepped forward and swung her into his arms. Her hands rested lightly against his chest, where she could feel his strong heartbeat. She caught a tangy scent that had grown familiar to her, that stirred memories she didn't want to recall.

She began to protest, but his voice silenced her. "Quiet, woman! Did you see their flag! It's a Spanish ship. You'll have to remain hidden when the Spaniards board our ship. Until they are gone, which won't be until we put into port, you're to remain quiet and in your cabin."

"I won't do either!"

"Indeed, you will." He reached down to open the door of a cabin. It was a narrow room with a hammock and a desk bolted into the bulkhead. It smelled dankly of damp oak timbers.

"I won't stay in this dungeon." He set her on her feet, pulling her against his chest.

"Don't push me too far!" he snapped in a deep voice. They looked into each other's eyes. While he gazed down at her, she saw the change in his countenance; the hardness softened, as did the lines around his mouth. His gaze lowered to her mouth, pausing with such intent she felt as if he had touched her lips. She moistened them with the tip of her tongue, then realized what she had done, as he drew a sharp breath.

"If I had time . . ."

"But you don't!" she gasped, unable to stop the hammering of her heart. "The Spanish should be boarding now."

"Ah, yes, the Spanish." He grinned mockingly. "You're not to make any commotion."

She tossed her head and opened her mouth to protest,

but before she spoke, he touched her lips lightly with his finger. "Don't refuse. Any disturbance from you, and I shall come"—he leaned down, the harshness returning to his features—"and thrash you. Do you understand?"

"You're a devil!"

"Be that as it may," he answered calmly, "don't make the mistake of pushing me too far, nor disbelieve what I threaten. I won't hesitate to do exactly as I have promised."

She regarded him with horror, seeing the cold glitter of determination. "You—"

He interrupted. "Don't tell me what to do or what not to do, Lianna. As soon as you understand that, we shall deal well together."

"I'm not interested in dealing with you at all!" she fumed. "I wish you had sunk with that ship!"

He laughed, a baritone rumble of mirth. His gaze lowered. "Why are you dressed in that black rag?"

"I have no intention of wearing your dresses!"

"I suspect you'll be delighted to wear them soon enough," he remarked dryly. "No woman cares to look like a crow day after day."

A crow! The man was infuriating! "What will happen to the Spaniards who come aboard?"

His eyes narrowed. "They may have information that I can use. We'll welcome the survivors and put them ashore in Spain."

"How can you be so treacherous?"

"I won't harm them; I've rescued them from the sea and I'll take them home. No treachery there . . ."

"Captain Raven, let me go ashore with them when you dock in Spain. Release me from this bargain." The words tumbled out and she held her breath, seeing something flicker in the depths of his eyes, and then his brows drew together as he frowned. "No, Lianna. You made your bargain with Quita." His eyes held a crystal coldness. "Now, no noise, do you understand?"

"I'll do as I please," she said angrily, furious with him for wanting her to fulfill Quita's bargain. "I won't be your mis—"

"Enough, Lianna!" he said, and left.

The door closed; a key grated in the lock. She glanced around the dark cabin at the small washstand, the single lantern, the tiny porthole. In the distance, voices could be heard, the commotion from topside filtering dimly to her ears.

Time passed slowly; the cabin grew darker. Growing hungry and hating the confinement, she paced the small area restlessly.

As she sat in the hammock, she thought about the captain from the sunken vessel. By this time he would be aboard ship, perhaps dining with Captain Raven.

If she could escape for a few minutes from the tiny cabin, make her presence known to the Spaniard, Captain Raven might have to relent, to give her freedom to go ashore in Spain. She could return to England, to Edwin.

She peered through the darkness at the door, contemplating a means of escape—and clearly, the image of glittering green eyes came. The warning of a thrashing was beyond her comprehension. Her father hadn't been loving, but he had never inflicted physical punishment, nor allowed his servants to do so. She realized Captain Raven was capable of violence, but she was willing to take the risk in order to escape.

It was impossible to leave the cabin except by the door, and it was locked from the outside. Then she saw the lantern. She lifted it off a hook, turning it in her hands. The smooth glass and studded copper were cold to the touch.

She ran her fingers over a sharp edge on the bottom, and decided it would be a satisfactory weapon. Her lips tightened in determination as she sat down to wait.

Hours passed and she grew weary. The steady rise and fall of the ship, the constant groaning timbers, made it difficult to stay awake. She leaned against the bulkhead and dozed, then woke with a jump as a key grated in the lock.

She grasped the lantern and stood, her heart pounding loudly.

The door swung open and light spilled into the room. Carrying a lantern, Captain Raven entered.

Lianna stepped behind him and brought the lantern down on the back of his head.

A dull thump sounded; Captain Raven pitched forward to the deck. His lantern crashed, and the light flickered crazily.

Fully certain that she had killed him, Lianna stared, for a moment aghast. She saw he was breathing, and relief, as well as reason, returned. Fleeing into a passageway, she raced for the captain's cabin, because his guests had to be quartered there or nearby.

11

Raven opened his eyes. His head pounded and the cabin spun around him. For an instant he stared ahead, dazed and hurt, until recollection hit him.

As he lunged to his feet, a wave of pain assaulted him. Staggering against the bulkhead, he steadied himself. He had to stop Lianna! She would try to get help from the Spanish—and might reveal his plans to them, thereby endangering the life of every man on board ship!

He stumbled into the passageway, fighting a surge of light-headedness.

He saw her running ahead. He hurried after her, trying to move quietly, yet clumsy from the pain. The passage wavered before him, and he felt faint. Gritting his teeth, he lengthened his stride to stop her. Damn the wench!

He almost fell. Straightening himself, he saw her glance over her shoulder, her eyes widening in fright. For a second she froze, and he narrowed the distance between them. Then she whirled and dashed around a corner.

He swore softly. He had to reach her before she found one of the Spaniards. While his head throbbed with hammer blows, it was clearing. He broke into a run, rounding the corner and sprinting after her. He reached out, slipping his arm around her waist to snatch her off her feet.

Lianna screamed, a shrill piercing cry that seemed like a dagger thrust through his head. He clamped his hand over her mouth. In seconds, he heard footsteps running over the deck.

Crushing her against him as she struggled, he dragged her down behind a cluster of barrels. Above them voices could be heard; there was clatter on the deck. A shout rang out.

"Not a sound from you, you vixen!" Raven hissed. He held his breath and listened.

The sound of footsteps close at hand tormented Lianna. She longed to cry out, to summon the Spaniards, but Raven's fingers bit cruelly into her flesh. Terror gripped her as she remembered his threat. Would he carry it out?

Gradually the ship grew quiet. Keeping her back pressed tightly against him, Captain Raven stood and nudged her ahead. They moved along the passageway until they reached his cabin. Once inside, he bolted the door and released her.

Her breath came in uneven gasps as she watched him cross to the wardrobe, open it, and withdraw a rawhide whip.

Her hand flew to her throat. He faced her, his eyes blazing with fire, his mouth set in a grim line. His hair tumbled over his forehead in an unruly tangle, only partially hiding a thin red cut he had received in his fall. Dust smudged one cheek darkly.

"You wouldn't!" she gasped, stepping back.

"My word is law on this ship," he said, fury lacing his voice. "What would happen if they learned of my plans?"

"I wouldn't reveal them!"

"Perhaps not deliberately—yet how am I to know I can trust your word? If they learned what I intend, I would have to murder every one of them or face prison if we docked in Spain! Did you think of the consequences of your action?"

Startled, she drew a shaky breath. "I wouldn't have caused trouble for your men. I would have just asked to get ashore in Spain so I can return to England."

"And how would you have explained your situation?"

"I could have done so without involving you."

"Or you could have taken your revenge. All I've seen from you is anger!" he snapped, stirring her wrath anew. His chest heaved; blood streaked his temple, running down across his jaw. Regret filled her, but it was useless to repeat that she wouldn't have revealed his plans. Their gazes locked and held like links forged together in a chain.

Captain Raven stood with his feet planted apart, his black seaboots gleaming dully in the light. His unwavering eyes, and powerful body, now held in check, reminded her that she faced a ruthless pirate, a man who had killed in battle. In a silent match of wills, tension stretched between them, pulling as tautly as an anchor rope dropped over the side.

She would not let him see her fear, yet her breathing constricted. Though her eyes burned, she refused to so much as blink. She wanted to turn and run, to defend herself, to escape from his rage, but too well she recalled the strength in his muscled arms, the speed with which he could move. In spite of her terror, she refused to cower before him

He walked slowly toward her. "Where are the tears or cries of terror?" he asked softly.

"I have none." She stared at him resolutely. "Do what you will. To me the pain of your whip is nothing compared to the indignities you have made me suffer," she said stiffly, praying he could not hear the loud hammering of her heart.

He reached out to touch her cheek, but she jerked her head away. "Leave me alone!"

"I warned you against stirring a commotion." He raised the whip and tapped it lightly against his hand. "Turn around. Will you disrobe—or do I rip that garment from your back?"

Lianna's pulse skittered and faintness welled within her, yet she refused to allow him the satisfaction of seeing her plead for mercy. She stared hard at him, and suddenly she felt that they were in a power struggle of another kind, a conflict that went beyond a ruthless captain and his unwilling mistress, past the present moment into a timeless battle between man and woman. A two-sided coin of anger and desire.

Instead of turning her back, she shook her head, swirling midnight tresses across her shoulders, and reached up slowly to free the ribbons of her black bodice. Her fingers trembled; she wanted to scream, to run. Instead, she faced him defiantly, and without taking her eyes from his, she loosened the front of her dress.

Her thin chemise did little to hide her full pale breasts or their rosy tips. For the first time in long moments, his gaze left hers. His chest expanded with his indrawn breath; his lashes drooped as his eyes burned over her body. Unwillingly, she felt herself respond to his look. The throbbing peaks of her breasts grew taut as his gaze touched them like a caress. She hated her reaction, yet she arched her back proudly, making her breasts thrust toward him. "Do what you will," she declared.

His eyes clashed with hers, only this time with fiery heat, built not by rage, but by passion.

She turned her back with a toss of her head, and clasped her hands together in front of her as she closed her eyes. Steeling herself for the first blow, she prayed that she would not cry out or beg for mercy. How she would like to put a dagger through his hard heart! She heard the whip whistle, slicing the air.

It cracked sharply on the deck at her feet. She jumped at the noise before whirling in surprise to watch Raven fling the whip across the cabin, where it struck the bulkhead and dropped to the deck. Quickly he strode across the room and pulled her roughly to him. The bristles on his jaw scraped her cheek as he lowered his head.

In a husky voice he murmured into her hair, "You're too lovely. Your beauty has bound me in fetters and my senses are drugged with you. It is I who am held in bondage, Lianna, not you," he whispered. "I'm bound by blue eyes, by full red lips that forever hold an invitation, by your fiery courage and a sweetness that warms me." His lips covered hers, his tongue assaulted her senses as he plundered her mouth to stop the words that he was afraid he might say. He was in bondage to her loveliness, to something fragile and intelligent—and he wanted her heart and soul even more than he wanted her body.

As his tongue stroked and delved and awoke a response

in her, he fought a raging battle against his desire. Why
didn't he throw her down and take her? She was his—
bought and paid for like a horse or a ship! Fury and
white-hot desire warred with a desperate ache in his heart,
a longing for something that he sensed he had found in
Lianna Melton.

As he buried his face against her throat, kissing her with
lips that were hot and searing, he felt her pulse race as
swiftly as his own.

She moaned softly. His voice dropped to a seductive
rasp that ran over her nerves like hot, sweet honey. "Lianna,
you are a lovely creature and I will have you, but I want
you to be willing and eager." His lips caressed her throat.
His fingers lifted heavy strands of black hair from her neck
and he kissed the delicate hollow between her throat and
shoulder.

Scooting away, she snatched up the black dress to cover
her breasts.

Admiration filled him as he looked at her wild blue
eyes. Thank God she was no wilting English miss—that
she had the courage to defy him, and the wisdom to almost
succeed!

He felt exhilaration and desire at the same time. His
loins ached with need of her, but he curbed his impulses,
knowing he wanted more than her lovely body.

"You blush," he stated with such satisfaction that her
anger flared anew.

"I have gone from a sheltered life to the life of a
dockside strumpet!"

"Strumpet? No, Lianna. 'Strumpet' is not a description
for you. Never." With each word his voice lowered and
his speech slowed until the last came out in a furred
huskiness that wrapped her in its warmth like a soft woolen
blanket. She trembled with a longing that she couldn't
combat. His strong tanned arms reached for her, slipping
around her waist. Remembering the night before, his rav-
ishment and her haze of pain and pleasure, Lianna was
torn with shame and remorse. She struggled, gripping
forearms that were as unyielding as iron. "Let me go!"
she cried. "Have you not inflicted enough pain?"

His voice was deep, a rumbling lion's purr. "Pain? No, love, I'll give you pleasure. You're a pleasure-kitten, a woman whose body is meant for love."

She twisted her face, and her long hair swirled over them as he kissed her throat. One arm held her tightly while Josh's free hand wound in her thick hair.

Her pulse drummed, yet she fought with all her strength, aware in the depths of her being that she fought more than Joshua Raven—she fought her body's wild, surging response to his every touch. She struggled to overcome her weakness, to deny what she felt, to resist what he was doing to her. "You've used your brute strength . . ."

Soon the protests became soft whimpers of pleasure. In spite of her determination to resist, she had no more control over her actions than when she had been intoxicated with wine.

Raven's lips reached the valley between her breasts and his tongue stroked her skin, tasting the sweetness of her flesh as he trailed a moist path around a trembling peak.

She was aflame. She felt as if she would burst with need. Protests were forgotten, circumstances no longer mattered.

She gasped as his indolent caresses heightened her fervor swiftly and pleasure spun through her in giddy waves. Suddenly he pulled the dress over her shoulders, tugging it high against her throat.

Dazed, she looked up at him. Beads of perspiration dotted his brow and she saw the tenseness of his shoulders. His voice was as ragged as his breathing.

"I promised you time. You shall have it."

He left, turning the key in the lock.

Lianna's heart pounded as she stared at the door, too startled to fathom his actions. *"I promised you time . . ."* The words swirled around her head like windblown snowflakes. Time? She licked her dry lips and frowned. If he had opened the door, she would have welcomed him into her arms!

The realization shocked her, and she felt a swift rush of shame. She was a hussy! There was no love between them, yet Josh Raven could easily demolish reason and make her desire him.

Suddenly she felt as if she had lost something. Tears stung her eyes. Why couldn't she have found this with a man who loved her instead of a ruthless pirate who would soon cast her aside?

The key scraped in the lock and he returned, hanging a lantern on a hook. "All is quiet now. You'll stay in your own cabin." He crossed the room and his dark brows drew together over the bridge of his nose. "Lianna?"

Unbidden, more tears sprang to her eyes. His thumb brushed her cheek and he lifted her chin. He sat in a chair, pulling her down on his lap. "What's this? Why tears?"

"Captain Raven . . ."

"Josh, love," he said with soft laughter.

"Am I wicked, a wanton?"

This time laughter caused his warm breath to fan on her cheek. "Wanton! Aye, that you are."

"Oh, no!"

"Don't say 'Oh, no!' You're delightfully wanton and that's the way it should be."

"Should be?" She opened her eyes wide to look at him.

He flashed a smile. "Aye, love. You were meant for a man—you take your pleasure as you give it."

"That's wicked, according to Doria, my betsy." Lianna blushed hotly.

His green eyes developed a devilish twinkle and she suspected he was enjoying himself. "What did Doria say on the subject?"

"She said that women who . . . enjoy men are wicked."

He chuckled softly. "No, my love. You're not wicked. You're sweet and fiery, as tempting as a flickering flame in the cold."

Suddenly his engaging smile worked its charm. She couldn't resist returning a smile. She caught his jaw in her fingers and held him lightly, her voice teasing as she said, "Then beware, Joshua Raven, that you don't get burned."

A startled look crossed his face, and his smile widened. He stroked her hair, his fingers idly brushing her shoulder beneath the silken strands. "Perhaps your warning comes too late, love."

She blushed and let him brush her hair over her shoulder. His voice dropped to a low timbre. "It can be so much better, Lianna. Next time, I won't hurt you."

She felt drawn to him and was shocked by her reaction. Why did he always win her over swiftly? She touched the bloody cut on his head. "I'm sorry."

"My head aches abominably, wench!"

"It is a head as hard as the deck, to withstand such a blow!"

He grinned and lightly kissed her throat, sending tingles spreading through her like lightning. "You're a vixen too, Lianna. Next time I'll beware—"

"Next time, sir? You intend to lock me up again?"

"I should retrieve the cat and teach you how to respect your captain. I paid handsomely—and not for a wench who downs me with a lantern!"

They both laughed. At the moment it seemed ridiculous that they had fought. She felt as giddy as she had the night before—and she cared not to explore why. She touched his forehead. "I don't see a bump."

"Here, a knot to make me look two-headed." His fingers directed her to the back of his head, where she felt a frightful lump.

"Oh, I'm sorry!" she said softly. His eyes looked at her accusingly, but a twinkle danced in their depths.

"Aye, you're sorry I hurt, but you'd gladly do it again if you had the chance."

She smiled, and he pulled her to his chest and leaned down. Lianna raised her lips, tilting her head backward. Her heart skipped a beat as his mouth dipped down, then paused inches from hers. "We'll go now," he said softly.

It took a few minutes for the words to sink in.

"Regretfully, I must take you back to the small cabin."

Startled that he hadn't kissed her, and shocked how deeply that disappointed her, she straightened her clothing. Why had he stopped? And why did she feel such an intense regret? Only an hour ago she had struggled against him with all her strength, yet now her heart raced and she longed to feel his arms around her!

He turned to look at her. Deep within her something constricted, taking all her breath. He was rumpled, his hair hanging free, his brown locks framing his face. His white shirt was open at the throat and his breeches hugged slender hips. As her gaze lifted, he leaned against the bulkhead and tilted his head, his smile knowing. She blushed because he had caught her looking so boldly at him.

"Lianna, how difficult you make it for me to move you to another cabin," he said huskily.

"You said I could go," she replied, yet she felt an unaccountable excitement.

"Can I trust you to go quietly?"

"For now, yes."

"Good. It will gain you nothing to cause trouble. Let's go quickly."

As soon as they were in the small cabin, she faced him. "I don't want to stay locked in here."

"Sorry, my love. You're no longer home, where your every wish is a command."

"My every wish never was a command."

His brows narrowed and his voice became gentle as he asked, "Were your parents unkind?"

"My mother died when I was a babe, and my father is . . . a cold man. He wasn't unkind," she said stiffly, hating the pinch of hurt she felt when she thought about her father's uncaring attitude.

"Yet he pledged you to a man you don't love, a Spaniard so far from home. Ah, my sweet Lianna," he said tenderly, stroking her cheek, and she was tempted to step closer, wanting his arms around her.

"How can you say that one minute, then lock me in here the next?"

He smiled. "If I didn't lock you in, we both know what might occur. Deliberately or accidentally, you could betray us all and bring down the wrath of Lucifer."

"How could I?" she asked quickly, feeling a flare of

excitement as she watched him. "You're Old Ned in the flesh!" The sparkle in his eyes made her smile.

"You call me Old Ned, yet I recall your lips pressed eagerly to mine."

"It was because of your devilish charm!" she teased.

He laughed. "So I'm charming! Lianna, how flattered I am."

"Don't give yourself airs! You know you can be charming."

"Every second makes parting more difficult. I want to take you back with me to my cabin."

"Then I won't say another word, so you will go."

A mocking smile made creases in his cheeks. "Good night, Lianna."

He brushed his mouth over hers and her lips parted as she closed her eyes and waited. She opened them to find him watching her. She blushed, knowing that she had wanted his kiss badly, and that he had seen her desire. He caught her chin between his thumb and forefinger, holding her, and she saw his intent in his eyes. Her pulse drummed as she realized he would kiss her.

"You want my kiss," he whispered.

She stared at him, unable to deny it because every fiber of her being quivered in anticipation.

"Say it, Lianna! Admit that you do."

She wanted to say no for so many logical reasons, but as she watched him, the word wouldn't come. Her gaze dropped to his mouth, and she felt longing tug at her like a net towing her along.

"Say it," he demanded gruffly.

"Yes," she whispered. She closed her eyes and his mouth came down as he pulled her into his arms, crushing her to him while his tongue thrust against hers. "Kiss me back, Lianna," he whispered. "Kiss me like I kiss you."

She was powerless to do otherwise, wanting him in a way she hadn't known she could want a man.

He leaned over her, his hand caressing the nape of her neck while his other arm tightened around her waist. She moaned softly, and suddenly he released her, looking at her intently. "I'll keep my promise to you," he said. He kissed her fleetingly on the lips and turned and left, locking the door behind him.

Her body trembled with desire as she listened to his footsteps fade away. She sat down on the bunk and gazed at the yellow glow of the lantern swinging from a hook. How Josh could charm her! The man's seductive ways melted her objections with total ease. "*I will give you time . . .*" she remembered. She wondered if in time she would be his completely, willing to throw aside everything for him. And suddenly she wondered how many broken hearts had been left behind by Joshua Raven in the past. She shook her head vigorously. What she felt for Josh wasn't love— love was reserved for the one man who had given it freely to her, to Edwin. Josh Raven had awakened her desire, taken her from girlhood to womanhood, but he didn't love her, and she knew he never would. He was a hard man, and one who had known many women—of that she had no doubt. Pity the woman who loved him.

She touched her lips with her fingertips, feeling her emotions war inside her. She loved Edwin and she shouldn't accept Captain Raven's kisses or return them, yet she couldn't resist! She flung herself down on the bunk, wondering why she couldn't control her own feelings, wondering again why Josh Raven could stir her in a manner Edwin never had.

Josh went above to check on the consequences of his fight with Lianna. Silently he took the wheel from Fletcher. Around them, gray fog rolled in off the sea, swirling and closing them into visibility of only a few yards.

With a hushed voice Fletcher said, "There were questions about a woman on board, sir. One of the Spanish sailors thought he heard a scream."

"Was an explanation given?" Josh asked in a voice as low as Fletcher's. Fine mist blew coldly against his cheeks.

"Aye, I explained that a cabin boy cut his wrist. The surgeon sewed him up and ordered sleep."

"You think that satisfied everyone?"

"Who knows?" Fletcher shrugged.

"She's back in her cabin, safely locked away. She hoped to reach the Spanish."

Fletcher swore softly.

"She's young, Fletcher."

"And beautiful," the first mate said bitterly.

"Do not distrust all women because of the treachery of one." Seldom did Josh refer to the unhappy love affair Fletcher had had before he joined the crew of the ship, but he now was goaded into the reminder. Against the rolling fog, Fletcher's broad shoulders were darkly outlined. His thick golden hair was a patch of yellow in the night.

"Hasn't this one already shown her treachery?" Fletcher asked. "She is supposed to be aboard a Spanish ship sailing to La Coruña to be wed to a nobleman, not here on *El Feroz.*"

"She said she only wanted to go ashore in Spain. She swore she wouldn't have revealed our plans."

"And you believe her?"

"Yes. She's young and she's truthful."

"Josh, take care. You're letting her addle your brains. She would do it again if she had a chance. She is a 'lady' and thinks only of herself. She's been reared in a pampered life, and to her the universe revolves around her whims. Do you think she cares a fig about anyone on board this ship?" Fletcher asked angrily.

"Fletcher, don't condemn all young women who have been born into wealth, because one used you wrongly and betrayed you."

"If it hadn't been for you, I would've been hanged in prison for the crimes her highwayman lover had done. My fine lady wanted a scapegoat, and all her vows of love were to keep me entangled to protect him. You'll see. They're all alike. This one will be the same."

"My head pounds," Josh said sharply. "Take the wheel while I see if I need stitches."

"Aye, captain," Fletcher replied.

Josh descended the hatchway, moving briskly down the passage toward the surgeon's cabin.

As the empty carriages and their drivers covered the final miles to the Melton manor, a rider appeared in the road ahead. Hatless and pounding down the lane, his cape flying behind him, he galloped toward them. Edwin was the first to recognize Byron, and his curiosity stirred. Byron pulled up sharply. "I ride for a doctor. The squire's had an accident."

"What happened to him?"

"His foot slipped and he stepped on his broken ankle and lost his balance. He fell down the main staircase, and we need a doctor desperately!"

Byron waved to them and the carriage moved ahead while Edwin mulled over the bit of news.

When they reached the manor, they found Squire Melton in as dire a shape as Byron had indicated. The doctor arrived that afternoon and took up residence there for the next few days. Squire Melton had injured his back and his leg seriously, and suffered internal injuries that Dr. Frampton could not identify and could not get to respond to his treatment.

It was time for Edwin to return to London, yet he wanted to see what happened to the squire because now the doctor said the squire's life hung by a thread.

Edwin paced the floor on sleepless nights while Byron sat late drinking ale with him. "You'll wear yourself thin," Byron drawled, watching Edwin move restlessly around the narrow room.

"I should be riding for London right now. Damn! What a turn of fate. If only this had happened months ago! Lianna may inherit everything."

"A lot of good it will do her if she has given Quita her identity."

"Quita will never return to claim it. She would run too great a risk—provided she tricks the Spaniard at all."

"I don't know how a Spanish peasant maid could pass herself off as an English lady," Byron said dryly. "She'll end up in a dungeon."

"She may succeed if she wants it badly enough," Edwin said, his mind momentarily on Quita. Then his thoughts went back to his own situation. "Should I go or should I stay? If Lianna inherits, I'll search this earth over for her."

"You said she is sailing where?"

"To a land called Chile that's on the other side of the earth."

"You're let in the attic with your wild thoughts of finding her or of gaining the squire's inheritance. Daft as bats, you are!"

"I'm going to London," Edwin said, suddenly reaching a decision. "It would be just like the old bastard to languish for months, and I'll miss my chance to sail with Captain Turner. Come with me, Byron. We have a chance to gain a fortune."

"Or lose our lives at the end of a knife. No thank you. I'll stick with simple pleasures."

Edwin pulled down his cape and hat and pocketed the money he had saved. He picked up the bundle of belongings he'd hidden in preparation for his departure for the sea. He turned to offer his hand to Byron.

"How I wish you would come with me."

Byron shook his hand. "No. It's not for me. I don't have the stomach for it."

"I do. I'm hungry. Try to send word to me in London at the Boar's Head tavern. Nan will save my letters."

Byron grinned. "You moan about Lianna and talk about Nan all in the same hour."

"They're different. Each serves a purpose in my life. I intend to find Lianna."

"She may be greatly changed if and when you do find her."

"Byron," Edwin said coldly. Byron's head snapped up. "Never a word that she has served a sea captain. No one in England knows except you and me."

"Of course, Edwin."

"And if she comes home before I do, tell her I'm looking for her, that I'll come back at the end of my voyage. Tell her I love her. Take care of yourself."

He left swiftly, wanting to ride away without encountering his father. At the end of the lane, he glanced back, feeling a swift rise of hope that Squire Melton couldn't live through this week. Lianna would own everything, including two ships. After this voyage, Edwin intended to know how to handle a ship. He would learn everything he could possibly learn. He turned the horse to the road for London.

When he dismounted in front of the Boar's Head at the end of his journey, it was late at night and he was weary from the hard ride. He had another eight hours before he had to board the ship. Eight hours. He entered the warm tavern and looked for his companions. Not spotting them, he sat down at a table and searched for Nan, catching sight of her as she stood filling glasses from a barrel of ale. She turned and saw him, and a smile lit her eyes. He was hungry and he intended to eat first, but when he saw her, his gaze dropped to the full curve of her breasts revealed by her low-cut gingham dress, his loins tightened, and he wanted her more than dinner.

He crossed the room to pay the tavern keeper for an upstairs room, then motioned to Nan. Smiling up at him, she said, "Yer back to see yer Nan."

"That I am. I have a room upstairs for the night, and I've paid for you to serve my ale there." He winked at her and her smile broadened knowingly.

"Yes, sir."

He tucked a coin in the front of her dress and smiled, feeling the warmth of her flesh. He went ahead, taking the stairs swiftly and finding the room he'd been given at the end of the hall. He lit an oil lamp and surveyed the simple room, which held only a washstand, bed, and one chair. A fire had already been built in the hearth, and the room held a cozy warmth. Laughter and muffled voices drifted up from below.

He moved restlessly around the room, looking out a frosty pane at the blackness, knowing beyond the buildings and rooftops was the sea and Lianna was sailing on it, sailing in the arms of a sea captain. . . .

He swore and turned angrily from the window, wondering what was keeping Nan, when he heard a slight knock.

"Come in," he said, and crossed the room.

She smiled as she swept inside. "I brought your ale, sir."

He closed the door and turned the lock, taking the tray from her hands. Suddenly he wanted her with a hungry violence. He turned her to him, yanking the dress off her shoulders.

Her eyes flew wide. "Sir! You'll tear—"

"Shut up. I'll pay you well," he murmured as he lowered his head to kiss her flesh while he shoved her dress to her ankles. The rough cotton shift was in his way and he ripped it down the center, seeing a flare of fright in her eyes, yet wanting to possess her and drive the demon images of Lianna from his mind.

Ten hours later, he watched Portsmouth recede into the coastline as the ship sailed out to sea. "Stafford!"

He turned to find the captain watching him, and suddenly, Edwin realized how inexperienced he was and what a task lay ahead of him. Captain Turner jerked his head, and Edwin hurried to him.

"You can sign on now. Here . . ." Captain Turner unrolled a scroll of paper and held it for Edwin, who read, "Articles of Agreement."

Edwin scanned the paragraphs, reading slowly in a soft voice the details that laid out everyone's responsibilities and shares. ". . . whoever first discovers a sail that becomes a prize shall receive one hundred pounds as a reward . . ." Edwin felt his pulse quicken as he read eagerly, ". . . whoever enters the enemy ship after boarding orders are given shall receive three hundred pounds . . ." He looked up and grinned at the captain. "I'll sign." Slowly he penned his name, then handed the paper back to the captain. Another seaman, a slender dark-haired man who looked only eighteen, stood beside them.

"Dunsten here will show you the ropes. Now, look alive or you won't sail long with me."

"Aye, sir. That I will. I want to know everything possible about sailing."

"Learn a little about fighting—it will serve you as well."

He followed Dunsten belowdecks through the captain's quarters, the galley, the berth deck with the cannon. Deep in the hold beneath the main hatchway Dunsten showed him where the shot and cannon balls were stored.

"This weight serves as ballast. There's the powder locker. It'll take a while, but you'll learn."

"I intend to learn fast," Edwin said grimly, giving his full attention to every detail. Dunsten showed him where the casks of drinking water and grog were stored. Top and forward of these were the provision barrels.

"I'll show you were to put your things," Dunsten said, leading him to the crew's quarters.

"How did you get into sailing?"

"I was a chimney sweep and an orphan as a child. I signed on as cabin boy early, and later I was on a ship taken by Cap'n."

As he looked at the dank, cramped space he would share with the other seamen, Edwin saw he would have to adjust after the comfortable quarters he'd had at home. "We all crowd in here?"

"No!" Dunsten laughed. "Cap'n's lieutenant, Pringle, the prize master, Gettys—they have officers' quarters down the port fore and aft gangway. Next, certain crew members have better quarters on the berth deck, where the boatswain, the gunner, carpenter, steward, and captain's clerk bed down. You'll sleep on a hammock here. Here's an empty sea chest left behind. It's yours."

"Thank you."

"And here's your best friend of all." He handed Edwin a cutlass. Edwin felt the weight of it in his hand. He shook his head. "I don't know how to use one."

"Just use it. It takes no special skill. You'll learn."

Edwin turned to slice it through the air, making several swings as he became more accustomed to the feel of the weapon.

"Wear it at your side when we sight another ship. Now, come along and I'll show you the ship and give you a task."

"I'm coming." Edwin put the cutlass in the chest along with his meager belongings and hurried after Dunsten. "Where's our destination?"

"The islands. Jamaica, to buy rum and sell English goods."

"Are these islands near Chile?"

"Great Hades, no! I'll show you a map." Dunsten shook the long braid of his dark hair back over his shoulder and straightened his canvas cap.

Edwin nodded. "Can I have a cap like yours?"

"Ask the sailmaker, Wooderston. It's made from ship's canvas and waterproofed with tar." He watched Edwin drop his things into the sea chest. "Each man gets a nooner, a gill of grog a day."

Edwin laughed as he stood up. "What's that?"

"A quarter of a pint of rum."

"We sail the same direction as if we were going to Chile, don't we?" Edwin asked, returning to the subject on his mind.

"Aye, for a time. Only we stop in the islands. If you were to go to Chile, you would keep sailing south down the coast of the New World and around Cape Horn—the most treacherous seas in the world. No, thank you, man. There's treasures enough to find not far from home. We don't need to risk our lives to sail to strange seas and enemy lands. No foreign ship can put into Spanish ports in the New World."

"But for now, we sail the same course," Edwin repeated.

"Yes, we do." Dunsten turned to look at Edwin with curiosity in his dark eyes. "What does Chile hold for you?"

"I was to be married, but the woman I was to wed sailed on a ship bound for Chile."

"We could encounter her. At sea, anything's possible."

"Have you ever heard of *El Feroz*?"

Dunsten shook his head. "No. A Spanish ship."

"No. It belongs to a Captain Raven—"

"The Sea Hawk! The man's not a raven, but a predatory hawk."

"You know him?"

"Captain's crossed paths with him once. He's a damned sea creature. He can outsail the devil himself! He cut our rigging to pieces and took everything we had aboard ship."

Edwin's curiosity was intense. "He let you live, though."

"Aye, that he did. He left us our ship and our lives. The

ship was a creaking wreck. We made it to port only
because we didn't encounter a storm.''

"So he isn't cruel. What does he look like?''

Dunsten paused, leaning his hand on a cask while he
grinned at Edwin. "Did she wed him?''

"No.'' Edwin saw the questions in Dunsten's eyes and
swiftly he related Lianna's plight and the exchange with
Quita.

"Damnation! She's cut her course now. He has a reputation with ladies dockside. They like him. Better than he
seems to like them. He has no ties that I've heard about.''

"What's he look like?'' Edwin persisted, wanting to
hear, yet dreading the answer.

"He's tall and fights like a fury and has the damndest
cold green eyes you'll ever encounter,'' Dunsten said, then
added slyly, "The world's full of women.''

"Not like this one.''

Dunsten grinned and jabbed Edwin in the ribs. "You've
never traveled far from home. Wait till we reach the
islands. You'll see some beauties that'll warm your blood
and make you forget your loss.''

As they reached the upper deck, Dunsten said, "*El
Feroz.* That's not his ship's name. He's up to something in
his journey to Chile. I'll tell Captain.''

"Would he attempt a fight with Captain Raven again?''

Dunsten shrugged. "Who knows what Cap'n will do?
We met him only once since we've sailed on this ship and
he didn't want to battle. Outran us. The man's a hawk, not
a raven. Now, climb up there.''

Edwin looked at the tall mast, the lines, and the rigging,
before he reached to grasp the footladder and scramble up.

In two days' time his skin was roughened by the wind
and sun, and his muscles ached beyond anything he would
have dreamed possible, but he was learning. He worked
diligently, stowing the hammocks early each morning—
doubling them, folding each at angles to the other until
they were packed away neatly. He paused now and then,
his gaze scanning the horizon.

"What're you looking for, mate?'' a companion asked.

"Another ship.''

"We'll find one soon enough. Spoiling for your first fight?"

Edwin smiled and turned back to stowing a hammock. *El Feroz* might not be too far ahead at all.

"Sails sighted!" came a cry from the lubber's hole high above.

Edwin's head snapped up as men began to swarm around him. Captain Turner moved to the bridge and took the telescope from a sailor.

"Unfurl sails!" he shouted, and men scrambled to obey. Edwin hurried beside Dunsten so he would learn what to do.

"What is it?"

"We're too far to tell yet. We're on the windward side."

"So what do we do?"

"We'll get on the same course and tack as the vessel we chase does." Dunsten squinted at Edwin. "You have the curiosity of a cat." Edwin glanced again at the white speck on the horizon, and his pulse jumped with the knowledge they were after a ship!

An hour later the ship was in plain sight and the distance was visibly narrowing.

"What kind of ship is it?" Edwin asked Dunsten, who came to stand beside him.

"An old Dutch ship, cumbersome and loaded with cargo. We'll catch her and we'll take her!"

"We've changed course and turned back toward England."

"That's the way the ship goes. We run northward toward Holland."

"And we run off our southern course."

"We'll get back on course later, and if we take her, you'll find it worth the time."

"How'll we get close enough to fight?"

"See." Dunsten pointed at the sails, then at the ship. "We tack whenever the ship is ninety degrees to beam. That way we'll meet."

Edwin went below to get the cutlass, feeling his blood pound with excitement. When he came above, the lieutenant met him. "You'll learn how to do battle now. You're one of the biggest men on the ship, so you get to the cannon. You'll go with the boarders. Kelsey will give you instructions. Stay with him.''

Edwin learned to place the hand spikes, rammers, powder horns, and matches by the side of each cannon. In another hour they caught the ship, their cannon blasting while the Dutch ship's cannon fired in return. Edwin helped a gunner, who stood to the right side of the cannon and rammed the powder cartridge down the full length of the bore. The powder was measured and rammed inside while he instructed Edwin to keep his thumb on the touchhole. Edwin worked feverishly, watching every movement, trying to store it in memory so he would soon be loading and firing a cannon, not assisting. A canonball hit the hull near his cannon, splintering it and making a resounding bang.

''We're moving alongside,'' Kelsey said.

''Prepare to board,'' the lieutenant called, and Edwin brandished the cutlass as he joined the others, swinging on grappling hooks.

The next moment Edwin was scrambling from his ship to the Dutch ship. A man rushed at him, cutlass raised. Edwin swung, putting all his weight behind his weapon. His knife sent the other man's clattering as it cut off the man's hand at the wrist and blood spurted over him. The man screamed, staring at his arm, and Edwin slashed his throat, moving on. He fought without thinking, as furiously as if he could overcome the demons in his life by winning this one battle.

Then it was over, and the ship was theirs. He heard shouts of triumph. Men stood in a cluster around the prisoners as Captain Turner boarded.

''We will take this ship and all its cargo. I don't want Dutch sailors. There are no survivors.''

''Aye, captain,'' a man said, and in moments the few surviving men were executed and tossed into the sea. Edwin's stomach churned at the thought of how little life was valued at sea. Yet how easy it had been! Men scrambled over the ship to discover what it contained, while Captain Turner picked a crew to man the stolen ship.

Edwin felt exultant. He felt as if he could take another ship single handedly. Dunsten came up from below, strings of pearls around his neck. "Look what I found in a sea chest. How'd you like your first fight?"

"It was grand!"

Overhearing Edwin, Captain Turner approached him. He clasped his hand on Edwin's shoulder, his laughter booming. "Listen to the green lubber! He has a thirst for riches and a damn strong arm. I saw you fight."

"Years of farming . . ." Edwin said, holding up his fist.

"You'll do well," Captain Turner said.

Edwin looked into the captain's black eyes. And someday I'll have my own ship, he thought, but he held back the words.

12

La Joya docked at La Coruña in February. As Quinta looked out the porthole, her nervousness made her hands turn to ice. Viewing the red tile rooftops of La Coruña and the thatched roofs of the nearby shacks, she thought how near her family was. Too near. She jumped at a rap on the door. Captain Lackly entered with a tall woman dressed in black at his side. Her dress was elegant, her features stern and frightening.

"Miss Melton, may I present Doña Vianta, who is to travel with you. She is a cousin of the Count of Marcheno. Señora, this is Miss Lianna Melton."

"Buenos días," Quita said, feeling terror shoot through her, wishing she had never committed a folly like exchanging places with Lianna.

"Buenos días," Doña Vianta returned, her cold black eyes studying Quita. "I understand your maid fell ill before you sailed, and you have traveled alone?"

"Yes, Doña Vianta."

Her frown became more fierce, and Quita could sense her extreme disapproval as Doña Vianta said, "You'll be accompanied by me as well as the servants as we ride to Madrid. Marcheno's carriages are waiting, and the captain has had your trunks loaded on the carriages. Everything is ready."

"I can go now," Quita said stiffly. Dressed in dark blue velvet trimmed in black, she wore the hat trimmed with the black gauze. As they started down the gangplank, she lowered the gauze to hide her face. Her gaze flitted over the docks from where she had sailed only a year earlier. She saw the lane she had ridden down when she had left Juan behind. Juan. She refused to think about him. She had turned her back on her past. With icy hands she climbed into the carriage behind Doña Vianta.

Sun shone brightly on the carriage as it rocked along the dusty lanes, carrying Quita through the town of her birth, passing the fountain where she had washed her clothes for her family. She sank back in the seat and soon La Coruña was behind her.

"Dispensing with our usual Spanish formalities, parties are arranged for the next few days so you can get acquainted. There are many relatives to meet."

Quita nodded, feeling the less she said, the better.

"Do you speak Spanish well enough to converse?" the older woman asked swiftly in her native tongue.

"*Sí*. I have had many years of study and a maid who spoke Spanish, as well as my mother, who taught me when I was small."

Looking relieved, Doña Vianta flashed her a chilly smile. "That's good. We'll speak in Spanish."

Each day became a stiff and tedious ride filled with awkward silences. They endured each other's company on the long journey to Madrid. The only moments Quita relaxed were at the inns where she was treated like royalty since she was traveling as the count's fiancee, so different from her past experiences as a maid. At night she would retire as early as possible to escape Doña Vinta's questions and forbidding presence.

Finally they neared Marcheno Castle outside Madrid. When Quita leaned forward to look out the window, and catch her first glimpse of the awesome structure, her breath stopped momentarily. Mammoth, with a multitude of parapets, turrets, and imposing towers, the castle loomed larger than she had imagined, covering an enormous expanse of ground. Sun splashed over its granite and limestone walls, and a red tile roof added to its warm appearance. Cypress and olive trees surrounded the outer walls. Quita thought it the grandest structure she had ever seen. Her heart thudded when she thought she would soon be mistress of the castle.

"How beautiful!" she murmured.

"It was built three centuries ago," Doña Vianta said proudly. "It's Mudejar architecture that was developed from a merging of Christian and Mohammedan traditions."

Quita clutched the window as she stared, unable to believe it would really be hers soon. And her children—a son who had her blood would someday be master of this castle. If only the count didn't discover the truth!

As the carriage rolled along a lane thickly bordered by olive trees, the sun went behind a cloud and a cold black shadow fell over the landscape. The chill ran through Quita, making her tremble. She glanced at Doña Vianta, who stared at her with hawklike black eyes. Quita drew herself up and leaned back against the seat. "I am weary of travel."

"You may rest as soon as we reach the castle."

And as soon as she had met the man she was to marry, Quita thought, conjuring up a vision of an older man; large, portly, and stern. Images of him had played through her mind countless times on her voyage. One moment she pictured a black-haired man, the next, a tall graying one, thin and gaunt. Then she would envision a white-haired man. At forty-one, the Count of Marcheno was almost her father's age.

When the carriage finally halted and she stepped down, she was aghast to discover an army of servants waiting to greet her. One by one, they were introduced by Doña Vianta. Then she was introduced to her personal maid, Yolana, and finally shown to her rooms.

As she climbed the broad steps to the wide polished floor of the hallway upstairs, her bewilderment changed to relief. She had not met the count yet and she would soon be in the haven of her room.

Her blood warmed, and her nerves calmed as she looked at the large room that was to be hers until the wedding. With shiny wooden floors, white walls, and dark beams in the ceiling, it looked magnificent to her. A canopied bed stood between arched windows, a dark mahogany armoire stood along one wall, and a brazier had been placed in the center of the room. She looked around at the washstand, the writing desk, things she had never possessed in her life or had at her disposal. It was far grander than Squire Melton's house, and for an instant she felt a twinge of sadness that Lianna would miss such a life for one of servitude. Then thoughts of her own rare good fortune crowded out consideration of Lianna. Again she was struck with a terrible fear that it was impossible for her, Quita Bencaria, to become mistress of Marcheno Castle. The count would take one look at her and see the truth, the serving girl who knew nothing of books or learning or society.

An oval mirror on a stand stood at an angle across the room from her, and as servants carried in her trunks, she glanced at her reflection. Her wide brown eyes looked full of fear. Taking a deep breath, she remembered how Lianna had treated her and tried to use the same polite tone.

"Please, set the small trunk by the foot of the bed. Thank you," she said, smiling at the boy who carried the smallest trunk.

In moments they were gone. Yolana said softly, "I'll get your bath ready so you can wash and freshen up. Tonight there is a ball. The count flouts custom—if you were a proper Spanish girl, he would have to conduct himself more circumspectly. It would be weeks before he could dance with you."

Fear rose along with a sense of helplessness as Quita stared at the girl. "I don't know how to dance." Her mind raced to think of an excuse. "I'm just out of the school-room, and my father never allowed me to attend a ball."

"Someone will teach you." Yolana looked at her and said shyly, "There are only two dances you will probably do. The count learned the waltz on a journey to France and he has it played at all the balls given here. They'll also do a Spanish dance, the fandango. I'll show you how."

"Please!" Quita said, wondering if she could learn the steps sufficiently to avoid appearing clumsy. She watched as the maid moved stiffly, then with a little more grace as she began to hum softly. Quita followed in step behind her until they both laughed. Remembering her position, Quita suddenly ended the moment. "I must bathe now. I'm tired from the journey. Thank you, Yolana. If you'll help me with this dress, please."

She turned her back to be helped to undress for the first time since she was an infant.

That night, she looked at herself in the long oval mirror and it was an effort to bite back a cry of surprise. Her own mother wouldn't know her. Her dark hair had been looped and twisted, and piled high on her head with long curls left hanging down the back of her neck. Fitting as perfectly as if it had been made for her instead of Lianna, the low-cut blue silk molded the curves of her high, full breasts, nipped in at her tiny waist, then flared over her hips. Rosebuds were pinned in her hair to match the velvet roses on the dress, and white lace trimmed its low neckline and short sleeves.

"How beautiful you look!" Yolana exclaimed.

"Thank you," Quita said, feeling a momentary pang of regret that Yolana was a servant and not a friend who could join her and share in the excitement. "Yolana, what is the count like?"

"El conde es muy macho, muy grande," she said swiftly, blushing slightly. "You are fortunate, as many hearts are broken by the news of your marriage to him."

"Señorita Melton," came a voice from the doorway. Doña Vianta, dressed in deep purple velvet from her chin to her toes, stood waiting. "You look lovely. You inherited much from your Spanish mother and little from your English father. Are you ready?"

"Sí," Quita said, feeling as if she were about to walk into a den of hungry wolves.

Side by side with Doña Vianta, she descended the steps to the grand hall. There, an elderly man who had black hair streaked with gray stood waiting, his long face changing from an impassive stare to a smile as she approached.

Her heart pounded because she was certain she was looking at her husband-to-be. He was less handsome than she had imagined, perhaps a bit older, although she had envisioned gray in his hair, but his smile was kindly.

"Señorita Melton, this is Don Felipe Acosta, the count's uncle. He will escort you to the ballroom."

Feeling a swift stab of relief that he was not the count, Quita took his arm and they crossed the hall.

She was announced, and found herself looking at a sea of curious faces, of handsome men in uniforms and fancy clothing, of women in elegant gowns. Beneath an *artesonado*, an elaborately carved wooden ceiling, chandeliers of lighted candles warmed the room. Doors to the terrace were thrown open. Musicians playing guitars softly sat on a dais flanked by greenery. The room was decorated with yellow roses, their sweet scent faintly carried in the air. Mirrors lined one wall, giving the room an illusion of vast spaciousness, and Quita felt too awed to move or breathe, knowing she stood in a place she did not belong.

Frightened to speak or act, she almost resisted when Don Felipe pressured her arm slightly to propel her forward. He leaned close to her to whisper, "*Señorita*, they are not lions you go to meet. They are curious and happy to welcome Marcheno's bride. They are all relatives and friends of the count's."

"Yes, sir," she whispered, finding it impossible to speak aloud. Her knees trembled and she suddenly feared someone would denounce her as an impostor, an impoverished maid banished from Spain by her own parents. She lifted her chin and took a deep breath as they moved forward.

In a daze she was introduced to one person after another, but none of them was the Count of Marcheno. Don Felipe asked her for the first dance of the evening and they lined up for the dance that Yolana had taught her earlier. Quita lost some of her fears as she concentrated on learning the complicated steps and following Don Felipe.

A soldier who was nearly Quita's age claimed the next dance and a well-dressed don led her out for the next. As she danced, trying to watch the dancers and follow the right steps as they turned in a circle, she felt compelled to look up.

A man stood on the sidelines talking to a group of people. A woman with golden hair stood beside him, but his attention was on Quita and she almost missed her step. His black eyes were as compelling as the wildest storm, capturing her attention and holding it momentarily. Thickly lashed, his eyes were unforgettable and as bold as a lion stirred to anger. She missed another step and pulled her attention away to watch what the dancers were doing, smiling at her partner.

In seconds they made another full turn, hands high. One hand behind her back, she met the same direct stare again, only this time, his gaze lowered, slowly drifting down over her, igniting tiny fires over every inch of her flesh. His black eyes seemed to strip away her blue silk dress. Quita blushed, her cheeks growing hot as her gaze flicked over him, taking in his magnificent green uniform decorated with ribbons and his fancy black boots, but it was the man and not the uniform that set him apart from the crowd. He was tall, his shoulders exceptionally broad; his black hair was thick and curly, framing his face, and a thick black mustache curved over his mouth. A nose with a crook high at the bridge contributed to the air of command in his appearance.

Someone spoke to him and he turned, laughing with a flash of white teeth. Then Quita had to turn again and lost her view of him. But from that moment, as the evening wore on and she danced with different partners, she was aware of the tall man watching her, of a current that ran between them. Once, she looked and saw his face in profile as he talked intently with two men, but as she watched, he turned, meeting her gaze as if he had been inexorably drawn to her.

Don Felipe took her arm again. As they whirled in a circle, she couldn't help staring across the room. The tall man's eyes followed her and her heart skipped a beat as she saw his watchful stare had become more open, more constant. Then he was gone from her view as Don Felipe led her in another turn. When the dance ended, a deep voice sounded behind her.

"May I have the next dance?"

The tone was low, strumming her nerves, and she caught

her breath when she turned to look up into a pair of velvet eyes that would have warmed the heart of a stone statue.

"Of course. May I present Señorita Lianna Melton. *Señorita,* I have the honor of presenting—"

"Armando Fuentes," the tall man said, never taking his eyes from Quita as he bowed over her hand, his warm lips lightly brushing her cold fingers. The music started and he slipped his arm lightly around her waist, holding her away from him.

"I've watched you. How lovely you are," he said softly in a tone that was entirely different from the one used by her other dance partners during the evening.

"Thank you, but I am betrothed, and you shouldn't say such things."

"You haven't been told that before?"

"Yes," she said, blushing. "But you say it differently from the others."

He arched a brow curiously, and her embarrassment deepened. Slightly flustered, she missed a step. Instantly his arm steadied her, and he apologized. She smiled up at him. "You are not the one at fault. My maid showed me the dances today. This is my first ball."

"One would never guess," he said gallantly.

"How polite you Spaniards are!"

"And Englishmen are not polite?"

She smiled, beginning to relax and enjoy herself. "I have little experience with men, either English or Spanish. And I have seen little of the world until now. Marcheno Castle is magnificent. Are you one of the count's relatives?"

"Yes. There are a lot of us here tonight! There are more relatives than servants, so you will have many names to learn."

"It seems I have everything to learn," she said, and he laughed. "I've been told that Spanish men and ladies are much more formal in their behavior to each other, but I find that difficult to believe."

"That's because the count doesn't see that it's necessary to follow all the old customs. Particularly when he's not a young lad. He's been wed twice, and the long, drawn-out courting customs are tiresome when one is no longer a youth.''

"Whatever the customs, everyone has welcomed me. Though it may take me long months to learn the names and the customs."

"Ah, you shouldn't sound so solemn on such a happy occasion as your introduction to Spanish society! Learn you will. You sound as if you have been shut away from all life."

"I feel as if I have. Even my lessons were limited," she said, hoping word got back to the count to explain her appalling lack of education, should he discover how little she knew. "My father traveled often, and I was left to myself. My tutor was as happy as I was to escape the lessons."

He laughed again. "I suspect you exaggerate, but I don't think Marcheno plans to wed you because of your schooling!"

She laughed with him and asked, "Will he appear tonight?"

"Yes, he will. I'll introduce you."

She slanted a look at him, smiling. "Perhaps you won't be near me when he arrives. You shouldn't make promises you don't intend to keep."

When he smiled in return, the faint creases around his mouth, the laugh lines around his eyes, only added to his appeal. "I don't make promises in vain. I've given my word and I'll keep it . . . if"—his voice lowered a fraction, and a twinkle appeared in his eyes—"I have to dance every dance with you between now and then."

Her heartbeat quickened, and she knew she was on dangerous ground because she felt a current of excitement stirred by this man. She looked down, trying to curb what she felt. "I think I should remind you again—I'm his betrothed."

He laughed softly. "I meant no harm."

"That is not what your eyes tell me!"

His brows arched, and he smiled, his teeth white in contrast to his dark skin and thick black mustache.

Suddenly she felt saddened that on her arrival in Madrid

she would meet a man who would immediately become special to her. The realization startled her and she looked up at him. He *was* special—from the first glance, he had been different from other men to her.

"I see dislike or regret in your eyes," he said.

Surprised that he could detect the change in her feelings, she answered, "Perhaps a touch of regret that you are not the Count of Marcheno, Señor Fuentes."

"Thank you. We will be friends," he said huskily, his dark eyes lit with fires that caused a tingling response in her.

"It is impossible for us to be close friends. But tell me about Madrid," she said, trying to turn the conversation to a safe topic.

"Why is it impossible that we become close friends?" he asked.

"I think you should tell me about Spain and Madrid," she replied stiffly.

He smiled at her, but gave her an intense look that burned with desire, and she forgot her question. The room became a blur, whirling around her as his arm tightened around her back and his long legs stretched out, making her steps longer.

"*Señor*, I don't dance well and this is unseemly," she said breathlessly.

"I know what displeases Marcheno, and this won't."

"Sir, people will stare! I've been told your people have very formal customs and manners, and I must not appear improper on my first day here!"

He slowed and his arm relaxed, allowing greater space between them. "Marcheno is a fortunate man," he said with a solemn expression on his handsome features.

"Thank you. I asked you about Madrid," she said desperately, fighting the response he stirred.

"Madrid is an old city. It was—" He broke off abruptly, looking beyond her. "I promised to introduce you to Marcheno."

She felt as if her heart had stopped beating. "He's here?" She dreaded the moment, and as she thought how it must have looked to him to have her dancing gaily with Señor Fuentes, her nervousness came flooding back.

"Yes, he's here." Suddenly he smiled. "Don't look as if the wolf will devour you in the next few minutes. He plans to marry you."

She smiled, feeling a slight easing of tension. "Thank you, Señor Fuentes. To tell you the truth, I'm frightened."

"You're eighteen. So very young," he said tenderly, making her momentarily forget about the count.

"You know my age?"

The twinkle returned to his eyes. "I suspect almost every relative and guest knows your age. They're curious about the lovely English girl. Now, I'll take you to meet Marcheno." He smiled and danced through open doors to the terrace. Instantly she tried to pull back as she protested, "*Señor*, I can't go outside with you. It isn't proper—"

"Marcheno's out here, and I said I'd introduce you," Señor Fuentes said softly. His smile was gone, and her heart pounded wildly as her emotions warred inside her. She suspected he was lying, that he was dancing her outside to try to steal a kiss. The thought heated her blood more than when Juan had reached for her. This man possessed a charm that touched some inner chord in her being, and she was drawn to him as a flower is drawn to the sun. She knew the danger of such an attraction. She pulled away swiftly, but his arm tightened and held her.

"*Señor*, I can't. You must release me!"

"I only introduce you to your future husband."

"You only want to steal a kiss in dark shadows," she said breathlessly, trying to look around his broad chest to see if another man were waiting.

He chuckled softly. "Lianna . . ." The word rolled off his tongue like a caress.

"Miss Lianna Melton, may I present the Count of Marcheno." He stepped back with a flourish and she saw only the darkened empty terrace with an olive tree spreading branches overhead, shadows intermingling with splashes of moonlight on the stone floor. She looked at him sharply.

"Armando Fuentes Cuevas, Conde de Marcheno," he

said, and bowed low. He straightened and smiled as she stared at him, forgetting momentarily that her mouth was open.

"You!" she breathed softly, feeling as if the heavens had opened and poured forth treasures at her feet. Her heart hammered violently, and she couldn't move or breathe, unable to believe her fortune. "You jest!" she whispered.

His smile vanished. "No, *querida*. For both of us, Fate has smiled. You are more than I dared dream of or hope for!" His arms slipped around her waist and he pulled her to him.

She placed her hands on his broad chest, still shaken by the discovery of his identity. He slowly tilted her chin upward and contemplated her mouth.

Her thoughts stopped; she felt on fire, wanting his kiss. Her lips felt swollen and hot as she gazed up at him and saw the lids of his eyes droop with passion while he studied her. Languidly he lowered his head. Her lips ached in anticipation, in eagerness for this man who was more handsome, more charming than any she had known. Hot tears from relief and joy sprang to her eyes.

His mouth grazed hers, and she willed herself to wait, to be still, to be the innocent, unkissed English maid she was supposed to be. He raised his head and his fingers brushed her cheek. "Tears, Lianna?"

"Of happiness! I had worried so—"

He laughed and dipped his head again. His warm lips pressed against hers, opening her mouth as his tongue thrust inside to stroke hers, and passion ignited. She stood on tiptoe, sliding her slender bare arms around his neck. Finally she pushed away.

"Sir, when we return to the ballroom, I'll be unpresentable," she said in a breathless whisper.

"The wedding will be in five days, *querida*. Five days of agony."

"*Conde*—"

"Armando is the name I prefer you to use. Men call me Marcheno, but I want you to call me Armando." His voice dropped to that timbre that became a sensual caress. "And perhaps I shall call you Lia." He kissed her lightly. "How happy I am! After your father left, I thought I had allowed him to convince me of the biggest foolishness of my life. Now, I'm overjoyed.''

He leaned down to kiss her again, this time lightly but hungrily, and she wanted more.

"I don't think I shall be able to stop smiling," she said, laughing up at him.

"Nor I."

"You ran a great risk. Suppose I had flirted with you earlier?"

"I wanted to know what kind of wife I had betrothed myself to. It is not too late to withdraw the offer, but now . . . beyond my wildest hopes, I'll wed my beautiful Lia."

Quita smiled up at him. "Shouldn't we go back?"

"Yes. The matrons' tongues will clack that we behave in an unseemly fashion, but in five days it won't matter. And in those five days, I'll show you Madrid."

Quita danced the next hours away with only one partner— Armando. Her heart beat in eagerness as each moment deepened their attraction. There were no more passionate kisses because they were in public until he bent low over her hand to tell her good night. She turned away to leave with Doña Vianta.

That night as she lay in bed, she was too excited to sleep. Over and over she remembered each detail of those moments on the terrace, the discovery of Armando's identity. She wriggled with pleasure, then suddenly felt a stab of fright that she should have a golden world dangled before her eyes. Five days . . . the vows could be canceled. She could hear his voice saying, ". . . *it is not too late to withdraw the offer* . . ."

In those words she saw the iron beneath his irresistible charm. For a man to withdraw an offer of marriage at this point could easily mean a duel or prosecution, yet she knew Señor Melton would do nothing. Thinking of Conchita's tales of the Count of Marcheno's cruelty and the dungeon where his enemies were imprisoned, she shivered. It was a side to him she had not seen; all she knew was the exciting man who had teased her and held her and kissed her—who had flirted and made her laugh and made her doubly eager for the wedding.

The next day Quita and Armando rode through the dusty streets of Madrid with Doña Vianta at Quita's side, ever watchful, as if she had to make sure no more kisses were stolen.

Nor were they. There were no more balls, only lavish dinners planned for the remainder of the week. The first dinner Quita sat down to stare in bewilderment at an array of silver. Panic struck her as she looked at the crystal, the china, the people watching her, including Armando. Doña Vianta, acting as his hostess until the wedding, sat at the end of the long table and Quita sat to his right. She waited, watching carefully to see what fork he would use, what he would do. Once she caught him watching her hands and she blushed, suddenly embarrassed and frightened. The ladies adjourned to a drawing room and Quita began to relax. There were no stolen kisses that night either, as Doña Vianta hovered at Quita's side like a bird over prey.

The next morning as Quita left her room to join Doña Vianta downstairs, a hand reached out to sweep around her waist.

Gasping with surprise, she looked into Armando's laughing dark eyes. "*Conde!*"

"No, Lianna—always when we are alone you are to address me as Armando, never my formal title."

"Doña Vianta waits for me. She watches me constantly."

"She's trying to do what your Spanish mother would have done had she been alive," he said gently. "*Querida*, don't be afraid here. Your father told me you had led a sheltered life."

She felt as if her heart might burst with her love for him. She placed her hands on his arms, feeling the muscles beneath the thin white silk of his shirt. She slipped her fingers higher. "I'm so fortunate," she whispered. "I thought you would be very old."

He laughed. "And I was terrified I had pledged myself

to a thin, pale English schoolgirl." Laughter vanished
from his eyes. "Three days, Lianna, and you'll be mine."

Her heart pounded, but as his head started to lower, she
slipped away from him. "Armando," she said, relishing
his name, aching to be back in his arms. "I mustn't keep
Señora waiting."

"A pox on my cousin! Come to me." He pulled her
back, catching her chin in his hand and holding her face as
he kissed her hard and passionately. Again, while her heart
thudded wildly, Quita fought to hold back, to try to be
reserved and shy, yet his kisses were like flames flicking
through her veins to scorch her raw nerves. She longed to
wrap her arms around his neck and return his kisses, but
she resisted, pushing against his muscled chest.

"Armando!" She whirled away and rushed toward the
stairs, hearing him say her name softly behind her.

Later that day, she received instructions from Doña
Vianta on which untensil to use when at a large dinner, on
how to greet guests properly and to summon a servant for
the carriage. She suspected that Armando had ordered the
lesson after watching her at dinner the night before.

The wedding day finally dawned with a glorious sunrise. Quita watched it from a castle window, for she had
been too excited to sleep more than a few hours.

Early that morning, Yolana appeared with several servants who were to help Quita get ready for the wedding.
Quita dressed in Lianna's beautiful white lace and satin
dress. It fell in soft folds around her legs, its rounded
neckline of satin hugging her curves, its white lace giving
her a fragile appearance. The lace ended in a high collar
beneath her chin and covered her arms in long fitted
sleeves. A hairdresser styled her hair so that it was looped
and twisted on top of her head, secured with tiny rosebuds
fastened amid her raven tresses. Last of all, Yolana helped
her with the veil of lace that was pinned to her dark hair
and trailed down to her waist. She would carry the white
orchids and roses Armando had sent from the sunhouse.

At the appointed time, Don Felipe appeared in the hall
outside the dressing room and offered her his arm. In one
of the count's carriages they rode past the imposing Palacio

Real with its Italian architecture of Guadarrama granite to the Cathedral de La Almudena beside it. There Quita walked down the aisle to wed the Count of Marcheno.

As they stood before the priest, she felt as if she couldn't breathe and her fingers trembled. It seemed an impossible dream. When she was to repeat her vows, she turned and Armando took her hand in his. Vows exchanged, he slipped a wide gold band with a huge diamond on her finger. Her other hand bore the golden serpent. The priest declared them to be man and wife.

Armando leaned down to kiss her lightly and they left the church for festivities at Marcheno Castle.

As she stood receiving good wishes from first one Marcheno relative, then another, she cast quick glances at her handsome husband. In his black coat and breeches, the red sash with decorations for his valor serving the army of Spain across his chest, his elegant shining boots, and his mass of unruly black curls, he was the most handsome man present, and she continually wanted to look at him and touch him.

Later, as she stood talking to three young unmarried cousins whom she had grown to like, Armando touched her arm. Drawing her aside, he whispered, "Go to your room and wait for me."

She glanced around and discovered that momentarily they had been left to themselves. She gathered her skirt and did as he asked, hearing the noise of guests' voices mingling with the sound of guitars fade as she mounted the stairs. No one was stirring in the upstairs hall. Her heart pounding with excitement, she rushed to her room and closed the door.

She could still hear music coming from below, both from musicians in the crowded ballroom and from the band on the lawn outside. She happily studied her heavy gold wedding band and its magnificent diamond. La Condesa Marcheno, mistress of Marcheno Castle, wife of Armando. She felt delirious with joy and then, only for an instant, sad for Lianna, who had given up the most wonderful future because of Edwin Stafford, a stableboy. Lianna would have forgotten Edwin by now. How could anyone

see another man when Armando smiled? A rap interrupted
her thoughts and she whirled to open the door.

Armando stood smiling on the threshold, his black eyes
devouring her as he extended his hand. ''Come quickly so
we can escape notice.''

She followed him and they wound up another flight of
stairs to the top floor of the castle, where they hurried
along the wide hall to the east wing.

Two servants guarded tall wooden doors at one end of
the hall.

''They are to see to it that we are not disturbed tonight.''

The guards nodded in greeting and opened one door,
closing it swiftly behind the newlyweds. Quita and Armando
walked down another hallway that had five rooms opening
from the end of it. Armando flung open the door to the last
room and scooped her into his arms to carry her inside. ''I
had this redone to give a better view of my land. These are
the bridal rooms, but they're also where I come when I
want to be alone.''

The huge room had Moorish influence in its architecture. Wide glassed arches gave a graceful openness to the
room. A breathtaking view of his grounds spread before
them, yet they were shut away on a high upper level of the
castle in complete privacy. Like the rest of the castle, the
room was magnificent, only far more so than her bed-
chamber. A massive, heavily carved bed canopied in deep
wine velvet stood at one end of the room. The chairs, their
curving feet as deeply carved as the bed, were upholstered
in wine velvet. A marble washstand held a large china
bowl and pitcher; a wide hearth had logs laid for a fire if
needed. An armoire as impressive as the rest of the furniture and an oval mirror stood along one wall. Beneath the
mirror was a table holding a tray of cut crystal decanters of
amber liquid and pale white wine. At the far side of the
room, a door stood open and through it Quita could see a
drawing room just as marvelously furnished in pale blue
damask.

Armando set her on her feet and crossed the room to
pour wine. Picking up two glasses, he handed one to her,

then raised his in a toast. "To a long and happy and fruitful union."

She smiled, touching her glass lightly with his, and watched him as she lowered her glass to sip the wine. Earlier in the week she had learned he owned several vineyards and the wine served at the castle was his.

His dark eyes seemed to bore into her soul. He lowered his gaze slowly, eyes drifting down her body. She couldn't swallow wine or think or speak.

"*Querida,* you're the most beautiful bride in Spain."

"Thank you," she answered solemnly, thinking he was the most handsome man on earth. "I'm a simple farmgirl. You bestow on me an honor beyond measure." He walked to her to take the wine from her and set both glasses carefully on a table. When he pulled off the scarlet sash with the decorations, shrugged out of his coat and draped them on a chair, Quita felt as if she might melt. His white shirt was elegant, with ruffles falling down the front and over his wrists, the cravat tied high beneath his chin, the steeped collar touching his firm jaw. His body was trim in the waist, narrowing to slender hips and muscled legs, a body of power and strength.

He walked to her and slipped his arms around her lightly, and the moment was agonizingly prolonged as he studied her features as if seeing her for the first time. "No, Lia, it is the other way. I'm the one who is fortunate. I have found my heart." His lips brushed hers, his thick mustache tickling slightly, and she silently thanked heaven that she had not met Juan by the river and run the terrible risk of losing her virginity. In Spain a woman was ruined, unfit for the most lowly marriage, if she were not chaste.

His mouth pressed firmly now, opening hers as his tongue touched hers, and safely wed, she began to give vent to the stormy passion he stirred, as she kissed him in return.

He gave a muffled groan and pulled away to look down at her. "I want this to be a special night for you," he said in a vibrant, husky voice that made the temperature in the room rise to suffocating levels. "I shall try to go carefully, slowly, Lia, but it is difficult." He leaned closer, his thickly lashed eyes closing. "It may be impossible," he whispered, and crushed her to his hardness, kissing her passionately.

She felt his hands remove the veil from the back of her head and fling it aside; then his fingers tangled in her hair and it came down like black clouds out of the sky, tumbling over her shoulders, curling on the white lace.

"Turn around," he commanded. She stood quietly while he unfastened the tiny buttons that ran from her neckline to her waist. He swore impatiently and kissed her flesh as it became exposed, his lips trailing where his eager fingers had been. In moments she stood before him, the beautiful dress and thin batiste chemise tangled around her ankles, her body bared for his eyes.

His bold look made her blush and tremble as he swept her into his arms to carry her to the big bed.

The coverlet was turned back. White silken sheets were cold against her bare flesh as he lowered her, then stood up to swiftly peel away his clothes. He was finely shaped, with a muscled body, caramel-colored skin, and a powerful chest covered by a thick mat of curling black hair that tapered to a thin line over his stomach. On fire, she reached for him, holding out her arms.

He caught her hand to kiss her fingertips, watching her. "*Querida*, I will love you now. You're mine, and together we'll experience all the pleasures of love." He lowered himself on the bed and pulled her against him, his flesh hot against hers as he began to kiss her slowly.

It was forever; it was fleeting seconds; finally he mounted her writhing form and spread her legs, watching her intently, his hooded eyes proclaiming his hunger. He lowered his weight and his hot thrusting manhood entered her soft warmth.

She bit back a cry, then gave a gasp of pain while he murmured endearments and kissed her.

For an instant she lay in agony as he moved within her. "Lia," he whispered, "I don't want to hurt you. Move . . ."

At last he cried her name and reached a shuddering release, his weight pressing her into the bed as he breathed deeply.

For a long time he held her, stroking her hair, whispering words of love. Then he rose on his elbows and looked at her. She adored him. Running her hands across his shoulders, she whispered shyly, "I love you, Armando."

He smiled. "My love. That was not good for you, but next time it will be, Lia. I promise you."

"I'm the happiest woman on earth."

He smiled and moved beside her. "But I can make you a much happier woman."

She felt giddy and happy, rolling on her side to face him. "Impossible!"

"It's very possible," he persisted.

She shook her head, wrinkling her nose at him.

"I'll show you," he said. "There are certain steps to follow. First, I must look at you . . . simple enough." He sat up and ran his eyes over her as she rolled on her back and lay still, feeling her nipples grow taut beneath his searching scrutiny. Her hips moved slightly.

"Armando," she whispered, amazed that she would want him again when it had been so painful.

"Ah, that is just the first step. Now, the second. I touch you, lightly, like this." His hand traced circles around her full breast, teasing without touching the pointed nipple. Then he leaned down, his hot breath brushing the peak, making her want to push his mouth down to cover the dusky pink tip.

"You torment me!" she whispered, and he chuckled deep in his throat.

"The next step, Lia, you must do. Move your hands on my thighs."

"Armando!" she whispered as she did as he asked, and then she was in his arms. His throbbing manhood was ready again, yet he kissed her and caressed her, until she gasped in urgent need.

He filled her softness with his heated shaft and this time he moved slowly. The sharp pain changed, and white-hot desire made her moan with longing. Her blood thundered in her veins and she cried out in rapture. She felt the hot rush of his seed and silently she prayed to conceive a son from this union, a son from this night to bind Armando to her irrevocably for all time, because she was bound to him. He possessed her body and he owned her heart.

Midmorning the next day, Armando rolled over and regarded Quita happily while her hands explored his flesh. "*Querida,* do you realize we have not eaten in twenty-four hours?"

"I don't think I need to eat in the next twenty-four days."

He chuckled and yanked her down on his chest so that her soft breasts pressed against him. "My lusty bride whose shyness has evaporated like mist beneath the hot Spanish sun."

"I'm your creation. You taught me to be wanton."

"I think I shall teach you more. But hunger gnaws at my insides. I'll summon the servants and we'll feast and love and take our time."

"How long will we stay here, Armando?"

He stood up and she rolled on her back to relish the sight of his naked body. "When we tire of these chambers, one of my ships will be readied, and we'll sail. I want to show you the wonders of the world. We'll sail to the New World, where I want to look at land holdings King Ferdinand has bestowed on me. I've heard of rumblings of discontent there and I want to see for myself that all is well. Also, my cousin Francisco is there."

Her bright, glorious world became clouded and she sat up in bed. She frowned, thinking of Captain Raven and Lianna, who had sailed for Chile.

"I would rather stay here, Armando."

He turned to look at her and laughed. "You're too lusty a wench to have been such a shy maiden only yesterday!"

Her mind raced, and she felt the return of old fears she had thought ended the moment the wedding vows were said. "No. I'm afraid of the sea. The voyage here was frightening. There was a storm."

He opened the armoire and pulled out a dressing gown that he slipped into and belted around his waist. He brought a pale blue silk gown to her and sat down on the bed, holding the robe open for her. "Lia, you will be safe. My ships have sailed for years and it's been a long, long time since I lost one due to a storm. We'll put in to the nearest port if bad weather threatens." He tilted her chin upward. "Now, no frowns. Give me a smile or I shall have to coax one out of you."

Suddenly the New World seemed a very distant threat and she forgot her fears. Mischievously she frowned and firmed her lips in an exaggerated pout. He laughed deep in his throat.

"So, I shall have to coax one out of you. What a task! Now, how shall I do this?" He leaned forward to kiss the corner of her mouth. "I fear I shall emerge from the marriage chamber a bare skeleton of a man who is weak and dwindling from hunger and fatigue."

She laughed and fell back on the bed, pulling him down on top of her. His arms slipped around her. "My world is perfect!" she said, forgetting about their coming voyage.

13

In her small cabin the hours Lianna spent shut away became long and tedious. Each morning the steward brought breakfast, a tray with oranges, a bowl of cold lobscouse, a thick stew of salt pork and burgoo, and oatmeal sweetened with molasses. Occasionally the tray bore a book sent by Josh, who in the dead of night came regularly to take her abovedeck for a stroll.

When midnight approached, Josh finished writing in the ship's ledger and leaned back in his chair, rubbing his hands across his reddened eyes. For the past week he had been toying with a notion and at last had come to a decision. When they stopped in La Coruña to let the Spanish sailors dock, he intended to wed Lianna.

For the first time he looked ahead. The future had always been an uncertainty in his life—one he had ignored. But no longer. Too much was at stake, especially the good life he wanted for Lianna.

He wanted her to be accepted, and knew that those who had shunned him and had closed their doors to him would treat Lianna the same way unless he was welcomed in society. He hit the table with his clenched fist, wondering how long his father's anger would haunt his life.

Crossing his feet on the table and locking his hands behind his head, he watched the lantern overhead sway with the rocking moton of the ship. They could sail together and establish a home in London between journeys. And later, there would be a child—the thought took his breath away. He hadn't thought about a family before in his life, yet now that he had started to contemplate it, he hungered for it. He wanted Lianna's love, he wanted children by her, and the thought made him willing to move heaven and earth to achieve his dream.

He wanted to declare his love over and over, but he couldn't. Where love was concerned, he was too vulnerable and his awareness of his vulnerability was no aid despite all logical thought. He'd had too many rejections in his childhood; he simply couldn't endure Lianna's mocking contempt nor give her a weapon to use against him.

Restlessly he stood up and paced the cabin, finally crossing to a porthole to stare out at the boundless sea. It was in his blood; for almost half his life it had been his livelihood. Lianna loved sailing as well as he, and she was a natural sailor. Yet if they had a home in London where they could go between journeys, could he make certain they would be accepted? He rubbed the back of his neck and watched steady whitecaps rolling by.

Planting his feet apart, he braced his hands against the bulkhead. He wanted her, but he wanted to give her a good life, not the closed existence of an outcast. He would fight in the Chiiean venture for his future and win his damned countrymen over in spite of the duke!

If only he could make Lianna come to love him! When she was happy, her laughter was magic. Her passion was deeper sorcery. His blood stirred at the thought, and turning abruptly, he reached for his cape so he might fetch her for a walk topside.

As midnight approached, Lianna's spirits lifted. Dressed in a woolen dress of deep blue, she was more impatient than ever to escape the confines of the narrow cabin. When a key grated in the lock, she dropped the book she was reading and sat up in the hammock, her heart leaping at the sight of Raven.

"Would you care for a walk topside?" he asked while his eyes lit with pleasure.

His thick brown hair and unwavering cool gaze reminded Lianna of the lion figurehead at the bow of the ship; it was a fitting symbol for Raven. Even though he lounged against the door, apparently relaxed, she sensed he held his strength in check.

When she approached the door, he continued to lounge in her path. Her steps slowed, then halted as she stared at his mocking green eyes tinged with an unnerving current.

"In exchange for a stroll and temporary freedom, I deserve a kiss of gratitude," he teased.

"Another of your cavalier demands," she answered, trying to hide the jump in her pulse.

"Such tact!" He laughed heartily.

"I think, Captain Raven, you're accustomed to swooning females who languish for your smile. You're sufficiently handsome. Why didn't you find a willing female who would be happy with you?"

"Thank you, love! How nice to discover you find me handsome!" With a twinkle in his eyes he said, "Blue flames are about to scorch me!"

"Well they should! The flames of Halifax should roast you for your confounded ways!"

"My, oh my! What a vixen! Or do I detect an effort to suppress a smile?" He leaned down to peer closely into her eyes and Lianna could no longer remain solemn.

Looking into each other's eyes, they both laughed. His white teeth were even; creases deepened in his cheeks. "You're an absolute ruffian," she said teasingly. "Neither words nor blows can dent your hardened hide. Shall we go?"

"When do I get my kiss?"

"How I'd hoped you would forget!"

"Not in the next thousand years could I forget a kiss from you!"

White teeth flashed in a vexing grin. She knew there was to be no escape from his demand. Her gaze lowered to his firm lips, her breath stopped, and her heart beat wildly. She forgot their teasing banter. She was drawn to him as a flower to sunshine, raising her lips while the world around them became a blur.

She stepped forward. Aware of his lean, hard body, she stood on tiptoe to place a light kiss against his cheek. Beneath her lips his cheek was warm and rough with stubble. The clean smell of soap and fresh linen assailed her, and her heart pounded. When she stepped away, he made no move, but merely arched an eyebrow.

His voice lowered to a husky tone that caused a ripple of heat to go through her. "I believe your instruction in kissing has been far superior to such bland touches."

He smiled lazily and waited. Then, wanting to destroy his image of her as bland, she reached up, caught the back of his neck, and pulled his mouth to hers.

Her lashes lowered as she placed her mouth over his and pressed his lips, teasing them with her tongue. When shyness gripped her, she stopped.

For an instant he did nothing; then he pulled back a fraction. "If that's the best you can do . . ."

Exhilarated by the irresistible challenge in his voice, she stood on tiptoe to place her mouth firmly upon his, her tongue thrusting between his lips in a scorching demand. Instantly his arm encircled her waist to crush her softness to him.

His tongue took up the dance, meeting hers, sending her heartbeat into a frenzy. She could not stop what she had started. She couldn't halt the response he stirred, the kiss that lengthened as it became more passionate, her wildly throbbing pulse that ignited like dry logs on the hearth. Nor could she halt an agony of need that grew with alarming swiftness. Through layers of clothing she felt his hard thighs press against her. She felt his warm flesh and a heart that thumped as rapidly as her own. When she became aware of his male arousal, panic gripped her. She pushed lightly, and he released her, raising his head a fraction. His fiery gaze made her tremble and cling to him.

Watching his hungry expression, she drew a sharp breath. His voice was hoarse as he asked, "If you'd known fully, would you have refused the exchange?"

It was a question she neither wanted to answer nor could, for her mouth became dry.

"I like being with you, Lianna." Each word was a scalding touch, and longing was transformed into a deeper emotion—one she didn't welcome because it frightened her.

"Have I earned my excursion now?" she whispered, shaken because she hungered for more kisses.

"A promise is a promise, love," he said in a mocking tone. "Sometimes I'm tempted to kiss you until you swoon," he said softly. "What would it take to make you swoon, Lianna?"

His question was filled with amusement, yet beneath it, she suspected a curious note. She thought of retorting, "Only Edwin!" but restrained herself easily. Edwin Stafford was beginning to seem very far away.

Josh knelt slightly so his eyes would be level with hers, and stared at her with curiosity. "You're thinking of the Englishman," he said flatly.

"Yes," she said, wondering how he had guessed. "Edwin seems like a part of my past." She was barely aware of Josh's quick frown, the stare that was unwavering as he straightened. "We promised to always wait for each other, to find each other someday again, but I wonder . . ." She looked up at Josh Raven, who had changed her life. "I've changed. I wonder if he has."

"No doubt, he has, Lianna," Josh said gently. "Life is full of changes. We seldom remain the same as time passes, and you were an innocent child when your father packed you up to send you away."

Josh stroked her cheek with his fingers while he talked, and Lianna tried to make sense of her own feelings. She realized she wanted to kiss Josh, to feel his lips on hers, and that Edwin was becoming a blurred memory. But she had promised to wait forever. Perhaps the time would come when they would both want freedom from their youthful vow.

He caught her face in his hands. "'How old is Edwin?"

"Nineteen. Two years older than I am."

"A country groom—Lianna, I was so sheltered until I left home. Edwin will change just as you have. Follow your heart."

"Edwin loves me. He is the only person who has always loved me."

As Josh listened to her, he wanted to blurt out that he also loved her, yet he'd never said the words to a woman before and didn't want Lianna to fling them back in his face. Instead, he lowered his head, looking into her wide blue eyes. "I'll make you forget him. You were both children, Lianna." He kissed her passionately, his hands stroking her shoulders, his fingers drifting to her breast to lightly touch the soft blue wool and feel the warmth of her flesh beneath it. She gasped as his fingers barely grazed her breasts and he knew he must stop or he couldn't keep the promise he had made to her.

"Ready to go above?" Josh asked in a breathless voice, seeing the dazed look in her eyes and knowing how swiftly her body surrendered to him. Now that she wondered about her feelings for the Englishman at home, Josh felt a swift rush of pleasure. She was changing. Her resolve to reserve her heart for a childhood love was weakening. Soon . . . so soon, she would be his legally.

She nodded and took his arm. As they entered the passageway, curiosity tugged at her. How much did Josh care for her? Logic told her he couldn't care a whit whom she had known, other than his wanting to possess everything on board his ship, yet there had been no mistaking the intensity in his voice when he'd said, "I'll make you forget him." Thrusting aside the questions, she sighed and walked beside him.

When they reached the afterdeck, the brisk wind was cool and welcome after the cramped dank cabin. Lianna looked out at the expanse of gray sea and sky. Captain Raven dropped an arm lightly around her shoulders and pulled her close. Her eyes adjusted to the night, and she saw clouds boiling over the horizon far in the distance. "Is a storm approaching?" she asked.

"It's blowing north while we run south. We'll miss it. By dawn we'll reach La Coruña and deliver our survivors safely home." As he spoke in a throaty voice, his breath wafted lightly on her ear.

"La Coruña! Quita's destination. And it was to have been mine. If I hadn't persuaded her to exchange with me, she would be here now."

"And you would be on your way to wed a monster," he said quietly. "At least I haven't been cruel."

"There are many degrees of cruelty," she retorted, regretting it immediately when she saw a fleeting look of pain surface in his eyes, then vanish in their depths. "But then, captain," she added shyly, "perhaps I did make the better exchange."

"M'lady, how grateful I am that you consider the possibility I might rank a notch above a barbarian! Your flattery overwhelms me!"

His cynical tone hurt. "I hope the Count of Marcheno isn't cruel to his wife."

"Probably he's not, but it's difficult for me to imagine him being kind to anyone."

"Why do you treat the Spaniards on board *El Feroz* as your friends?"

"I have no reason to quarrel with these men. I shall have revenge in my own way," he said so coldly that Lianna shuddered.

It was on the tip of her tongue to confess her lineage, to tell him that he had a Spanish mistress, but she remained silent, fearing what he might do. He had his tender moments, but his voice rang with hatred when he spoke of the Marchenos.

He leaned against a bulwark and watched her.

"You take to the sea as if you were born to it," she observed. "Don't you grow weary of it?"

"No. I can't remain in one place, settled in one house . . ."

Her mouth curved as she finished for him, ". . . or love one woman."

He laughed softly. "I think I could love one quite easily."

Flustered by his answer, she asked quickly, "Will this be a rough voyage to the New World?"

"Aye, the worst waters in the world are at the Horn. We'll sail through the straits if possible."

"You risk your life in a cause for people you don't know. How did you meet Miranda?"

"Miranda has enlisted aid from many—he has even contacted the czarina of Russia and our prime minister." As he spoke, he traced circles on her hand. "I've sailed here once before and have seen the plight of these people. The Spanish have divided the land. They have great estates, *estancias*, with thousands of Indians who serve in wretched conditions. The system is called the *inquilino* and it is comparable to the serfs under a feudal system. It is unjust, Lianna.''

As he propped his elbow on the rail, his voice developed a distant quality, as if his thoughts were far removed from the present. ''Workers on these *estancias* are free, but by an unwritten agreement among the wealthy landowners, if a worker leaves one *estancia*, he is refused work elsewhere.''

While he talked, the wind tumbled locks of his brown hair over his forehead. Curbing the impulse to brush them away, she drew closer to him. ''In Chile, do you intend to pose as a Spaniard?'' she asked.

''Aye,'' he answered, relaxing his shoulders slightly. ''I shall pose as a Spanish nobleman, a *marqués,* with an estate awaiting my arrival.''

''You mean you already have a home in Chile? How did this come about?''

''It was arranged.''

''Was there actually a *marqués* who owned this estate?''

He saw the accusation in her wide blue eyes. How innocent she was! And how lovely! He felt a kindling of desire for her. ''There was a *marqués*—Don Cristóbal Esteban, Marqués de Aveiro.'' He added coldly, ''The *marqués* is dead.''

''So you're a murderer as well!''

''No. Others have laid plans. I merely stepped in at a time when I was needed. Remember, Lianna, this is a revolution—an overthrow of tyrannical rulers, not an afternoon tea. The *marqués'* life was part of the battle.'' He thought how sheltered her life had been, and a protective longing rose in him. Startled at the reactions she produced, he studied her. He did wish to shelter her, to keep her from harm, but first he had to wipe the angry look from her eyes. There were moments when she smiled and her eyes heated with desire. How he yearned to see something deeper in them! He thought about his plans for her, and his pulse juumped. He knew she had no inkling what La Coruña held for her. If she did, she wouldn't be standing quietly beside him.

Forcing his thoughts to their conversation, he asked, "Have you ever seen families with young children subsisting on a diet of weevil-infested bread? Or watched men die like insects in wretched mines to satisfy the endless Spanish greed for gold?"

Her brows drew together in a scowl, but in his need to make her understand, he continued relentlessly. "Have you ever seen children living in dirt hovels while Spanish ladies dress in fine silks, spend their time in idle amusements? Or have you seen children who are forced to carry bricks and work like beasts of burden?"

"It can't be so dismal!"

"Ah, but it is," he said. "It is vile in England for many. Surely your sheltered life hasn't hidden that fact. This is much worse. The Spanish word is absolute; they do as they please, and in areas where the men in charge have lost all sense of fairness—you have a situation like Santiago."

At that moment the ship's bell clanged, marking the half-hour. "What time does that indicate?" Lianna asked.

"The even numbers mark the hours, the odd numbers are struck on the half-hour, up to eight bells, which is four o'clock, then the sequence begins again. At the moment it's one-thirty." Unable to restrain himself from touching her, he lifted a thick strand of hair from her face, his fingers brushing lightly across the warm flesh of her throat. He saw her lashes flutter and suspected she had more reaction to his touch than she cared to show. His breathing quickened as he longed to pull her to him.

"What kind of country is Chile?" she asked.

He wondered if it were his imagination that she sounded breathless. Did she feel as tense as he? Beneath her innocent demeanor was a sensual woman, for whom he ached, yet he answered her question as if it were the only thing on his mind. "Chile is magnificent—and it is terrible. It's a land of mountains, deserts, volcanoes, snow, and glaciers. There are ancient Indian civilizations and many ruins from tribes which have disappeared from the earth. Others still exist such as the Araucanians, a fierce people who have never been conquered."

"Unconquered," she said bitterly, and for an instant he wanted to remind her that the Count of Marcheno might not have shown kindness or patience. Instead, he reached to stroke her cheek. His fingers slipped lower to her throat, resting quietly while he discovered her pulse skittered like a butterfly. She did feel something for him!

Gazing into the distance, she said in a level voice, "I've read of the Spanish explorers Vasco de Balboa and Hernán Cortés."

If he hadn't had his hand on her throat, his fingers over the vein that beat so frantically, he wouldn't have known she was aware of his existence. He smiled as he said, "A Spaniard named Francisco Pizarro came with Balboa. Pizarro conquered much of Peru and sent Pedro de Valdivia into Chile. He founded the largest city, Santiago, so named for Saint James."

"Will we go to Santiago?" she asked. "It sounds exotic, and I've never been far from Wiltshire."

"You'll go far from home now. As I understand it, Valdivia's mistress led the fight to defend Santiago against the Spanish, as Valdivia was gone at the time. Where would I find you, Lianna, if I had to leave in such circumstances?"

"How can I answer that question?"

He laughed, his clear baritone voice floating on the wind. "What do you fear? I have a feeling it would not be a military battle."

"Do you expect an answer?"

He laughed again, enjoying the pink that rose in her cheeks. She was brave; she had faced him when she expected a beating; she stood still without tears when he knew she had been terrified. As he continued talking, his fingers trailed to her ears. Although she paid him no heed, he knew she was as aware of each touch as he. "The natives didn't like their Spanish conquerors," he went on. "Valdivia forced a young Indian to be his groom. The boy escaped and organized a band of followers. They raided Spanish settlements until Valdivia was taken prisoner and tortured to death. According to the tales I've been told, Valdivia was forced to drink melted gold."

"How dreadful!"

His fingers followed the rim of her ear. He caught up a dark curl and twisted it in his hand, relishing its silkiness. He moved closer to her, and loosely slipped his arms about her waist, trying to keep the heat she inspired out of his voice.

"Chile is a country of many different people. Spanish, Creoles—people of Spanish blood who were born in the colonies. There are the mestizos, those of mixed blood." His voice lowered a notch and he couldn't prevent the raspiness brought on by passion. "The *conquistadores* brought few women with them to such a remote place, so they took natives as wives."

She started to move away, but he tightened his arms. "Do you want to go below?"

"Not yet," she answered. "This is the first fresh air I've had today, and the water is so beautiful at night, so dark and mysterious, except where the moon dances across it with silvery streamers."

Josh wondered what lay ahead for both of them. Then his attention shifted to her features, and his mouth felt dry.

"You'll see Wiltshire again," he promised. "How old were you when your mother died?"

"I was three. My father was a merchant and met her in his travels, married her, and brought her to England to live."

Barely hearing her words, he watched her. Her mouth was raised, her full soft lips parted. Drawn by an invisible force, he started to lean down to taste her sweetness, to commence the tempest that was as stormy as the most violent wind, when beyond them he glimpsed one of the Spaniards emerge from below. Standing beside the main-mast, the sailor stopped with his back to them. Josh swept Lianna into his arms and started down the companionway.

Misinterpreting his motives, she gasped, "Put me down!"

"Shh! A Spaniard came on deck." Rushing to her cabin, he stepped inside and kicked the door shut behind them.

"Were we seen?" she whispered as he set her on her feet, far more aware of Josh than of danger. As his hands lingered on her shoulders, she raised her chin with determination. "When we dock at La Coruña, you could set me free."

"Is that what you want?" he asked.

The question danced between them and caused her emotions to swirl, changing as swiftly as quicksilver. Silence lengthened and his brows arched while his fingers tightened slightly on her shoulders.

Was that what she truly wanted? She looked at the tall, hard man who watched her. She wanted to be loved—and Edwin Stafford was the one man who loved her. Josh Raven desired her, but no words of love had ever passed his lips. Yet . . . suppose Edwin had changed? And suppose it mattered to him that Josh Raven had possessed her? The thought of leaving Josh made her hurt in a manner she wouldn't have believed possible. Yet, she was nothing more than his mistress. She could be tossed aside in any port at any time.

"Lianna?" he coaxed, his eyes now knives, cutting to her heart. Her breath caught at the manner in which he watched her.

"I don't know . . . Everything has changed."

"Do you want to go home?" he persisted.

"Yes," she said, thinking it was the only future she really had. Disappointment seemed to flare in his eyes, but it fled so swiftly she wondered if she had mistaken it, if she had seen it because she had wanted to see it. His voice was harsh as he said, "You can't go home. You can't stay in Spain. No, Lianna. I need you at my side."

"You don't need me—you want me!" His hands drifted higher, to her throat, and his thumbs caressed her to distraction. The feelings he stirred drove her to plead with him, and while she talked, a silent battle waged within her. "I beg you to release me from this bargain before I'm with child! Have you stopped to think if I have a child, it will be your bastard! You talk about freedom and high ideals, then you risk a child's life in this world as a bastard!"

His lips curved in a slight smile, an inscrutable expression crossed his face, and suddenly she wondered what was in his thoughts.

"There'll be no bastard child. I promise." Then, winding his fingers in the knotted cord that held her cape fastened, he drew it free while his green eyes flamed.

She didn't want to respond to him. She wanted to protest, yet his seductive emerald gaze captivated her and invisible lightning charges sparked between them.

"Do you make promises you can't keep?" she asked, her voice dropping to a lower pitch. He pushed the cape off her shoulders and it fell to her feet. "No, Lianna. I won't go back on my word." His fingers wound through her hair, sending the pins falling. Strong arms wrapped around her, molding her to his body while he kissed her until her head spun, until she slipped her arms around his neck and yielded to his touch.

His kisses destroyed reason, wiped out consciousness of all else except his hard, exciting body. For an instant she was befuddled when he released her, gazing down at her with parted lips, his chest rising and falling.

"I have to stand watch. Good night, Lianna."

In seconds the key grated in the lock and she was alone. The captain standing watch? She didn't believe him, yet why had he stopped kissing her? It wasn't lack of desire; she had felt the swift surge of his manhood as he held her against him. Why had he gone so abruptly? Was it her talk about a bastard child? She found that unlikely. What was Captain Josh's intention, and why could she not resist him? She burned with embarrassment when she thought about the past few minutes and how eagerly she had responded. Yet a deeper warmth fanned through her as she remembered how it had felt to be pressed to his hardness, to have his arms around her. And in all truth, she had to admit that Joshua Raven was an exciting man.

She gazed through the small porthole at the stars until the steady motion of the ship lulled her, and then she stretched on the bed to sleep.

14

———•◦—••◼•——•◦•———

Farther north, Edwin stood watch at night, looking at the stars high overhead and wondering about Lianna. They had pulled into port in Plymouth and sold the Dutch cargo and the ship, which Captain Turner deemed too cumbersome to sail with his *Adrian*.

They had been there long enough for Edwin to learn of Squire Melton's death. No doubt a solicitor had sent word to Quita, yet Edwin didn't think Quita would dare come back to England to claim the estate.

No, it would be waiting for Lianna, and his blood raced when he thought of the possibilities. Santiago, Chile—the same southern course the *Adrian* sailed!

When they had been in port he had asked many questions about why an Englishman would sail to Santiago. He discovered that there was unrest and some Englishmen intended to aid in overthrowing the Spanish. There was a group in London.

He leaned against the rail and looked at the water rushing swiftly below, the endless whitecaps and the expanse of dark seas. His future was unseeable, yet so many opportunities could be his! Soon he would get his own ship, for he was learning so fast that Captain Turner had remarked on it more than once and had given him more and more responsibilities. And he was learning to use the cutlass better, practicing belowdecks when no one was around. He learned the Dutch ship was a cargo ship, loaded with chests of indigo balls, vanilla beans, raw sugar from the islands, cowhides and beaver pelts from French Canada. What the crew dreamed about were Spanish ships loaded with gold from the colonies, treasure that wouldn't be hauled into port and sold, but hoarded away, each man having his own secret uses for his share.

In port Edwin had found a comely wench, Lila, who was prettier and more lusty than Nan. Warmth filled him as he remembered their nights. He would go back to Plymouth, back to Lila.

And he had learned about Josh Raven—a man who filled women's eyes with a longing that made Edwin's insides knot. He wanted to slit Raven's throat! He knew he would have to learn how to handle the cutlass better. It was one thing to attack a merchant ship and to use brute strength to hack his way to claim a prize; it was another to fight a man who stirred awe in other hard, experienced seamen. And adding flames to his anger, men were in awe of Raven. Edwin hoped he would have the chance and ability to run the man through! And if Lianna developed that look in her eyes at the mention of his name, if she had come to love him—

He abruptly snapped his thoughts away from that. He would hold her to her promise! He prayed Raven would not win her love, and if he did, little good it would do her if Raven were killed!

When his eyes swept the horizon, he thought he saw a speck. He peered up at the lubber's hole but decided if sails were in sight, they would have been spotted. Relaxing, he leaned his elbows on the rail. Lianna had inherited everything. A captain's mistress. It made his stomach churn, yet it was done now. And it made it easier for him. Even if she returned to England long before he did, men would be reluctant to marry her. She was no longer innocent, but had no man's good name. She was too sheltered to have the kind of social contacts that would help her overcome ostracism. No, she would wait for him. And if he could, he might sail on another ship for this faraway Chile.

His gaze swept the horizon, and this time the speck was

a dot, dark but real. He straightened to watch, then found a telescope and had a look.

"Sails sighted!" he bellowed, his pulse jumping because he relished another encounter, and the sighting might earn him extra pay. The last battle had furnished him with more wealth than a year of farmwork would have brought.

Men sprang to life, and in seconds Captain Turner appeared, coming up from his cabin below.

"Sails sighted, sir. I'm sure that's what I see."

"You sounded the call?"

"Aye, sir."

"What the devil is Betters doing?" Turner grumbled, looking up at the lubber's hole. He snatched the telescope from Edwin's hands.

Edwin stared at the dot so far in the distance. He would attack anything if it would make him richer and move him closer to Lianna. He lifted his chin. "The north wind has come up."

"Aye, and the ship runs northwesterly. We'll give them a merry chase!"

The ship was faster than the Dutch, a trim bark that went swiftly, but the *Adrian* soon came within firing range. Edwin worked beside his cannon, but he continually questioned the gunner about their position. As Dunsten levered a handspike against a carriage step to heave up the barrel breech and aim the gun higher, Edwin asked, "We'll have to board to leeward, won't we?"

Dunsten squinted at him over the barrel. "You learn fast. Yes, we will."

"How'll we do it?" Edwin persisted, wanting to be everywhere at once so he could learn.

"When our forecastle is abreast of their mainmast, we'll luff sails and put helm hard alee to close in."

"Won't she blast us out of the sea?"

"Not if we pass her lee quarter close enough. Haul on the left training tackle to get this into position."

In a short time when they were ready to board, Edwin spotted the yellow-and-red flag of Spain. "Spanish!" he exclaimed, and then he was boarding his second ship, swinging the cutlass with a cold determination, thinking of

Joshua Raven and wishing each man he fought were the captain of *El Feroz*.

This time, they found what the crew had talked and dreamed about since Edwin met them for the first time at the Boar's Head. Gold from the New World! Edwin didn't think he could ever stop staring at his share, as he ran the cold, hard coins through his fingers. The bark had been so badly damaged by cannon that it went down, but not before they had time to unload most of the cargo. Three sailors had begged to be taken on as crew members, and Captain Turner had agreed—something Edwin would not have done. There would be no loyalty from those men, he thought, rubbing two gold coins between his fingers.

"Still dreaming, Stafford?" Dunsten said as he sat down on a hammock.

"It's beautiful! And so easy!"

"Don't be fooled. We've had two easy encounters and lucky shots. The old Dutch ship was on its last legs. Tonight we were lucky. It's not always so easy."

"Easy or not, 'tis the best way I know to make a living!"

"You're a bloodthirsty one. I've seen you fight. You fight like a madman."

"Perhaps I am," he said quietly and saw two men who were mending clothes turn to look at him while Dunsten frowned.

"It won't always be so easy, and you've gone without a scratch. Wait until you get your first wound. It will seem a different matter then."

Edwin stood up abruptly and walked away as another sailor called to him, "Captain wants you."

Edwin dropped the gold into the sea chest and locked it, pocketing the key. He'd bought his own new chest at Plymouth and he kept his things locked now.

In the captain's cabin he was motioned to a chair. It was a tiny cabin with a bunk along one bulkhead, a desk bolted to another bulkhead, and a chair bolted to the floor. Captain Turner looked up from the ledger on the desk and pushed a drawstring purse toward Edwin. "Take this."

Edwin picked it up and felt the heaviness and heard the clink of coins. His brows arched inquiringly.

"It's your share for sighting the sails first and for saving my life when a man came at me with his sword. You killed him as I reached for my pstiol, and I want to reward you."

"I don't remember. Thank you, but you don't need to pay me."

"Take it. You're a mean fighter, Edwin Stafford. I thought a farmer would be a poor fighter." He shrugged. "Perhaps I don't know everything about men."

"I'm barely aware of what I'm doing."

"Well, you do damned fine! I wouldn't be here if you hadn't. You like sailing, don't you?"

"It's the thing I know best."

Captain Turner laughed. "Best? I heard about you and the tavern wench."

Edwin laughed in turn. "Very well, second best."

The captain's smile faded. "Well, take care in battle."

15

In the captain's cabin Josh stood bare-chested in front of the washstand. Fletcher eyed him as he entered and closed the door behind him.

"You sent for me, sir?"

Josh ran a washcloth across his jaw and waved the long razor. "Fletcher, sit down."

"Aye, sir." Fletcher dropped into one of the wooden chairs, stretched his long legs in front of him, and glanced at Josh lathering his jaw.

"Are you fully awake?" Josh asked.

"Aye, ready to sail into La Coruña. I shall be heartily glad to see the Spaniards ashore and us at sea, safely away from there."

"We'll stay a few nights before we sail."

Fletcher's head whipped around. "Why in hell take the risk? If the Marcheno family or the soldiers learn your identity, you know what they'll do. There's a price on your head, on each of us, still."

Josh cut a swath through the leather. "I intend to take Miss Melton ashore and wed her."

"Damn! She consented swiftly enough!"

Josh paused. "She doesn't know about my offer yet."

"In the name of heaven then, why will you offer for her?"

Joshua laughed softly. "It's time I had a wife. She's beautiful—"

"And already yours as long as you please. Why bind yourself to a woman who doesn't love you?"

Josh turned slowly and faced Fletcher. "I want a wife, and I want to have a family."

"You'll regret this alliance!"

Josh clamped his jaw tightly. "You're soured on women."

"No, I just keep a level head because I've learned a bitter lesson. I think you know as well as anyone that I find the fair ones delightful—in their place."

"We'll go ashore to be wed in church, and then return to the ship. I want the men given leave so I may have the ship to myself tomorrow night with my bride."

"Damn!" Fletcher jumped to his feet and walked closer. "You'd put these men ashore and risk their getting foxed and revealing who we are?"

Joshua met angry gray eyes. "Watch your tongue, Fletcher. Their lives are at stake as much as mine. They'll keep their mouths shut and they'll welcome two or three nights ashore."

"Aye, sir!" Fletcher flushed and whirled to a porthole and gazed outside. "Sir, there is more than a bond of blood between us. You could have left me to fend for myself. Instead, you've treated me as you treated Phillip. You saved my life when I was injured in battle. I wouldn't be here this moment if you hadn't risked your own life for mine. Don't—"

Josh turned, dropping a towel over his bare shoulder. His voice was firm. "Fletcher, I want Lianna always."

"Zounds! You sound foxed. Sir, you educated me, allowed me to move in a society that had turned its back on you. I know women like Miss Melton better than you. If you tell her you love her—this cold English maiden— you'll create your own hell."

"That's enough!"

Fletcher stiffened. "Aye, sir."

"I'll be up to take the wheel shortly. We'll summon the men, tell them about leave, and sail into La Coruña."

"Aye, sir."

"That's all," Josh said softly, and watched the first mate leave in long angry strides.

Josh let out his breath and looked at his reflection in the mirror. Was he committing the greatest folly of his life? Instead of his own green eyes and brown hair, another image swam before him. He saw wide blue eyes the color of the sky on a clear day, midnight tresses that floated over pale shoulders. He felt a quickening in his loins. Lianna was in his blood. Damn, how he wanted her! He thought how responsive she was, how quickly she lost her reluctance and her inhibitions. If one gained her love . . .

His blood pounded and he blinked, seeing himself again. He laughed at the image. "You besotted fool! Taken in by big blue eyes." Should he follow Fletcher's advice? He owned Lianna's body. He shook his head, his smile fading. Her body wasn't the ultimate prize he was after—it was her heart.

He dropped the towel and turned from the mirror without questioning his motives any deeper.

Abovedeck, Fletcher stood in the early light of dawn and spotted land in the distance. Trying to curb his anger, he gave orders to the helmsman as they approached La Coruña. A brisk wind drove them swiftly toward their destination. By the time Josh appeared to take charge, they were approaching the dock.

Near Marcheno Castle the wind whipped against Quita's cheeks and she smiled, feeling exhilarated as she watched Armando riding ahead of her. She thought she would never tire of looking at him. Beneath a warm morning sun, he wore a broad-brimmed cap on his head, his long dark hair curling over his wide shoulders. He turned in the saddle to flash a grin at her, and she felt a skip in her heartbeat.

Suddenly a rabbit dashed from the woods and a hound glimpsed it. He turned, baying as he ran, and the other hounds ran after him.

The rabbit ran in a zigzag pattern as the riders changed direction to follow the hounds. There were two noblemen and their wives riding in the hunting party. Quita turned her horse, loving the feel of the beautiful gray animal beneath her. He had been a gift from Armando, and she treasured the horse as something very special.

She watched as the rabbit dashed desperately ahead of the hounds. It was small and brown; once it looked back as the dogs began to narrow the distance, and suddenly Quita hated the chase. She had ridden with Armando before to hunt, but this was different. The rabbit was soft and it looked small and helpless with the dogs barking and galloping headlong after it. As she watched, her dislike mushroomed, because she could clearly imagine what it would be like to be the rabbit. It reminded her of the nightmare she'd had several times since her arrival in Spain, a dream of running from faceless men who chased her. Her mouth became dry and she tugged on the reins, wanting to avoid seeing the kill as the dogs closed in on the helpless hare.

She turned her horse, letting it walk into the pines. She would catch up after they had ridden ahead. She heard a high squeal and realized the rabbit must have been caught. In the cool shadows of the pines, she shuddered and stared at the riders, now slowing and milling around.

Suddenly Armando separated from the group and rode in her direction. Her heart beat swiftly, because she always wanted to avoid displeasing him. She urged her horse forward to meet him.

As he reined beside her, she forced a smile.

"What happened to you?" he asked, a quizzical smile on his face.

"Sorry, I stopped to cool in the shade."

His brows came together and he stared at her intently for a moment. Her heart began to pound, because he looked at her in a cold manner like never before. He turned in the saddle to wave to the others. "Go ahead. We'll catch you."

Her breath stopped and she wondered if she had angered him by staying behind.

He turned his horse toward the trees and she followed. They rode quietly into the cool shade until they came to a stream. She began to relax, deciding he had wanted to water the horses—or perhaps kiss her. She had learned by now that she had married a lusty man.

He dismounted and reached up to pull her down, resting his hands lightly on her waist. His features were stern as he said quietly, "Why did you turn back?"

She felt a shock, realizing he had known so easily that she had lied to him. Her heart thudded in sudden fear because of his fierce expression. "I didn't mean to displease you," she whispered.

"Lianna, don't ever lie to me." Her fear grew larger, and she nodded, unable to answer him, wondering how he had known. "I will tolerate many things, but be truthful with me."

She trembled, thinking what a monumental lie their marriage was! Her name, her lineage—she hadn't been truthful to him in the most elemental and important way.

"Why did you turn back?"

"I couldn't bear to see that tiny rabbit chased down and torn apart by the dogs," she whispered, barely able to get out the words beneath dark eyes that seemed to see every thought. For a moment she felt like Quita Bencaria, a peasant girl.

His features softened, losing all their harshness, and her racing heartbeat began to slow. "Lia, it was only a rabbit. You've hunted with me and enjoyed the kill."

"But a deer or a bird killed by a clean shot is different. The rabbit was smaller than the dogs, alone and defenseless . . ."

"Oh, *querida*," he said, crushing her to him and laughing. "I'm sorry if we upset you. You don't have to watch the dogs kill a rabbit!" He held her away, his eyes filled with curiosity. "Why didn't you say so when I first asked?"

"I didn't want to displease you," she answered softly, and her heartbeat quickened for a new reason as she saw the flare of joy in his eyes.

"Ah, Lia, how I love you! You'll never displease me," he said, tilting her chin up.

"I pray not." She wound her fingers in his hair and stroked his neck, feeling a swift, hot rush of desire.

His dark eyes focused on her mouth and she stood on tiptoe. His eyelids lowered and he bent to kiss her, murmuring, "You always please me."

His hands fondled her breasts, pushing aside her riding coat, tugging at the laces at the neck of her silk blouse.

"Armando, the others—"

"Won't disturb us. Shh, touch me, Lia."

His hands were callused and rough, but his touch was gentle and magic, a silken torment that made her forget where she was or what was happening or anything else except Armando.

He swung the full cape off his shoulders and swirled it, spreading it on the leaves. He sat on it, tumbling her down in his lap, her clothing half off as her own eager fingers pushed his garments aside.

As he entered her, she watched him for an instant, seeing his hard shoulders, his smoldering gaze, hearing only bird cries as dappled sunlight played over their bodies through pine boughs. She closed her eyes, lost in a swirling vortex of passion that took all her senses. She heard his cry only dimly, and her own voice sounded as if from a distance. His weight came down and he held her, stroking her face, murmuring endearments.

"Armando, I shall die of shame to join the others again! My hair . . ."

He laughed, kissing her and silencing her protests. "We'll ride straight back to the castle."

Late that afternoon Quita lazed in a tub of hot water that had been brought to the bedroom. They were still living in the bridal rooms of the castle and stayed in seclusion most of the time. Quita had dismissed Yolana because she wanted to soak alone. As she stepped from the tub and started to pull on her pale blue velvet robe, she paused, glimpsing her reflection in the oval mirror. Her black hair was loosely fastened on top of her head. She lowered the robe to stare at her flat stomach. They had been wed over a month now and she had not conceived.

Suddenly she became afraid she would lose Armando's love if she bore him no children. He talked constantly of an heir, a son. She closed her eyes to pray there would be one soon.

"Lia."

She whirled around, pulling the robe up to her chin, and saw Armando filling the doorway. His countenance was solemn, and her breathing stopped, because she knew something had happened.

"Lianna, there has been a messenger from England."

16

For an instant the room swam before her eyes while she wondered if Squire Melton were coming to visit. As Armando approached her, she knew she couldn't hide the truth from him if he questioned her.

"Lianna," he said sadly, placing his hands on her shoulders, "your father had an accident. He's dead."

Dizzy with relief, Quita closed her eyes while his arms enfolded her. She tried to summon tears and found it was easy to cry with relief. She lived with threats turning up in unexpected ways and unexpected moments, and each one seemed to pull her nerves more tautly than the last.

Armando picked her up and carried her to a chair, where he sat with her on his lap, pulling the robe over her to cover her.

"I'm sorry, *querida*."

She sat up, wiping her eyes. "Armando, my father was my parent . . . but he was a cold man, not cruel, just cold. I don't think he loved me." She was afraid to look into midnight eyes that could discern the truth too frighteningly well. She toyed with the laces on Armando's shirt. "He loved money and ships more than all else on earth."

"I know, Lia," he said so gently that her eyes flew wide. He smiled. "What kind of father would have married off his daughter in the manner yours did?"

"Thank heaven he did!" she said, love welling up inside her. "Armando, I don't want to go back to England. This is the first happiness I have known. I don't want to remember a honeymoon spent on a long journey back to a cold English home where I was always lonely!'' Her plea tumbled out as she kissed his throat between words and felt his arm tighten around her waist.

"Then you won't go back. It's unnecessary now. Someday you may want to see to your inheritance. I don't care if we never see it. In the meantime, I'll send word to your father's solicitor to appoint someone to manage the estate.''

She raised her head to stare at him, and his brows arched quizzically. "What's the question I see in your eyes?''

"You must be a man of great wealth to treat my inheritance so casually!''

He laughed. "*Sí cara,* I do have wealth. And I want to give it all to you. Give me a son, Lia,'' he said, and suddenly she knew the one thing he wanted that wealth could not buy. His dark eyes were intense, and her body trembled with desire and an overwhelming longing to produce the heir he wanted, to bind him to her so tightly that if he ever learned the truth, he could forgive her.

He pushed the blue robe away, his hands following the path of the material as it slipped off her naked body.

A week later, he wanted her to travel with him to La Coruña to see the progress on a new ship he was having readied for them to sail on their coming voyage to the New World.

She didn't want to make the long journey to La Coruña, but she was terrified to protest even slightly. Armando could far too easily detect when she wasn't telling him the truth, so she agreed to go, but each day of the journey brought her that much closer to danger.

As the carriages rolled into town, again she had a feeling of dread, fearing that the Fate that had given her Armando and a life of wealth might snatch it away as swiftly.

From the shadows of the carriage she stared at the women who washed clothes in the fountain, and to her relief, she didn't recognize any. She felt somewhat better when their carriage rolled down the dusty lane to dockside and she saw the great ships. She leaned forward, her spirits lifting, for it was unlikely she would see a familiar face aboard ship. Her gaze fell on a prow with a familiar figurehead—a lion's head with a flowing mane and teeth bared. Her eyes searched for the name—*El Feroz*—and her heart stopped beating.

She stared in disbelief, as if a specter had risen up to haunt her. Turning to ice, she wondered what conspiracy would bring them all together—did Armando know and intend to confront her with Lianna Melton? The world spun and spots danced before her eyes until Armando spoke in a lazy voice.

"For someone who fears ships, you seem fascinated by them."

She glanced at him. He lazed back in the corner with one booted foot propped on the seat, his elbow resting on his knee while he watched her with a slight smile.

"I felt faint. I'm weary of riding and needed fresh air," she said, suddenly realizing whatever had brought *El Feroz* to Spain, Armando knew nothing of it.

"Lia, I'm sorry. We're almost there," he said, at once solicitous as he sat up.

She glanced again at *El Feroz*. Lianna Melton was on that ship, only yards away. Quita trembled, wondering if Lianna had changed her mind—yet she doubted that happening. What had brought *El Feroz* to La Coruña?

She forgot as arms closed around her waist and she was pulled onto Armando's lap while he nuzzled her neck. "We're almost there. I should have left you at home, but I want you with me."

"I'm all right. I'm glad I'm here," she said, winding her arms around his neck, feeling safe.

Within the hour, as they started up the gangplank of his ship, Quita glanced over it. Her gaze drifted over the three masts rigged with lanteen sails and the extended quarter-deck, then along to the bow, and she gasped with delight. "Armando!"

He grinned as they both looked at the name freshly painted, *La Lia*. "You named it for me!" she exclaimed, squeezing his arm.

He laughed and hugged her shoulders in return. "Come look at her."

They walked the deck of the ship he was having redone for their trip. It was magnificent, yet Quita couldn't shake her fears. It made her nervous to have *El Feroz* so close at hand, yet not know why it was in Spain. Once, when Armando finished giving instructions to his men and linked his arm in hers, she pointed to the ship. "*El Feroz*. Is that one of your ships, Armando?"

"No, Lianna. I've been told they rescued Spanish sailors whose ship had gone down and brought them into port. I want you to see the rest of the ship." He took her arm to help her down a companionway, and *El Feroz* was lost to sight.

Relief that the presence of *El Feroz* had nothing to do with her mixed with new worries. Squire Melton was dead. If she let Lianna know her father had died, Lianna could go home and claim her inheritance. Armando seemed to have no interest in the English possessions—and Lianna would not have to spend a life in servitude. Edwin Stafford was at home—the man Lianna loved—and Quita realized how fortunate a woman was if she were able to marry the man she loved. Compassion and gratitude warred with caution, because the wise course would be to let it go, to let Lianna Melton struggle in life in her own way. Yet how much she owed to Lianna!

Emotions tugged at Quita. She didn't want to risk anything that might disturb her precarious hold on Armando's affections, yet Lianna might be safer tucked away in England than sailing to the New World. Armando held no love for England, telling her more than once he had found it a cold country with cold people. She barely heard what Armando was saying and realized she must pay closer attention. They spent the night on the ship in a half-furnished cabin and the next day they planned to start for home with Quita still worrying about Lianna.

The problem seemed to solve itself because she had no opportunity to get word to Lianna. But midmorning Armando helped her into the carriage for the ride home, and he was suddenly called to go back to the ship, leaving her alone. It was hot in the carriage and she stepped out to walk, moving to the shade of small shops yards back from the waterfront. As she sat on a bench and stared at the ship, wondering where Lianna might be, she made a decision. Hastily she penned a note and took coins from her reticule. She looked around and saw a lad tethering a horse nearby. *"Un momento, por favor,"* she said softly, and motioned him over, knowing she was out of sight of Armando and his men.

An hour later, she climbed into her carriage and they headed for Madrid. She turned once to look back through the window, wondering if the message would get delivered and what would happen afterward. She had asked the lad to wait until *El Feroz* looked ready to sail, but already second thoughts were besieging her that she had made a mistake. If Lianna claimed the inheritance and Armando wanted to go to England . . . Quita shoved the thought aside. It had been far more risky the other way. The New World was Armando's next destination, Santiago, Chile— the exact place Mr. Summers had said Captain Joshua Raven intended to sail!

Now Lianna could go home to Edwin and live a life with the man she loved, just as she had given Quita the opportunity to do. Quita smiled at Armando, slipping onto the carriage seat beside him and turning to him as she dropped her hand to his thigh.

The sun climbed over the horizon, and the air warmed. Midafternoon they passed through a pine forest and the coolness was welcome. As they left the edge of the woods, moving into sunlight again, a commotion started. Shouts and a gun blast deafened Quita as Armando sat up.

"What the hell?"

The door burst open, and a ruffian thrust a pistol inside.

Quita screamed. Armando lunged, kicking at the man. The pistol fired, its noise blasting Quita's ears in the confines of the carriage.

As soon as the man had fired, Armando hit him and the man fell from the carriage.

A man on horseback rode alongside the carriage, and to her relief, she saw it was one of Armando's men. Her relief was short-lived as Armando started out the door.

"Armando!" she cried, and grasped his arm.

"It's bandits!" He shook free and grabbed the man riding beside them, pulling himself onto the back of the horse behind the rider.

"Armando, come back!" she cried, knowing it was useless, but unable to keep from calling to him.

He shouted to the rider and the man reached for the coach, pulling himself off the horse and clinging to the side of the coach. He scrambled up toward the box out of sight while Armando slipped into the saddle and turned the horse to go after a bandit who was riding away. He aimed a pistol and fired and the man toppled off the horse, then got up and began to run.

The door banged and air rushed in as the horses plunged ahead. More shots were fired and then the carriage slowed while Armando and his men brought three bandits together.

Quita climbed out of the carriage as Armando dismounted and waited while a fourth thief was rounded up. She expected Armando to return to the carriage, to let his men shackle the bandits. Wind tugged at his white collar, blowing it against his dark jaw, and he turned, seeing her watching him.

"Get inside the carriage, Lianna," he said.

For the first time she realized and she stared at him, seeing him as the man she had heard whispered about, the cruel man of iron who was so unyielding.

"Lianna!"

She climbed into the carriage and shut the door, staring stonily ahead, realizing he had another side to him that was as harsh and cruel as the stormiest sea.

Four shots were fired. Each one made her flinch, and she clasped her fingers together. If Armando ever discovered her identity . . . In that moment she lost all illusions that he would forgive her.

The carriage door opened and he climbed inside, slamming shut the door as he sat down and looked at her.

"You shot them," she said, knowing she shouldn't say anything.

"Perhaps word will travel that the Marcheno carriage is one to leave alone. They were thieves, Lianna. That man would have shot you or me if I hadn't kicked the pistol and ruined his arm. They're brigands. Only a little over a year ago soldiers spread across this land trying to drive the French out. Wellington's men, our men, French soldiers, men from three armies overran Spain in the fight against Napoleon. There has been riffraff on the road in abundance ever since. They wouldn't treat you with kindness and they don't deserve any. Forget them.''

She looked down at her hands, knowing he was right about the thieves, yet it frightened her to see how callous he could be.

Silence lengthened between them, and as the carriage lumbered along, warmth began to return to her again. She glanced at him to see him staring out the window, a scowl on his features. She leaned forward to take his hand.

''Armando, are you angry with me?''

He turned and his features softened as he reached for her to pull her to him.

''Of course not!'' He smiled at her, his black eyes developing lusty fires. ''Lia, we have a long, leisurely journey home, and I will show you how happy I am with you.''

Aboard *El Feroz*, as Lianna brushed her hair, Captain Raven appeared carrying a kettle of hot water.

For a moment she gave no thought to the object in his hands, so taken was she by the sight of him. His wide smile dazzled, but below the smile, his clothing made his appearance breathtaking. Instead of the customary black breeches and linen shirt, he was wearing an elegant white silk shirt with a snowy white cravat. The shirt tapered to flawless fawn-colored breeches and gleaming black Hessians, all of which looked incongruous on a man tending to the chore of filling a tub with water.

She couldn't think of a male acquaintance who would look as appealing as Captain Raven did this moment. The clothing was, without a doubt, expensive and carefully tailored. She watched with open curiosity. As soon as the tub was filled, he crossed to the wardrobe, searched among the dresses then produced a filmy white gauze dress shot with silver, and her woolen cape. Placing them across a chair, he made an elaborate bow. "This cabin is yours, love. I'll return shortly."

With that, he left, and Lianna remained perplexed. Why the fancy dress? She rose and lifted the white dress, fingering the delicate material. Why was he so well-dressed? What did he plan? Rushing with eagerness to discover what lay ahead, she bathed.

They were in Spain. Perhaps he intended to put her on a ship bound for England! And briefly the idea brought a pang of regret that she would never see Joshua Raven again. There were moments when he was exciting and more fun than anyone she had known in her life. And when he touched her . . . She drew her breath sharply, shaking her head as if to clear it of such thoughts. She wanted to go home, but she would miss him—and remember him forever.

She dressed, gazing at the lovely gown. It was a ball gown, not a morning dress, and her curiosity increased. The door opened, and Captain Raven stepped inside.

"How beautiful you are," he said, and the warmth in his eyes made her smile with pleasure. He crossed the cabin to place his hands on her shoulders, and the faint contact, merely fingers resting lightly on her shoulders, was as jolting as if the ship had been suddenly rocked by a giant wave. His clothing smelled fresh and clean, his hair was drawn back, framing his face.

"Will I be allowed to go ashore?"

"Aye, you'll go ashore with me."

Curiosity was rampant. His eyes twinkled with devilish satisfaction. She tilted her head to study him. "I suspect that you are up to something wicked!"

He laughed. "Hardly, love."

"Where are we going?"

He ran a rough thumb lightly along her chin. Suddenly he swept his arm around her and bent over her. "Miss Lianna Melton, will you marry me?"

17

Aghast, Lianna stared at him. His mouth quirked in amusement. "Ah, my love, such burning rapture, such eagerness to become my bride!" he said sardonically, stirring a shocked reaction.

"I have no inclination to wed a jackanapes pirate who most likely came from the London slums and stowed aboard ship at age fifteen!" Her mind reeled while the words she hurled at him had far from their desired effect. With a flash of white teeth he laughed. She continued relentlessly, "You're very handsome, and quite entertaining, but I have no desire to wed you. You're also a cutthroat pirate and a ruffian, as ignorant of the refinements of life as any dog on the wharf!"

His grin widened. Was the man immune to insults? In a sweeping gesture he waved his arm. "And all these books count for nothing?"

"I suspect you gained them in a raid upon another ship!"

" 'Ser o no ser . . .' " he quoted.

"I can't wed you!" She shook with anger and fright. And another emotion rippled like a surging wave, yet she wouldn't recognize it or the breathless effect it had.

"Aye, you shall." Laughter faded from his eyes. He straightened and held her. "Lianna, our destinies are entwined. We can have a good marriage. You have no home to return to—I need a wife."

Her mouth felt dry, and her heart pounded. His green

eyes held her captive and it was an effort to think. "Let me go to a Spanish convent. Then I'll get passage on a ship to England."

"And then what? You can't return home, can you?"

"No, but I—"

"Lianna, wed me before we sail to the New World. We can't wed there. It can be annulled when this is over."

"I can return to England if you'll let me. I don't have to go home."

A flinty, shuttered look crossed his features. Emerald eyes became slivers of ice, hard and unyielding. "Would you rather sail as my wife—or my mistress?"

She drew in her breath sharply and clenched her fists. Trembling, she probed his cold eyes. "Do you want a wife whom you have coerced into marriage?"

For a fleeting moment a look of pain crossed his features, but it vanished swiftly, replaced by an impassive coldness.

"Why, when you've taken me and made me your mistress—in truth, your captive as much as any slave—why do you want to wed me?"

"I can be a far more convincing *marqués* with the Spaniards in Chile if I arrive with a wife," Josh stated simply, wanting to wipe the hurt expression from her face. Didn't she realize the precarious position she was in?

"You could lie as you had planned, and they wouldn't know. Why are we to wed?" she persisted, and he felt a deep ache. He had given her time and he had hoped she would change.

He closed his mind to the thought. "It's time I have a wife," he said flatly. "You're young and healthy and very beautiful." An eyebrow quirked as he added, "As well as passionate."

Something hurt inside, yet what choice did she have? As if he saw her dilemma, his features softened.

"Love, it can be good between us. Give me your trust."

His voice was gentle, but Lianna wanted something more. "You won't gain my loyalty by a forced marriage!"

"And the possibility exists that you're *embarazada*, already with child."

"I pray not!" she gasped. Searching wildly for something to dent his cool manner, she cried, "I love another man! I love Edwin—"

Hard fingers locked around her arms, lifting her to her toes.

"Don't say his name! Dammit, you're not his! Did you pledge your love to him?"

"Yes!" It wasn't true, but it might stop the wedding. Her answer brought an unexpected reaction. Captain Raven paled, his eyes narrowed. He looked as if he truly cared! Startled, she drew a deep breath, peering at him intently.

"Enough of this!" he snapped, his patience waning. He placed her cape around her shoulders. "Come along. A priest awaits us."

Scooping her into his arms, he strode across the cabin.

"Put me down!"

"No, you're light as a wren, and we're off to our wedding!"

He lifted her into a hansom carriage. The driver closed the door behind them. As the carriage began to roll, Josh held her on his lap, her gauzy white skirt billowing over their knees. She couldn't be deeply in love with Edwin Stafford if all she had told him were true. Her blue eyes danced with excitement now, and while she frowned at him, he saw the vein in her throat pulse rapidly.

"Lianna, I'll try to make you happy."

"Your arrogance is beyond bounds!" she snapped, but her voice sounded breathless.

"Lianna," he said huskily, "it can be so good between us. No South Sea or summer sky ever held the clear blue of your eyes." His voice was a rumble that made her blood heat.

Lianna wondered at the many facets to the man. A seafaring pirate who was hard and scarred from battle, yet now said poetic words to her while he gazed warmly at her. If only, deep in his green-gold eyes, there was another emotion. . . .

While she studied him intently, her thoughts swirling like tossed leaves, the moment changed. The sparkling tension that could flare quickly between them ignited. All her nerves pulsed to life. She became aware of every contact of her flesh with his, even though separated by thin layers of clothing. And it seemed that he felt it as much as she. His eyes narrowed while his fingers drifted over her, sliding beneath her cape, touching her throat and moving down over her shoulder. "Mrs. Joshua Raven, my wife. I . . ."

She waited, holding her breath while her heart, her lungs, ceased to function.

"I'll have a beautiful wife," he finished abruptly.

A constriction squeezed her heart, and she felt a flicker of disappointment that she couldn't understand. What had she expected from him? What had she wanted—a declaration of undying love? Ridiculous! She tossed her head and slipped off his lap to face him across the aisle.

She tilted her head to regard him. Would there be any last chance to talk him into letting her go? She leaned forward to place her cold fingers over his warm ones. "Please, Captain Raven, release me from this arrangement."

"I couldn't if I were dispositioned to do so," he answered flatly.

"Why, in heaven's name?"

"Because we're in Spain. I'd run too great a risk of you relating my plans to the Spaniards."

"I swear I wouldn't! Who would believe me anyway?"

"They would believe you, all right. The Spanish have spies spread in ports from here to New Spain, to the Cape and back. Almost three centuries ago a papal decree—the Line of Demarcation—gave them claim to half the world. Since that time, they've protected their territories. Ships can't gather against them, countries which send forth their ships toward the New World know they can't put in to shore for long periods. The Spaniards dominate a large portion of the world. They would get wind of my mission and it would be useless then."

"I swear I won't reveal a word. And if you'll release me to go back to England, I'll return your payment." She didn't know how, but if he agreed, she would find a way.

"Why do I doubt that?" he said with infuriating stubbornness.

"You already have taken my purity," she said.

One damnable eyebrow climbed, giving him a wicked, devil-may-care appearance that set her teeth on edge. How could she melt beneath the onslaught of the rogue's kisses!

"You would repay me fully? Ten thousand pounds' worth?"

Stunned, she felt as if he had plunged a knife in her heart. "You paid that price for Quita?" she gasped.

"Aye," he answered calmly.

She stared at him again in wonder. The man must be wealthy as Croesus to hand over such a figure for a mere serving girl. "It is an incredible amount!"

"It is, and I intend to get what I paid for."

She sank back and looked out at the Spanish city, the buildings with their plaster walls and red tiled roofs and Moorish architecture, so different from London. She could never earn such a sum to repay him. Even if she could go home and ask her father, he would refuse. Her father's love of gold exceeded his love of all else.

"Lianna."

The word rolled off his tongue slowly, drawn out with a velvety tone that brought back her acute awareness of him as a man. She raised her lashes to watch him lean forward to grasp her chin, his face only inches away. "Lianna, this will be a good marriage if we both try."

She wanted someone who loved her, who wanted to marry her because he loved her, not because it was convenient for a revolution! Something tightened in her throat. She remembered the nights as a small child when she had cried herself to sleep after sessions with the maids or her father, when they had made it clear she was merely tolerated, not loved! And Edwin came to mind, the look in his eyes as he swore helplessly over her departure. Edwin, the one person in her entire life who had cared!

"Dammit," Captain Raven said in a low voice so filled with fury that her thoughts immediately jerked back to the present. "You're thinking of him, aren't you!"

An angry flush darkened his cheeks, turning them the

color of weathered copper, and his eyes were sharp dag-
gers, threatening her with fiery pinpoints of gold. He
reached out to grip her shoulders painfully. "I'll drive
him out of your thoughts if it's the last thing I do!"

"Why do you care if I love another?" she cried. "All
you want is my aid in your deception of the Spanish."

"I don't care to share my possessions!" he snapped.

She drew her breath and turned to the window. His
possession! The man was arrogant, impossible, as contra-
dictory as snow falling in a tropical wilderness! Mrs.
Joshua Raven. What lay ahead? What life would she have
from this forced marriage? His head turned and green eyes
wrapped their clinging tendrils around her heart. Oh, why
couldn't they have met under other circumstances? Why
couldn't there have been a chance for love to grow?

His brows narrowed and she held her breath. The man
had the most uncanny way of guessing her thoughts. At
the same time, his were absolutely unreadable.

"What are you thinking, Lianna?"

"I wondered the same about you, captain."

"It's Josh." His voice lowered to that furry depth that
came over her nerves like soft cat paws. "Let me hear you
repeat it."

"Josh." It came out breathlessly and she was ensnared
in clouds of emerald, drifting above earth without a solid
footing, drifting toward a golden sun that blazed into her
soul. She couldn't breathe, couldn't move. His lips parted,
his firm, well-shaped lips. He leaned toward her, and her
breath stopped as he whispered, "We can have happiness,
Lianna."

The carriage jerked to a halt and she blinked, reason
returning to her. She watched while the door was opened
and Captain Raven jumped down, then turned to take her
hand.

As Lianna stood before the priest, her icy fingers held
by Captain Raven, she heard dimly the vows intoned until
the priest stated, "And do you, Joshua Cathmoor Brougher
Raven, take this woman as your lawful wife . . ."

A jog of memory took Lianna from the present as she
recalled her father's fury one winter's day not so long ago.

He had paced the library, waving his fist in anger, his blue eyes snapping, while he denounced the snobbery of two English peers, the Marques of Cowden and his grace, William Brougher Raven, the Duke of Cathmoor.

Orphans and street urchins, commoners, seldom bore names such as Joshua Cathmoor Brougher Raven. Who was this man? Why would he leave a life of wealth and ease, give up a title, for the danger and discomfort at sea?

He raised her hand to slip a band of gold onto her finger. A tiny golden ring of slavery, binding her to an iron-willed rogue whose green eyes bewitched and whose lips enchanted, when all she had ever wanted was love.

The priest gave permission for a kiss, and her new husband leaned down to whisper, "My love . . ."

His lips brushed so gently and she looked up to see him smiling at her. He was handsome, this tall man who could be charming—if only he loved her! Her throat tightened with an ache because she had no illusions. Joshua Raven had married her for convenience, for some purpose in his scheming plans. In spite of that knowledge, her heart beat faster as she walked down the aisle, out of the church with her new husband.

As soon as they were in the carriage to return to *El Feroz*, Lianna asked the question foremost in her thoughts. "Who are you?"

"Captain Raven of *El Feroz*, and now, your husband."

"Who's your father?" she persisted.

He laughed, a harsh, mirthless sound. "So, you know the duke?"

"No," she replied. "I've heard my father speak of him."

As he gazed steadfastly at her, she wondered what had caused the rift between Josh and his father. It occurred to her that Captain Raven's childhood might have been as devoid of love as her own. Was that what had driven him to sea? "Why did you leave home at such an early age?"

"The duke was a very cruel man," he responded flatly.

So Josh Raven was vulnerable too! Her sympathy stirred; she reached across impulsively and touched his hand. "I'm sorry."

Something flickered in his eyes and he gazed at her intently. She withdrew her hand swiftly and locked her fingers together in her lap. "You're the son of a duke. Do you have other brothers?"

A cynical note came into his voice as he answered her, "No, but I won't be the Duke of Cathmoor." She drew a quick breath at the smoldering anger in his expression. "Don't raise your hopes, love. I've been disinherited."

"My hopes!" she snapped, forgetting the rising tide of sympathy she had felt for him. "I'm here now because I fled from marriage to a nobleman, one of the wealthiest in Spain! There is only one reason I'd want to marry, but unfortunately, I had no choice."

"And what is that one reason?"

She raised her chin defiantly. "Marriage should be because of love."

"There are some fine substitutes," he answered sardonically, leaning forward, his dark coat falling open over the ruffled expanse of his white shirt. Her heart skipped as he tilted her chin up and placed his mouth on hers with deliberation.

Her arguments dissipated into nothing, burned away by the passion he could arouse effortlessly. He shifted to look at her, arching an eyebrow in satisfaction.

She blinked, her befuddled senses reeling before she realized he had proven a point. She flounced her skirts, turning to the window while he rode in silence for the remainder of the journey back to the ship.

Catching sight of *El Feroz*, with its gun-deck ports closed, the snarling lion's head at the black prow, and its tall masts stretching skyward, Lianna again experienced a bounding feeling of adventure when she gazed at *El Feroz*. What lay ahead in the New World? Excitement rippled in her at the prospect of seeing new lands and new people.

"You like my ship," Josh observed softly.

She brought her gaze down and her spirits lowered as swiftly. "It's a prison."

One corner of his mouth raised in a crooked, cynical smile. "Nay, my love. I've seen sea captains and sailors with the same gleam in their eyes. You love adventure, my lady, just as surely as you draw breath." He reached out to stroke her chin. "It can be so fine between us, Lianna."

With his words came awareness of the deep possessive way he said her name. It sent a warmth into her being. He swung her into his arms, and his long legs covered the gangplank in easy strides. One of his men caught sight of them and whistled, then shouts went up from the crew for their newly wedded captain. As they came aboard, Fletcher stood beside a keg of rum, unplugging it to pour the first deep flagons for Captain Raven and his bride.

"Here's to our captain and his new bride—may they embark on a successful venture and happy life!"

As the men cheered and drank, Fletcher gazed with solemn gray eyes across the rim of his cup at Lianna. "Here's to the captain's beautiful bride—be good to him," he said softly.

"You ask that I be good to him. If only you knew the circumstances—"

"I do."

Startled, she peered intently at the first mate. "He told you?"

The answer was lost as Josh turned around to circle her waist with his arm. Looking down at her, he said, "To a long, happy life—together."

She lifted the silver flagon as he lightly touched his against it, and they both drank. She couldn't fathom his expression. Did he hope she would love him? Did he think someday he would feel love for her? What an unreadable man she had married, this tall stranger whose life was now forever linked intimately with her own. He sipped, lowering the cup to smile at her, a radiant, flashing smile that brought one to her lips in return. Captain Josh Raven had his winning moments! She felt breathless as she thought of how charming he could indeed be.

For the next quarter-hour they drank toasts with the men; then Josh lifted her into his arms again to carry her below, and her heart began to pound violently as she remembered their first night. Inside his cabin he set her on her feet, holding her close.

"My wife," he whispered, reaching up to remove the

pins from her raven hair. Lianna's heart pounded. She was wed to him, yet at the moment fears rose to haunt her. All she could think about was his cavalier treatment, the pain and embarrassment she had suffered from him, and never again would she see in a man's eyes the look of love that she had seen in Edwin's. Certainly not in the eyes devouring her now. Captain Raven wanted her, but it wasn't love.

"Lianna," he breathed huskily, leaning forward to kiss below her ear, then letting his warm breath fan over her throat as his lips trailed downward to the soft hollow between her throat and her shoulder. He paused and raised his head. "Seldom have I looked back with regret, but now I do."

She opened her eyes wide. "You regret bringing me!"

"No, I regret that we didn't meet in England, that I couldn't court you."

He sounded so sincere that Lianna was touched. And how deeply she wished their pasts had been different! With each brush of his lips, his breath, his hand stroking so lightly on her nape, her voice became breathless, the words difficult to pronounce. Her lids became heavy. She tilted her lips up to her husband and closed her eyes, her arms circling the strong column of his neck.

"Please, give me the time you promised. This isn't love." The idea that he would possess her when he didn't love her frightened her.

"I care, Lianna, and when I look at you, I can't get my breath."

She didn't believe him, but she couldn't argue. Words fled. Adeptly his fingers unfastened the white gauze and pushed it from her shoulders, down over her tiny waist, over her hips. As it floated down in a billowing whisper around her ankles, Lianna's reserve fell with it. Lost in the dazzling onslaught of his seductive touch, she forgot their differences.

He lowered his head, his hair pressing softly against an upthrusting breast as he turned his face to kiss the other pointed peak. She gasped and wound her fingers in his hair, pulling free the strip of leather that held his brown hair bound behind his neck.

"Lianna, Lianna, my sweet love . . ." he murmured, and she wanted to cry out and tell him to stop whispering endearments that he didn't mean. At the same time, she relished his words. If only he meant them!

His hands were magic, roaming everywhere, each foray bringing golden sorcery, driving her to an abandon she didn't dream possible. This wedding night she was not befuddled with wine, no longer struggling against a captor. He made love to her as if she were the most precious part of his life, and Lianna responded fully.

Beneath his hands her shift drifted away; then he pulled off his coat; the white cravat and shirt went next. Bare-chested, he stood before her, bronzed, his skin taut over muscles honed to perfection from years aboard ship. One look at the short brown curls that matted his chest, and she remembered fully their texture against her bare breasts.

His black breeches bulged with his aroused manhood; his hands lowered to pull off his gleaming black boots. She licked her dry lips as she stood mesmerized by a marvelous body, by the hungering fires dancing in his eyes, by her body's quivering response to his languorous gaze.

"How beautiful you are. Fate meant our paths to cross, gave you to me . . ." His voice was husky. And, heaven help her, she wanted him so badly! Even if there were no words of love, some part of her already belonged to Josh Raven, and how easily he could claim it.

Tight breeches were peeled away, and then he lifted her in his arms to carry her to the bed. He stood over her, his eyes burning with passion at the sight of her lush pink-tipped breasts, her pale flat stomach, and her long, slender legs.

"Lianna, love," he whispered huskily. He lowered himself to the bed and pulled her into his arms, crushing her to his chest. His hands and mouth dallied with breathtaking thoroughness, building an aching need in her that drove her to abandon.

"Josh!" Lianna heard her voice dimly as she cried out

his name and tugged his shoulders, pulling him down over
her. She ached with need for him.

Josh relished her hips thrusting up to meet his, her
slender arms clinging so wildly. His heart pounded, and he
felt a primitive desire that he had never known. He wanted
this woman for life—forever. Her lush pale breasts, her
slender hips, were made for him, to bear his seed. In one
brief second before he too was lost in sensation, he gasped,
"Ah, Lianna, now you're mine!"

He thrust inside her, and giddy waves of sensation
wiped out all thought. She cried out in rapture as waves
of pleasure burst over her. Her voice mingled with his
harsh groan. She felt his hot, shuddering release, and
clung to him as their breathing slowed.

Holding her close, he turned and they lay entwined
while he stroked her hair away from her damp brow.

Later, he shifted and raised himself on his elbow to look
down at her, and he felt a rush of pure joy. "Lianna . . .
beneath the shyness and the reluctance burns a passionate
nature."

She placed her hand along his cheek. Immediately he
turned to kiss the palm, to touch it lightly with his tongue.

She waved her left hand, looking at the small golden
band glinting in the moonlight. "It is difficult to believe
that I am wed."

"Ah, love." He chuckled, a brief rumbling sound that
was full of male satisfaction. "Married you are, and for
eternity."

She looked up at him solemnly. They had just bonded
in the closest physical union, yet she wanted more. He was
so handsome with curls tumbling over his forehead, his
teeth white in the darkness. If only he loved her!

She caught his hand. "You have so many scars, Josh."

"Do they frighten or repel you?"

Never had she felt repelled by his physical blemishes.
She caught his hand to kiss it. "No. I hate it that you
fight."

"I hope that means you care. I didn't lose part of my
finger in a fight. It was because of my father."

She gasped, staring at him in dismay. "Your father did that?"

While he told her about his childhood and the beatings, his running away from home, Josh smoothed her black hair away from her face, smiling down into wide blue eyes that gazed at him as if her life depended on watching him. What ran through her mind? He was overjoyed with her—and was her captive far more than he could claim her as his.

Each time he started to tell her the depth of his feeling, he stopped, halted by memories of her declaration of undying love for Edwin. She couldn't love another and lie in his arms and give of herself so passionately. Yet, she thought she loved Edwin. And Josh could hear Fletcher's bitter voice: *"Tell her you love her, this cold English maiden, and you'll create your own hell . . ."* So he smoothed her hair and kissed her forehead, trailing his lips down to her throat, to her soft breast, and held back the words he wanted to say, instead revealing his childhood and youth.

She framed his face in her hands. "I'm sorry. My father was cold and unloving, but he wasn't cruel. I'm so sorry." Lianna pulled Josh to her to kiss him tenderly, feeling an ache in her heart for the life he had had as a child. What kind of father would threaten his son with an iron trap?

He held her in his arms and his voice became as cold and harsh as she had ever heard it. "He's effectively barred me from every club and decent home in London, as well as disinheriting me. That's why I intend to fight in this cause that interests my fellow countrymen—I want their regard when I return to London."

"Oh, Josh!" She raised up on her elbow, her black tresses falling over his chest and shoulder. "It is so dangerous to fight in a revolution just to win the approval of men who are snobs. You said you have friends."

"I hate having things closed to me simply because he hates me for taking Phillip."

She sat up to look at him, feeling sympathy, and understanding some of his agony. "I always wanted my father to care. Until the very last, I hoped he would be interested in me, but he wasn't. I suppose it's the nature of children to hope." She caught his hand, turning it to kiss the knuckle of his little finger while he lay in the moonlight and watched her. She saw his chest stop its steady rise and fall as she trailed her lips across the back of his hand. "I'm sorry. Josh, if there is a child from our union, we must give it love."

He swept her hair over her shoulder, his hands caressing her. "If I thought you cared . . ." he whispered, and pulled her down to kiss her, and sympathy changed to flaming passion.

Later, she tucked her head against his shoulder and clung to him, shyly stroking his chest. "How quiet the ship is," she whispered, wanting to ask what he had meant earlier when he had said, "If I thought you cared . . ."

"My men are ashore, so we're alone. They'll return at midday tomorrow, hopefully sober enough to sail." He caught up strands of her black hair to run them over his cheek. "When we dock again, away from Spain, where it's safe, I'll buy you whatever your heart desires. What would you like, Lianna?"

"I don't know what to ask for when I don't know where we're going or what they'll have."

He stretched out beside her, pulling her into the crook of his arm and fitting her to his side. "We'll go to exotic ports as we sail around the continent that holds Chile. There will be golden jewelry, wines, rum, silk and satin, dyes, spices . . ." The teasing note entered his voice. "Perhaps a cask of pepper for my fiery wife."

She laughed and sat up to look down at him. He placed his hands behind his head and gazed at her with such open delight that she trembled. "I'll sprinkle it over your food and your bed!" she threatened, reaching for the sheet. His fingers caught the sheet and pulled it away.

"I want to look at you."

Her heart jumped, and she gazed down at him. With his hands behind his head, his muscles bunched beneath smooth skin, he looked so male, so pleased with her. She felt a flame kindle in her loins and singe her nerves as it raced through her veins.

His eyes caught hers and held, and the moment transformed again when she had thought it impossible to happen again tonight. Tension pulled like rigging holding a sail. He moved his arms from behind his head and reached for her. "My love," he whispered. "How beautiful you look with your dark hair spilling over your pale shoulders. I have to kiss you, Lianna, to hear you cry my name again . . ." He pulled her down, and her gaze lowered to his sensuous mouth. She met his lips eagerly, welcoming his demands.

A great white moon rose in the heavens while the ship rocked gently in her moorings, and Lianna spent the night in ecstasy. Again Josh Raven drove her to a peak of rapture, discovering new ways to elicit a wild response, while in turn, she discovered his body intimately.

At last, as the pink-streaked rays of sun lightened the sky, they slept wound in each other's arms, a smile on Lianna's lips. She woke to Josh's kisses on her throat, and their thundering need commenced.

Finally she began to hear men on deck and realized the crew had returned. "Your men are back," she said.

He groaned. "If only we weren't in a Spanish port where danger lurks, I would stay in this bunk with you for the rest of the week. I can never get enough of you, Lianna—not in one lifetime."

"Yet you risk both our lives in this endeavor." She sat up in bed, drawing her knees to her chin with the sheet spread over her. "Give it up, Josh. Sail as other men and deal in ordinary trade."

He looked torn with indecision for the first time in her acquaintance with him; then the expression in his face was gone as swiftly as it had come. "It is a tempting thought." He traced his finger over the curve of her cheek. "Now I have a reason to want to turn back, but I can't. No, love, I'm committed. And when we return to London, I don't want to be ostracized."

"I'm sorry for what your father has done to you." She wrapped her arms around his neck to hug him, but he pulled back, studying her intently.

"Lianna, you care!"

She blushed and wound her fingers through the hair on his chest. "Yes, I care."

His fingers tilted her chin up, forcing her to look into his eyes, and it made her breath stop.

"How much?" he asked hoarsely.

Suddenly she felt confused. It wasn't a question she could answer, even to herself. She tried to answer lightly, to tease, as she tilted her head and asked, "How much do you want me to care?"

"With all your heart and soul," he said quietly, yet with such feeling that her heart slammed against her ribs. Blood roared through her veins as he leaned close, his lips taking hers. And she started to tell him that she wanted the same, that she wanted him to care for her as deeply, but his arms crushed her to him, pulling her against his long, bare length, and the moment was swirled away on tempestuous winds.

When Josh washed and dressed, Lianna watched him, then turned to look outside. "The sun shines now, but storm clouds gather on the horizon."

She didn't hear him come across the cabin on bare feet, but he turned her chin to face him. "There are no storm clouds on our horizon," he said solemnly, and bent down to kiss her. Later, she would recall his words with desperate clarity.

While the breeze tugged at her hair, Lianna stood on the deck beside the rail, watching the sights as they prepared to hoist anchor and sail. All commands were given in Spanish; to the casual observer, *El Feroz* was a Spanish ship.

Noticing a frantic haste to the work, as Josh passed her, Lianna halted him. "Everyone is rushing about his task."

"We have our spies. We've been warned to sail as quickly as possible. Spanish soldiers may come to search the ship. And right over there, Lianna, is one of Marcheno's ships. How I'd like to put my men aboard her in the dark of night and sink her!"

He strode away, leaving her with questions swirling in her mind, wondering how Quita had fared.

A few moments later, at Josh's reappearance, Lianna's thoughts changed to heated recollections of the night that made her heart beat faster.

A seaman's voice behind her said, "Captain Raven, sir, there's a man looking for a Miss Lianna Melton. He has a message from someone named Bencaria."

Surprised, Lianna turned. A youth dressed in coarse gray clothing and dusty boots gazed solemnly at her, then back to Josh, who nodded in her direction. "The person in question is my wife now. This is Lianna Melton Raven."

The man removed his cap and nodded. *"Buenos días. Aquí, señora.* I'm to deliver this message to you and you only," he added in Spanish, and held out a paper.

She gazed at the paper that was rolled, tied, and sealed. Reluctantly she reached out to take the message. *"Gracias,"* she whispered as she untied the black string and unrolled the paper.

Tight, cramped handwriting read: "Miss Melton, When I heard *El Feroz* had sailed into La Coruña, I knew I must send word to you. A messenger has come from England to tell me the sad news that your father is dead. You may claim your inheritance." The message was from Quita.

Lianna's head swam. A dark shadow fell on the paper, and she looked up to see Josh reading over her shoulder.

A sharp pain squeezed her heart as she remembered her father. No matter how cold he had been, he was her parent and she had loved him. Following the rush of grief came the blinding knowledge that she would inherit, she was free, bound by no parental demands. "I'm free," she whispered.

"I'm sorry about your father, Lianna," Josh said solemnly.

"I'm free," she said aloud. "I can go home." As she turned away from him, an arm ensnared her, wrapping around her waist to hold her firmly.

18

Startled, she looked up at Josh's darkened countenance. In the shock of reading Quita's message, she had completely forgotten him.

"Let me go! I can go home now!"

"Mrs. Raven."

The words fell with the sharpness of a sword. They stabbed into her heart and brought the cold sting of reality. The arm holding her tightened, and Josh swung her around to face him. "You're my wife . . . my legal wife, bound to me, not to that damned Edwin!"

"You have to let me go home!" The situation had changed so swiftly, she reacted without stopping to think.

His scowl sent the men around him scurrying away hurriedly, yet Lianna paid no heed. He snapped, "Mate, hoist anchor. We sail from Spain now!"

"No!" she cried, and wrenched free to dash toward the gangplank. Josh's arms shot out, and he snatched her up against his chest, his face set in determination.

Lianna's hands pushed uselessly against his chest. "I can go home! We can dissolve this marriage!" she cried.

As Josh dragged Lianna down the companionway, emotions tore at him. Wisdom and fairness and all he had tried to live by told him to set her free. But he wanted her and he thought there was a chance for love. And there were moments when he thought he was winning her over. In bed she returned passion fully. Time was what he needed, and he intended to have it! He entered his cabin, kicked the door shut, and crossed the room in swift strides to drop her onto the bunk.

Breathlessly she jumped to her feet to face him. "Let me go!" She looked at the expression of the man whom she had married and saw his determination to hold what was his. As irrevocably as the possessions in his cabin, he had placed an invisible lion's stamp on her, and she belonged to him.

"You're my wife, Mrs. Raven. You agreed to this journey."

"It was a mistake. It can be undone now."

"No."

"Damn you, Joshua Raven."

A look of pain crossed his face, but his jaw set in a resolute thrust.

"I want England and home, not a revolution and battles in some far corner of the world!"

Josh drew a sharp breath, and his dark skin flushed. A pounding at the door forestalled his reply. Fletcher called, "We've a boarding party sent by the king. They ask to come on board and speak to our captain."

"Dammit to hell!" Josh's brows drew together.

"I'll scream, I'll reveal everything!" she cried in desperation to get him to yield. "If you'll just let me go . . ."

"You little fool! Don't you know if they find I intend to fight them in the New World, that I'm a privateer who's robbed Spanish ships, they'll confiscate my ship as well as you! You'll endanger your own life, my men's, Quita Bencaria's . . ." Suddenly he called, "Fletcher!"

The mate entered and Captain Raven picked up Lianna, crossing the cabin to hand her to the startled first mate.

"Don't let her make a sound, if you have to choke her until she faints!" Josh snapped. He left and slammed the door behind him.

Stunned, Lianna gazed after him, then looked at the tall man holding her. Fletcher asked, "Can I trust you if I put you down?"

She closed her eyes, the tears coming in a hot spurt, stinging her eyes and making her throat ache. "I want off this ship. I can't fight you both. I can't escape him, but I want to go."

"I can't free you, Mrs. Raven," Fletcher said coldly, emphasizing her name. "If I could, I would, but I have my orders. I'll put you down, but if you scream, I won't hesitate to do as the captain ordered."

"I won't scream," she whispered. He set her on her feet, and Lianna walked to the window.

"The captain is a damn good man," Fletcher said coldly.

"Good, perhaps, to his men." She turned to look into angry gray eyes. "You don't like me, do you, Fletcher?"

His dark scowl gave her an answer before he spoke. "Women are pure trouble if they're pampered!"

"Pampered!" she rejoined bitterly, wondering at Fletcher's dealings with women. He was handsome in the same rugged way as Josh, and now that she knew about their blood relation, it was easy to see the similarities in their features. Their wild life showed in their dark skin and the determined glint in their eyes. She guessed Fletcher to be several years younger than Josh. After a long silence, she said, "He owns me. I'm a mere possession and he won't give me up, but I mean nothing to him."

"You don't know him," Fletcher said harshly. After a moment he said, "He took me out of nothing—out of misery and shame and squalor. I was an outcast with the village children, my mother . . . was degraded by the duke. Josh took me to London and placed me in a home with people who cared for me. He saw to it that I had the education he never had."

The door opened suddenly and Josh reappeared. "Thank you, Fletcher. They wanted to thank us for saving the men from the sinking bark—or so they said. They invited the entire lot of us to a banquet to celebrate, and I accepted."

"You *what?*"

"Only to gain time. If you'll go above now, we can sail. Let's do so quickly. When they see us go, they may come in pursuit."

"Aye, sir."

After Fletcher left, Josh stood with his feet braced, his fists doubled on his hips, staring at Lianna. He looked as angry as he had the night he had produced the rawhide whip, and her heart beat just as wildly because she felt him capable of violence, yet she faced him steadfastly.

"I need to go above," he said in a flat voice. "A storm brews, and we're in for a rough sailing. 'Twill be choppy leaving the harbor."

"Please, let me return to England."

"And our marriage?"

"It means nothing to you. Have it annulled."

"You know I can't. It was consummated and it was entered into willingly enough."

"Can't! You won't!" Fury shook her and she wanted to penetrate his stubborn arrogance. "I don't love you! I love another man."

He swore and left, slamming the door and setting a lantern swinging.

Lianna stood stiffly with her fists clenched while tears burned her eyes. Finally she pushed her disheveled hair from her face and noticed Quita's note lying on the floor. She picked it up, smoothing the crumpled paper in her lap to finish reading: ". . . I know if you return to England, my risk deepens, but now there should be no reason for you to betray me. Protect me from your side of the sea. I wish you well. Now you have all you want. Your servant, Q. Bencaria."

Lianna crumpled the letter, crying over her father and her home. Shortly she rose to stride back and forth in the cabin, her fury mounting over Josh's treatment. He could have taken a wife so easily, one that would love him. The man was handsome and had his charming moments, but he didn't love her, and he courted danger as if it were a lady. She thought of her English home. Her inheritance—what would happen to it if she didn't return to claim it? Captain Joshua Raven, his revolution, stood in the way of home and England.

Topside, Josh crossed the deck angrily to take the wheel, to give his stormy thoughts over to the immediate problems and try to forget the woman he had locked in his cabin.

The black clouds on the horizon had billowed and moved

faster than he had expected, and already the sun was hidden. Whitecaps topped the rising waves, and breakers crashed when they swept in against the wharf. Judging from the looks of the sky, it would be bad through the night and next day. Word circulated that a ship had been lost some hundred miles to the north of La Coruña—and the storm clouds were moving to the southwest swiftly.

Josh turned the wheel, maintaining a grim silence. No one was allowed to speak to the helmsman unless giving orders, and there was no one to give the captain an order. No one save the fiery temptress locked below. He swore, glancing at Fletcher standing beside the binnacle, making compass readings. The wind carried *El Feroz* swiftly out of the harbor, and Josh set a due westerly course to try to outrun the fury of the storm. Finally he turned the wheel over to the helmsman, then went to the rail to peer ahead gloomily. He braced his feet, riding the ship with each rise and fall. Fletcher stopped beside him, handing him a spyglass. "It is as bad to the west as it is in the north."

"We'll be caught in a gale."

"Captain . . ."

Josh turned. "Put her on board an English ship and send her home. There are others who are gentle and loving."

"It's my business, Fletcher!" he snapped angrily, his throat tightening until it felt raw as he thought about Fletcher's suggestion. Guilt over keeping Lianna tore at him. He should give her her freedom, but he couldn't. He closed his eyes while pain constricted his chest. He couldn't let her go. She was in his blood, as necessary as breathing.

"Aye, sir," the mate said.

Instantly Josh said, "Sorry."

"Aye. Women are like cats; they hold allegiance only so long as 'tis convenient. And they have claws."

"I shouldn't have coerced her into this marriage, but I thought . . ." He ached as if he had received a wound. "Damn, I can't let her go, no matter how much I know I should!"

A fork of lightning streaked across the sky, and the first spatters of cold rain hit Josh in the face. "The air grows worse by the minute. We'd better batten her down and get set to ride it out.''

"Aye, captain," Fletcher answered, and started to turn away. Josh dropped his hand on Fletcher's shoulder and squeezed.

Josh clutched the rail as the ship canted. A cold wave rose and fell, splashing over his boots. Lianna had never been in a storm. Now, from the looks of it, her first storm at sea would be one of the worst. "Dammit!" he swore, the wind catching the expletive. Lianna was a natural sailor; he suspected she would ride out the storm wrapped in her fury. Most women would be in screaming hysterics. He gave a sardonic laugh as he clung to the rail. How cruel fate could be! He was lost to a pair of wide blue eyes, to silky raven hair. The thought of her slender arms around his neck, her mouth raising to meet his, made his blood sing, and he clenched his fists angrily. Damn the Englishman! Damn him to hell!

With a resounding bang, the cabin door slammed against the bulkhead, and Josh swept in, bringing a rush of cold air. He peeled off his wet coat and faced Lianna while the lanterns swung, making the light dance wildly. His linen shirt was damp, clinging to his powerful body, molding rippling muscles that looked fit to combat a storm. Lianna stood beside the table, her fists on her hips.

"You will drown me at sea, confound you!"

He laughed, his spirits lifting merely at the sight of her. Her blue eyes flashed with fire, and he ached to reach for her.

"I knew I would encounter anger! Most women would have fainted dead away or be in screaming fright by now. Instead, you rail at me for getting you into the storm while you stand as coolly on a rolling deck as a seasoned sailor.''

She thought she detected a note of respect beneath his sardonic words. Thank goodness he didn't know how fearful she had been minutes earlier as she had peered through the porthole at the boiling clouds and sea! She watched silently while he changed his boots.

"We're in for it this night," he said. "Secure the cabin, love."

"Wouldn't it be safer to sail back to La Coruña?"

"No, the wind sweeps us on. Besides, it will be hazardous at dockside. Ships slam into each other and break up. I suggest you eat, because it may be the last chance you have until the storm abates. We'll need all hands; the cook can do little when it gets rough." He stripped off the damp linen shirt to drop it on the oilskin, and orange lantern light flickered over his broad chest.

"It's dreadful to wait helplessly and not be able to do anything!"

He gave her an unreadable glance; then his voice changed, coaxing softly, "Lianna, forget our differences for a moment. Give me a farewell kiss. I could be washed overboard so easily."

"Saints of heaven! You'll survive, and you don't need a kiss. Why should I kiss a scoundrel who's brought me misery?"

Creases fanned from his eyes, his lips twitched, and he looked as if he were attempting to smother his laughter. "Lianna, after last night? I go above to face the cruelest danger."

She blinked, staring at him. Was the man jesting or in earnest? The tossing ship made her believe him.

His voice lowered to that husky baritone level that could cajole honeybees away from flowers if he wanted. "Come, love. You can give me one kiss."

Cautiously she stepped to him and wound her arms around his neck, conscious of his broad bare chest. Suddenly he seemed a bulwark against all fear, and she clung to him.

He wrapped his arms around her, and his eyes glittered with an expression she couldn't understand. "Give me a kiss to remember when I go out into the storm. I may not return. Please, Lianna," he urged, ignoring a twinge of guilt over his lie. The storm would be rough, but he would survive. Of that he had no doubt.

"Josh, surely . . ."

"One kiss."

She stood on tiptoe and placed her lips over his, feeling their warm firmness. His arms tightened, and he pulled her against the length of his body while his tongue slipped into her mouth in a heated kiss that made her momentarily forget their danger and their disputes. The ship tilted, and his thighs pressed against hers as he braced his legs. When his lips moved away, she opened her eyes.

"Full worth it," he whispered. "That was a kiss a man could store in memory and go to the bottom with a smile on his lips."

She moved away, far more disturbed than she had expected. Why did his kisses always shake her to her soul? Was he in mortal danger? She turned to watch him through narrowed eyes as he picked up the dry shirt.

"You're a brave one, Lianna."

His soft words were her undoing. All the calamities and fears crowded upon her, and she closed her eyes.

He was at her side at once to scoop her into his arms. He sat down on the edge of the bunk, holding her close.

"Josh, I said some cruel things to you . . ."

"Perhaps we've each dealt wickedly with the other. I survived, Lianna."

Shocked at his admission that he might have treated her unfairly, she held him tightly while his hands stroked her back. His gentle touch, the emotional upheaval of the past day, took their toll. Suddenly she burst into tears and tightened her arms around his neck.

"My home, Josh. My father, my home, England—all are gone."

He rocked her, stroking her hair and holding her. "I swear to heaven, I'll try to make it up to you. Lianna, I want you." He buried his head in her thick black hair, and his words were muffled while her sobs came without check, and he knew she didn't hear when he whispered his love for her.

The ship rolled, rising, tilting, then dropping with a shuddering crash that slammed them both down on the bunk. As they sat up, Josh pulled away. "I'm needed above. You may have to tie yourself in to keep from rolling about the cabin." He handed her a coil of rope.

After dropping a shirt over his head, he lifted down another oilskin coat. He crossed the narrow space to take her chin in his hand. "We shall ride out this storm, but 'tis a vastly different way than I hoped to spend this night."

He gazed at her, and she felt the silent challenge. For the past few minutes she had seen another side of him, a gentle side. She reached out to touch his hand shyly.

Josh's brows narrowed, and he leaned down to give her a swift, hard kiss. His voice was hoarse as he searched her eyes. "Lianna, I'll make it up to you," he said, and his voice sounded firm with the promise. "I have to go above."

As he crossed the cabin, she followed him toward the door. Then the ship rose, and the quadrant slid across the surface of the desk. Lianna snatched it up and knelt to place it in the chest. She raised the lid and pushed aside a folded shirt. Her hand brushed something cold, and she looked down. A golden ring of a striking serpent with a blood-red ruby eye lay on the shirt.

Gasping, Lianna yanked her hand away, her eyes shifting to Josh.

"What happened?" he asked.

Her mouth felt dry, and she shivered, looking again to see if imagination had tricked her, but the evil serpent was there, the dark ruby eye glittering. Lianna didn't want to touch it. Josh came to look down, and picked up the ring. "You know the Marchenos' ring."

"I gave one like it to Quita." She stood up as his expression became flinty.

"Someday I'll return this ring and exact payment from the Count of Marcheno." It lay in Josh's palm, and he ran his thumb across it. "A serpent ready to strike."

"How did you acquire it?"

"They placed it on my brother so I would know beyond any doubt whom we had crossed," he replied. A pained expression played over his features. His voice was hoarse as he said, "They carved the serpent in Phillip's flesh."

"Oh, no!"

"I'm needed above, Lianna," he said roughly. He dropped the ring in the chest, slammed the lid, and left.

The creaking of the ship and the violent rise and fall

increased along with the noise of whistling, howling winds and waves beating *El Feroz*. Lianna clung to the bunk in terror.

Finally, chilled to the bone, she pulled on one of Josh's woolen capes. She rushed to the porthole to gaze outside, and pure cold terror gripped her. A solid wall of black water beat against the pane, blurring the glass. Was the crew on deck—or washed overboard? She despised waiting helplessly. Nervously she pulled the woolen cape close beneath her chin and opened the door. Water splashed down the ladder and eddied in the passageway, and she wondered how the ship held together. It seemed impossible that men could be on deck facing the raw elements of nature.

The ship canted and she lost her footing as a wave crashed down the companionway, knocking her off her feet. Thoroughly soaked, she struggled into the cabin and slammed the door.

Shivering from the cold, Lianna changed into another woolen dress and climbed into the bunk, to cling while the ship rode out the storm.

Later, her own wild cry stirred her out of sleep. Her breath came in ragged gasps caused by a nightmare. Instantly arms went around her. "Lianna, shh, love! 'Tis but a dream.''

She shivered violently, clinging to Josh, yet only dimly aware of him. His cool hand rested on her temple. "You burn with fever.'' He held her close, cradling her in his arms as his warmth flowed into her chilled limbs.

She dozed, then awoke to fling off covers from her heated body. The bed was empty as she moaned softly, the cabin suffocating in its warmth. Nights and days melded, became unreal. She lost all sense of time, the grip of sickness blotting out all else.

Occasionally she was aware of gentle hands moving her, helping her to sip hot broth, washing her face, but reality blurred into her dreams and nightmares. Once she dreamed she rode down the lane at home behind Edwin as they used to do when children. He raced ahead on Taddie, his sorrel gelding, while she followed on Midnight, only Edwin's eyes were green and his hair dark. He raced into a hedge-row and she couldn't find him.

Finally she opened her eyes and gazed at sunlight pouring through the panes. Lying still, she became more alert and cognizant of her surroundings. The ship rode quietly. Josh sat by the table, his unreadable green eyes watching her carefully. "Lianna?"

"Good morning."

He stood up, unfolding his long frame with an easy grace to come sit beside her on the bed. "Ah, perhaps the fever has cleared. You sound better."

"Better? How long did I sleep?"

"The storm was five nights ago."

"Five!" she exclaimed, looking at the stubble on his chin. With a shock, she realized he must have given constant attention to her. "Josh, you look as if you've slept little." She scooted up to look at him more intently. "You do care for me," she murmured.

He caught a lock of her hair to run across his cheek as he lowered his head, and she couldn't see his eyes. "Yes, I care," he said roughly.

Her heart felt as if it were unfolding to a dazzling warmth. "Josh," she whispered, and framed his face in her hands. Her heart pounded as she looked into eyes red from sleeplessness. She slipped her arms around his neck to hug him. "You do care! Oh, Josh, perhaps we *can* have happiness." Shyly, with a degree of uncertainty, yet filled with hope and gratitude, she whispered, "I love you."

His hands stroked her face while his eyes searched hers. "I see uncertainty and I pray someday you'll say those words to me and mean them with your whole heart."

He crushed her in his arms, holding her while he buried his head against her throat. He knew he ought to tell her not to say the words unless she meant them absolutely, but he couldn't. They were the best words he'd heard in his life and he wasn't about to break any tenuous hold on her heart. "I love you, Lianna," he whispered, and prayed the two of them could let love unfold.

Her arms tightened around his neck and he turned, his mouth seeking hers, but she pushed him away.

"Josh, I'm a fright and you might catch something."

He smiled at her and stroked her forehead. "I'll wait, but you're not a fright."

She laughed, feeling a giddy happiness as she smiled at him.

He kissed her knuckles, watching her. "Soon you'll be well and you can sleep in my arms, exhausted by fever of another kind."

Her cheeks flushed, but she reached out to stroke his throat and his pulse drummed. He moved away abruptly. He wasn't weakened by fever and her looks and touch stirred him swiftly to a burning need for her. "I'll fetch a steward with something for you to eat."

"I feel as if I could eat part of the bedding, I'm so famished."

He laughed. "You're better! I'll be back, love." He kissed her temple lightly and left. Within a few minutes he returned. "Jason is cooking stew and will be here with it soon."

"Thank you for your care," she said softly.

He stared at her with a warm expression in his eyes, and nodded. "When you're able, we'll go topside to get you into the fresh air. We sail south, where the sun grows warmer and the air more pleasant."

A few days later, Lianna and Josh were on deck when he led her to the bow, where Fletcher handed over the telescope. "A battle—there are two ships on the horizon."

Josh squinted into the telescope. "We'll have to get closer." He raised his voice to shout, "Southward! Twelve sail."

"Wouldn't it be safer to avoid a battle?" she asked.

"Safety is not what I always seek."

Within minutes the sails filled with wind and *El Feroz* gained speed, drawing closer to the ships and the pounding guns.

Josh raised the telescope to peer at the ships. "A British ship, the *Adrian*, and a Spanish schooner." Lowering the glass, he said to Fletcher, "Mount a swivel gun on the poop deck. Move to the windward quarter, cross the stern and luff sails with the helm alee. We'll rake her stern with the biggest guns as we pass.''

"Aye, sir."

"Pass the word to aim for the rudder, their tiller, and block and tackle."

"Aye, sir. Grappling irons?"

"No. No boarding party from our side. We'll leave the spoils for the English frigate. You better get below, Lianna."

"Do I pull down the red-and-gold, sir?" Fletcher asked.

Josh looked up at the Spanish colors flying above them. "No," he said. "Not until I give the word."

"You'll sink your countrymen!" Lianna gasped.

Green eyes glittered with anticipation. "No, we'll come about on the other side of the Spaniards. Then they'll be caught between two English frigates who will send them to the bottom. Come along, Lianna. Call for battle posts, mate. Clew up sails when we draw alongside. I want the main topgallant furled."

"Aye, aye, sir!" Fletcher answered.

Josh hurried Lianna below, then crossed to the sea chest to remove a sword and belt, which he buckled around his hips. She watched as he opened a box with a brace of pistols and began loading swiftly.

"Kiss me, love. I go to battle for you."

"Not for me, Josh. You love battle," she said. With a smile she stood on tiptoe and brushed his cheek.

His eyes glowed warmly and his gave her a quick hug. "How glad I am that you're well." He turned and left, and she knew the lull between them, while he had waited for her to mend from her bout of sickness, was over. And she burned with conflicting emotions as the full significance dawned on her. Excitement drummed within because she realized he would return to claim her as his wife.

A gun blast shattered her thoughts. She dashed to a porthole to watch the battle. *El Feroz* drew alongside the unsuspecting Spanish ship. The volley of guns was deafening as the English and Spanish fought. Suddenly *El Feroz* shook with a blast of cannon and the Spanish mast cracked, falling to the deck. Within minutes men were screaming and battling on deck while Englishmen from the other ship swarmed on board the Spanish vessel.

The Britishers fought Spaniards hand-to-hand, with cutlass and pistol. She felt sick, watching the carnage, and was ready to turn away, when a golden head of hair captured her attention.

Lianna's heart missed a beat. She rubbed her hand over the glass and stared at the deck of the sinking ship as two men fought with swords, one clumsily, yet determined to win, his golden hair blowing in the sun. "Edwin!" she gasped. It couldn't be! Edwin Stafford was at home on the farm in Wiltshire.

She blinked and strained to see as the combatants battled toward the rail, closer to *El Feroz*. Her hand flew to her throat as the Britisher ran the Spaniard through and turned away. There was no longer any doubt—it was Edwin!

She dashed for the door and raced up the ladder to the deck. Confusion reigned. Men were shouting victoriously as *El Feroz* began to draw away, its sails billowing while Englishmen on the sinking Spanish ship waved and called their thanks. Lianna rushed to the rail, pushing her way between startled men. "Edwin! Edwin!" she cried.

"Lianna!" Josh snapped, and the crew faded from the rail. Josh's arm closed around her.

"Let me go to him!" Lianna cried, twisting helplessly against arms that held her like iron.

"Lianna!" The call came again and she turned to see Edwin posed at the rail; then he jumped into the sea to swim toward *El Feroz*.

"If he comes aboard, I'll run him through!" Josh ground out the words savagely.

"No! Don't hurt him!"

"Fletcher! Take her below!"

As Fletcher reached them, Edwin made it over the side.

Drawing his sword, Josh whirled to face Edwin. "Get below!" he commanded Lianna.

"Never! I must see him! Edwin!" she cried.

Josh snatched up a sword from one of his men and flung it to Edwin who caught it easily. "She's my wife now!" Josh shouted.

Lianna screamed as Fletcher carried her down the companionway. She pounded against his broad shoulders, struggling to break free. His arms tightened until she thought she would faint. When he reached the cabin, he set her down. His fingers locked on her shoulders and he shook her, his gray eyes dark with rage.

"If I were Captain, I'd run the man through and come down and beat you senseless!"

"You're as barbaric as he!" she cried. "You haven't a shred of kindness!"

"It isn't ruthlessness that will be Josh's downfall, but desire!" He slammed the door and locked it behind him.

Lianna's head reeled as rage and fear surged in her. "Edwin! Oh, Edwin!" she cried helplessly, pounding against the locked door. Tears streaked her face. If Josh killed him, she would get revenge if it took her last breath! Why had Edwin been on an English ship? What had happened after she had sailed?

She sank down, the muslin billowing around her legs while she cried. And her feelings took another seesaw turn as uncertainty over what she felt swamped her. How good it had been to see Edwin! He was home and childhood and the awakening from young girlhood all blended together, and she loved him dearly. And when she had seen him, it made Josh and everything that had happened diminish. She wanted to be in Edwin's arms. To ride with him and to hear him declare his love for her again. To have him kiss her until she fainted with desire. Tears assaulted her again and she put her head in her hands to cry.

Shortly she moved to first one porthole, then another, trying to catch a glimpse of Edwin, but it was impossible. Dusk settled and still she did not know what had happened. She paused in front of a mirror to gaze at her reddened eyes, her rumpled blue muslin with a white fichu tucked around her shoulders, her tumble of black hair.

Behind her the cabin door opened and Josh filled the doorway.

She looked up, questions rushing into her mind. "Edwin. Is he . . . ?"

He turned the key behind him, locking them in together.

Her heart pounded wildly when she saw the hard set to his features. His anger became waves of heat that flickered and scorched her. As he crossed the cabin, he unbuckled the scabbard and tossed it aside. He pulled off his coat and undid the laces of his shirt.

"You can't . . ." She backed away, seeing his intention as clearly as if he had announced it.

"You're my wife, Lianna!"

"I don't love you! I love Edwin Stafford!" As he reached out to pull her to him, she asked, "What happened to Edwin? Did you murder him? Is he alive?"

"I want to drive Edwin Stafford out of your mind. He's alive. I wouldn't kill him and have you mourn forever."

"Where is he?"

"He swam for his ship when we parted. You're mine, not his. We're wed! Can't you understand that? Wed and consummated, and you wound your arms around me and cried out in joy—and you will again."

"Don't remind me!" She blanched and tried to wrench free from the clamp of his hands on her shoulders.

"You may be with child now!"

Startled, she looked at him and fury blinded her. To bear his child as he sailed into a revolution and danger, to be compelled to go along on a mission that meant nothing to her, to part from the only man to truly love her—white-hot rage shook her and she lost all caution.

"And if I am, captain, you'll have a Spanish heir!"

The fingers gripping her shoulders bit deeper as his eyes filled with fire. "You're English! If you've lied to me, if you're actually Quita Bencaria—"

"No, I'm Lianna Melton, daughter of Charles Melton and his Spanish bride, Josefina Rosa Carmelita Anastacio!"

She heard the hissing intake of Josh's breath. "Damn you, woman! You're lying to me!"

He glared at her, feeling a stinging hurt because she had lied to him about her heritage. What else had she lied about? He felt betrayed that she hadn't told him before.

"It's the truth. I told you, my father met my mother in his travels as a merchant. Now, will you let me go—or do you want to sire a Spaniard with your name and your blood?''

The words floated in the air like a black storm cloud in the sky. She wondered what ran through Josh's mind—if this revelation would give her the freedom she cherished and finally drive him from desiring her. Was it a blow to him, as she intended it to be?

Suddenly he gathered her effortlessly into his strong arms. In long strides he went abovedecks to the rail and swung her out over the sea.

19

Lianna's breath stopped as she gripped his arms. Moonlight shone fully on his face and the sight of his stormy features frightened her as badly as being held above the dark water.

"I can drop you, Lianna, and end all possibility of producing a Spanish heir!"

"You pirate!" she snapped, unable to get her breath.

"If you're English and this is a lie, you'd best speak quickly."

"I've told you the truth." She shook with fear, but his words rekindled her courage. If she were to die at his hand, she would say her thoughts first. She returned his gaze without wavering. "Go ahead, you ruffian! Fling me into the sea."

"Then you're Spanish, but you're Lianna Melton, not Quita Bencaria?"

"*Sí, señor,*" she said with relish. Beneath the tight grip of her hands she felt the bulge of iron muscles in his arms. Josh Raven had hurt her and forced her into marriage. For the moment she could retaliate. Wind whipped black strands of her hair across his arm, caught the white fichu at the neck of her dress and snatched it away. Tumbling in the air, the fichu, ignored by both Lianna and Josh, fluttered and dropped into the foaming sea, pulled out of sight into the water.

Just as swiftly as he had lifted her out, he swung her back to the deck. "You're damned brave," he said in a

voice that was as guttural as a growl and so filled with
agony that she wondered what havoc she had wreaked, and
suddenly she regretted hurting him. She had spoken in a fit
of anger and she began to regret the callous words she had
flung at him.

"And your words of love were also lies, weren't they,
Lianna?" Before she could answer, he continued, "Your
love is still Edwin Stafford."

She stared at him with conflicting emotions. The shock
of seeing Edwin had made her want to be with him and
talk to him. And the turmoil over Edwin's appearance had
made her uncertain about what she truly felt for Josh.

He stared at her, feeling his blood heat in spite of his
anger. What other lies had she told him? What other
deceptions did she weave? And it occurred to him how
easily she could betray him in Chile. He saw he must
never reveal all his plans to her; how could he trust her?

"Spanish," he said flatly, wondering if she had an
English father. Everything she had told him could have
been a lie. She stared back at him coolly and he thought
about how she had faced him moments ago when her life
had been threatened. He remembered her cries for Stafford, and anger gnawed at him. Suddenly his arms tightened and he carried her below, kicking the door shut
behind them as he set her on her feet.

"Now, you leave me alone—" Lianna started to say, then
bit off the words at the sight of his face. He reached out,
catching the throat of her dress as he ripped it away from
her body in one swift movement. The tearing sound was
loud in the silence, and she gasped, trying to run, fear
surging through her, but his arms caught her.

As she struggled, he said softly, but in a voice filled
with the sharpness of a knife, "Now we'll see how long
you resist or cry out Stafford's name or try to escape."

His head came down as he kissed her neck, and she
struggled furiously, wanting to fight him and the insidious
fire that started the moment his lips moved on her flesh.
Why could he always destroy her resistance? It seemed
unfair when they were at cross-purposes half the time. She
wanted to give her love to a gentle man, to someone who

loved her and wanted her love, not this man who would bind her to him by passion.

His arms were iron bands that wouldn't yield, but other than holding her, he used no force. And he needed no force. His lips trailed over her, one hand moved to fondle her breast, and slowly, slowly, Lianna felt all anger burning away in searing caresses that set her aflame. And finally she was in his arms, holding him, stroking him in return, her body aching for him when he possessed her with fiery thrusts until she felt his hot release.

She lay with her eyes closed, her arms around him, words of love almost ready to surface, when he rolled away and stood up, snatching up his breeches as he looked at her in the lantern's glow.

"All I can think about is to wonder what else you have lied to me about." He stood staring down at her. "You'll get your wish about bed, Lianna. I've paid a king's ransom for your body. I've given you my name—now I have the benefit of neither. We can't turn back, but you'll get your freedom when this is over."

His boots clacked on the boards as he dressed swiftly and strode away to take over the helm. She closed her eyes. She had won her freedom from Josh Raven.

She gazed at the empty space beside her on the moonlit bunk, and an unwanted memory came to mind swiftly, of Josh Raven's vigorous bronzed body stretched beside her as he kissed her passionately, his green eyes looking at her with joy. She thrust the thought away and wondered if he would move her to the small cramped cabin again.

The chill she experienced worsened. She gathered a coverlet around her to huddle uncomfortably. She had won! He would not take her to bed—he would return her home and end the marriage. Suddenly the victory rang hollow. How pained he had looked! How could he be anything besides vexed at her admission? Why had he looked agonized? Did he truly hate her Spanish heritage so much? Or had he been so angered because he had discovered she had been untruthful to him? She felt hot tears sting her eyes and fought them, deciding it was the culmination of everything that had happened that day, but she hurt more than she had ever hurt over Edwin or anything else in her past.

Finally dawn's gray light filtered through the panes, dimly lighting the cabin. Outside, Josh stood with his hand against the door a moment before he stiffened his shoulders and entered. "You'll move to another cabin," he said, and hated the slam of his heart against his ribs at the sight of her. Why couldn't he get her out of his system? She had deceived him; she loved another man and had cried out for him desperately, yet she was like a heady wine that took all reason and thickened his blood. And while he seethed with anger, he had to fight the temptation to look at the soft swell of her breasts rising above the neckline of her muslin dress. Her wide blue eyes met his unflinchingly, forcing his grudging respect.

"Get everything you want," he said.

"Of course," she answered with a toss of her head. She gathered her clothing, dropping the portmanteau.

In two long strides he crossed to scoop it up and take the clothing from her. Wordlessly he held the door and slammed it behind them.

Swirling the cape around her shoulders, Lianna lifted her chin while his silent rage swept over her like a winter storm. He held open the cabin door, followed her inside, and flung the portmanteau onto the hammock.

"I should have guessed why your father pledged your hand to a Spaniard," he said. "I was so bedazzled with you that I accepted your answer and everything else you've said to me without question."

"If I'm without child, you've lost little, Captain Raven, once you dissolve this marriage."

To her surprise, her statement made his scowl deepen. He gave a dry, mirthless laugh. "So I have bound myself in a web of my own weaving. I should have known better—"

"You're not bound by anything!"

"If only that were true!" He turned and left.

Lianna stared after him, then sank down on the hammock and shook with an aftermath of reaction. Josh, bound by anything—impossible! What lay ahead when he was so furious with her? They sailed into a land of intrigue and danger—and she rode with a man who despised her, who wanted to be free of her. How long would she be safe if danger threatened?

Thereafter, as much as possible aboard ship, Josh Raven ignored her. Days ran together while they sailed southward, and Lianna found a friend in an older member of the crew, Morley, who had a daughter nearly her age. Morley provided paper and pen and Lianna whiled away the long days at sea sketching pictures of the ship and crew, carefully avoiding its captain, yet aware down to the tiniest nerve when he was present.

Finally, at the end of May, they anchored in the bay of Valparaiso, and Fletcher appeared at Lianna's cabin.

"The voyage is over," he stated.

Members of the crew mounted horses to ride ahead and behind the carriage which was taking Josh and Lianna to their destination. Fletcher and another sailor named Simms drove the carriage. It was the first time since that fateful night so long ago that Lianna had shared close quarters with Josh. She smoothed the brown cloak over her green silk dress, keeping her gaze on her clothing, on her hands, out the window, anywhere away from him. In spite of her cool manner, she was acutely conscious of his elegant brown leather breeches and brown coat. His white shirt had cuffs that fell over wrists as hard as iron. And her heart hadn't calmed since the first moment Josh had entered the carriage. She fought the urge, yet was irresistibly drawn to glance at him.

Her breath stopped as she discovered his unwavering gaze focused on her. Sparks danced along her veins, and she locked her fingers together in her lap.

Josh said, "We'll soon reach Santiago and our home. Once there, you're to speak Spanish."

"And how will you prevent me from betraying you?" she asked coolly, yielding to the temptation to ruffle his composure and aware that he assessed her brazenly.

"You won't, if you want to return to England. And to Edwin."

In spite of the bitterness in his voice, the constant, dull

anger in her, she felt the tension pull between them, an invisible current that burned in the air.

"If you value your life, you won't betray me," he continued dryly. "*Señora,* I know how deceiving you can be." Cold eyes sliced into her heart as she blushed from his stinging words. A corner of his mouth lifted in a sardonic grin. "You never lack bravery. You've tempted, provoked, and defied me. You're damned fortunate not to be at the bottom of the sea."

"Instead, I'm riding into a revolution with a bloodthirsty pirate who cares nothing for me. I wonder if I'll ever see England."

"You—afraid?"

"I cannot imagine you mourning my loss!"

To her amazement, his expression changed. Something flickered in his eyes and he leaned forward, so close, breathtakingly near. His voice was husky as he said, "I'll get you back to England. I promise."

She held her breath. His lips were near and the ache she felt almost made her moan.

He jerked back, sinking into a corner of the carriage and turning to look out a window.

Lianna did the same, but emotions seethed like a boiling kettle. She stole a quick glance and saw his fist clenched upon his knee. She stared at the whitened knuckles, and shock waves struck her that he might be drawn as irresistibly as she.

Then she reminded herself that he had been many long months at sea and he would feel the same in the presence of any woman, but she hurt and was torn, wanting to reach for him, wishing it were different between them.

As they rode in silence, the carriage lumbered through small villages with adobe huts lining dusty lanes shaded by eucalyptus trees. The wide brown eyes of curious children stared at the noisy carriage while chickens and an occasional thin mongrel fled from its path. They passed barefoot peasants in bright clothing. Others, dressed in dirty rags, squatted in the dust in front of shacks made of palm fronds.

The carriage traveled a winding road down out of the

mountains to a flat plain as they approached Santiago. The town lay beneath snowcapped Andes mountains, their jagged peaks glinting whitely in the sunlight. For miles on either side of the road fields of sunflowers stretched out of sight, blossoms raised toward the sun, their golden petals contrasting with the distant blue-shadowed slopes of mountains beyond the town.

Like a sea of gold surrounding the carriage, the brilliance of the flowers lifted Lianna's spirits. She gasped with delight. "Josh, look how beautiful! Miles of golden flowers like the buttercups at home!"

He drew his breath sharply when she addressed him as Josh. Sunshine bathed her face, half-turned so that he could see the dark fringe of her lashes, the faint pink on the curve of her cheek, and he ached to reach out and touch her. After all these months, when he had been congratulating himself on forgetting her, in a few short hours' time he was as deeply ensnared as ever. He had promised her freedom when they returned to England, but he questioned his own motives now. England was far away; if they were landing on English soil now, he knew he wouldn't want to let her go! On impulse he signaled Fletcher to stop the carriage.

Knowing he was a fool, and hopelessly lost with love for her, Josh dashed into the field and snapped off blossoms. He laid the bouquet in her lap. *"Para tí, con todo mi amor,"* he said mockingly, his words taunting himself more than Lianna. He wanted to crush her in his arms and shower her with kisses.

She blushed, emotions swirling within. While she was aware of the falsity of his words, the Spanish rolled softly off his tongue in his deep baritone voice, sending a message that made her tingle from head to toe. She couldn't understand him. He had just railed at her with his biting comments, then had jumped blithely from the carriage to pick a bouquet of wildflowers for her while the whole entourage waited. Captain Josh Raven was a complex man. She gathered up the blooms as he slammed shut the door and the carriage began to roll.

"Thank you," she said. "They're beautiful!"

"Don't breathe deeply—their beauty lies in their color, not their fragrance. They're not what they seem when you get close."

She gazed into glacial eyes, certain his words mirrored his feelings for her.

In Santiago, along the wide central Plaza de Armas, they passed the yellow stucco Governor's Palace. "There's the Church de San Francisco, built over two hundred years ago by the conquistador Pedro de Valdivia," Josh explained.

She looked at the red Spanish church, then turned to meet Josh's smoldering gaze.

"And now," she said bitingly, "I'm Doña Lianna, Marquesa de Aveiro."

"*Sí*, and once we leave this carriage, we must speak only Spanish unless we're in complete privacy," he said harshly. "I think it would be safer if you take another name, something less unusual."

"Whatever you say, sir," she answered too sweetly.

"Lita is close enough. Is that acceptable?"

"None of this is acceptable," she snapped, and he drew a sharp breath.

"Lita it is," he stated, unperturbed by her answer. "Also, once we arrive, my men will take up varying positions. Fletcher will be a butler, Simms a groomsman."

He turned to look out the window. "There's the new La Moneda Palace, the mint. And there's the prison."

The harsh note jarred her as they passed a building with a facade broken by deeply recessed arched windows secured by iron grillwork. While the wide double doors were elaborately carved and painted a pale blue, they couldn't hide the cold lines of the building. Its shadow fell across the lane and over the carriage, momentarily a cloud on a sunny day.

They turned down another dusty lane, Avenida Real, where elegant homes presented a solid front to the world. Red tile roofs showed above tall trees, the houses half-hidden by green foliage and solid, massive walls. In front of sun-faded yellow plaster walls, the carriage halted. Josh stared at them, wondering now about his driving ambition to get London society to accept him. The notion was bitter without Lianna, yet he knew he must achieve it if he wanted a future in England. He had memorized the names of three other Englishmen who were playing double parts just as he, posing as Spaniards. Two in particular, he was to find as soon as he was settled. There was an English earl who had a taste for adventure, Lord Timothy Paddington, who posed as Don Alfredo Todaro. The other was an English duke, his grace, the Duke of Brenthaven, who posed as Don Gerado Davio.

He had more than a dozen other names memorized, members of their staffs, Spanish and Creole men who intended to play a part in the revolution. Miranda had been persuasive, and many Englishmen were eager to help.

Brenthaven was a deep believer in human rights. Another Englishman, Lord John Bannister, had been a brief acquaintance Josh had met through William Craine. What a dull victory it would be without Lianna's love! Yet the nagging knowledge of his father's causing him to be excluded everywhere always strengthened his determination to win over the Englishmen's respect.

Josh alighted and offered his hand, their first physical contact in months. The moment their fingers met, Lianna's fascination with the new land dwindled to nothing as every nerve became aware of the tall man before her, his large fingers holding her slender ones.

He dropped her hand to take her arm, and the touch burned through her sleeve. She walked with Josh through doors opening onto the *zaguán*, a long hallway. Off the hallway she glimpsed a salon and paused in surprise. French chairs, as handsome and delicate as any she had encountered in England, covered in pastel shades of damask, sat beneath oil paintings. On thick plastered white walls gilt mirrors ran from the floor to the high cedar ceiling that was carved ornately in baroque style, different from her home with its bare floors and sparse furniture.

"Do you like it?" Josh asked politely in Spanish, but his eyes were full of curiosity.

"It's beautiful, so different from my home."

A frown replaced his curious stare as they moved on. Josh watched her closely, and he hurt with a slow-grinding, steady pain that their arrival hadn't been different. Her eyes sparkled as she looked at the house, and he could tell she was impressed with its beauty. He wondered about her Wiltshire home and childhood that must have been cold and devoid of love. It made him want to shelter her and give her whatever he could to keep the sparkle in her eyes, yet he knew how foolish he was being. She loved Edwin Stafford and she wanted free of her marriage, and the sooner he learned to adjust and accept the knowledge, the better off he would be.

While they walked through the rooms, Lianna discovered the house formed a square, with all inner rooms opening onto a courtyard with fragrant jasmine, Indian laurel, banana trees, palms, and graceful fountains. Around the second floor was a corridor overlooking the courtyard.

"This is so lovely!" Lianna gasped in her fluent Spanish while she took in the bougainvillea growing rampant along balcony columns, spilling its paper-thin yellow blossoms in a spectacular display. Climbing copihue, with bell-shaped red flowers, entwined a tall palm. "It's a wonder world!" she exclaimed, suddenly wondering what her life would have been if she hadn't insisted that she loved Edwin.

"So, you can be pleased somewhere in the world other than your precious England."

"Yes, of course I can," she answered quietly, and saw a cynical arch to his brows.

The staff waited in the large kitchen, lined up like an army of servants. Mestizos with brown skin and large brown eyes were soft-spoken as they welcomed the master and mistress of the house. Josh took charge quietly and efficiently, as he had aboard his ship.

He escorted Lianna upstairs to their bedrooms, two rooms with a connecting door, each room opening onto the corridor overlooking the courtyard.

With white walls and a dado of inlaid blue and white tiles, Lianna's room was the smaller of the two, but she loved it immediately. Sunny and light, the room had intricately carved cypress furniture; the four-poster bed stood high enough from the floor to require a small step stool.

Josh waited in the doorway, then moved near to Lianna. "Your hair shouldn't be hidden beneath a bonnet," he said in a deep voice, untying the ribbon and tossing the hat on the bed.

"Thank you," she answered quietly, fighting the urge to place her hands lightly upon his chest. "Don't you fear some of the Spaniards might have known Don Cristóbal?"

"No, our plans have been well laid. We have spies."

"And now, am I to be a prisoner in this house as I was on *El Feroz?*" she asked, her thoughts running in a jumbled confusion of why she was so drawn to him. Was she that starved for love?

He nodded. "Aye, for a time. If I see I can trust you"—he waved his hand—"then you may go elsewhere. Otherwise, you'll remain home."

Her gaze went past him to the ornately carved bed in his room, and she imagined Josh stretched upon it.

He followed her gaze. "You'll have privacy, but for both our sakes, I must have freedom to move around. The door won't be locked." His eyes raked her insolently. "Your body will be safe," he drawled.

She stepped back as if he had delivered a blow. "You're blinded by your anger, Josh! I didn't tell you sooner about my Spanish mother because I was afraid of your deep hatred of anything Spanish."

"You've known from the first night that my quarrel is solely with the Marcheno family." Quietly he added, "I'm blinded, all right! Sometimes I think in Portsmouth I received a mortal wound."

"How can you say that?" she could barely ask, as all her breath was taken by his answer.

"Perhaps we both did, Lianna, in different ways."

A knock interrupted them. Josh stepped into his room and closed the door while Lianna turned to face a slender young maid whom she had met earlier in the kitchen.

The girl curtsied. "*Buenos días,* Señora Alveiro. *Yo soy* Madryn Huancayo. Do you want the trunks unpacked?"

"*Sí,* Madryn. *Muchas gracias,*" Lianna replied, wishing she could have continued her discussion with Josh while she puzzled over what he had said. Josh blinded in

Portsmouth? Could he still want her? Or was he merely starved for any female and blinded by something physical? She stared at his closed door and wondered what was in his heart.

By the time Lianna descended the stairs to eat, she felt refreshed. With word from a servant that Don Cristóbal had gone out, she dined alone and afterward strolled through the house, exploring the rest of the rooms, wondering what kind of home Josh had grown up in. It must have been even more elegant and larger than this one, as he hadn't seemed to give his surroundings much notice today. And her home—what had become of it? She entered a library which was disappointing to her because it held few books and most of those were ancient ones Lianna had already read. The room was long with a beamed ceiling and white walls which ran halfway down to meet squares of colorful tiles. At one end of the room was a massive curved fireplace; its mantelpiece held a pair of tall gold candlesticks. Lianna selected a book. As she turned, she glimpsed one of the maids stepping swiftly out of sight in the hall.

Lianna hurried into the empty hallway, but saw no one. Was she spied upon by someone for Josh? Or was it someone for the Spanish government? The only certainty was that Lianna was sure someone had been at the door.

When she went upstairs to bed, she paused beside the connecting door. Unbidden memories taunted her. She remembered Josh's husky laughter, his quiet competence at sea—and she acknowledged a deep-running longing. If she had controlled her reaction to seeing Edwin, would Josh have grown to love her and she to love him? She closed her eyes, feeling an all-consuming loss.

She dressed in a high-necked white gown and climbed into bed. While she lay there unable to fall asleep, the connecting door opened and yellow light from Josh's room spilled into the darkness.

20

"What are you doing here?" Lianna sat up, pulling the covers up to her chin as her breath caught in her throat.

Josh's coat was gone, his cravat untied, the ends dangling loosely.

"I intend to sleep in this room. I'll sleep on the floor."

"Why?"

"I explained to you how much is at stake. These men will allow nothing to stand in the way of their ambition for power. We have to look the part we're playing. If I slept in one room, and my beautiful young wife in here, it would be a subject for speculation and gossip. I want to avoid any undue attention, therefore we share a room."

"How will anyone know?"

"There are spies everywhere. The maids will know in the morning when they come to clean our rooms."

He stood watching her. Vaguely she wondered if he could hear her heart pound. In the shadowy room his features were dark, his expression unreadable. The silence wasn't broken until he turned his back abruptly.

Lianna lay down. His reasoning made sense, as it always did, but how could she sleep with him only a few feet away? A rustle made her turn her head.

Josh slipped off his shirt; moonlight highlighted the rippling musculature of his back, and at the sight of his bare torso, desire shook Lianna. He was furious with her; she wasn't in love with him, yet she'd shared more intimacy with Josh Raven than any other man in her life.

She turned her head, puzzling over her feelings for him. When all had been good between them, he could be more fun than anyone else. He was intelligent, competent, strong—and exciting beyond measure! And even if there hadn't been love on their wedding night, there had been joy. She had been happier with Josh than ever before in her life. If only . . . She broke off her thoughts abruptly.

The covers rustled and she stiffened, remembering to the finest detail the healthy male body stretched nearby.

Every turn, each whisper of his movements, sent a sizzling current of awareness along her veins. She lay as stiffly as a block of ice, trying to quell her body's longings, the searing memories that persisted. Finally she turned and glanced down at him.

Josh lay quietly with his chest rising and falling in regular deep breathing. Lianna wanted to scream with frustration. How could she get through night after night like this? She wondered just how deep his mistrust for her was.

She propped herself up on her elbows to look at him more closely, then silently pushed back the sheet and stepped out of bed as if irresistibly drawn. She walked the few steps to his side and stood looking down at him.

Josh knew she was beside him, and beneath the covers he clenched his hands into fists and willed his eyes to remain closed. He counted each breath, trying to ignore the faint, sweet scent of rosewater she wore, trying to avoid looking at her bare ankles. If he looked into her blue eyes he would be lost.

Each breath was torture. He reminded himself over and over that she loved another. When she turned to go back to bed, he risked a glimpse. Her midnight hair fell around her shoulders in a cloud, swaying slightly with each step. He saw a slender shapely leg as she climbed into bed. He closed his eyes and tried to think of the three cannon he had to move from *El Feroz* to the mountains to the patriots. Yet how hard it was to ignore the clamorings of his body, to forget how it felt to have Lianna's softness beneath him as she cried out in ecstasy.

When Lianna awoke in bright sunshine, Josh had gone. He didn't appear until shortly after noon for the main dinner, a *cazuela* of chicken, potatoes, beans, onions, and parsley.

During the meal, Josh announced in his smooth, flowing Spanish, "We're invited to a reception and ball at the Governor's Palace."

A ball! With Josh! Her heart skipped in anticipation. She had never attended one because her father wouldn't allow it. Then practicality brought her back to earth. "I won't have an appropriate gown."

"There are seamstresses here who do excellent handwork. I brought material for this purpose. It's a precious commodity in this land where dresses are willed from one generation to the next."

"You jest!"

"No." He leaned back, his hand resting on the table.

"If only Melissa could know!"

"Who's Melissa?" He tilted his head to study her while he waited for her answer.

"She was my best friend at home. The Hardestons lived on a neighboring farm and occasionally I was allowed to visit her or Melissa to visit me. She teased me for being so careful with clothes, for patching my plainest muslin dresses, but my father insisted on it."

Josh said warmly, "Your eyes sparkle when you smile."

"Your mind does jump from one thing to another!" she answered, hiding the sudden rush of pleasure. "When is the ball?" she asked.

"In two weeks. It's in our honor."

"Why our honor? We don't know anyone."

"Because we're new arrivals and because of my wealth and nobility." The cynical note that was becoming more and more familiar to her crept into his voice. "And when they see you, my beautiful Spanish wife, they'll rush to have more parties."

"Thank you." She smiled at him, and he nodded his head coolly.

"There are paints and canvas in the sunroom for your use."

"Thank you," she said again, and wondered if Josh had

furnished the paint and canvas or if he had found them available.

"This afternoon," he said, "I'll visit our *estancia*. It's a short journey from town."

"Will you be gone long?" To her amazement, the prospect of his absence was unsettling.

"I have no idea." He shrugged. "Long enough to look over our one hundred and eighty thousand acres."

"Merciful saints!"

"The land's been divided and given to the conquerors," he explained. "A relative came with Pizarro, consequently today, as his descendant, I have vast holdings here. There are stables behind this house. Soon I'll make arrangements about a horse for you. I recall you said you like to ride."

"So you remembered," she said.

"I'll always remember—everything, *cara*." His eyes were the color of green moss, and as unreadable.

A maid appeared to pour more wine. As she worked, her long black lashes were downcast, but Lianna recognized the face as the same she had glimpsed watching her in the library last night. As soon as the woman returned to the kitchen, Lianna asked Josh her name.

"Juanita."

"There are so many servants here," she said, not yet ready to tell Josh what she suspected.

"What caused your sleeplessness during the night?"

"Perhaps it was the new surroundings." She tilted her head to observe him closely. "To have heard me turning, you must have lain awake as well." In a voice dripping with innocence, she asked, "Did the new surroundings disturb you too?"

"As a matter of fact, yes."

"But you didn't toss and turn." Instantly she wished she could take back her words, as his eyebrow arched.

"How amazing to discover that we both know, down to the smallest detail, how the other spent the night," he said dryly.

"You can be the most . . ." She closed her mouth.

"Oh, don't stop now! The most what? I'm breathless with suspense."

"Are you through eating?"

"The most what? My mind reels with possibilities," he teased.

"The most aggravating man on earth!"

"The most aggravating on earth," he mused, as if she had paid him a compliment. "That makes me unique . . ."

"Will you stop!" she said, tempted to yield to his merry banter. For the first time she saw how easily she might lose her heart to Josh—and how painful that would be.

"I'm pursuing the conversation," he continued. "It's not often a beautiful woman has informed me that I'm so singular."

"You have a skin like a pig's hide!" she said, hiding laughter. "Nothing pricks it!"

He grinned, his white teeth flashing. Then he reached up to touch her cheek and the mere brush of his fingers was torment. "One thing—you don't have a pig's hide, *mi amor.*" His voice lowered softly. "No, 'tis soft as the petal of a flower."

"You're impossible!" She barely knew what she said. His touch stirred a wild tingling, and the warmth in his eyes invaded her senses like wine.

He arched an eyebrow. "What thoughts run through your mind when you look at me like that?"

Her mind raced for an answer, frightened of the feelings surfacing. She said, "I'm thinking of a new ball gown."

He stared intently, then pushed back his chair and came around to stand beside her. The sun slanted in through the high windows and splashed across his white shirt, and she smelled a faint, fresh scent like woods on a summer day.

"The material is in a trunk in my room; I'll find a seamstress for you. *Adiós,* I won't be back for several days." Josh's lips brushed her cheek lightly, and then he was gone.

Juanita came to clear the table and Lianna looked at her impassive features, the large black eyes and long thin nose. Would she be in danger without Josh? The room felt cold, as if it were a place suddenly deprived of sunshine. And as she left to go to Josh's room, the touch of his lips on her cheek lingered.

At the foot of his bed stood the sea chest and a brown trunk with a high curved lid. Lianna tried the chest and discovered it was locked; then she opened the trunk and removed three bolts of white, pale green, and soft rose silk. Beneath the silk she found white tulle. Two more bundles of muslin lay near the bottom of the trunk, but these Lianna left untouched.

She unrolled a few yards of rose silk and held up the material, turning and twisting in front of a pier glass. Josh had bought this for her. He would get a horse for her. Could he truly be indifferent and still shower her with gifts? And she knew that the material was necessary for his own purpose. He could not take his wife to the governor's ball without a ball gown. Why did it matter? Was she losing her heart to Joshua Raven?

The notion shook her, and Lianna leaned forward to peer at her blue eyes as if she could read an answer in them.

"I'm not," she said firmly, her voice loud in the silence. "I'm not and I won't." Grimly she clamped her jaw closed. If she did fall in love with him, it would be heartbreaking. He was an iron-willed, ruthless pirate who would not bend an inch, and the woman who loved him would be left waiting at home time after time while he was at sea risking his life as a privateer. For the first time she thought beyond the moment and looked at Josh's future. "I won't love you, Josh Raven," she whispered, but the words sounded hollow.

Within the hour, Madryn appeared, accompanied by her mother, Teresa, to commence the sewing. Lianna sketched a dress, showing them what she wanted, and in spite of her resolve, all the time she worked over the dress, she considered how it would look to Josh. She had to admit to herself she wanted to make him take notice of her, to soften the coldness she saw so often in his green eyes.

Josh rode away from the house, turning up the long street, his thoughts going back over each word with Lianna, her smiles, her teasing. If only . . .

He shut his mind, knowing that he should face reality

and stop longing for what could not be. He was ushered into the wide, cool hallway of an elegant house set behind high, thick walls. He waited, hearing a fountain splash in the courtyard, and then the butler reappeared to usher him into a salon where three men turned to face him.

As his gaze ran swiftly over them, instantly recognizing the long slender face of Lord Bannister, the three stood up. Josh wondered how he would be received, aware all of them knew his past as well as his father.

"Don Cristóbal," Lord Bannister said in a jovial tone, watching as the butler closed the door. His voice lowered. "Joshua Raven, come meet our friends," he said, stepping forward to shake Josh's hand. Josh looked into warm brown eyes that seemed to hold no animosity. John Bannister's handshake was firm.

He turned to introduce Josh to the others. "This is Lord Brenthaven."

Josh met the direct stare of wide hazel eyes. With large features and a square, heavy jaw, Reginald Brenthaven was a taller, larger man than Josh. He smiled and shook hands.

"Welcome to Santiago. We're glad to have you. I've heard about your exploits and we can use your wits."

"Thank you, your grace."

"No, none of that. Reginald—or use the Spanish name Gerado. We need each other's friendship."

Josh began to relax, the tenseness leaving his shoulders. He had braced for the same rejection he had always found in London, and when it wasn't forthcoming, he felt an enormous relief. The relief was short-lived as he turned to meet Timothy Paddington. Josh looked into icy blue eyes and saw scorn that was plainly visible.

"Lord Paddington, Josh Raven."

The handshake was brief and limp as Timothy Paddington withdrew his hand swiftly. "I hope we can count on your loyalty. Your reputation precedes you."

The words were enough to warrant a calling-out, and Josh's temper flared, but he curbed it swiftly as Lord Brenthaven stepped closer.

"Come now, Timothy. We have to band together if

we're to accomplish anything.'' He took Josh's arm. "Come sit down while we bring you up-to-date on the troops and the people in Santiago.''

Josh listened while they discussed San Martín, but part of him seethed with fury that his father's wrath could follow him halfway around the world and still cause him difficulty. The sea was the only place he could find total acceptance. He glanced at Timothy Paddington. Of the men in the room, he would have guessed Paddington to be the last to adhere to London society's values. He'd been told Lord Paddington was an adventurer. He appeared younger than Josh, and his long slender form was dressed with a careful elegance. Josh knew both Paddington and Brenthaven had reputations as excellent shots as well as being expert in the art of swords.

Timothy Paddington glanced at Josh, and their gazes clashed. Josh felt the hatred in cold blue eyes, and anger rose in him. He wanted to slap the arrogant face and challenge him, but he knew that would bring ruin on him and harm their cause as well.

He gave his attention to Lord Brenthaven, who was turned to him. "I've been here over a year now. Timothy and John came about six months ago. We'll give you names to remember, but you're not to write anything down. Commit them to memory and don't trust anyone unless you're absolutely certain about him.''

Josh caught Lord Paddington watching him again, and arching an eyebrow with a sardonic grin. Josh returned his attention to Lord Brenthaven. "Yes, sir.'' He listened carefully while they went over the names of local people whose sympathies lay with the patriots' cause. He learned of known enemies, of spies for both sides.

Lord Brenthaven stood up. "Enough of this. I'd like tea, but we'll have brandy instead. Your head should be swimming with facts by now.''

Josh laughed and stretched out his legs. "Aye, that it is. I have to get cannon unloaded and moved to the mountains.''

"We'll provide help when you need it. One man you should contact is Pedro Méndez.'' Lord Brenthaven moved to a table to pour brandy into glasses, and the others stood up to join him. As they stood by the window drinking the brandy, Lord Paddington moved to stand by Josh.

"I hear you're wed now."

"Yes. Word travels fast."

"A farmgirl, isn't she?"

Josh smiled, refusing to let Timothy Paddington stir any visible ire. "From Wiltshire. Miss Lianna Melton."

"How nice for you. Now you'll have a home when you go back to England."

Lord Brenthaven stepped between them. "I want you to see the courtyard. The flowers here are breathtaking, although I'd give a great deal for some nice English roses."

Josh chuckled. "This is a paradise of flowers and color."

"I want you to meet Celeste. She'll call on your wife soon. We're fortunate men to have women who'll travel into danger at our sides."

"Yes, sir," Josh said flatly as they entered the courtyard.

An hour later, he told them good-bye. "I want to talk to Pedro Méndez before I ride for our *estancia*. Good day, gentlemen."

The three men told him good-bye and sat in silence as the door closed behind him. Lord Brenthaven turned to Timothy. "Keep your damned opinions of the man to yourself, Paddington! We have to pull together here if we're to succeed."

"It grates on my nerves to know I'm trusting my life to a rogue!"

"You won't have a life if you keep taunting him! The man's a deadly shot."

"I'm not afraid," Timothy said with a smile as he stood up. "I must go home. I hope he doesn't betray us all."

"We have to trust each other," Lord Brenthaven said solemnly. "I know about his past, and as far as I can learn, he's trustworthy. His conflict lies with the Duke of Cathmoor and no one else."

"He's a damned pirate! What kind of honor does a ruffian have?"

"We agreed to welcome his help," John Bannister said. "I intend to have him watched closely."

Lord Brenthaven shrugged. "If you want, but I trust

him. Marcheno's cousin in Spain killed Raven's brother Phillip. He has an old quarrel with the Marcheno family and that's the reason he's here. That and the fact that he wants to help liberate the Chileans for self-rule."

"Bah! A pirate—he wants something for his own use, and I intend to find out what."

"We've a good group of men here. Don't cause dissension and slow us down," Lord Brenthaven urged.

"I won't. I just want to eliminate Joshua Raven," Timothy said. "Well, until we meet Wednesday night, good day, gentlemen."

He turned and swept out of the room, mounting his horse to ride away, his eyes soon spotting the figure in the distance ahead. He tightened his hands into fists and shook his head.

For the next few days Madryn and Teresa cut and sewed while Lianna stood through long fittings. Without Josh, the house seemed empty and lonely. Lianna tried to pass the time as she had on board the frigate, by painting. One afternoon as Madryn stitched, Lianna sat down nearby to sketch, reproducing on paper a likeness with flowing black hair and wide-set black eyes. Finally Lianna laid down her brush.

"Madryn, it's time to stop for today. Want to see your picture?"

Madryn folded the material and came to look at the drawing. She laughed. "It is truly me! I like it."

"Good. I'll work on it tomorrow. There's still a lot to do. I'm just getting started." She glanced up to see Juanita cross the patio.

Lianna frowned. While her conversation with Madryn was inconsequential, it wore on Lianna's nerves to know that she was continually watched.

Lianna and Madryn began to have two sessions daily, one for the sewing and the next hour with Madryn posing while Lianna sketched. Within a short time a close friendship began to develop between them.

One afternoon after Madryn had gone, Lianna continued to paint. The only sounds on the patio were the gurgle and splash of water in the fountain and the soft scrape of Lianna's brush on the canvas. A shadow fell across the palette. Lianna glanced up and her heart skipped. Josh, staring at her sketch, stood directly behind her. He was dressed in dusty leather breeches and wore a brown coat over his shirt; a stubble of whiskers covered his chin. "Your sketch is charming. Madryn's a beautiful girl."

"Thank you." How good it was to have Josh home! To hear his voice again. "You've been gone a long time. Far longer than I expected from what you said."

"Put down the picture a moment and come with me."

Upstairs in his bedroom, Josh shut the door, pulling the heavy drapes. "Sit down, Lianna."

He crossed to step into her room and she heard her door close. When he returned, she looked at his furrowed brow, the unfamiliar lines that bracketed his mouth.

"What's happened? Are you having difficulty?" she asked.

"More than I would have imagined possible." He shed his coat and removed a dagger from a hidden inside pocket. "It's not going well for the patriots. Santiago's defenses are strong." He tossed the dagger onto a desk and sat down to pull off his boots. "The Spanish have spies everywhere; they're as abundant as fleas." Green eyes raised and bore into her. "Be cautious in your conversation with Madryn. She could betray us so easily."

"I'll be careful," she answered, "but I feel Madryn can be trusted. She's unhappy with the Spanish royalty."

"Has she admitted that?"

"No, but it isn't difficult to guess."

"Still, be wary," he instructed.

"Why did you ask me upstairs?" she asked abruptly.

"I've been gone six days now. If we were in love, what would be the first thing I'd do when I returned?"

She blushed, momentarily disconcerted. "One of the servants, Juanita, follows and watches me," she blurted.

"She would turn us over to the authorities instantly if she had a reason."

"You knew her loyalty to Spain and you didn't tell me!"

He shrugged. "I warned you to be careful. I know some, but I don't know all who are spies. Just take care." He lay down on the bed, his hands behind his head. His long lashes lowered. "I've ridden all day and all last night," he said, his voice filled with weariness, and Lianna longed to move to the bed and stroke his brow.

"You sound exhausted. Did you meet other Englishmen?"

"Yes. I'll go over the names with you. One of the wives, Lady Brenthaven, Señora Davio, will call soon." He ran his fingers across his brow. "My past follows me. One of them, Lord Timothy Paddington, despises me."

"Oh, no!"

He opened his eyes to stare at her. "I'll try to control my temper, but he's pushing. I think he wants me to call him out. It seems the man hates me."

"I'm sorry," she said.

"If only you truly did care, Lianna," he said so tiredly that she stared at him. She had never seen him bone weary or heard him sound defeated as he did at this moment.

"I must sleep," he murmured, and within seconds his chest rose and fell evenly. Lianna sat quietly beside him, her emotions warring. She wanted to reach out and touch him, and finally leaned forward to turn a lock of his hair around her fingers. "Josh," she whispered softly, her gaze resting on his mouth. Abruptly she went to her room and closed the door. Later, when she went up to freshen for dinner, Josh was gone and she dined alone.

That night as she lay in bed she heard a scrape and turned to see Josh step through the open window from the balcony. Sitting up, she asked, "Why come in through the balcony?"

He peered down at the darkened courtyard. "No one must know I've been gone, or where I've been. Someone could be watching the courtyard."

A shiver ran down her spine, and she worried over the weary note in his voice. "I didn't hear you leave."

"I met with patriots." He sat beside her on the edge of the bed. "If anything should happen to me, if you need help, tell Fletcher or Simms or our majordomo, Carlos."

She clutched her bended knees, gazing at Josh with fear in her blood. To hear his solemn tone now, when he had faced danger so recklessly in the past, increased her concern over the threat surrounding them.

"There are adobe huts in the foothills of the Andes out of Santiago, where patriots hide. They would take you to safety, back to *El Feroz*." His fingers brushed her shoulder and a sense of danger was replaced with consciousness of Josh Raven sitting so close, his fingers lightly playing with her hair, his gaze on her hungrily.

"Does the revolution draw closer?" she asked, barely aware of the conversation, far more conscious of the intimacy of the darkened room. She could detect a masculine scent of leather in his clothing, and suddenly she ached to feel his arms around her.

"No, there are too many obstacles. The Spaniards have a ring of defense around Santiago to the north, east, and south. To the west is the natural barrier of the Andes," he answered, unable to remove his hand from her shoulder. The warm flesh beneath her gown was a torment and he felt a swift surge of desire. She was warm from the bed; her hair held a sweet scent that assailed his senses.

"If there's no revolution, will we return to *El Feroz*? How long will you wait?"

"You'll get home to England."

She bit her lip and turned her head away swiftly, her hair swirling over his hand.

"That's what you want, isn't it?"

"You taught me the ways of love, then abandoned me."

Stunned, he drew a sharp breath and his fists clenched. A muscle worked in his jaw. Suddenly he stood up and moved away, fighting with all his will the urge to pull her into his arms, to push her down beneath him and caress her. He swore softly, trying to gain control, keeping his back turned so she wouldn't see his obvious rise of desire.

"I did us both an injustice. But you should have told me your love for Edwin ran deep. And you should have confessed your Spanish ties."

"And have you slit my throat!"

He turned. "I wouldn't have, and you know it! As it is, how do I know what you've lied about? I've promised you your freedom," he said harshly. "And then you can go home to Edwin, who will love you."

The promise that once would have sent her heart soaring now inflicted pain. Pain that she didn't fully understand, but she understood something else. Josh Raven's body couldn't follow his heart. He desired her, and the knowledge made her burn with longing.

He went to his room and closed the door between them. Lianna sank down, pulling the sheet to her chin, hurting with an empty ache.

Two nights later it was time for the governor's ball. Lianna's anticipation outweighed her dread. Governor Francisco Marcheno would be there, but what sent her heart into a flutter was the prospect of getting to dance with Josh, to be held by him.

As Madryn laid out Lianna's dress on the bed, Lianna studied the yards of white gauze caught in swags held by tiny blue satin bows. With exquisite lace flounces edging the low-necked bodice and the elbow-length sleeves, it reminded Lianna of her wedding dress. She turned the simple gold band that bound her to Josh. To her amazement, the more time that passed without his kisses, the more acutely aware of him she became. She could not help but wonder what Josh's reaction would be when she appeared.

"I'll comb your hair now, *señora*," Madryn said in her soft voice.

"This is my first ball," Lianna said as she sat down for Madryn to work.

"You'll dazzle your handsome husband." Madryn piled black curls on top of Lianna's head, pinning them carefully while she continued to talk. "How wonderful it must be to be wed."

"Madryn, you're in love!"

The pink in Madryn's cheeks gave an answer as well as her words. "*Sí.* And we'll marry soon."

"Do I know him?"

"No." Madryn smiled. "He's Rinaldo Sepulveda, a blacksmith."

"And he's very handsome," Lianna said, making Madryn giggle.

"Oh, *sí! Muy simpático*—as is your husband. How fortunate you are, *señora*."

Lianna looked down a moment, fearful that Madryn might see the truth clearly. "Madryn, I had my seventeenth birthday just before the voyage here. How old are you?"

"Eighteen last month." She combed the long curls that tumbled down the back of Lianna's head, then fastened tiny fresh gardenia blossoms in her hair. Their deep-scented sweetness and velvety white blossoms were a stark contrast to Lianna's raven locks.

Once dressed and ready, Lianna waited until the ponderous chime of the clock downstairs sounded, and she knew Josh would be ready.

She descended the stairs to find Josh in the library. He stood before the empty fireplace, his broad back to her. Clad in an elegant coat cut away at the waist with the tails falling to the backs of his knees, he turned to face her. As tangible as if she had touched hot coals, a flame ran through her and it made her afraid. What if she came to love him, this man who was a pirate and lived only at sea?

While he studied her languidly, Lianna assessed him as thoroughly. He looked every bit the Spanish grandee. The richly fashioned coat was cut in the Spanish style, with large wing lapels. His white cravat made his dark skin more appealing than ever; the points of his stepped collar covered the lower part of his firm jaw. In his hand was a glass of Madeira, which he placed on the table.

"You're very beautiful, Doña Lita," he said, approaching her.

"Mil gracias." Her pulse sounded as he stopped inches from her. His gaze flicked past her to the open doorway, then returned.

"You'll conquer these Spaniards in a manner the rebels can never achieve," he whispered, and her throat became too dry to answer because he meant what he said. It was not a flowery comment for the benefit of listening ears. It was a whisper of open admiration.

"We must go." He stepped into the hall and waited while Fletcher assisted Lianna with a velvet cape.

Once on their way, Lianna asked, "What will happen tonight if you encounter someone who knew Don Cristóbal in Spain?"

"Then I'll go to prison," he said flatly.

"If you go, then I too will be taken prisoner."

"Don't fret. We're a world away from Spain, and the Marqués de Aveiro had an unsavory reputation as an inveterate, dishonest gambler, which brought about his banishment to the colonies. He'd been forced to liquidate many of the holdings he had in Spain to meet his debts. The only living relative was a married sister who long ago refused to claim any relation to him. I don't expect trouble from that direction."

"But if you're wrong?"

His voice was cool. "Then you'll be arrested too."

"I pray I come out of this alive."

His mouth curved in a wicked grin. "And you don't pray for my safety? Your husband, who every day treads an increasingly dangerous path?"

" 'Tis your own choosing!"

"But you should pray for me as well! I'm the barrier between you and danger, *mi amor*! Pray for me to save your precious skin."

"I pray you don't abandon me here when you go! You're ruled by hatred."

He flushed and leaned forward, startling her. "Lianna, I'd like to see you unmoved if people you loved, your own blood kin, were treated as Phillip and Terrence were. My crewmen had been with me on voyages, some since I was a lad . . ."

The words poured out with such pain she wished she could help him erase the memories. His voice shook with grief, and she saw again the vulnerable side to him.

"If I began to describe the horrors to you, you'd retch."

"Josh, I'm sorry," she whispered, touching his arm and suffering over his expression.

He leaned closer, his fists doubled, more handsome than any other man she had known, racked with agony. "When I think of what we could have had, Lianna, I . . ." He flung himself back against the seat.

Lianna was stunned. There could be only one reason he was so distraught—he cared for her to some degree.

Her thoughts swirled and spun; then the carriage halted.

Josh clenched his jaws, stiffening his shoulders. The evening would be tedious, because they always ran a risk of discovery, more so tonight in the crowd, when they would draw so much attention. Lianna would turn heads. Her wide blue eyes were filled with shock.

How close he had come to admitting the struggle within. He couldn't get her out of his blood! He thought he had succeeded on board ship, only to find when he caught her scent of roses, when he saw her blue eyes warm with laughter, his heart stopped beating for a moment. And each night in his room was torture. Would he ever get over her? Grimly he stepped down and offered her his hand. Lianna took his hand. The harsh set had returned to his features, yet she realized he was suffering an inner struggle.

Later, when she watched him move through the crowd, acknowledging introductions smoothly, it seemed impossible that he had sounded hurt.

The large hall was ablaze with lights. They moved into the ballroom to the receiving lines, and each new face was a momentary threat to Lianna. Josh leaned close to whisper, "There, my dear, is the man who was to have been your relative by marriage—Governor Francisco Marcheno."

Curiosity made her study the black-haired man, who was as tall as Josh. His nose was long and thin above his thick lips. When Lianna reached him, he took her hand to welcome her.

"Bienvenidos a Santiago!"

His protruding cold black eyes glittered like small bits of obsidian, with pouches of fat beneath, causing Lianna to think he resembled an evil toad waiting to swallow an unsuspecting insect. A chill touched her, as if a draft of cold air had blown across her nape. Briefly she forgot her surroundings and saw only Governor Marcheno. Perhaps the Count of Marcheno resembled his cousin. And instead of being wed to such a man, she had married Josh Raven. Something constricted around her heart. A feeling of relief was matched by a dull pain. Home and England were far away. They were beginning to lose significance.

Governor Marcheno's eyes narrowed and he looked at her quizzically. "How lovely you are, *marquesa*." He raised her hand to his lips.

"*Gracias*, your excellency," Lianna replied, and as she withdrew her fingers, her gaze lowered to his hand. A golden ring circled Francisco Marcheno's thick index finger: the familiar serpent's head with a ruby eye, its fangs bared.

Beside her Josh commented lightly, "My wife is intrigued by your serpent ring."

"The serpent ready to strike—the Marcheno crest. And you are fortunate enough to be the *marquesa*'s husband, eh? Welcome to Santiago."

"Thank you. I've waited a long time to get here."

"I hope it's everything you expect. Later we'll talk."

They walked along. Josh's hand on her elbow steadied her. "I thought you might faint before," he said. "Are you ill?"

She glanced up, expecting some more of Josh's mischief, but his expression was solemn. "I realized what my future might have been," she answered. His eyes darkened, but he said nothing.

"*Buenas noches*," a feminine voice intoned. Lianna turned to face a tall black-haired woman. Her softly modulated Spanish was spoken in a sultry voice, and she looked at Josh with open approval, barely giving a nod to Lianna while she introduced herself as Salina Marcheno, the governor's wife.

As they walked away, Lianna said, "You court danger."

"Aye, I like a challenge—and accepted one too many."

"And that was?"

"You have to ask?" he said softly.

"I can't be a challenge to you."

He leaned back, his brows arching as he looked at her.

"My dear wife, your big blue eyes throw out a constant challenge. The words between us dredge up a gauntlet."

"That's absurd!" she protested, yet her pulse skittered with an exhilarating swiftness.

"No, it's not. You've just heightened it," he drawled with a lazy smile. "See what happens when we look into each other's eyes? When we touch our fingers together. The slightest contact is provocation, Lianna."

He watched her closely while he talked, and she couldn't deny what happened between them. His smile was mocking as he turned to walk beside her. They moved down the receiving line, then various guests approached to meet and chat with them. The profusion of new names and faces swirled in Lianna's head, but several stood out from the crowd. Young matrons, both Spanish and Creole, promised to call on Lianna. One, Señora Vachon, took Lianna's arm. "*Marquesa*, General Farjado insists on an introduction."

Lianna looked into the black eyes of a handsome Spaniard. His green uniform was decorated with a chest full of medals. He smiled and took her hand to raise it to his lips, while his eyes never left hers. "Santiago has gained a ravishing new flower."

"*Gracias*," Lianna replied, slightly amused by his compliment. "Santiago is a beautiful town."

He released her hand and smiled. "When the dancing commences, will your husband allow me the privilege?"

"*Sí*," Lianna replied, sure that Josh wouldn't care.

"Ah." General Farjado's eyes burned with satisfaction. "Were I your husband, I fear I wouldn't be so generous." He glanced beyond her at the receiving line. "I see the reception is over—shortly it will be time for the dance."

She realized her experiences had changed her since she had sailed from Portsmouth. Her father had never allowed her to do frivolous things. Because of her youth and inexperience, not too many months earlier, this lavish ball, men flirting, and the new, intricate dance steps would have frightened her. Now she could accept all with a poise she had acquired during the last year. Girlhood seemed far behind her, and she wondered how much she had changed due to Josh's influence.

While General Farjado remained beside her, Lianna watched as the musicians gathered on a dais behind a row of potted palms. With the strumming of guitars, the governor led off the first dance with his wife. Within minutes, others began to drift to the dance floor.

Lianna's gaze drifted across the room to the dark head that showed above most of the guests. Josh stood half-facing her, talking to a striking brown-haired woman. His white teeth showed as he smiled broadly, a quick glance flicking toward Lianna. He laughed, and Lianna wondered what the two discussed. The same constriction she had experienced earlier returned. One look at him made her heartbeat change. Breaking into her thoughts, General Farjado made a slight bow and offered his arm.

"Your hsuband is occupied. May I have this dance?"

She smiled, and General Farjado took her into his arms to dance, whirling her around the floor. Lianna studied his thick black hair, the convex curve of his nose and full sensual lips. She decided he was slightly taller than Josh, heavier, yet handsome in a swarthy manner, and far younger than she would have guessed a general might be. She voiced aloud her thoughts about his rank, bringing a smile to his lips. "Sometimes one moves up rapidly in war. I fought in the Spanish Army against Napoleon. And there are many opportunities in the colonies. That's why I came, as well as three of my brothers." He glanced across the room. "Your husband has already seized upon the opportunities."

"How's that?"

He raised an eyebrow in surprise. "You don't know? Perhaps I've revealed a secret. I refer to the estate he won at the gaming tables. He's a formidable gambler." His black eyes bore into hers. "One must never underestimate an opponent." The words were cold, yet General Farjado smiled disarmingly. A foreboding of danger ran secondary to her surprise at learning about Josh's gambling prowess.

The general danced in a wide circle, and she glimpsed Josh, now standing beside a golden-haired woman dressed in blue silk. He looked into Lianna's eyes while the woman leaned forward to whisper something to him, making him laugh. Then Lianna turned, and Josh was gone from sight.

The dance ended, and Governor Marcheno claimed the next one, his hand damp as his fingers closed over Lianna's, and she felt as if an aura of danger surrounded him. "Tell me about Spain, *marquesa*."

"Spain is the same as always. When we sailed from La Coruña, I wondered if I had left all happiness behind. Now that I'm here, I think I won't miss Spain so badly."

"Good. We're glad to have you. I left Spain four years ago."

"The people here have been gracious."

"How fortunate for Santiago that Don Cristóbal decided to claim his inheritance and bring his new bride. I know your family hated to part with you."

"I love my husband very much." The sentiment rolled off her tongue with shocking ease. The dance stopped, and a Spanish officer claimed the next one and asked for another. Just as the music commenced, she heard a deep voice behind her.

"Sir, if you don't mind, I'll claim my wife."

Lianna tried to hide the swift excitement that came when she felt Josh's arm circle her waist. The officer nodded. "Of course, Don Cristóbal. *Marquesa, gracias*."

Josh turned her into his arms and smiled, dazzling her, and for a fleeting second she forgot that he was doing it to keep up the appearance of a happy, newly married couple. And she forgot the danger in becoming entranced by Josh Raven.

"Every man in this room wants to dance with you tonight."

"They've been polite."

"Politeness has little to do with it. You're the most beautiful woman here."

The words were roses tumbling at her feet and she wanted to believe he meant them. "Thank you," she said softly, "but it isn't so. And anyway, I'm married."

His voice acquired a cynical tone. "That makes you all the more enticing to some."

"Why? I'm bound to you."

"Your life couldn't have been so sheltered that you've never known married women to take lovers. It doesn't take long for a perceptive man to discover if a woman truly loves her husband." Lianna frowned at him, wondering if he were speaking from firsthand experience. His cynical tone shattered the bubble of warmth, and she tried to keep up her guard. He looked past her. "And Farjado is no fool."

Josh turned on the dance floor and Lianna cast a darting glance at the general, to find his gaze resting on her. She drew a sharp breath.

"Surely you don't fear the general?" Josh asked derisively.

"No, but he makes me uneasy."

"My brave wife, uneasy?"

"You tease about bravery."

"No," he replied, sobering. "I've commanded men since I was nineteen years of age and have seen great brutes cower at my anger, yet upon more than one desperate occasion you've faced me without a qualm. You're very brave."

"Thank you," she whispered, wondering how triumphant he would feel if he knew she was in danger of losing her heart.

He smiled and pulled her close against his chest. "Smile, Lianna, and these Spaniards will think we're in love."

She smiled eagerly. How easy it was, because she didn't have to pretend. In his arms she could smile forever, yet wisdom warned her to take care. If she fell in love with her husband, it would mean the cruelest loss when they parted.

Josh held her close and whirled her around the dance floor, watching her cling to him, following his steps perfectly. She was breathtakingly beautiful tonight, and every time he had watched her dance in the arms of another man, it had taken all his control to keep from charging to the dance floor to claim her. In the carriage, he had almost lost control and declared his longing to keep her bound in marriage. "How many balls have you attended, Lianna? How many brokenhearted suitors have been left behind?"

"None. My father was a frugal man. Balls and ball gowns were a frivolity he wouldn't allow."

His heart twisted. He could imagine a small blue-eyed girl growing up in an empty house with an uncaring father. A little girl who wanted love. And now he had hurt her badly in this forced marriage.

"If there were no balls, Lianna, how did you learn to dance?"

She smiled, a smile that was warm and bright, a smile that made everything inside him glow. "My friend Melissa talked her poor brother Thomas into teaching us. How put-upon he was!"

"If he could see you now, he wouldn't be put-upon."

"Oh, yes, he would! Thomas thought I was a nuisance. Besides, he's the father of two now."

Involuntarily his arm tightened more, crushing her soft breasts to his chest.

This time she resisted. "No, Josh, not too close."

"How beautiful you are. Beautiful and self-willed."

When she tried to pull away a fraction, his muscles tightened, holding her. "Perhaps we're two determined people, each unwilling to yield," she said.

Softly he whispered in English, "Aye, love, and one of us must lose."

The music ceased, yet still he held her. "Josh, this is unseemly."

"Not for happily married newlyweds."

"You have danced until the music stopped, and still you hold me close. You won—now release me."

"No, *cara*. The music will commence again. I won this time. If only I could always win . . ."

A waltz started and Josh swept her with him. She slanted a look at him. "General Farjado says you are an expert gambler."

Josh smiled, but the cynical hardness had returned to his features. "He's quite good. And very careful."

"Is that where you go at night?"

"Sometimes."

"You didn't gamble before."

"On my ship?" He laughed. "Hardly. This is because

the real *marqués* was a gambler, remember? And it gives
me an excuse for odd hours. And an invitation to certain
houses. And I must win to keep up the *marqués'* unsavory
reputation, but one gamble I lost.''

"And what was the prize?"

"Our marriage."

She missed a step, and his arm steadied her. Her smile
vanished. "If you did, it is because of your own forceful-
ness!" She tilted her head to stare at him with wide,
curious eyes. "You lost? From the first day, you told me it
would be annulled."

"How your blue eyes flash. Smile again. Otherwise it
will look as if we argue."

"I find little to smile about."

"There are worlds of things to make one smile."

"And what makes you smile—the beautiful ladies?"

He laughed softly. "Better! Now you sound like a
jealous wife if anyone overhears us." His voice dropped
suddenly. "You smell like a garden, a heady fragrance.
I'd like to pull each white flower out of your hair and
watch the tresses tumble down."

Lianna's pulse tripped as she pulled back slightly. "I
wonder, do you say that so that the Spanish will be
satisfied with our appearance?"

His voice deepened to the husky tone that created a
storm of its own. "I said it to see your blue eyes darken,
to see your lips part, to feel your pulse quicken. For a few
minutes, Lianna, let's forget the world and tomorrow."

With a dazzling smile that took her breath, he tightened
his arm and whirled her around the floor. "You've not
spent all your days at sea," she said breathlessly. "You
dance as if you had spent years at it."

"Too bad we're not in England dancing at a ball." His
voice changed to a merry tone. "Miss Melton, how delightful it is to get to know you."

"Thank you, sir." She entered into his game, relieved
from the earlier tension.

"Do you like to ride?" he asked.

"Yes."

"Splendid! I have a fine new stallion, and spring's

almost here. Some morning soon, I'd like to call and we can ride in St. James's Park. May I have permission?''

"Josh Raven," she said softly with laughter, " 'tis the first time I've heard you inquire of anything in such a fainthearted manner."

"Fainthearted! I must repair my image, Miss Melton." He whirled her through the wide doors to the courtyard.

"Josh, you will stir gossip!"

"But I won't be called fainthearted!"

"I take back my words. Do be serious!"

"So now I'm silly as well as fainthearted!" He danced over stones into a shadowed corner.

"You're incorrigible!"

"Incorrigible, silly, fainthearted! Miss Melton, I'll show you, I'm corrigible, earnest, and lion-hearted! How can I convince you?"

"I'm convinced!"

"Oh, no. I'll have to prove my mettle. I know—I'll steal a kiss!"

"Josh," she laughed, and placed her arms on his. Her heart skipped as she looked into his smiling features, the creases bracketing his mouth, his white teeth showing in the dusky light. "Oh, Josh, why can't it be like this all the time?"

"It can be," he whispered. Then his head dipped and his mouth touched hers and all laughter vanished.

With the slightest contact, a burning attraction flamed. His arms closed around her waist and he hungrily possessed her mouth with his.

Josh tightened his grasp, losing control. He wanted to taste her sweetness; he had to crush her softness against him. His blood roared in his ears as he kissed her deeply. With a groan, he tore his mouth away. They stood with arms entwined as they tried to regain their breaths.

"Danger lurks on all sides."

"And the greatest danger isn't the Spanish," she whispered in a daze. She saw the curiosity in his expression. Suddenly uncertain, she drew back and said stiffly, "Let's go back."

As they stepped into the ballroom, General Farjado smiled at them. "Enjoying the governor's patio?"

"Very much," Josh answered smoothly. "My wife wanted a breath of air." He pulled Lianna into his arms for a dance. They were both quiet. She wondered if he were as shaken as she. And as she danced with him, she became aware that the room was filled with lovely women whose eyes followed his every step.

Her mind went over every word said on the terrace, and her pulse jumped each time she thought about what he had admitted.

Finally the music ended. Josh shifted his hand to her arm. "I think we can leave now. We should have convinced anyone watching how in love we are. Love is always an excuse to depart early."

Josh took her arm, and Lianna felt disappointment cut into her heart. He had danced and kissed her, laughed and flirted to present a good show to the Spaniards. What had she expected? She had warned herself before the evening started to guard against his charm. After telling the Marchenos good-bye, they started toward the door, when a voice stopped them.

"Leaving?" General Farjado asked.

"The evening grows late," Josh answered, and turned to the butler to request their carriage be brought to the door.

General Farjado took Lianna's hand to kiss it briefly. "How nice it is to have you both in Santiago. I'd like to show you some of our sights." He looked at Josh. "Would you care to go tomorrow afternoon?"

"I have an appointment with Governor Marcheno, but thank you."

"Oh? Then would you allow me to show your wife Santiago?"

A smile curved Josh's lips as he looked down at Lianna. "Regretfully, I think my wife has an appointment tomorrow afternoon."

"*Sí,*" she replied quietly, aware of the tense atmosphere, the contest developing between the two men. "I thank you too."

"Perhaps another afternoon soon. *Buenas noches, marquesa.*" He bowed and Lianna smiled, relieved to have the conversation end. The two men nodded good night, and Josh took Lianna's arm.

In the carriage they rode in silence, with Lianna acutely conscious of Josh sitting only a few feet away. Gone was his teasing charm, reinforcing the realization that his conversation, his dancing, and his kiss had been for show, to prove to the Spaniards he was what he appeared.

Again she wrestled with an unwanted emotion. She wanted Josh to return to an earlier topic, to talk about their marriage. Did he want her love? One look at his harsh expression convinced her how foolish she was.

She told herself her feelings were stirred for a multitude of reasons that she might be mistaking for love. It could be because the evening had been exciting and fun, or because she was far from home and Josh Raven was becoming familiar as a friend. It could be because he was a handsome, charismatic man. Silently she waged a mental argument, trying to convince herself of the possible reasons her heart jumped every time he looked her way.

"In spite of tonight, General Farjado will come to call," Josh stated. "The general was taken with you and he'll politely appear until he's absolutely sure you're wildly in love with your husband—or until he sees an opportunity."

"That's absurd."

"No, love," he answered cynically. "You're a babe where intrigue is involved. Take care. He's a dangerous, evil man."

A commotion sounded outside. A woman screamed and the carriage halted.

"What the hell?" Josh swung open the door.

21

Lianna wanted to climb out behind him, yet part of her attention was on his hand holding to the inside of the carriage, only inches from her. She wanted to touch him, to trail her finger over each rough knuckle, to feel his arms around her . . .

She bit her lip and shook her head as if she could shake off the longing that plagued her. Josh sat down on the carriage seat, and Fletcher thrust his head into the carriage. His voice was tight was rage.

"Soldiers are arresting someone. A man's donkey cart collided with a nobleman's carriage. They're arresting the man and trying to clear the way."

"Fletcher, we'll be able to give more aid here if we're free. Don't get involved," Josh said quickly in a low voice.

"Aye. I know, but it's damned difficult to sit and watch."

Fletcher's head disappeared; Lianna heard voices as someone asked Fletcher who rode in the carriage.

"Don Cristóbal and his wife," Fletcher snapped, "the Marqués and Marquesa de Aveiro, on their way home from the governor's ball."

"*Perdón*. This will be cleared within minutes."

A soldier looked into the carriage.

"A thousand pardons, Don Cristóbal. You'll be on your way in seconds."

"*Sí.*"

The soldier closed the door, but it didn't shut out the sounds of a woman weeping, begging soldiers not to hurt her husband.

Lianna drew her breath. "There's nothing we can do except watch?"

"That's right, and it's a damned helpless feeling." Fury laced Josh's voice and he sat with his fists clenched. The carriage started to move, and Lianna looked out the window as a child screamed. A Spanish soldier had his fingers locked in a small boy's hair, the mother sobbing and pulling on the soldier's arm.

Hard arms yanked Lianna from the window and the leather flap dropped down. "Don't look!" Josh ordered.

He moved back into his corner and gazed stonily ahead. All became silent again except for the horses and carriage, and Josh's heavy breathing gradually returned to normal.

When they entered the large hallway at home, Josh lifted her cloak from her shoulders and leaned down to kiss her throat, his warm breath sending sparkling tingles down her spine as he whispered, *"Es guapa, cara mía."*

She guessed the display of affection was for the benefit of a valet, Geraldo, who moved silently behind them with Fletcher, both men putting away the cloaks.

"Gracias, Cristóbal," she answered with a smile.

He dropped his arm across her shoulders and strolled beside her up the broad stairs; then, at the top, he swung her into his arms.

Lianna's heart thudded violently. Pressed against his chest, she felt his pulse race also. She curled her arm around his neck, gazing at him, so close at hand.

They entered her bedroom and he closed the door behind them with his foot. Two small candles burned, the bed was turned down, and a nightdress was laid out for Lianna.

As soon as the door clicked shut, Josh set her on her feet. " 'Night, love." She looked up into eyes that burned into her soul. His gaze dropped to her lips. "In a while, I'll slip out and see if anything can be done for that family."

It took a moment to realize what he had said, and she stared at him blankly. "Won't it be dangerous?"

He shrugged. "Lianna, beware the general."

It wasn't the general who was a threat. It was stormy eyes and lips that could drive her into a world of fiery passion. It was a man whose quiet laughter and quick wit could delight. And in some ways, she had discovered, he was as vulnerable as she. As if she had no control over their movement, her fingers drifted to his hands.

Instantly his dark brows drew together, and he glanced down at her pale fingers resting as lightly as a lily bloom placed in his grasp. He drew his breath in a hiss and turned to go to his room, closing the door behind him.

Dazed, Lianna stared blankly at the door. Had she escaped something she would have regretted later, or was she falling deeply in love with her husband? Still, all too clearly she could remember the moment at sea when she had discovered Edwin. All else had vanished and she had wanted Edwin's arms and Edwin's kisses. Would that happen again when she saw him?

She stepped out of the ball gown, letting it drift to the floor before picking it up. The dress would hold special memories, and she placed it carefully over the chair, then pulled on the nightdress before she reached up to take a gardenia out of her hair.

Without warning the door opened, and Josh paused there, one hand pressing against the jamb while he watched her. His coat and cravat were gone, the white shirt with ruffles was unfastened over his coppery chest, dark hair on his chest curling against the white ruffles. Flickering candlelight gave a subdued rosy glow to the room, and silence was complete. Everything inside her constricted, and she trembled slightly.

"If I had given you the choice of going on that ship with Edwin, would you have gone?"

The question lay between them, and Lianna realized her answer was important. For a moment she was tempted to lie, but she faced him and answered, "Yes, I would have."

Josh straightened, jamming his hands into his pockets.

The movement pulled his breeches tautly across his loins and she saw the hard evidence of his desire. She held her breath as he crossed the room to her.

His hands rested on her shoulders; the drumming in her ears was an ocean's roar at the height of a storm. She fought the impulse to wind her arms around his neck, to pull his mouth down. Her breasts grew taut; longing burst low inside and spread a heated warmth through her veins.

With a shuddering breath Josh's chest expanded, and his brow furrowed as if he fought a silent battle with himself. Suddenly he yanked her to him, leaning down to open her mouth with his, to thrust his tongue deep, to wind his hands in her hair. Gardenia blossoms tumbled down as midnight locks fell. Glorying in his kiss, she locked her arms around his neck and stood on tiptoe.

Time vanished; through her thin nightdress she felt Josh's hard thighs, his throbbing shaft, his heated body. Heartbeats joined into hammer blows while tongues slipped together and raging fires erupted. She moaned and clung to him. His strong hands drifted slowly down her back to cup her buttocks, to tilt her hips fully against his.

He raised his head, and torment or anger, an emotion she couldn't fathom, filled his eyes. He whispered, "Good night, love."

His chest heaved with his ragged breathing as he released her and left in swift, angry strides. The door closed with crushing finality.

In shock Lianna stood rooted to the floor, her senses pulsing with desire, with hot flaming need for Josh's kisses and hands and body. Why had he come in to kiss and torment her? Why had he gone so swiftly? Her body yearned for him, but what about her heart? Troubled, she climbed into bed to stare into the darkness and fight the turmoil in her thoughts.

In the middle of the morning, Lianna opened her eyes to see Juanita enter the room. *"Buenos días."* She nodded at Lianna.

"Qué tal?" Lianna answered sleepily, wondering where Madryn was. She usually came in the morning. Juanita's black eyes lowered and she looked at the gardenias and

hairpins strewn over the floor. Lianna blushed as the woman turned to open the drapes.

Madryn entered, greeting Lianna; then she said to Juanita, "I didn't know you were in here."

"I thought I would open the *marquesa's* drapes. The *marqués* has gone. You may finish. I'll clean his room."

Juanita left, and suddenly Lianna wondered if Josh had deliberately kissed her to give him the opportunity to scatter the gardenias across the floor. It was a convincing sign that she had been loved by her husband. Had he done it for a purpose or merely because he wanted to kiss her? And to her disappointment, the first reason seemed the more likely.

Madryn picked up the gardenias. "You had a good time at the ball," she said dreamily.

"Madryn, save a flower for me. One gardenia."

"Of course," Madryn replied as she picked up the white dress and shook it. "How beautiful you looked."

"Thank you."

"My parents announce our engagement tonight."

Lianna came more awake and sat up in bed. "How nice! I must meet him. Tell me where to find Rinaldo."

"At the stables at the end of Avenida Blanco."

"I hope you're happy."

Madryn giggled, so unlike her usual composure that it was infectious, and Lianna laughed. "With Rinaldo I will be in heaven!"

"I hope so." A crushing weight of envy dealt Lianna a blow, and she knotted her fingers in the covers.

Madryn picked up a book, glanced at the cover, and idly read the title aloud.

"You can read?"

"*Sí.* My father taught all his children to read. Tonight we have a party. All my cousins, my parents and grandparents, everyone in both our families will come."

"And what will you wear?"

"I have a dress I've made."

Lianna looked at her white dress and realized if she kept it, each time she looked at it would only serve to make her long for Josh and the brief, happy moments at the ball.

How much better to put it to use where it would bring more happiness, so she said, "You may have mine that I wore last night."

Madryn's eyes widened. "This beautiful dress? Your husband had it made for you."

"I'd like for you to wear it also, if you want."

"Oh, *gracias*!" Madryn picked up the dress to hold it in front of her before the mirror. "*Gracias,* Doña Lita." She became solemn. "I cannot. Your husband will be angry."

"No, he won't. He'll be pleased because it makes you happy. Take it and be happy with Rinaldo." Something constricted around Lianna's heart as she looked at Madryn's glowing eyes. She threw back the covers and stood up. "I'll bathe now," she said, to escape her thoughts.

"Oh, *sí*!" Madryn went back to work to help Lianna dress.

When Lianna went down to breakfast, she was informed that the *marqués* had left for the *estancia.* Disappointment was tempered by relief. She sat down to eat alone. And, as they had promised the night of the ball, young matrons came to call. Lianna found her mornings taken up in stiff, formal visits.

To her dismay, most of the women she met bordered on illiteracy, having been raised with only one purpose in mind—marriage. They knew nothing of politics or literature, but plied Lianna with endless questions about the latest hair and dress styles in Spain, to which she related in detail the latest London fashions.

Invitations came to dinners, which were given to Josh, and the decision to accept or refuse was his.

In the afternoons Lianna shopped and rode in the carriage, enjoying the sights. Occasionally she encountered General Farjado astride his white stallion. Sometimes he would ride beside the carriage, leaning down to chat with her through the open window. On several afternoons she met Josh, who stopped to talk briefly before he would ride away, sitting tall and straight astride a sorrel stallion.

Two weeks after the ball, they attended a dinner given by the Marqués Dantas, where Lianna was seated at a long banquet table between General Farjado and Señor Bucarica, an older retired diplomat. Even though Josh was seated at the opposite end of the table, between two beautiful women, an invisible chain of awareness bound her.

On solid silver plates they were served an elaborate dinner of *centollas,* delicious sea crabs, and turkey *mole* with piquant sauce. As Lianna lowered her fork to comment on the food, General Farjado leaned close.

"The *mole* is made of as many as fifty ground-up ingredients—it can include cloves, cinnamon, aniseed, slivers of bitter chocolate . . ."

"The cooks have been busy."

"Do you like Santiago, my dear?" the man across from her asked.

"*Sí,*" Lianna answered, finding her enjoyment partially dampened by the persistent attention of Captain Fernando Caribe. His watery brown eyes openly studied her and he had plied her with questions, his heavy jowls working as he chewed while he talked.

"I don't know how I've missed seeing you around town."

"I'm home with my husband most of the time." She stressed the word "husband."

"An excellent shot," the general added cheerfully, and Caribe's eyes narrowed.

"You've seen my husband's ability with pistols? I'm surprised he's had occasion to use one."

"There is always an occasion," General Farjado said, then changed the topic. "Have you seen the Church de San Francisco?"

"I've passed it," she answered, relieved to turn from the attention of Captain Caribe. She looked up into brown eyes that flashed with satisfaction.

"Then I must show it to you. You should see the interesting places here with someone who knows the background."

"I think my husband knows the history fairly well."

General Farjado's black eyes twinkled. "*Sí,* to be sure, but your husband is a busy man with many interests— gambling, riding, ranching. And you share him with a most demanding mistress—politics."

"Kindly phrase it another way, general!"

"*Marquesa, perdón!*" He laughed. "I regret my choice of words, but I'm dazzled by your beauty."

"*Gracias*, but also remember, I'm very happily wed."

"And does the lady protest too much?"

She glanced down the length of the table as Josh laughed with a flash of white teeth over something said by the golden-haired woman next to him. If only he would look her way and confirm her statement to General Farjado! And each time she declared her love for Josh, every time she mentioned their happily married state, she felt a rising panic. If she fell in love with her handsome, reckless husband, it would mean misery far beyond any she had experienced before in her life. Misery that would have no end, that would be unbearable, because Josh Raven was a sea-loving pirate and a man of iron. He would neither change, nor bend, nor yield. Nor would he care, and that hurt most of all.

She knew she courted disaster each time she was with him, because every moment together, every contact, forged another link between them. A link that bound her to Josh . . . how tightly?

"Doña Lita," General Farjado said, his voice husky. "What a lovely name you have."

She turned and gazed into black eyes with thick, long lashes. And it occurred to her that if she had more male acquaintances, she might not be so vulnerable where either Josh or Edwin was concerned. She smiled slowly, and something flickered in the black depths of General Farjado's eyes.

"Perhaps you can show me that church after all," she said.

His full lips parted, revealing white teeth as straight as Josh's. "Ah, excellent!" He seemed to think a moment, then asked, "Wednesday afternoon after *siesta?*"

Wednesday Josh would be at their *estancia*. She looked into the waiting black eyes. Did General Farjado know Josh's plans? Josh's warnings rose like mist from a river: "*Beware the general . . . he's a dangerous, evil man.*"

How could viewing a church be dangerous? She smiled.
"That will be a good time."

"Ah, my week has improved vastly!"

After dinner, when the men had joined the ladies, she
stood at Josh's side as several men and women talked. She
was aware of a cold aloofness in one of the men in the
group, Don Alfredo Todaro. Josh was talking about a
horse he had acquired in a recent gambling venture, laughing with Don Jorge Suárez.

"You won my black stallion, but this week, perhaps I
shall win him back."

"Or perhaps I shall win the bay you ride," Josh teased,
a twinkle lighting his eyes.

"You seem to know what you'll win. Perhaps, Don
Jorge, you should watch closely how the cards are played,"
Don Alfredo said.

An instant silence fell on everyone in that part of the
room. Josh's dark brows flew together, and he frowned
while Lianna held her breath.

"I haven't heard a complaint from Don Jorge," Josh
said evenly, and Lianna could feel a slight easing of
tension. The insult had been enough for Josh to call Todaro
out, and she was surprised he had let it go by, but she was
thankful he had.

Todaro smiled thinly. "Perhaps I don't fear to call a
man a cheat if I know he is."

"I think you need to prove what you say," Josh said
quietly, and now the entire room had become silent.

Todaro shrugged. "I can't prove it when I don't gamble
with you."

"Nor can I prove what a liar you are," Josh said, and
turned his back, taking Lianna's arm.

She saw the swift flush that turned Todaro's cheeks pink
and she held her breath as she walked across the room with
Josh.

"Señor . . ."

Josh turned, and Todaro slapped him, his eyes flashing
angrily with an unruly lock of hair curling on his forehead.
"How soon can we meet?"

"Tomorrow morning at sunrise," Josh said coldly. "Pistols." He turned to cross the room to their host to offer apologies for the disruption of the party, and then minutes later they were in the carriage on the way home.

"Josh, you can't fight a duel!"

"I have to. Todaro pushed me into it."

"Why? What have you done to him?"

His head snapped up, and she looked into his angry eyes. "My father, love," he said quietly, his voice tight with anger. "Always, my father. He's determined to get his revenge."

"I don't understand."

"Don Alfredo Todaro is actually Sir Timothy Paddington from London. He's despised me since the first moment I met him, because of my father. He wants this duel; he wants to kill me."

"Oh, Josh!" She threw herself across the carriage to hug him.

"Lianna!" His arms went around her, and he squeezed her while shock at her reaction struck him.

"Josh, I'm so sorry. I don't want you to be killed! Can't we run away to *El Feroz*?"

He laughed and held her away to look at her while he settled her on his lap. "Lianna, love, I have no intention of dying!"

"Then you'll have to kill Don . . . Paddington!"

"I might, but he gave me no choice."

"Oh, Josh!" She threw her arms around his neck and pulled him to her to hold him.

"Lianna?" She heard the question in his voice as he stroked her hair. "You care?"

"Of course I care! I don't want you shot and killed!"

"Someone will get you home if that happens," he said dryly.

"Josh, let's go home now. Let's go before you have to fight this duel."

He pushed her away, tilting his head to stare at her questioningly. "You say you love Edwin Stafford, yet you cling to my neck and beg me to run away."

"I don't want you to die!"

"I have your pity," he said, his voice full of curiosity.

"Yes! And I care for you."

"And you care for me?"

"Of course I do!"

"Lianna, this might be my last night on earth," he said, watching her intently. What the hell did she feel for him? She was hanging on his neck and pleading with him to run from danger, yet in the next breath she could be telling him how much she loved Stafford! Josh wondered if she knew what she truly wanted. She had been young and sheltered and he had swiftly forced her into bed and marriage. Perhaps she wasn't as certain about Edwin as she acted. He stared at her in momentary curiosity. Fair or foul, she was on his lap and in his arms, and he faced a duel with the dawn. This was one night he intended to take Lianna to his bed and not question motives. For tonight, he would settle for her body. Her blue eyes widened endlessly as she looked at him, and she caught her lower lip in her teeth. Tears sparked her eyes, and if he hadn't known all too well that the Englishman had her love, he would think he might be winning her heart.

"Josh," she whispered, stroking his cheek.

He kissed her throat. Now that he had made the decision to possess her, all the heated desire he usually fought so hard to ignore burst into scorching flames. "Lianna," he murmured huskily. "Love me tonight. Paddington is a deadly shot."

She cried out and stroked him, showering kisses on his throat. He trailed his lips to the softness of her breasts while his hands sought her flesh beneath her skirt. She gasped and softly moaned as he stroked her.

The carriage rolled to a halt, and he climbed out, pulling her into his arms to carry her inside. He dismissed the servants except Fletcher. He asked Fletcher to go to Don Gerado Davio and ask if he would be a second for him in a duel at dawn. Then Josh carried Lianna upstairs to his bedroom.

Her pulse pounded while protests fled at the thought that he might be killed at dawn. She didn't want Josh to die in a duel, and she stroked his chest as he set her on her feet. Looking into his eyes, she felt a blast of heat as if she had

looked directly into the summer sun. His gaze drifted
down, and every nerve quivered in anticipation.

"Lianna, a duel will be worth this," he whispered, and
slowly began to unfasten the tiny rows of buttons that ran
down the front of her bodice.

As he peeled away her dress and chemise, she forgot the
duel. She trembled and gazed at him through half-closed
eyes while her hands pushed at his clothing. He slipped off
the evening clothes, dropping the cravat carelessly on the
floor, the shirt following, and Lianna was lost as he began
to kiss her slowly, temptingly, moving over every inch of
flesh.

"I'm going to make you cry my name over and over,"
he said in a slow, heated drawl while she wound her
fingers in the silky thickness of his hair.

He picked her up to carry her to bed, and Lianna's heart
drummed violently as he stood over her, his eyes devouring her until he put his knee on the bed and his weight
came down beside her.

Lianna stirred, murmuring Josh's name and turning to
run her hands sleepily across the bed. "Josh, love . . ."
Her eyes flew open as she remembered. She sat up, gazing
around the dusky room. Josh was gone.

She threw aside the covers and tugged the bell-pull to
summon Madryn, asking her to send word to ready a
carriage and then come back to help her dress. Madryn
rode with Lianna only moments later as the carriage careened down the road. Lianna sat stiffly in the corner, her
eyes closed while she prayed for Josh's life.

22

Josh rode in the carriage in silence, listening as Lord Brenthaven swore steadily in a flat voice. "Damn the man! He hasn't the wits of a flea! We need each bit of help we can get, not to kill each other off before the fighting commences! The bastard has pudding for brains."

"I tried to avoid this."

"Dammit, I know you did. I wanted to slap the bloody fool's face." He paused, and his voice dropped. "He's supposed to be a good shot. He's fought several duels."

"I know. I don't intend to die. Nor do I want to kill him. I have no deep quarrel with Paddington. It's my father's hatred that's caused the trouble. Whatever the outcome, it would make my father laugh. He's a damnably cruel man."

"I know him. I can understand why you ran away."

Josh looked at Lord Brenthaven, who stared back stonily. "I hate to lose Paddington, but I hope you win. We need cooler heads than his for the coming battles."

"He's young."

"He's a childish popinjay!"

Josh laughed, momentarily gazing out at the mists rising off the fields, thinking of Lianna and the raptures of the night. If it were his last night, it had been worth every moment. How she had clung to him! He thought of her wild abandon and felt a swift renewal of desire. He forced his thoughts elsewhere, knowing he had to have a cool head for the next hour.

When they stopped at the edge of a grove of trees, he climbed out. In moments Paddington's carriage came into the clearing, and he stepped down.

As Paddington crossed the open space to them, Lord Brenthaven snapped, "You damned fool!"

"I didn't think I'd find you here as second," Timothy said coldly.

"You have, and you'd better lower your voice. We may not be surrounded by friends! You fool, don't you know we need every man?"

Timothy's cold blue eyes looked with haughty disdain at Josh. "We need every reliable man. We don't need a dishonorable pirate who's shut out of every club in London for his thefts!"

"Dammit!" Lord Brenthaven snapped, and Josh put his hand on his arm.

"Let's get this done and over," Josh said.

"Say your final prayers, rogue!" Timothy snapped, and walked away.

Josh patted Lord Brenthaven's arm and said, "He's young and foolhardy. There's nothing you can do now."

"I know. Kill him before he can harm you. I need a man with intelligence to help me. I'll see to the pistols." He left to join Paddington's second. As he walked away, another carriage emerged from the trees and halted. When the door flung open, Lianna stepped out, pulling her cape close around her.

"What're you doing here?" Josh asked, feeling his breath catch. Momentarily he remembered the night, and his parting this morning while Lianna lay in bed.

"I had to come. I wish there were some way to avoid this."

"Get in the carriage." He leaned down. "If I don't survive, Fletcher has instructions. He'll go with you right now to get you back to *El Feroz* and England."

"Josh!" She sounded stricken, and his heart pounded violently. She stood on tiptoe to kiss him on the mouth, her tongue thrusting into his mouth, startling him with her reaction. His arms tightened around her, and he kissed her for long moments. He wanted her desperately. Finally he remembered the occasion and released her, looking down at her dazed expression. "Last night was heaven, Lianna . . ."

He turned quickly, striding back to find the men waiting for him. He walked to the center and picked up his pistol as he looked at Timothy Paddington; then they turned their backs to each other and listened to the count as they stepped off the long distance.

"Turn and fire!"

The call finally came, and Josh whipped around as Timothy turned and raised his pistol to fire at him.

Josh yanked his pistol up and fired, blasting the pistol out of Paddington's hand.

It was over. Paddington snatched up his injured hand and looked at Josh, who could have reloaded and killed him if he had wanted to do so. Lianna ran to Josh to fling her arms around his neck and cling to him with relief.

He held her, kissing her temple, thinking about the night that was ended. With his survival, would her thoughts turn once again to Edwin? He watched Lord Brenthaven approach, and talked to him over Lianna's head. "I want to take my wife home," he said, the words ringing in his heart in an echo. His wife—how he wished she truly loved him!

"I'm sorry. Remember, we're moving the cannon today from your ship to Santiago, and we'll hide it in town until we can move it to the mountains. We need you to ride to the coast with us."

"Give me an hour."

Lord Brenthaven clamped his hand on Josh's shoulder. "You should've killed the stupid pup, but I'm glad you didn't. He may have learned a lesson today. Thank God, you survived!"

"Thank you. I truly thank you for being my second." As he looked into Reginald's eyes and saw only friendship and approval, Josh felt a swift rush of warmth. Perhaps he would win a few of them over! It would be worth every hint of danger, every threat, to overcome the hatred of his father.

He wrapped his arms around Lianna and led her to his carriage.

Inside, he pulled her onto his lap, and in the warmth of the carriage, as reaction to the past hour, the memories of the night stirred Josh to passion. In moments he had her clinging to him as he turned her beneath him on the carriage seat and took her swiftly and passionately.

Within the hour he kissed her good-bye and left her to meet Lord Brenthaven. Lianna listened to his fading footsteps as he went down the hall, and her heart beat with warmth and relief that he had survived the duel. Beyond that, she wouldn't search her feelings.

Two days later, Lianna summoned the carriage and rode to the stables on Avenida Blanco, where she halted the carriage. A bronzed young man, shorter than Josh but with broad shoulders and powerful muscles, worked over an anvil. When her carriage halted, he straightened, wiped his hands, and approached. Lianna leaned out the window.

"*Buenos días.* Are you Rinaldo Sepulveda? I'm the Marquesa de Aveiro."

White teeth showed against Rinaldo's brown skin as he smiled broadly. "Marquesa, Madryn has told me about you. She gave me a picture you drew of her."

While they chatted, hoofbeats approached. Lianna's smile widened the moment she saw Josh astride his horse. Dressed in a brown leather coat and breeches, a broad-brimmed Spanish hat low over his eyes, he drew rein beside the carriage and smiled down at her.

As soon as Josh had been introduced, the men talked. Lianna's attention was barely on the conversation; she was far too aware of her husband. His horse stood near the carriage, and it was impossible to ignore him. Lianna waged an inner struggle with her emotions, aware that her feelings for Josh were intensifying every day. As Rinaldo and Josh talked, a crowd gathered down the street, where shouts and laughter rang out.

"What's happening?" Lianna asked, noticing the commotion.

"I'll ride down to see," Josh said.

"Take me with you," she said on impulse, and opened the carriage door.

Laughing, Josh looked down at her. "You have a devilish taste for adventure, Lianna!"

She smiled, feeling lighthearted. He swung her up on his horse and held her close in front of him. "We'll make tongues wag today."

"I don't care. It's a beautiful day, and I'd like some excitement. Let's see what the laughter is about."

"How happy you sound!" With a long, searching stare that made her momentarily forget everything else, he looked at her, and they both smiled. Near the square the noise grew louder. A crowd had gathered in front of a building where the flag of Spain was displayed prominently over the door.

A small brown monkey swung from the pole, tugging on the flag. The flagpole jiggled; then the flag was scooped up and thrown over the pole, to wrap around it.

The crowd cheered the monkey on, applauding and laughing at his antics in twisting the flag of Spain into a turban while he danced on the pole.

"Josh, look at him! What a funny little fellow."

Josh rode toward the group, but as they approached, he suddenly turned his horse around.

"Wait—"

"Look, Lianna, soldiers," he said tersely. For the first time, she noticed soldiers approaching from the opposite direction.

"There's General Farjado," Lianna said. As she watched, the general draw his pistol, and a cold realization dawned on her. "They're after the monkey." She wriggled free and slipped down.

"Lianna!" Josh snapped.

Paying no heed, she hurried forward as General Farjado called commands and a soldier raised his pistol. Those in the crowd who had become aware of the soldiers and the general stepped back; some turned to go.

Lianna pushed past a cluster of people and started to call to the general. Her breath was crushed out in a gasp. Josh's arms locked around her violently, and he swept her up before him. "Hush, Lianna. You'll endanger us."

"But they'll shoot the little beast. He means no harm."

"The monkey is destroying the flag of Spain, and the crowd loves it. Soldiers won't stop if you call—or if they do, the general will wonder about your loyalty. Don't look—"

"We can't abandon a simple animal! I don't care!"

Josh wheeled the horse, his arm locking around her waist until her head swam and blackness threatened. She struggled to break free as they rounded a corner. He relaxed his grip, and her breath returned in gulps.

"It's only a monkey—and we would risk a multitude of lives if we interfere. I'm sorry."

A shot rang out; screams were heard. Josh urged the horse forward. "We have to get out of here!"

Another shot was heard, and Lianna clung to his arm. When they reached the carriage, Josh tied his horse to the back and told the driver to start home. He swung Lianna inside and climbed in to ride with her.

She was ashamed of her reaction. "I know it was only a monkey, but it seemed so unnecessary. I didn't think about endangering you or others."

"I've dealt with men like this before, Lianna."

They rode in silence, and she became aware of his glances, his knee lightly touching hers—and she exchanged one hurt for another. He was home so seldom now, she barely saw him, and she missed him with an ache that was intense. And she attributed it to being alone, so far from Wiltshire and all she had always known.

When they reached home, Josh alighted to help her out. Within seconds after she reached her room, the door opened from Josh's rooms. He stood in the doorway holding a pistol in his hand. He motioned with his head. "Come here."

Startled, she crossed the room. He lowered his voice. "I think it's time I showed you how to use a pistol. I'm gone too often; you may need to protect yourself. As soon as possible, I'll take you out to let you practice. Let me show you how to load this."

They went into his room, where a rod and powder lay on the desk. She listened, watching his hands move competently. He gave her another pistol and waited while she did as he instructed.

"Don't hesitate if you have to do something to protect yourself," he said grimly. "If anything should happen when I'm gone, any of my men will take you to the coast. I'll leave these pistols in the trunk. I have others."

"I don't think I could shoot someone," she said.

His mouth curled in a sardonic grin. "Pretend it's me, love."

She looked up sharply. "You think I hate you, Josh?"

His brows arched, and the gentle rise and fall of his chest stopped.

"You have a right to, Lianna," he said quietly. "I shouldn't have forced the marriage. There are grounds, so we can have it annulled when we reach England. Then your life can go on as before."

"With one great change," she said.

"If Edwin loves you, your virginity won't matter."

She bit her lip, watching him, wanting to shout that that wasn't the great change, but she held her silence, wondering how strongly he wanted out of the marriage.

"I regret bringing you into this danger. I was so—" He bit off the words. "Use this gun if necessary. Take care," he murmured, brushing her cheek with his lips as he left in long strides.

As soon as she was alone in her room, she sat down by the window and gazed out the front at the wide tree-shaded street. It looked so peaceful, yet not far away, soldiers had murdered a monkey because it had played with a bit of cloth. What evil undercurrents ran through a place that appeared so calm on the surface? She shivered and felt cold. Josh Raven, again mounted on his horse, rode into view, leaving to go down the street.

She looked at his straight back, the breadth of his shoulders. Would he sacrifice her as easily if a choice had to be made to save his cause?

Lianna didn't see Josh again that day or night, and learned he had gone to their *estancia*. As Wednesday approached she was torn by conflicting emotions, but fi-

nally the time came and she went downstairs to meet
General Farjado. Dressed in black lace with a mantilla on
her head, she entered the salon to find him waiting. His
black eyes flashed with admiration, and he smiled. The
green uniform set off his swarthy skin, his handsome
features.

"How beautiful you are!" He took her hand to kiss her
fingers. "And how fortunate I am for a few hours."

"Thank you." She smiled. "Perhaps next time Don
Cristóbal will be here to go with us."

He smiled. "Perhaps—and perhaps not. I prefer it this
way. Just you and I, Doña Lita."

"You make me regret my decision to go."

"Never! Come, let me show you the sights of Santiago."

He took her arm and they left to climb into his elegant
carriage, and she waited to feel that swift current of excitement she always felt around Josh. From the first moment
Josh Raven had opened his cabin door, every encounter
had stirred dazzling responses. His slightest touch made
her breathing alter. She willed the same with General
Farjado—heaven knows, the man was handsome by all
standards. As if seeking what she found with Josh in
another man, she moved her hand so that it brushed General Farjado's arm. He turned and smiled, but she felt
nothing. Absolutely nothing.

When they emerged from the carriage, they entered the
Italian Renaissance church, stepping through the heavy
doors into a cool, darkened interior.

With each step she took, the skirt of Lianna's black
dress rustled in the silent church. Beside her, General
Farjado's boots were loud on the stone floor.

"This church was started in 1568, but not completed
until years later. See the statue there on the altar—it was
brought to the New World by Don Pedro de Valdivia."

As Lianna studied the small carved wooden statue, a
shaft of sunlight came through the high stained-glass window, giving a warmth to her cheeks. She turned and
caught the general's gaze on her, an undeniable flame in
the depths of his black eyes. He took her arm to stroll to
the cloister to point out certain pictures, and again she

hoped he would stir some flicker of response, but there was nothing.

Later, when they had returned home, he said, "Tomorrow we'll ride up Santa Lucia hill."

"I shouldn't go out again . . ."

"Oh, but you will. It's better than sitting home with your sewing. I'll call at the same time." He turned to go without waiting for an answer from her. Lianna watched him climb into his carriage, regretting the day. All it had done was confirm her fears.

Josh stayed at the *estancia*, and as the days passed, General Farjado's visits came with regularity.

23

Dockside in London, Edwin paused on the deck of the *Adrian*. "We made it," a deep voice said at his elbow, and he turned to nod at Steedham. Edwin's gaze swept the ship, the broken mainmast and tattered sails, the splintered and burned deck. "But I don't know how," Steedham added.

"More than the first half of the journey was smooth as a windless sea," Edwin said. "I thought it would all be easy."

"Can't count on anything at sea," Steedham said.

Edwin thought about their days sailing toward the islands, where they had crossed paths with a Dutch ship. This one was not old and weighted with cargo, but a fighter that had almost blasted them out of the sea. They had turned back for England, and then had run afoul of a storm. The storm wreaked its own havoc and the surviving crew was down to twenty men. One night when they were at the height of the gale, Edwin had thought his life was over as waves crashed over the ship. Remembering the howling wind and freezing water, he recalled the moment he had encountered Captain Turner as they both had clung to starboard lifelines.

In the darkness on the wind-tossed ship, Edwin had seen his chance and shoved Captain Turner into the foaming sea. Remembering the swift decision, he clenched his fists, dismissing fleeting regrets.

Before that night was over they were down to nine men

and no captain. Of the nine, four were as new to sailing as Edwin. Edwin had proclaimed himself captain, saying he had as much right as any of them, and if anyone wanted to challenge him, he would meet the challenge.

After his announcement, the seconds he'd waited had been the longest in his life. Once again he had felt as if his life hung in the balance, and when they nodded their heads in agreement, a flare of satisfaction went to his soul. And he had learned an unforgettable lesson—to the bold belong the spoils.

"Damned ship's a wreck. Most of the cargo is gone, the ship's barely afloat . . ." Edwin said.

"You're going to fix her?"

"I'll see what I can do," he said, despising the small molelike Steedham, who had immediately tried to become friends with Edwin when he had taken over the *Adrian*.

Edwin suspected the main reason the men hadn't threatened him as captain was simply that they hadn't expected to get safely into port and didn't want to risk their lives over a hopelessly battered ship. It was no longer seaworthy and would take more than all of them had gained to attempt to repair it.

The moment they had docked in London, three of the sailors disappeared from the ship, and Edwin knew they wouldn't return.

Nor did he care. He had his own plans. "I'll be back in two days," he said, knowing the men might see to it that he was no longer captain if he returned.

Carefully retrieving his hoard of gold from the successful ventures, he packed. The moment he left the ship, the first thing he did was to find lodgings at a comfortable inn. Next he went to see a tailor to be fitted and order clothes.

Then he sought out a fencing instructor. He faced Monsieur Toussaint, a thin, dark-eyed Frenchman. Plunking down his money, Edwin said, "I want lessons. I don't have long between voyages, so make the lessons twice a day."

The wiry Frenchman looked at him and smiled. "Would you like to begin now?"

"Yes," Edwin said, and shed his coat, following the

man to the large room where an array of weapons were displayed along one wall.

By the next week he had learned what he wanted to know about Santiago, Chile, and what man to contact in London. And at midmorning several days later, he sat in a comfortable chair in the corner of a London club while he faced a white-haired man who watched him with curiosity in his pale gray eyes.

"I've heard about the Laturo Lodge and your interests in Santiago, Chile. I've come to offer my services as a mercenary."

Lord Quimby smiled. "You're very young to be a mercenary soldier. And while I'm deeply interested in the Chilean revolution, all our fellow countrymen have been volunteers."

"That doesn't mean a mercenary won't fight just as hard."

"Of course not."

Edwin sipped the hot tea from a fine china cup and forced himself to relax, to take his time. He'd studied Lord Quimby well before approaching him. He knew Lord Quimby's interests were in creating further markets of trade for his ships. He was wealthy, with a fleet of ships and an adventuring nature that was hampered now by age and his wife's health.

Edwin gazed beyond Lord Quimby at the green fronds of a potted palm that partially hid them from the view of other men in the room.

"What could you do for us in Santiago?"

"I could take a ship filled with arms and supplies. Once there, you have men working toward the revolution. I could do what the patriots need. I could bring back whatever you want me to carry—men, supplies, cargo."

"You make me wish I were going myself. Once you develop a taste for far-off places, it's damned difficult to get it out of your system."

"Yes, sir."

"What's your background, Mr. Stafford?"

"I worked on a farm for Squire Melton in Wiltshire."

"Oh, yes. I knew him because of his ships. He's dead now, isn't he?"

"Yes. I was a groomsman," Edwin said, and noted with satisfaction the brief, flickering glance Lord Quimby gave his clothing. Edwin felt comfortable with the elegant fawn breeches, the tailored dark blue coat, and the white silk cravat. His clothes weren't a groomsman's clothes, and the fact had to be quite obvious to Lord Quimby. Edwin continued calmly, "I left him in the winter of 1816 to sail on the *Adrian,* a privateering vessel. I'm now the ship's captain."

Lord Quimby's stare gave Edwin another flare of satisfaction, this time greater than before, because shock was evident in Lord Quimby's features.

"Captain? That's remarkable!"

"Yes, sir. I feel fortunate, although my good fortune was at the expense of my fellow seamen. As you well know, the sea can be very unpredictable. We were engaged in battle and fared poorly, then hit a gale. There weren't many of us who survived to bring the ship home, but I was one of the survivors and I was made captain."

Lord Quimby stared at Edwin, who gazed back with a faint smile. Lord Quimby's gaze dropped, and he sipped his tea. "What ship did you say you command?" he asked politely.

"The *Adrian.* You can see her dockside."

"Why would you leave your own ship and fight in Santiago?"

"The *Adrian* is a wreck. We were fortunate to get her into port. She won't sail again."

"Ah!" Lord Quimby nodded as if Edwin's answer had settled some question in his mind. "How much would you want to earn to fight in Santiago?"

Edwin placed his teacup carefully on the tray in front of them, sat back, and said, "When I'm through, I want my own ship."

"So that's the prize! You're a captain without a ship. Do you think with your brief experience at sea you could get a ship around Cape Horn?"

"If I had the right crew, yes, your lordship, I think I could."

Lord Quimby smiled. "You're a daring one, Edwin Stafford. I'll give the matter thought. Where can I contact you?"

"I'm at the King's Inn until I sail. Thank you, Lord Quimby, for giving me your time. I hope we can work together."

They stood up and shook hands and Edwin left, his glance going over the tasteful furnishings that made him hunger for the things he wanted. He couldn't tell if he'd made any dent on the crusty old man, and now he'd just have to wait and hope. He stepped outside into a chilly fog, putting on his beaver hat as he headed back to the inn to change clothes for his fencing lesson.

He kept busy, his nerves growing raw as a week passed without word of any kind from Lord Quimby. Edwin cursed the man for his slowness in replying. He fought the fencing master with a fury that made the Frenchman swear and exclaim on Edwin's mastery.

"More finesse!" he cried once as Edwin sent a rapier flying from the his hands. "You go at it as if you wanted to murder me and everyone else in London! Use some grace."

Edwin laughed. "To hell with grace! I want to be able to fight with the best of them."

"You will, m'sieur! *Sacrebleu!*"

Whenever he remembered the shipboard encounter with Josh Raven, Edwin burned with embarrassment. How swiftly Josh had disarmed him, and could have run him through if he'd been so inclined. Instead, he'd sent him scrambling from the ship and raging with the knowledge that Raven had wed Lianna.

Edwin would have given her up if he hadn't seen her rush toward him and heard her scream his name. Whatever kind of marriage she was bound in, it was not her choosing and she didn't love Joshua Raven. And in a revolution it would be just as easy to be rid of Raven as it had been to eliminate Captain Turner. Perhaps easier.

Edwin slashed the rapier through the air. How he longed

to meet Josh Raven again. This time he wouldn't be a
green lubber who didn't know how to handle a sword! And
afterward Lianna . . .

His mind jumped to contemplation of the fortune waiting for her to claim at home in Wiltshire. There was the
prize! -

After his lesson, he picked up his coat and entered the
anteroom, where he passed Lord Gwyn, an aging man who
came for the exercise of fencing and left his young wife
waiting. His bored, beautiful young wife who was more
than happy to spend an hour talking with Edwin. Harriet
Gwyn gave more than subtle hints about the nights she
would be alone while her husband was gone to the club,
but Edwin didn't want anything to turn Lord Quimby aside
and carefully avoided agreeing to come visit her, yet he
also tried to appear deeply regretful. The moment he got
the word from Lord Quimby, whether yes or no, Edwin
intended to sample the delights so visibly promised in
Harriet's dark, flirtatious eyes, her pouting red lips, and
her high, full white bosom.

He left before Lord Gwyn was finished, and as he
stepped outside, a man moved away from a waiting carriage and approached him. "Mr. Stafford?"

"Yes? I'm Edwin Stafford."

"Lord Quimby sends a message. Would you be able to
meet him at his club tomorrow morning at eleven o'clock?"

"Yes, of course. I'll be there," he answered, eager to
finally get an answer. He spent a restless, sleepless night
after tumbling a wench from the inn. Lord Quimby had
made his decision, and Edwin's nerves were on edge with
the suspense of waiting and worrying.

The next morning Edwin was there promptly on time,
this time wearing his second new pair of breeches, dark
blue, with the dark blue coat. He greeted Lord Quimby,
who introduced him to a dark-eyed, dark-skinned man
named Vicente Garansuay, and the three sat down to talk.

At Belém along the Brazilian coast, a Spanish ship lay
at anchor in the estuary of the Amazon River. Lush green
mangoes crowded down to the sluggish, muddy river's

edge and parrots squawked, their raucous cries starting
early in the day, while small brown monkeys scampered in
the treetops. Inside *La Lia*, the Count of Marcheno's ship,
in a large cabin given over to the owner and his wife,
Quita stepped out of bed to dress. She paused in front of
the long mirror fastened securely to the bulkhead and
pulled off her gown to look at her body. She was slender
as a young tree and she suffered a sense of panic that came
more and more often.

Armando and she had been wed more than seven months
now and still she was without child. And she knew the
situation was beginning to disturb Armando.

She had seen him studying her figure with smoldering
looks. There were moments when he made love to her, his
thrusts hard and frenzied as if he would force her to
become impregnated with his seed. And his disposition
sometimes was cross. It was seldom, and he apologized
swiftly, but she knew what was worrying him. Another
birthday approached and he would be forty-two and she
knew he wanted an heir desperately.

And she wanted one equally desperately. They sailed for
Santiago, Chile, and Quita was fearful of crossing paths
with Lianna. Constantly she prayed that her note had been
delivered to *El Feroz* and that Lianna had returned home to
marry Edwin Stafford. But she couldn't rid herself of the
fear that the boy might not have delivered the message. Or
Captain Raven might not have let Lianna go. And Armando
had told her that Francisco had written there might be
rebellion from the Chileans, and thus an immense loss of
gold and wealth to Spain. If there were to be a fight,
Armando wouldn't run from it, and she feared for him and
their future.

A more immediate fear gnawed at her. They had been at
anchor at Belém for three weeks now. Armando liked the
river and the hunting, the wildness of the area. And last
week while he had been hunting animals she couldn't
describe, she had visited the village, where she had learned
of the magic practiced near there, a mixture of beliefs that
included sorcery.

Carrying a bolt of material Quita had asked for, Yolana entered.

"Has Don Armando left the ship?"

"*Sí.* The men left an hour ago. They've gone upriver."

Quita pulled on her robe and belted it around her waist. "Help me dress and come with me today."

Yolana nodded, her black eyes wide and round, and Quita knew she was afraid. Quita felt equally afraid, but she was willing to try anything to provide Armando with a son.

"Doña—"

"Yolana," Quita interrupted firmly, too aware of the maid's fear, "I need you!"

"*Sí.* I will go."

Two hours later, as the sun rose high in the sky over the village of Belém, Quita and Yolana followed a native woman, Maria, down to the river, where they sat in the rough-hewn log canoe. A man pushed them away from shore and rowed silently.

They branched off on a narrow tributary, and overhead, interwoven branches shut out the sunlight. Shrill bird cries, the screech of monkeys, and the steady dipping splash of the paddle were the only sounds. Quita watched as a snake as large as Armando's arm slithered into the water and began to swim, leaving a forking wave of ripples in its wake.

The tributary narrowed swiftly, and the canoe glided silently in chocolate waters. Quita looked down at the rush of the brown water slipping past and shivered, wondering what was below its murky surface. Momentarily she wished she were back safe on board Armando's ship, but with a lift of her chin, she knew it was too late to turn back now.

They landed and followed João and Maria down a narrow path. In moments the sound of a drum came and they reached a clearing. Chickens were in a yard in front of a house built of wood and palm fronds. A young boy, his black skin shiny with perspiration, sat with a drum between his knees; his eyes were half-closed as he thumped a steady rhythm.

They were motioned to wait on the porch, then in

seconds ushered into the house. Smells of food and something sweet assailed Quita and she thought of her home in La Coruña. Yet at the same time, this was different, with other, unidentifiable odors. While João remained on the porch, Quita, Maria, and Yolana were led to a dark windowless back room that was stifling in the heat. Several women were seated cross-legged on the floor and stared at Quita with round black eyes.

Quita felt perspiration bead her brow, and the muslin clothing began to cling to her body. Growing louder, the steady drumbeat reminded her of a heartbeat, until it felt like her own throbbing pulse. The women in the room chanted in a low, steady monotone that became as overwhelming as the heat in the air.

At one end of the narrow room a woman sat on a chair on a platform. Quita had heard about her in the village and knew she was called Mama Iriri. Her dress and turban were white and she wore shells around her neck. She motioned them forward, then pointed at Quita to come closer.

Quita couldn't understand Mama Iriri's words, but she knew what the motions meant. She moved closer and the woman stood up to gaze down at her, holding her chin in her hand.

"You want baby?" Mama Iriri asked in Portuguese, but Quita understood.

She nodded. "Yes, badly."

A harsh word was spoken in Portuguese, yet was enough like Spanish that Quita knew she was to remain silent. The women's chanting grew louder, the heat became more oppressive, the air was cloyingly sweet, all combining to make Quita feel faint. A jar was passed, each woman raising it to her lips to drink. Quita took it when they thrust it into her hands and took a sip of something sweet, yet afterward it left a faintly bitter taste in her mouth.

Mama Iriri moved to a chest and removed something, holding it in her fist. She closed her eyes and chanted unintelligible words, then shook her head.

Cowrie shells fell at Quita's feet and Mama Iriri knelt to

poke at them. She looked up at Quita. "You will have a child."

Quita swayed, wishing the words could be true. Mama Iriri stood up and waved her hand, and Quita heard a rustling behind her, but she didn't look around. The chanting rose in volume, and the drumbeat increased its tempo. Two women moved beside Quita and began to unfasten her clothing until she stood naked.

Mama Iriri got something out of the chest and began to sprinkle a powder on Quita's body, murmuring incantations.

Quita felt the perspiration run in rivulets between her breasts, felt the faint, light sprinkling of the powder as she watched through half-closed eyes. The drums and chanting wove a spell around her.

Mama Iriri tilted her chin up. "Your man's name is . . . ?"

"Armando Marcheno."

"Armando, Armando . . ." Everyone began to chant it softly while Mama Iriri produced a jar of ointment and rubbed it on Quita's belly.

Then two women worked swiftly, helping her to dress again while Mama Iriri pulled a small bag out of the chest and thrust it into Quita's hand, murmuring, "Sprinkle on your bed tonight. You need strong gris-gris." She gave Quita a shell necklace. "Wear this."

Next she moved to the chest and came back with another bag she put in Quita's hands. "Bathe with this." She stepped down off the platform to look into Quita's eyes, and Quita felt caught, as if in a web, by large black eyes.

"Do you love him?"

"Yes, very much."

"Love him, daughter. Love your man with your heart and body."

Hands turned her, and Quita was led out of the room. The chanting and drumbeat stopped while they walked out in silence to follow João back to the canoe and glide swiftly downriver.

Quita felt as if the past hour had been unreal, as unreal as her surroundings seemed. She saw an animal that looked like a small coarse-haired pig come to the river to drink. A giant butterfly with wide yellow wings dipped in a lazy spiral over the river, and her senses seemed to be in a similar giddy swirl.

Once she was back on board ship, she stayed alone in the quiet cabin for a long time, thinking about all that had happened; then she summoned Yolana to help her get ready for Armando's return.

She bathed in water as hot as she could stand, emptying part of the contents of the bag and smelling a sweet, heady odor as it spread across the top of the water.

As soon as she had finished bathing, she dressed in a red satin gown that Armando had given her, wrapping herself in a red silk robe while she waited for him.

He had sent word he would join her in time for dinner, but Quita had asked the galley to leave them undisturbed until summoned.

She waited, then felt her heart skip as Armando came in.

His black hair curled damply against his head as if he had just bathed, and he wore an unlaced white shirt and tight black breeches. He carried a bright red blossom in his hand, and his eyes lighted with delight as he looked at her.

"Lia, what a surprise!"

"I've missed you," she said, going to him to twine her arms around his neck.

"I picked the right flower," he murmured, tucking the red blossom behind her ear. He kissed her long and hard, his hands pushing away the silk robe and roaming over her body.

"Lia, how beautiful you look." He swung her up in his arms and crossed to the bed, which was turned down. He started to lower her, then straightened. "What the devil?"

He stood her on her feet and brushed his hand over the bed, coming up with white powder coating his palm. "There's something all over the damned bed."

"Armando, ignore it," she whispered, pulling his hand as she put her knee on the bed.

"No! I don't want to roll in powder!"

"Armando . . ." She began to fear his anger. "I put it there."

He turned around to stare at her. "You did? What is it?"

"I went to a woman in the village. They say she has magic. I want your baby."

Suddenly he threw back his head and laughed. "Lia, my foolish love! That's nonsense! And I'm not going to kiss that damnable powder off your body!" His eyes narrowed and he reached out to pick up the shell necklace, his knuckles resting on her collarbone. "Did she give you this?"

"Yes."

He yanked it off, spilling shells over the floor.

"Armando!"

"Let me show you . . ." He dropped down on the floor and stretched out, pulling her down with him. "This will get us a baby more quickly than flouncing around in dust!" He pushed a thin red strap off her shoulder.

"Wait, Armando," she whispered, remembering the words *"Love your man with your heart and body . . ."*

"Let me tonight," she whispered, and knelt beside him to stroke him with her hands. "Let me love you," she said, standing up and slipping off the red gown before she knelt beside him again, watching fires ignite in the depths of his black eyes. She waved her hand in front of her breasts. "See what you do to me by a mere look. . . ."

24

In Santiago, as the weeks passed, Lianna saw less and less of Josh, who was busy night and day. One night as he returned home, looking forward to seeing Lianna and hoping she was still awake, he was met at the door by Fletcher. "A man waits in the library, sir. Elias Reyes, a servant of Don Gerado Davio."

Josh crossed the hall swiftly to enter the library. A man stood by the window and turned, waiting until Josh had closed the door before he spoke.

"I brought a message from Don Gerado," Reyes said swiftly, crossing the room to speak in a low voice. "They are moving the cannon tonight from Santiago to the mountains. Don Gerardo had planned to supervise, with Alfredo Todaro assisting, but this afternoon Don Gerado was issued an invitation to dine with the governor. Can you go in his place? He said it was urgent or he wouldn't ask."

"Of course. When?"

"Can you come with me now? We'll join them."

"Yes," Josh said, trying to keep a note of weariness out of his voice. He had barely been with Lianna for endless weeks now. He knew she was seeing more and more of General Farjado. He didn't think her interests could be stirred by the man, yet it grated on his nerves to think of her continually in Farjado's company. And he wondered if she knew what danger she was in and what a risk she ran associating with the Spaniard.

"Is there a way to leave other than by the front?"

"Yes, this way," Josh said, wondering if he could work several hours alongside Paddington without the man starting another fight. Brenthaven had carefully kept them apart on assignments, but they were continually thrown together at social functions, coolly ignoring each other, although Timothy Paddington made no effort to hide the hatred in his eyes.

Josh and Reyes rode to the stable where the cannon had been hidden. Inside the stable, Rinaldo Sepulveda came forward to greet them.

"They just took one cannon and are moving down the lane. If one of you will ride after them, we need one of you here to help us with the next cannon."

"I'll catch them," Josh said, and turned his horse, leaving Rinaldo giving instruction to Reyes. He moved in the shadows, letting the horse walk.

Suddenly he heard a spate of loud Spanish and then a muffled cry. He slipped off the horse and ran alongside a wall, pausing at the corner as he listened to sounds of a scuffle.

He leaned around to see a straw-covered horse-drawn cart. A man was slumped in the street, a knife protruding from his back. Two men fought, and as they tumbled to the ground, Josh recognized the pale hair of Lord Paddington.

A Spanish soldier had him by the throat, choking him and banging his head on the ground. Josh reached into his boot to withdraw his dagger and ran across the road swiftly and as quietly as possible. Without hesitation, using all his force, he drove the knife into the back of the Spanish soldier. The man collapsed at Josh's feet.

He pushed the soldier away and pulled Timothy to his feet. Timothy gagged and coughed, leaning on the cart while Josh hoisted the body of the slain patriot onto the cart.

He pulled his dagger out of the Spaniard and swiftly took the man's valuables, tossing them into the cart. "If I take his things, maybe his murder will seem to be because of theft. Get into the cart and pull the straw over you. I'll get us out of here."

He caught Timothy's horse and tied it and his own to

the back of the cart, then climbed up to drive the team of horses. The cart was old and creaking, and Josh's nerves became raw as they moved slowly along. If a Spanish soldier were to stop them, it would be imprisonment, because Josh couldn't hide the contents of the cart. And only blocks away behind him lay a dead Spaniard. How long before the body would be discovered and a search begun?

They left Santiago without mishap. They had picked a dark night with a sliver of a moon, but Josh felt as if a hundred eyes watched him as they wound across the plain to the mountains. He heard a rustling of straw, and Timothy Paddington climbed to the seat beside him.

After a moment of silence Timothy said, "Thank you, Captain Raven."

"We're on the same side," Josh said dryly.

"You could have easily let him kill me. I thought maybe . . . your shot when we dueled was an accident. I realize now it wasn't. I owe you an apology, sir."

Josh turned to look at him, and Timothy extended his hand. "I'm sorry."

"We'll forget it." Josh shook his hand.

"I listened to your . . . well, I didn't think you were a man of honor, but you are. And if you are, then the other gossip I've heard about you must also be untrue."

"Forget it, Lord Paddington—"

"No, sir. Timothy, please."

Feeling a glint of satisfaction and a flickering hope that maybe he had begun to cause cracks in the solid opposition in London, Josh glanced at Timothy again. "Very well, if you'll address me as Josh."

"Fine. And thank you again for saving my life. That was damned brave."

"That's why we're here." Josh looked over his shoulder. "I'll be glad when we're across this plain."

Finally the mountains were close, and when he looked back toward Santiago, to his relief, no one was following.

They rode back together, but parted on the edge of town. Josh hurried home, slipping in through a gate at the back and climbing the iron grillwork to the bedroom. His eyes had fully adjusted to the night, so he stood a moment looking at Lianna stretched on the bed, her hair fanned over her pillow.

Desire struck him as strongly as a blow. He reached out and caught a silky strand of hair to let it twine through his fingers as he thought of a woman he had recently met. Luisa Otero was eager to make him forget his married status, and he was tempted to see if he could forget Lianna, because as soon as they returned to England he would have to do so. He turned away abruptly and went to his room to undress, cursing the fact that he was to ride for the *estancia* in the morning to meet with the patriots who hid in the mountains. He wanted time with Lianna. Instead, he was caught in a web of intrigue and a coming revolution that took more of his attention every day.

Gradually Lianna saw the sights of Santiago. She wondered how the general managed the knack of appearing only when Josh was gone—was it spies in the household, or Josh himself who told the general when he would be gone?

One afternoon after a carriage ride, General Farjado accompanied Lianna inside, closing the doors to the salon.

As he faced her, he said, "It's unfortunate that the ride to the coast is so long. I'll be gone from here for the next few days."

Lianna placed her gloves and reticule on a table. "Do you have to leave because of the army?"

"*Sí*, a Spanish fleet has docked at Valparaiso, and we're to meet it to bring back supplies. I'll talk with a representative of the Spanish crown."

Lianna's mind was still on the thought of a ship to Spain . . . so close to England and home! Josh's neglect could only mean he had lost interest. The last time they had been together he had promised to end the marriage when they returned to England. He hadn't asked, but had merely said he would. And she knew him well enough to know he did what pleased him. Every day was becoming a greater heartache and more lonely. "Will the fleet return to Spain soon?"

General Farjado lifted her chin and gazed down into her eyes. "You would like to go home."

She looked down quickly, suddenly afraid of what she might have revealed. "This land is far from home—there are moments I miss Spain terribly."

"You're much too lovely to waste away locked in this house with no man to make you happy."

"You know I have a husband!"

"A husband who is never present for a wife who was meant for love." His hand slipped around her waist, and he drew her close.

"General, please release me!" She pushed free and walked to the window.

"Very well, but someday you'll tire of being left alone by a husband who entertains himself continually without thought of you." His head tilted, his eyelids drooped, and he gazed at her heatedly. "You're the most beautiful woman in Santiago and you remain closed up in an empty house with only the servants. You need a man's lips and caresses—"

"Sir, please!" She turned to look outside. "I have to ask you to go. Good afternoon."

General Farjado came to stand behind her, his breath warm on her neck. His fingers touched her hair lightly, stroked across her shoulder. "Why don't you want to hear the truth?" He leaned down to kiss her nape.

"You know my husband will challenge you if he learns what you've said to me." She turned around to face him.

"You can't really care what he does," he said mockingly.

"You don't know my feelings!" she snapped, surprised at the assurance behind his remark.

His black eyes glittered in a manner that sent a chill through her. He answered, "You're not a happily married woman."

"How can you possibly know that?"

"Were I your husband, I would not spend evening after evening in dull political discussions with the governor. Nor spend my time at the gaming tables. Nor kiss a certain dark-eyed *señorita*."

Lianna felt as if the earth had vanished beneath her feet.

Her voice was an angry whisper. "General, I don't care to hear more about my husband's activities!"

"You'll change," he replied with assured complacency.

Lianna said farewell without being aware of his words. After he had gone, she remained standing, her emotions in a turmoil. Why should it matter if Josh kissed another? Why did it give her an overwhelming sense of loss? Was it true, or deceit by the general to get what he wanted? The questions began to grate on her nerves. Was Josh gone because of politics—or because of a woman? Now Lianna had to face what she truly felt for him.

Several weeks later Madryn was late for her sitting. Lianna touched up the portrait while she waited, and finally heard a step. Madryn moved gracefully across the patio and sat down in the chair to pose. The portrait was sufficiently finished that Lianna could give up her model, but she enjoyed the afternoon visit with Madryn more than the mornings spent with young matrons.

As Madryn apologized for keeping Lianna waiting, she twisted a fold of her white cotton skirt nervously. Her face was pale, and there was a pinched look to her mouth which caused Lianna to ask, "Is something disturbing you?"

Madryn's black eyes clouded, and she whispered, "No, Doña Lita."

It was such an obvious lie, Lianna was sorry she had asked. "I didn't mean to pry."

"Oh, no! It's not that." Madryn paused and her gaze swept the courtyard. With a chill foreboding Lianna glanced around and saw Juanita watering a plant.

"Madryn, there is a task upstairs. Come with me, and I'll show you what I want done," Lianna announced, and set down her brush.

Madryn followed Lianna upstairs to her room, where Lianna closed the door and faced her. "We're alone now, there are no listening ears. Is there something I can do to help?"

Madryn stared at Lianna in silence. Suddenly her composure vanished as she put her hands over her face and trembled. "There is nothing anyone can do. Nothing."

Lianna crossed the room to a carved chest, opened a drawer to find a handkerchief. "Here, Madryn. If it's an argument with Rinaldo, then I'm sorry," Lianna said while the maid wiped her eyes.

"Oh, no! Never that." Madryn pushed her long black hair away from her face and shuddered. "It is the privilege of royalty . . ." Her voice was bitter. Then her voice faded and her eyes widened. "*Dios!* Doña Lita, I am truly sorry. I forget because you're so good to me—*you're* royalty."

Lianna gave an impatient wave of her hand. "Madryn, tell me what troubles you. Perhaps it's not as bad as you think."

Madryn twisted the damp linen handkerchief in her hands. "I'm a mere servant, and we're little more than slaves. A Spanish nobleman has seen me. He made inquiries and learned that I'm to marry Rinaldo soon. He sent a servant to fetch me to his house. Before . . . before my marriage . . ." She raised a tearstained face. ". . . I must be his."

As full understanding dawned on Lianna she whispered in dismay, "I can't believe such a monstrous thing! You're no slave. Don Cristóbal will protect you. You don't have to consent."

"Oh, yes, I do!" Madryn answered bitterly.

"How could he force you?"

"Through my betrothed. If I inform Rinaldo, or if I do not willingly do as he asks, then Rinaldo will be arrested for disloyalty to Spain, for being a heretic." Madryn placed the handkerchief over her eyes and wept silently.

Lianna studied her. It was another bit of evidence that what Josh had said about the rulers in Chile was true. Lianna asked, "Who is the man?"

"I cannot reveal his name."

"In heaven's name! How can I help you if you won't reveal who he is?"

Madryn lowered the handkerchief from her reddened eyes. "It's Captain Fernando Caribe."

Instantly Lianna recalled his leering face across the dinner table at the party given by the *marqués*, and her stomach churned with distaste. "Madryn, no one can do something so vile. If they arrest Rinaldo on a false charge, won't it be easy to prove his innocence? If we tell the full story to the governor, won't that end the trouble?"

Madryn's mouth twisted. "The governor is just as evil. They are friends; Captain Caribe helped bring Governor Marcheno to power." She added angrily, "This is not the first time. I've heard girls talk and I know exactly what will take place if I don't do as Captain Caribe wishes."

Lianna sat down on a velvet chair and studied Madryn. "How long until you must go to Captain Caribe?"

"Four nights from now," Madryn answered.

"Dry your eyes. I'll do what I can to help," Lianna said.

"There's nothing you or anyone else can do. If I tell Rinaldo, he'll kill Captain Caribe."

"What would happen if you and Rinaldo ran away?"

"I see you're not familiar with the rules of the country," Madryn answered bitterly. "We're not allowed to own horses. We would have to steal them, and wherever we'd ride, they would know we were on stolen animals. If we were caught, it would go harder on us—if such is possible."

"Suppose I gave you two of our horses as a gift?"

"By law, you cannot do so." She shook her head. "It is hopeless, truly. I've been warned. If we try to flee, then my mother and father will be arrested."

"We'll find a way," Lianna said grimly. "That miserable man mustn't touch you."

Madryn reached out and touched Lianna's hand. "You're good, Doña Lita. Thank you for your kindness."

Lianna gazed into the girl's dark eyes. "I'll help you, I promise."

Long after Madryn had returned to her work, Lianna paced the library to contemplate the problem. She began to fully understand Josh's anger and involvement with the patriots.

Pulling her concern from her own problems, she returned to Madryn's. Madryn's plight was desperate. There was one hope—Josh.

Lianna spent the day and evening pacing through the house, nervous and restless, aware of Juanita's curious stares. Josh had been gone for weeks, and Lianna had no notion when he would return.

The next morning, three liveried servants came to the house, as was customary, to leave invitations.

Lianna watched Fletcher place one in a bowl by the front door. She stopped to pick up a card that was an invitation to coffee on Thursday morning next week. Next she opened an envelope that held an invitation to a dinner. Lianna didn't recognize the name and left it for Josh. She picked up a thick white envelope that bore the governor's crest. Tearing it open, Lianna read the invitation to another dinner and ball. Her gaze drifted down over the words, and she stiffened as the black lettering seemed to leap up at her: ". . . request your presence . . . dinner and ball . . . January 20, 1817 . . . in honor of his excellency's cousin and wife, the Conde and Condesa de Marcheno."

"Señora, is something wrong?" Fletcher asked politely, his arm steadying her.

"I'm sorry," she whispered swiftly in Spanish. "I feel ill." She held the invitation where Fletcher could see it and watched his brows draw together as he scanned the announcement.

"*Dios!*" he whispered. "Let me help you to the salon or summon a maid."

"I'll go to the salon and sit down."

Behind them a female voice said, "May I help?"

They turned to face Juanita, whose dark eyes rested on the announcement in Lianna's hands.

Fletcher said calmly, "Doña Lita feels ill. If you would help her to lie down, Juanita . . ."

"*Sí.*" Juanita moved beside Lianna, who was regaining her composure. She tossed the announcement into the bowl casually.

"I will finish reading the cards and invitations later."

"I can read them to you, *señora*, if you prefer," Juanita offered.

"Gracias. After I lie down, *por favor."*

Lianna stretched on the sofa. The Count of Marcheno and Quita in Santiago! Lianna had been so upset over the news that she hadn't noticed the date of the dinner. When would Josh return? She had to find him and warn him. Now what would they do? Give up this venture? Flee to *El Feroz* and home? Or stay and gamble on the risk? Their lives would be in Quita's hands. Quita would guess instantly that Josh was a spy for the patriots—she would know they were not the Marqués and Marquesa de Aveiro. It would give away Quita's secret if she revealed their identity, yet could she remain quiet knowing they were a threat to the life of her husband and his cousin?

Juanita sat close by and read the invitations. Lianna lay with her eyes closed, and when the maid had finished, said, "Juanita, *gracias.* I feel too ill to think about dinners or parties. Will you please return them to the silver tray for Don Cristóbal? He can see to them and let me know which we will accept."

"Sí."

"I'll go to my room to rest."

"Do you want help?"

"No, *gracias."* Lianna rose, paused for the benefit of Juanita's watchful gaze, then left to go upstairs. Fletcher stood at his post, looking unconcerned, his handsome features impassive.

The moment Lianna closed the door, she moved nervously to the window. First, Madryn and her problems; now the arrival of Quita and the count. Lianna clamped her lips together and shoved aside worries over Quita. More immediate was the problem of Madryn. Lianna's gaze searched the quiet street. "Josh . . ." she whispered, "come home. Please, come home!"

The night was long. Lianna paced the floor in her room, then lay in the darkness, her ears straining for sound of Josh. She dozed fitfully and woke early to gaze out the window as if she could conjure Josh up out of the gray sky. Something had to be done, and she couldn't wait.

There had to be some place of safety for Madryn and Rinaldo. She tried to think what she would do in their place. Where could they hide? Where could they live? They would have to leave Chile, but where would they find refuge?

El Feroz.

Lianna threw back the covers and went to sit by the windows while her mind raced. The ship could be a temporary haven until some decision was made about the future.

Two hours later, when Madryn came to make the bed, Lianna was waiting with her plan.

The day was one of the longest in Lianna's life. She prayed that Josh would come home, that she could turn everything over to him, but when sundown came and he hadn't appeared, she went ahead with her plan.

At midnight she dressed in the boy's clothing that Madryn had supplied earlier. Tugging on high black boots, she smoothed her black coat above breeches that were loose in the waist. She remembered the night Josh had climbed in the front widow, and left the house the same way.

Aware that she risked everything, that Josh might be furious with her, nevertheless, Lianna was compelled to save Madryn from Captain Caribe's lust.

She climbed down the tree slowly, then stood behind it in dark shadows, her heart pounding with fright. Dread washed over her, and she fought the urge to return to the safety of the house. She ached for the security of Josh's strength and commanding presence—the night would hold no terrors for him. But for Madryn's sake, Lianna had to see the plan through.

Gritting her teeth, she walked cautiously, remaining in the shadows until she stepped outside the gate. Madryn had told her the way to go to Rinaldo's, where they would meet.

Lianna's breath came in short gasps and her palms were damp, because if soldiers stopped her, she knew how little chance she would have to deceive them and escape. Another worry plagued her. If Josh returned and discovered her missing, what would he do? She had left a note that she had taken a walk, but how ridiculous it had sounded.

She hurried along, moving quietly yet trying to walk purposefully and stay hidden. The moon was perfect for her needs, a mere sliver that left the town in darkness. With tall poplars and full *alerce* trees lining the street, her path was shadowy. Lianna's eyes adjusted gradually, and she could make out pale walls and houses.

How long would it take to escape safely from Santiago? Her seething worries changed abruptly when she heard a footstep behind her.

It was slight but unmistakable. Her heart thudded against her ribs. She paused and strained to listen. A bird's melodic cry carried in the night. Lianna moved forward, walking close to the high wall of a house, staying in the shadows. And she heard the footsteps commence again.

Her breathing became ragged. She trembled as her thoughts raced frantically. It was many more blocks to her destination. Who followed? And why? If it were soldiers, they would have come forward to accost her, so it must be someone else.

Was it a thief? Someone from the house who had followed her out? She walked faster. The footsteps increased, now easier to hear.

Lianna racked her mind to think of some escape. The houses were walled, protected from intruders. She might try a gate and step into a patio, but she would be hemmed in.

She turned a corner, stepped into a recessed doorway, and waited. A scrape sounded.

Lianna flattened herself against the rough wall that still held heat from the afternoon sun. She held her breath, hearing her heart drum in her ears.

A man came into sight, moving silently. A wide-brimmed Spanish hat was set low on his head, hiding his features; a serape was flung across his shoulders. He was as tall and broad-shouldered as Josh or the general. He passed her swiftly on quiet feet in spite of his boots. Lianna let out her breath and forced herself to count to ten.

She bit her lip as she cautiously leaned forward and looked out. Nothing. The dark street was empty, full of shadows that could hide anything.

Quickly Lianna slipped out of her hiding place and rushed back around the corner in the direction she had come. She had to get away from the man who followed her.

There were other routes to her destination. She paused in another doorway to listen. Only silence. Far in the distance a horse whinnied. She stepped out again, wiping her damp palms on her breeches as she turned to retrace her steps.

Behind her a footfall sounded. Lianna glanced over her shoulder as hard arms locked around her. A hand clamped over her mouth.

25

―――••――▪▶━━▪━━◀▪――••―――

"Lianna!"

She recognized Josh's voice and closed her eyes. Faintness came, and her weight sagged against him in relief. As his strong arms held her, he pulled her into the shadows of a wall.

"I'm sorry I frightened you. I had to find you without making noise." He removed his hand from her mouth and held her. "Fletcher knew what you'd planned and got word to me. When I arrived home, I read your note and saw the window open. The wax was warm from the candles, so you couldn't have gone far."

"I prayed you'd come!" She clung to him tightly, relishing holding him, her fear momentarily forgotten.

"I was watching out the window and saw you go through the gate. I couldn't call, so I had to follow and try to catch you."

"Why didn't Fletcher let me know he could reach you?" she asked.

"There wasn't time or opportunity. We're watched constantly. Fletcher didn't have details, he simply said that you planned to help Madryn escape with Rinaldo. I came as soon as I could."

"I didn't know what to do, and tomorrow will be too late. All I could think of was to get them to *El Feroz*."

"You can't take them to the coast!"

"I had to try. I couldn't think of anything else to do. I'm going now to Rinaldo's. One of your men, Simms, will lead them, and he's waiting there now."

"There'll be trouble."

"I couldn't bear to think about Madryn going to Caribe. I'm sorry if I've endangered you, but the man is foul."

"I'm glad you did," he said softly. "A year ago you wouldn't have done this."

She was startled at the satisfaction in his voice. He frowned as he said, "I'll have to do something, because they'll arrest her parents."

"No. They're going too."

He held her away and looked down. "They're going? Four of them and my coxswain? Five people?"

"What's wrong with that?"

"They're trying to hide and escape. Each additional person cuts their chances."

She drew a breath, bracing for his anger. "There are more than five."

"Who else, for heaven's sake?"

"All their relatives on both sides of their families," she answered rapidly.

There was a moment of silence; then he exclaimed, "I'll be damned! And I thought *I* was daring! How many, Lianna?"

Her face burned in the darkness, but she raised her chin defiantly. Josh couldn't stop them! "Forty-three."

"Forty-three people!" he swore softly. "Forty-three to hide for miles across Chile?"

"If they reach *El Feroz*, it'll give them time to plan their future safely."

He chuckled, holding her away to lean down and look into her eyes. "And now who's foolishly risking all to help people you don't even know!"

She blushed, and warmth raced through her that he was so pleased. "Madryn is my friend."

"You've changed, Lianna," he said quietly.

Always, at every encounter, a dazzling invisible tension flared between them, and something in his solemn observation shook her to her soul.

Josh held her, momentarily lost in thought over how much she had changed since that first month on his ship. Right now, when they needed to get off the street, to meet

Simms and the others, he wanted to step into the shadows and pull her into his arms and kiss her.

"Come, let's get this over," he said abruptly.

Lianna hurt when she heard the harshness return to his voice. If only he weren't so strong-willed, so bent on this revolution that he was blinded to all else! She gripped his wrists. "Josh, did Fletcher tell you about the Count of Marcheno?"

"Yes," he answered as if he relished the news. His reaction was far different from what she had expected. "Yes, Lianna, I heard he's brought his new wife to Chile on their honeymoon. Now I shall get my revenge."

"You are possessed by it! It makes a devil of you!"

"You can't understand. The Marchenos are barbarians, and particularly the count. I have a score to settle."

"I understand your loss and the terrible things Don Armando did, but you let revenge rule your heart," she said violently.

"You do protest!" He looked at her intently. "What causes you to feel so strongly about the matter?"

She blushed hotly as she answered, "You are consumed with hatred, which benefits no one."

He caught her chin in his hand, holding tightly while he raised her face to peer at her. The darkness could not reveal much, and she gazed back unflinchingly.

"I wonder what runs through your mind," he said softly.

It was on the tip of her tongue to cry out, "I love you!" But if he laughed at her or made a sneering gibe, she wouldn't be able to bear it, so instead she asked, "What if Quita reveals our secret before you can do anything?"

He released her and answered, "She won't reveal our identity because we can reveal hers."

"How can you be sure? She'll know instantly what you're doing. Can she sit by and watch you pass the Spaniards' secrets about military strength and defenses to the patriots, or cause her husband's life to be in danger?"

"That's all she can do if she wants to survive and remain the Countess of Marcheno. I'm gambling on time."

"So our risk grows! Where'd you learn about them?"

"I hear what happens in Santiago, what ships dock at Valparaiso. Our plans are forming. Now, we must see about Madryn."

The grim note in his voice made her fear increase, but he was correct. At the moment, more pressing problems concerned them.

He held her hand, and together they went on to bid Madryn and Rinaldo good-bye and to watch the group start for the coast.

Finally they were back at home, climbing in the front window so the servants would not see them. As Lianna clung to the windowsill, Josh reached down to place his hands around her waist and lift her inside. While he turned to light a candle, she closed the shutters.

Light danced to life in a small circle, leaving dark corners in the room. When she looked at Josh, her heart thudded violently. The black hat was pushed behind his head and a serape was flung across his broad shoulders over a brown leather coat and breeches. His boots were dusty, and short locks of hair escaped his queue. A gunbelt was fastened around his hips.

Even dusty and disheveled, he looked so appealing, so virile, that she trembled. She held her breath as his gaze lowered leisurely, drifting down to appraise her boy's clothing. One corner of his mouth curved in a crooked smile.

"You would fool no one, *cara*." His voice was husky, strumming over her nerves like a summer wind across a pond, stirring ripples in its wake. And she knew without question what an enormous, disastrous folly she had committed.

It wasn't Edwin Stafford who held her heart, but Josh Raven! She was in love with a man who was dangerous, reckless, and tough, who would never leave the sea that he loved more than all else. Lianna knew Josh desired her; it showed in his eyes. But she wanted more, and she didn't want to wait at home while the man she loved fought battles at sea. She had flung her heart to a savage man who would laugh in her face if he knew. He was as hard as stone, and all the smiles and kisses from now until they reached England wouldn't melt his iron heart or change the way he lived—and it wasn't the kind of life she wanted.

He crossed the room to remove the hat from her head, and in spite of the reasons she didn't want to love him, her pulse fluttered. As he lifted the hat, locks of her hair tumbled down. Flickering candlelight danced over Josh's features and she couldn't get her breath. The room was hot; her knees felt weak. Josh put his hand in her hair and slowly tugged, gently pushing pins free. He removed his fingers, and the remaining black tresses cascaded over her shoulders.

With a bemused smile he pushed her coat off and flung it aside, then tilted her face up. "Forty-three people you helped to escape because of one peasant girl. You always amaze me. You risked your life for Madryn tonight. Do I recall a taunting question about why I would help these people?"

She couldn't think about his question. Her mind was captured by his long thick lashes, his mouth that made her ache to be kissed.

Josh looked at her more intently. He saw the candlelight reflected in her blue eyes, watched her lips part and her tongue dart across her soft, full lower lip. He felt as if all his senses were drowning in blue. The look in her eyes was a blatant invitation. She wanted to be kissed.

His blood heated and desire surged through his loins, making him long to crush her in his arms. And as always, the specter of her love for Stafford rose to haunt him.

He shook his head as if to clear it. Never once had she declared her love for him. She loved England and Edwin. Desire, her own lusty nature, consumed her in intimate moments, but her heart was elsewhere. He would not bind himself to a woman who didn't love him.

"What will we do about the Count of Marcheno?" she asked softly.

Josh's gaze rested on her mouth. When he didn't answer, Lianna looked up at him. She felt empty, and only Josh could make her feel whole, complete. She drew her breath and held it, wanting him more than she had ever dreamed possible.

He reached up to frame her face with his hands, his thumb drawing lazy circles over her cheek. "Lianna, I want you."

She clung to his hard wrists, closing her eyes. "You make me melt. Feel me tremble—it's because I want you."

"Look at me," he demanded, watching her closely.

They faced each other in the dusky light of the flickering candle. Her breath was ragged as she gazed at him. "You have taught me the ways of love. I'm human. I'm a woman . . . with an appealing man . . ." Her voice trailed off in a whisper.

"You know the risk you run!"

She frowned as if in pain. "Yes," she whispered, aware the risk was not in having his child, but in loving him with her whole heart.

He felt as if his heart had stopped beating. "You want me to touch you, don't you?"

"Yes," she whispered, and his pulse drummed. "You know I do."

His mouth came down on hers violently, opening hers to his hot demands. Lianna met his fire with her own flame. Eagerly she wound her arms around his neck and kissed him, trembling at his touch. Desire exploded in her, consuming her like dry brush burning in summer heat. Josh wound his fingers in her hair and pulled her head back to look at her. His chest heaved with his ragged breathing, expanding to proportions that made her want to run her fingers over him.

"My treacherous Spanish lady, is it your tempestuous blood that boils and makes you cling to me? Or are you after something?"

She fought back a sob. She wanted him, more than she had ever wanted anyone else's love . . . more than she would have guessed possible to need someone.

"I know how much time you've been spending with Farjado. Have you given him your kisses as freely?"

The question was like a blow. Lianna gasped. Shocked and hurt, she reached up to slap Josh.

The sound broke the silence. She stepped back as a startled look flashed across his features.

"Get out," she whispered, shaking to hold back her tears. If only he would go before he saw her cry!

His eyebrows arched, then drew together. She expected anger, not curiosity, and her fear rose. "Get out!"

"Lianna . . ."

She looked at him intently. "And you, Josh, have you kissed another?"

His face flushed. "Perhaps I have, to get you out of my blood! And there's only one way you could have learned about it— Farjado!"

"There's a Spanish fleet at Valparaiso now. Let me go—"

"It sailed," he said curtly, and left, slamming the door behind him.

Hot tears streamed over her cheeks as she stared after him. How close she had come to revealing everything! She must never tell Josh of her love. His derision would destroy her. He had kissed another! Perhaps he now loved another and wanted out of the marriage. If only she could forget him, but it was the same as forgetting to breathe— impossible. In spite of everything, she ached for him, clenching her fists as she stood without moving, long after he had gone.

And she knew how angry he had been by the way he had slammed the door. He was so careful to keep their movements quiet, to keep up the appearance of newlyweds who loved each other.

She discarded her dusty male clothing, sponging off and dressing in a white nightgown. She brushed her hair, gazing out the window at the night, thinking about Madryn, who was with the man she loved, safely aboard *El Feroz*—in the same town as Quita and her husband.

What a shock it would be to Quita to learn that Lianna and Josh Raven were wed and posing as Spaniards. Lianna's curiosity heightened as she wondered if Quita were happy with the exchange.

Was Josh correct? Would they be safe from Quita's betrayal because it would reveal her identity also? Lianna turned to stare at the door to Josh's room. Beyond it he lay stretched in bed, asleep. The mental image came of Josh sprawled on the bed, his coppery skin dark against the white sheets, his long legs stretched out. With a groan she tried to force her attention elsewhere.

The next morning, the servants drifted through the house in silence, moving quickly about their jobs, until Lianna realized they were acting in an unnatural manner.

She summoned Maria. The girl curtsied and stood before her with wide eyes. "What ails this household?" Lianna asked.

The girl appeared on the verge of tears. "Doña Lita, I know nothing about it."

At that moment Lianna heard voices in the entryway. She rushed into the hall to meet Josh, who looked so handsome in a black coat and breeches and high polished boots that she was momentarily distracted.

"I see you have discovered our loss," he said quickly.

Another figure in a green uniform emerged from the shadows of the *zaguán*. General Farjado came forward with a frown on his face.

"*Buenos días*," Lianna greeted him, her gaze returning to Josh. "What loss? What's happened?" Lianna asked, realizing that it had to be the disappearance of Madryn and Rinaldo. Suddenly panic gripped her. Suppose they had been caught! Josh looked grim, his features set solemnly.

With a scowl Josh answered, "The servants have taken four of our horses and run away, but they won't get far before they're caught."

"Run away!" Lianna repeated breathlessly, hiding her relief. "Who?"

"The maid Teresa Huancayo and her daughter Madryn are gone. Also a stablehand, Rinaldo Sepulveda, along with his younger brother, Lucas. The general assures me they won't get far before they're caught."

"But if they wanted to leave, why didn't they tell us?"

General Farjado answered, "They're worthless people who most likely don't want to work. The blacksmith is a heretic. We'll find them and your horses, which are more valuable."

With smooth composure Josh said, "Lita, I'm sorry you were troubled with this. Don't let it concern you." He smiled and turned to the general. "This way. We'll have coffee in the salon." Both men nodded to her and left.

All through the morning and early afternoon soldiers and officers were in and out of the house, talking with General Farjado and Josh. That afternoon she heard Josh's boots clatter on the stones in the courtyard. She waited breathlessly in the corridor upstairs, watching his dark hair as he climbed the steps swiftly, taking two at a time.

"Buenas tardes, cara," he said. His arm went around her waist and he drew her into his room, closing the door on prying eyes and ears. The moment the door closed behind them, he released her.

"Where are Rinaldo and Madryn?" she asked.

"They divided—the able-bodied men, including Rinaldo, went to the mountains to join the Chilenos, the patriot army of Chile. The others are safely aboard *El Feroz.*"

"Thank goodness!" She sank down on the edge of a chair, folds of her yellow muslin dress billowing and settling over her legs. "Do you know if they encountered difficulty?"

"No, they didn't." He smiled. "There isn't anyone left in either family who would be of interest to the authorities—a fact which became apparent just this afternoon and is causing increasing irritation."

He straightened. "I'm due at a meeting with the governor."

"Is there any suspicion about how they escaped?"

"None that I'm aware of." He crossed the room to tie a cravat. His gaze in the mirror shifted to her. "Captain Caribe is dead."

"No! You didn't—"

"No. I suspect Rinaldo or one of his brothers. It was caused by a snakebite, and many people will see no connection, but General Farjado and Governor Marcheno won't be fooled." Josh craned his neck as he folded the wide cravat. Lianna couldn't resist crossing the room to stand beside him. "Turn around. I've tied my father's cravats on occasion."

He faced her, and she carefully avoided looking into his watchful eyes. She twisted the smooth cloth, conscious of her hands resting on his chest, of a vein in his neck pulsing with each heartbeat. A faint, enticing woodsy scent assailed her, bringing swift memories that made her fingers fumble the bit of silk. Her mind raced for something to say to break a silence that was all too swiftly being filled by her pounding heartbeat.

"I should pay a call on Quita. Perhaps it'll give us a chance to talk alone before we're in the eyes of the public at a formal dinner."

"You're having difficulty tying my cravat," he said softly.

She clamped her jaw together. "You should stand still."

"I haven't so much as taken a breath."

She shot him a glance, and the effect was like a blow to her midriff. "Perhaps you should tie it yourself," she said, and started to turn.

His arm caught her. "Oh, no! Tie it, Lianna. I'll stand here until there are rainbows in hell if necessary."

She laughed at his teasing, excitement bubbling in her while she began again. "It's been a long time. I don't remember how." She carefully straightened it around his neck and smoothed it in place.

"Any woman who can whisk forty-three people out from under the Spaniards' noses should be able to tie one cravat."

"The cravat is infinitely more difficult," she answered lightly, yet she felt as if she were on the brink of a yawning chasm.

"Now, why on earth is that?" he asked in great innocence.

"Because, Josh, I must fasten it on you," she said.

He tilted her chin up, but she kept her eyes on his cravat, working faster. "Be still, I'm almost—"

"Look at me."

Her blood heated at his commanding tone. His green eyes probed mercilessly, then narrowed, and she knew she couldn't hide anything. If he laughed at her she would . . .

Desperate to avoid his curiosity, she moved away and asked, "How are the patriots faring?"

He leaned against the mantelpiece, studying her while he answered, "We draw closer to conflict."

It was almost impossible to think about the Spanish when her thoughts were tumbling over Josh. "You think there's a way to fight the Spaniards after all?"

"Yes, there is," he answered, and his expression altered. "San Martín is daring. He's quartered in Mendoza, gathering an army, while others help here."

"How can they help in Santiago?"

"By spreading false rumors about the coming conflict. Then perhaps the Spanish will center their forces at the wrong points."

"And you're one of those spreading rumors?"

"Yes. General Marco del Ponte and General Farjado will be in charge of the Spanish troops. Hopefully, both of them and the other Spanish officers will be misled."

"You know what San Martín plans?"

His frown vanished and his eyes glittered like emeralds under a midday sun. "Look, Lianna . . ." Pulling off his coat, he dropped it on the floor as he sat on a chair facing her. Pointing to the coat, he said, "Here's Santiago." His hand circled the coat. "Spanish soldiers reside in town, their armies surround it to protect it." He touched her knee. "Where you sit is the sea, with the Spanish guns trained on it."

"And behind it all—an impossible barrier, the Andes," she said.

"Right. Behind Santiago to the east, where I am, are the Andes. Rugged, snow-covered, a natural fortress. Now, how will San Martín surprise the Spanish and gain control?"

She looked at the coat spread on the floor. "Everything is protected." Questioningly she suggested, "A fleet that is powerful enough to withstand the guns?"

"No. There is one English ship willing to help, Admiral Cochrane's, and word has it two more will arrive any day now, one a mercenary who is an Englishman. But no. From the sea it's hopeless."

"I'm not a soldier, Josh. How can the Spanish be attacked?"

"I've been gone, supposedly at our *estancia*, but actually I met with men who've been with San Martín. He is brilliant, Lianna!''

She looked at his eyes sparkling with anticipation, the leanness of a body physically fit, ready for action. ''You're a pirate who loves battle!''

''No, I want to succeed when I set out to do something.''

''And you always do succeed,'' she answered.

His chest expanded as he drew a sharp breath. She was held by his gaze, her voice fading to a whisper. ''Where are the Spanish vulnerable?'' she asked, but was only dimly aware of the question.

Her attention was on Josh, on her awareness of him as an appealing man, a man who could love her until all thought was gone, until she gasped and ached and cried for him. . . . She trembled and clenched her fingers.

When he didn't answer, she frowned and asked again, ''Where are they vulnerable?''

''I feel as vulnerable as the Spanish Army,'' he said softly.

She drew in her breath. ''Your heart is an iron fortress and nothing can melt it.'' His eyes darkened and her blood raced in her veins. ''Josh, answer me about the Spanish. Where can San Martín attack?''

With an unwavering gaze he doubled his first and placed it against his chest. ''Here. We will come this way.''

As what he was saying dawned on her, her eyes widened. ''Across the mountains? He would bring an army of men and horses over the *cordillera!*'' She thought of the jagged mountains, their snowy peaks often hidden by clouds. ''That's impossible!''

The determination in Josh's eyes gave her an answer. ''Lianna, the army of the patriots will cross the Andes. The Spaniards will never expect it.''

''Of course they won't, because it can't be done! No army can accomplish such madness. The slopes are filled with snow and ice,'' she said, suddenly terrified of what lay ahead for Josh.

''San Martín is training his men in the mountains at Mendoza. They're gathering supplies, making portable bridges and slings to carry the cannon.''

''Where's Mendoza?''

''Across the border in Argentina. A monk, Fray Luis Beltrán, is aiding San Martín. They've melted down the church bells to get iron for machetes and cannon.''

''The church bells—to use for weapons to kill men?''

''To gain freedom from tyranny, Lianna! He's made more than fifty thousand horseshoes. Women have given their jewelry to have it melted down. They're weaving dyed blue llama wool and goat hair into uniforms.''

Suddenly Lianna felt desolate. Her days with Josh Raven were numbered, drawing to a close. She held her breath as she asked, ''Will you be with them?''

''Of course,'' he answered solemnly, but she heard the exhilaration in his voice. ''We'll leave soon. I'll send you to *El Feroz*, then I'll ride south to a pass to cross to Argentina and go back north to Mendoza.''

''It's impossible!''

''No,'' he whispered, and knelt on one knee to pick up his coat. He paused, looking into her eyes, his face only inches away. ''I think it can be done, when the first of January comes—Chile's summer, and as good as the weather will ever be in the mountains. There are two passes to the north of us and west of Mendoza. They've mapped out the way they'll cross.''

''When you're lost down a mountainside, how do I get back to England?''

''Come now, Lianna, for Madryn's escape you accomplished the impossible!''

She was pleased with his words, but they didn't vanquish her worries. ''I didn't do it alone.''

''I've pledged my aid to San Martín.''

''And I shall be hopelessly lost here.''

He reached out to take her hand, and the touch was a brush of fire. ''No. Simms will escort you to *El Feroz* when I leave. I promise you'll be delivered safely back to England. You'll get your freedom,'' he said. ''The patriots' army of Chile is ready to move. I'll go join them. By spring you will be on *El Feroz* sailing for England.''

He knelt before her, his hand over hers, his wrist resting on her knee. Lianna gazed into his thickly fringed green eyes and quivered. An ache that was becoming more and more familiar to her spread hotly inside. It wasn't England she wanted . . .

His brows arched and he leaned closer, his gaze lowering to her mouth. She whispered, "You don't have to fight. You court danger as if it were a lady."

"Danger is a beautiful blue-eyed lady who would destroy me if I let her."

She blushed. "You're too strong for me to destroy you. I couldn't inflict the smallest wound."

"The wounds you've already inflicted torment, yet there is something between us that draws you as much as it does me."

He leaned closer, and Lianna could no more draw back or resist him than she could get up and walk out. She leaned forward, her lashes flutterd, her gaze rested on his mouth. She trembled with desire and closed her eyes.

His lips touched hers, and longing seared every nerve. As his arms went around her, Lianna slipped her hands across his shoulders, winding her fingers in his hair. She paused to look at him. "I can't resist you."

"Nor I you, Lianna. If only . . ."

His words trailed off as he kissed her and they slipped to the floor, Josh pulling her down on top of him. Her long hair tumbled over her shoulders and his; her heart pounded in her ears, drowning out all sounds.

She couldn't breathe, she couldn't get close enough, get enough of Josh. She ran her fingers through his silky hair, she touched the strong column of his throat. Through her skirt and chemise, through the petticoats, she felt his arousal. Her hips moved against him and she moaned softly. She wanted to rip away all the barriers, to touch his solid muscles, to claim his friendship, his love.

She caught his head with her hands. "Oh, Josh, it doesn't have to be this way. Would you give up the sea?"

His green eyes darkened as his brows narrowed and his breath seemed to stop. "You care?"

"Of course I care! I love you," she whispered, feeling her heart thud as his eyelids fluttered. His dark brows came together in a frown, and he sat up, holding her shoulders. His eyes bored into her as if he wanted to see her soul.

"What about Edwin Stafford?"

"Edwin was part of my childhood." She met Josh's searching stare. "Life changes, and it isn't Edwin who has my heart."

Josh's eyes closed as if he were in pain, but his arms slipped around her waist, pulling her to him as he crushed the breath from her lungs. His voice sounded agonized. "Lianna! I'd given up waiting to hear you say the words! I think I've loved you from the first night. That's why I couldn't let you go."

She pulled away to look at him, unaware of his fingers tugging at the buttons on her dress. "Why didn't you tell me? Never once— "

"Never, because you didn't love me. You haven't loved me since that first month at sea. Admit it."

"No, it took time for me to recognize what I feel," she whispered, "and I think I fought it constantly," she said, her words slowing as he pushed her dress off her shoulders and cupped her breasts in his hands.

"Why?" he asked, looking up at her. His thumbs flicked over nipples that were taut with desire. At the moment, all she could think about was that the man she loved was inches away, his hands caressing her.

"I do love you," she whispered, and tilted her face upward as his mouth came down.

He loved her passionately, making her cry out in eagerness. Josh felt as if he would burst with need and love. He wanted to stir her to the heights of passion, to give love to her endlessly. Her hands moving on his legs made him burn with need. Her fingers drifted over him, caressing him, and he closed his eyes, whispering his love to her until he could stand no more.

He moved between her legs, wanting to feel her softness engulf his senses, wanting to possess her as if he could make her his forever.

Passion racked him in shuddering waves as he gasped, "Lianna, my love!"

She cried out, clinging to him, her hips meeting his thrusts in a blinding union.

He held her tenderly afterward, as their breathing returned to normal. He kissed her shoulder, his arms holding her close. "I love you," he whispered over and over.

She caught his face in her hands. "Josh, we need to talk about our future," she said solemnly.

He smiled, rolling on his side and propping his head on his hand with his elbow resting on the floor. "I think I was supposed to meet some men about half an hour ago."

Lianna's heart felt as if it might burst with joy as she looked up at her handsome husband. She couldn't resist touching him, her fingers moving lightly over his shoulder and chest, along his bristly jaw. "Josh," she said, trying to find the right words, wanting to wait and worry about them later, yet knowing that every day increased the danger he faced. "You asked me why I fought loving you."

"Mmm," he said as he kissed her throat and looked at her curiously. "I thought it was because of Edwin."

"Not for a long time now."

"Why?" He waited, studying her more intently.

"I was an only child, and my father was always at sea, even though we had a farm. Here you are, fighting in a revolution that grows more dangerous by the hour. You risk your life daily."

He raised his head to watch her, a slight frown on his forehead as she continued, "Take me home to England and away from this, please! Let's settle on the farm. I can't . . . tie my life to a pirate!"

"Sailing is all I know, Lianna," he said, sounding so agonized that she felt torn apart.

"You know all I can do is sail and be a privateer," he said, feeling a crushing blow. He wanted her to love him no matter what he did—as he loved her.

"I can't live that way," she said, hot tears stinging her eyes while his scowl deepened. "Our children wouldn't know their father any more than I knew mine. I have a farm when I go home and claim my inheritance."

He sat up to look down at her. "I haven't farmed since I

was a fifteen-year-old lad. I can't take your farm and settle there to do something I know little about."

She could feel the bubble of joy that had held them for the past hour bursting, leaving them both more vulnerable than before. Desperately she said, "You'd remember what you knew and learn the rest as quickly as you learned to sail!"

"We can have a house in London, where we can have friends. That's why I need to stay and fight here, Lianna. I'm beginning to win over men who had listened to my father and shut me out at home. I'm doing this for you too."

"I'd rather have you!" Her blue eyes widened, and he felt pulled apart, seeing in her eyes what she wanted, but knowing what he had to do. "You may lose your life in this battle. The patriots have been defeated every time they've tried to fight. And to cross the Andes—you know it's an impossible trek filled with danger. I want you, Josh."

"We'll work it out, Lianna, if we love each other," he said tenderly, wanting to do what she asked, yet knowing he couldn't.

"No," she whispered. "What you're saying is we do everything your way or not at all. I don't want to give my heart and love to a pirate!" She closed her eyes wearily. "Go, Josh . . . go now!"

"You hold me with your kisses, you send me away with your words. What do you want?" he asked, the pain he fought becoming so bad he was tempted to capitulate to her wishes.

"Go fight your damnable battles, Josh! You love battle more than all else. Go!"

Swearing, he rose, snatched up his clothes, and went to his room, slamming the door behind him. Lianna rolled over to place her face in her hands, lying on the floor while she cried silently. Finally the tears stopped, yet she lay still, stretched on her stomach, her cheek on her arm until a woman's voice asked, *"Señora?* Doña Lita, are you well?"

Startled, Lianna sat up and looked at Juanita, whose black eyes swiftly took in her appearance.

"May I help you to bed?" Juanita asked.

"Thank you, Juanita, no. I'm all right. I'd like to be alone."

"*Sí, señora.*" Juanita left quietly and closed the door behind her, a smile hovering on her thin lips.

Lianna stared at the blank door. Had Juanita eavesdropped? And if she had, how long had she listened? Whatever else she had learned, Juanita would pass the word along that all was not well between her master and mistress. Would it matter? Would it increase the danger they were in?

Lianna went to the window, gazing out as the sun set and darkness fell. Across the treetops and rooftops of Santiago was the Governor's Palace, where Quita would stay. All of them were caught in events beyond their control. Their lives would change because of a man named San Martín, because of an army of determined people, men who were willing to risk their lives for freedom. She herself would leave soon, sail for England, but what lay ahead? Would it be years of emptiness?

Lianna ran her hand across her flat abdomen. Why hadn't she been with child since the few wild nights of love with Josh? Her heartbeat quickened as she thought about a baby. If one of them didn't yield—Josh give up the sea or she give up the demand to have him at home— Josh would still dissolve the marriage once they were back in England. Lianna knew his resolve wouldn't waver, but if there were a child . . . The thought made her heart skip. The baby would have a name, it wouldn't be illegitimate, and at home there waited an estate. There were her father's two ships and his house, sufficient to care for both her and a baby. She turned to stare at Josh's door.

Her throat felt tight. She thought she had shed all the tears possible, yet more threatened. She looked out the window again.

"Josh . . ." she whispered.

Christmas came and went, a forlorn holiday called La Noche Buena, the Good Night. Gifts were exchanged later on El Día de los Reyes, Twelfth Night, an occasion when

Josh presented her with a diamond necklace while she gave him a new set of dueling pistols.

She turned the sparkling diamonds in her hands, feeling a tug on her heart. They were the first lavish gift she had received in her life, and she was breathless looking at them, yet their cold glitter reminded her of her dilemma. She wished Josh had cared enough to fasten them on her.

"They're beautiful! Thank you."

"You don't sound sure, *cara*," he said.

"I've never had such a gift. It's overwhelming."

He stared at her solemnly until she blushed and said, "Open your gift."

He unfastened the wrappings and opened the box. "Pistols! They're excellent." He lifted one to examine it. For a moment a sardonic grin crossed his face. "You see me only as a cutthroat pirate! Well, perhaps I am. There's little else for me to be." He rose swiftly, taking the pistols with him, leaving her with an empty feeling that seemed to haunt her days.

Then two days later she saw him briefly. She heard a rustle and opened her eyes to see him rise from the pallet on the floor.

Lianna had been uncertain if he still slept in her room. He came and went at odd hours, and if he were there, he came while she was asleep and left before she awoke, taking all traces of his presence with him.

He glanced at her. "Sorry if I woke you."

Her gaze flicked down across his bare chest, his tight breeches, and she became too hot to breathe.

"Lianna," he said softly, making her pulse drum, "any day now I'll leave for the mountains and Simms will take you back to *El Feroz*. You can't pack many things, because it'll reveal our plans. Put the things you don't want to leave behind where you can get them at once."

"All right." She had barely heard what he said. They would leave. It was over. She felt no elation, merely regret, loss, desire.

She wanted him desperately. "Josh . . ."

He turned around. "Yes?"

Her heart thudded as she looked into his cool green eyes. She shook her head. "I'll be ready."

He turned and left the room, closing the door behind him without a sound.

Tuesday morning more than a week later, Quita sat in the courtyard of the Governor's Palace. She watched the fountain, waiting for Marie, one of the servants, to tell her when the men were finished with their meeting.

They had been in Santiago a week now and parties were being planned to introduce them to society. Quita was beginning to relax because she hadn't seen any sign of *El Feroz* or heard of a ship with an English captain; adding to her relief, she had learned that Spain wouldn't allow any ships to put into ports of the colonies except their own, so perhaps Captain Raven had to sail on to other places.

She laughed softly, thinking nothing could disturb her now, yet she still hoped she could persuade Armando to sail soon for Spain. She didn't like Santiago, but she couldn't admit to him why. Francisco and Salina Marcheno were gracious to them—particularly Salina to Armando. Quita would have had to be blind to miss Salina's obvious flirting with Armando, yet he was gallant and nothing more. Quita smiled, sure of holding his love now, so very sure. And with the threat of Lianna Melton and Captain Joshua Raven evaporating into nothing, life held bright promises. She frowned, momentarily thinking of the one cloud. Armando had hinted there might be an uprising—and that he could give Francisco help. Quita didn't want to lose her dashing, handsome husband because of unrest in a colony across the world from Spain! She wanted Armando back at home where life was safe, and she intended to use all her wits to persuade him to return.

Marie's quiet footstep was impossible to hear as her shadowy form drifted past the fountain; the slender maid halted in front of Quita.

"Condesa, the men leave the salon."

Quita's pulse quickened in eagerness. "Good. Will you tell my husband I am ill and need to see him? I'll be in my bedroom."

"Sí, condesa."

Quita hurried, moving as swiftly and quietly as Marie had, while her heartbeat hammered in happiness. "Now, Armando . . . you will be mine forever!"

She hurried into the bedroom that was part of the quarters she and Armando had to themselves in the east side of the Governor's Palace. The bedroom had baroque black wrought-iron torchères on both sides of the intricately carved rosewood bed. There was a niche in one wall with a shell motif carved above it, forming an altar on one side of the room; on the wall beside it was a tin carving of a saint. A brazier with a copper bowl stood in the center of the room if they needed warmth.

Quita had put a bright red silk coverlet on the bed. Armando's sword was in one corner, his books on a table. The room held their personal touches and she felt satisfied with it. She turned to look at herself in the oval mirror, to make certain her appearance would be right and would please Armando. She wore a soft white batiste dress with lace at the throat and along the sleeves and around the hem. It was the dress of a young girl and made her look sixteen again. Her black hair fell free and she had picked a bright red hibiscus blossom downstairs to tuck behind her ear. Around her neck she wore a simple gold cross Armando had given her when they had been in port in Bahia.

Without warning, the thickly carved wood door burst open and with a clatter of his boots and spurs on the stone floor, Armando swept into the room, a scowl on his face. He closed the door and halted abruptly, his features softening. "Marie told me you were ill." A faint smile played over his mouth as he watched her, and Quita smiled in return.

"I wanted to be alone with you. Forgive me because this one time I had to tell a tiny lie."

He laughed softly, the sound deep in his throat as he crossed the room to look at her. Her heart quickened as she looked at her handsome husband with his white silk shirt open at the throat, a gunbelt slung low around his narrow hips.

He rested his hands on her shoulders. "Shame on you

for worrying me, Lia,'' he said huskily. ''Perhaps I shall worry you a little in return.''

''You knew it could be nothing serious. You left our bed only an hour ago.''

''You cannot imagine what worry you caused! And I told you, I want only the truth—although maybe this once I'll take my revenge and then forgive you.''

She smiled, winding her fingers in his hair.

''You little witch!'' he murmured, and his fingers caressed the underside of her breast, making her gasp and look up at him through eyes almost closed.

''Armando, stop a moment. Wait—''

He chuckled again, a husky male sound that tickled her senses. ''Ah, you don't want to be tormented, yet you unnecessarily cause me woe . . .''

''Armando!'' She caught his hands and stepped back. ''I have something to ask for and something to tell you. I've never asked you for anything, have I?''

''Only to stay in Spain.'' His brows arched while he gazed at her with curiosity. ''So what do you want from me?''

''Take me home to Spain.''

He laughed and dropped his hands to his hips. ''I will soon enough, but now there's trouble here, and Francisco needs me.''

''That's all the more reason to go! I want you! I love you!'' She threw her arms around his neck. ''Please . . .''

''And what did you have to tell me,'' he asked flatly, and she suspected he was growing impatient with her requests to go home, making him remember things he had planned to do at the moment instead of staying to talk to her.

She slipped out of his arms and spun away from him to face him, feeling her heart pound against her ribs. ''I had to wait to tell you until I felt sure.''

''Sure of what?''

''How do I look?'' She held out her arms and turned slowly in front of him.

The faint smile returned to his features and he unbuckled his gunbelt. ''You look,'' he said, and his voice lowered, "good enough for me to make Francisco wait for me a little longer."

"Armando, look at me!" She placed her hands on her hips and stared at him.

His brows arched again and he paused, his fingers tangled in the laces of his shirt. He frowned. "Lia . . ." he said impatiently.

She reached behind her to gather the fullness of her dress and pull it tight so it molded her figure. His gaze drifted down slowly, making her breasts grow taut and the nipples harden.

"You're lovely," he whispered.

"And you're too slow for words!"

His head snapped up, and she laughed. "Armando . . ." She caught his hands, placing one on her breast and one on her stomach. "Now, look at me," she whispered. "And feel . . . feel what we have made together, feel how my heart beats . . ."

His dark eyes seemed to widen endlessly, and his breath left as if he had received a blow. "*Querida!*" he whispered. "A child?"

She laughed. "Yes, Armando! Your son!"

"*Mi amor*, Lia!" He crushed her to him, showering her with kisses while she clung to him and laughed with joy.

"Armando, suppose . . ." she whispered while he knelt and buried his head between her breasts, kissing her, his breath hot on her skin even through the batiste. She caught his dark head to turn his face upward to her. "Armando!" she whispered, shocked to see tears in his eyes.

"I've waited so long, Lia. Finally you give me an heir."

She felt as if she would melt with love for him as she held his head to her breasts. "Suppose it's a girl?"

"There have been strong women in history. Our baby will be strong whether a boy or a girl." He stood up and laughed. "And hopefully, we will have both!"

She laughed with him, clinging to him. He stepped back to unfasten the tiny buttons and laces and hooks, swearing as his big fingers fumbled and delayed him. Finally he pushed away her garments to hold her at arm's length while he looked at her.

"This is when a woman looks most beautiful—now," he whispered in a raspy voice.

"Armando, come here."

"Un momento, querida," he whispered. "How beautiful you look."

"I hope you think so months from now!"

"I will." He scooped her up and placed her on the bed to stand over her, looking at her until she held out her arms.

"Armando, please . . ."

"Shh . . . you carry our child, my heir." He sat on the bed to kiss her stomach, saying softly, "Lia, I will give you the world in exchange."

His kisses set her on fire, but she knew she should persist now. She reached down to tangle her fingers in his hair and turn his head. "Give me the one thing I've asked for—take me home to Spain. I don't want our child born here or at sea."

"Dios!" His chest expanded with a deep breath. "We'll go. Give me two weeks to help Francisco, then we'll start for Spain."

She closed her eyes. Two weeks. Fourteen days, and she would be headed safely home. What could harm them in such a short time? *"Gracias,* Armando!"

"Shh, don't thank me! I'm the one to thank you. And I will show my gratitude like this," he whispered as his tongue touched her nipple, ". . . and like this." His head lowered and his lips and tongue trailed over her flat stomach while his hands began to move on her. "You're a woman now, *querida,* my woman. How fiery you are! You make my heart dance like the fandango." He kissed her thigh, his warm breath fanning over her while she moaned and shifted.

"Armando, please . . ."

"Shh," he whispered, his tongue stopping her words and thoughts.

Wednesday morning Lianna smoothed the folds of her green silk dress, took a deep breath, and entered the Governor's Palace. Last week she had sent her calling card, leaving it for the Countess of Marcheno. She had received an answer, that Doña Lianna would be happy to meet her Wednesday morning.

The reply lay folded in Lianna's reticule, embedded in her memory, her own name signed in Quita Bencaria's tiny script. What a winding path each had taken. Lianna refused to look back, to think what might have been if she had loved Josh from the beginning.

She was frightened about the meeting with Quita. She prayed they would be alone, that no one would witness the first moment Quita would see her, and she wished there had been some way to warn Quita who she was.

Lianna stepped into the long hall with its white walls and dark log beams in the ceiling, and she stiffened. Near a doorway down the hall stood Governor Marcheno, General Farjado, a soldier, and another man. All glanced in her direction, murmuring greetings.

"Buenos días." Lianna nodded, replying stiffly, barely aware of her words. All of them could see and hear everything! She prayed they would go before Quita appeared. She wanted to turn and run. There was nowhere to stand where the men couldn't see her.

Swiftly she considered pleading ill or returning to the carriage immediately. She couldn't face Quita with the four men watching. General Farjado was quick and shrewd. Lianna's pulse raced in fright while she stood waiting.

"Marquesa . . ." came a soft-spoken greeting from a voice Lianna recognized instantly.

She turned to see Quita appear in a doorway on her left. Quita wore an elegant silk dress, her black hair piled high on her head, her neck adorned in rubies, and her brown eyes widened alarmingly as she screamed.

Then Quita, who had become the Condesa de Marcheno, collapsed in a faint.

26

"Lianna!"

Lianna's head jerked up. A handsome man who was fully six and a half feet tall rushed to pick up Quita.

The Count of Marcheno. Lianna felt as if she might also faint. Her head spun, and she glanced at the others hastily approaching. A pair of black eyes watched her with the attentiveness of a swooping hawk. General Farjado reached out to steady her.

"Are you ill?" he asked.

"No. I can't imagine what happened," Lianna answered. "I merely said hello."

The count lifted Quita effortlessly and walked into a salon. Lianna's mind raced as she glanced at the governor and the general.

"Perhaps . . ." She paused and frowned.

"Yes?" General Farjado snapped the word.

"Perhaps it is a woman's matter. Let me go help."

While the general frowned, the governor waved his hand. *"Sí, por favor."*

As she entered the room, the count was fanning Quita. Lianna's fingers locked together. She wanted to run from the house, from the hostile people around her. Instead, she tried to keep her voice calm.

"Conde."

Chocolate-brown eyes rested on her curiously, and she looked at the man who would have been her husband. He was unbelievably handsome, with bright eyes, a black mustache, and thick curly hair, a stature as fit as Josh Raven's, and a sensual mouth. For a fleeting second Lianna felt a sense of relief that Quita might not have been disappointed with the exchange.

She said swiftly, "This may be a woman's concern. Let me help."

He frowned, then stood up as General Farjado introduced them.

"Doña Lita, this is Don Armando, the Conde de Marcheno. This is the *marquesa,* the wife of Don Cristóbal, Marqués de Aveiro."

"Ah, I am sorry we meet under these circumstances."

Quita moaned, and Lianna's terror rose. "If you will allow me, sir. Will someone please fetch a damp cloth?"

"I'll summon the maid," Governor Marcheno said, and left the room. The two men moved away, but Lianna was conscious of General Farjado's presence, his steady, questioning eyes.

"Condesa?" Lianna patted her hand. "Are you all right?"

Quita's dark lashes fluttered, her eyes focused, and she gasped.

Lianna talked quietly and steadily. "Ah, I told your husband this might be a womanly matter. I understand these things. Would you like privacy? I've sent for a damp cloth. Just lie quietly. Don't try to talk." Lianna squeezed Quita's hand as she made the request, and saw a flickering response in the dark eyes focused solemnly on her.

"Just lie quietly and you'll feel better. Much better. I'm the Marquesa de Aveiro, Doña Lita."

"Buenos días," Quita whispered.

Behind her Lianna heard voices, then the count handed her a damp cloth.

"Lianna, are you all right?"

Quita's gaze shifted to her husband, and she smiled stiffly. "I'm sorry. I felt faint and had a sudden pain."

"If you're all right, I'll join the men again," he said, but his unwavering gaze never flickered as he watched his wife closely.

"Sí," she whispered to him. "You go. I'll be fine."

Lianna sponged Quita's brow as the men left the room.

As the door closed quietly behind them, Lianna wondered if General Farjado had actually gone or if he were standing outside the door, listening for a snatch of conversation. She placed her finger on her lips and asked Quita, "Would you feel better if you had fresh air? If we walked in the garden?"

Quita stared at her so long that Lianna became afraid. One word of truth, and she could be imprisoned along with Josh and his men.

Quita ran her hand across her brow, aware that Lianna was waiting for an answer. "*Sí,*" she answered finally. They crossed the room silently, to open the door and face General Farjado. "Do you feel better, Doña Lianna?"

"Yes," Quita answered, trying to sound composed. "We go to the courtyard where the air is cooler."

"Can I be of service?"

"*Gracias,* no."

His dark eyes shifted to Lianna. "Doña Lianna and Doña Lita. How similar your names are."

"*Sí,*" Lianna answered, and Quita received another shock. Lianna was terrified. Fear plainly showed in her features, and her skin was pale. "If you'll excuse us, general, Doña Lianna needs to sit down."

"Of course." He stepped aside, but as they left, Quita knew he continued to watch them and she had a feeling of dark undercurrents between Lianna Melton and General Farjado.

In the courtyard they sat down near a three-tiered fountain whose splashing water would prevent anyone from overhearing their conversation. Quita looked into frightened blue eyes and felt danger swirling around her like a rising fog.

Listening to the water splash in the fountain with a dim awareness, Quita felt as if someone were slowly closing clawlike fingers around her throat. Fear overrode all else after the first shock of coming upon Lianna face-to-face without warning—the moment Quita had feared and dreaded since Armando had told her they would sail to Chile.

Her thoughts tried to sort themselves out as she realized Lianna was posing as the wife of a *marqués*, a fact that could mean only one thing: Captain Joshua Raven was a spy for forces opposing Spain!

Quita knew little of the politics in Santiago, but she had gleaned enough from Armando to learn there was enough unrest among certain Chilenos that Spanish officers feared an uprising.

She stared at Lianna, torn by the knowledge that Lianna could destroy her marriage to Armando with a few words—yet at the same time aware that Lianna and Captain Raven's presence meant that Armando's and Francisco's lives might be in extreme danger.

"Why are you here?" Quita asked.

"If you'll keep our identity secret, we'll be gone soon," Lianna said, evading the question.

"Your husband must be posing as the Marqués de Aveiro—the only thing he could be doing is spying," Quita said, studying Lianna, realizing Lianna had changed in subtle ways. She looked like a woman, not a girl. And she was more beautiful than before, but she looked frightened and worried. "And that means he's a threat to my husband's existence, to Francisco and all other Spaniards!"

"Quita, you and I have been caught in circumstances we can't help," Lianna whispered, leaning closer. "The men in our lives have a destiny, and you and I are part of it whether we like it or not." Then, as if surprised, she said, "You look so beautiful—you must be happy."

"I am—and I'll protect what I've found at all costs," Quita said, thinking what a dilemma they were in. She couldn't reveal what she knew of Lianna and Josh—yet how could she sit by and watch them destroy something vital to Armando? "Armando thinks I'm Lianna Melton. This is our honeymoon, and we'll sail from here around the world and home to Spain. He gives me almost anything I desire, and I am carrying his child now."

"How grand!"

For a moment both women were silent; then Quita said, "I assumed you had returned to England. Did you get my letter?"

"Yes, thank you. Josh wouldn't let me go. I'm thankful

you're happpy," she went on, "but please don't betray us.
We'll leave Santiago."

"I can't betray you—yet I know you're a threat to my
husband's life!"

"You don't want Armando to know your identity."

"Of course not! He's a hard man; he would destroy
me."

"As soon as possible, I'll try to talk Josh into leaving.
Give us time!"

"Josh? Are you his mistress?"

"I'm his wife."

They stared at each other and Quita realized that Lianna
was a threat to her own existence and to her child.

Lianna blinked, and Quita wondered if her anger and
fear showed clearly in her expression. She looked at her
hands knotted tightly in her lap.

"Quita . . ."

"It's Lianna!" Quita snapped nervously. If Armando
were to overhear Lianna, he would wring the truth from
them! "It's Doña Lianna. I don't want to hear another
name!"

"Lianna, don't betray us. Don't have me arrested now
or I will reveal everything about you," Lianna said coldly,
yet her blue eyes looked full of terror. "I can prove what
you've done, and you know your husband will be furious."

Quita frowned and licked her lips, knowing the only
choice at the moment was to agree with Lianna. "Very
well. But can I trust you?"

"We'll have to trust each other. What would we gain
except arrest? Keep your silence, and we'll leave Santiago."

"You promise, swear that you won't reveal our secret?" Quita asked.

"I swore secrecy to you once long ago. I'll keep my
promise. Just give us some time."

"I feel ill," Quita said. Her gaze drifted nervously
around the courtyard. "This is a dangerous place, filled
with intrigue. We'll sail from Chile in two weeks, sooner
if I can persuade Armando, but until we go, don't cause
trouble. Now I hold more power than you. And I won't
give it up!"

"I understand." Lianna nodded, wanting to get away as quickly as possible, feeling as if Quita was barely controlling her anger and hatred.

"I must go to my room now," Quita announced, and stood up.

Relieved that the visit had ended, Lianna stood and gazed into angry eyes. Was Quita determined enough to try to find a way to destroy them? Lianna desperately wanted to get Josh and leave for *El Feroz* tonight, but could she convince him of the added danger?

"I'm glad you've found happiness," Lianna said, and meant it. How fleeting it would be, she didn't know. She hurried out, shaking with reaction when she climbed into the carriage.

At home, her fright increased when she learned that Josh had left town, and worse, she remembered she had promised to go on a carriage ride in the afternoon with General Farjado. She gazed at Fletcher's impassive features and said rapidly, "I need to see Don Cristóbal. Do you know when he returns?"

"No, Doña Lita. I'll find out for you."

"Please, it's urgent."

She went to her room, to pace the floor. She had to warn Josh that Quita's actions were unpredictable. She looked down the empty street and wished he would return home. And she regretted her acceptance of General Farjado's invitation for the afternoon. She would have to appear as carefree as possible, because she knew his curiosity had been stirred this morning.

After his arrival, Lianna caught up a filmy fichu and adjusted it in the neck of her rose silk dress, then went to the salon. The moment she entered the room, General Farjado's black eyes appraised her. He bowed low over her hand, boldly allowing his kiss to linger.

"How lovely you look. You should always have your hair down." The general rocked on his heels. "I thought you might enjoy an outing. There are Indian ruins nearby that we can visit."

Lianna started to refuse. Before she could, he added,

"Unless you are still too upset from the incident this morning."

The words carried a threat. He watched her intently, and Lianna answered casually, "I'd enjoy an outing. After all, it was the *condesa* who had the difficult morning."

"Of course. But you, too, looked pale for a time."

"She surprised me. Would you like for someone to greet you, to have her take one look at you, and faint?"

He smiled. "No. I wouldn't like it at all." His voice was full of curiosity. "And I would wonder greatly what had caused it."

"You'll have to discuss that with Doña Lianna. I'll have the maid fetch my shawl."

In the carriage, General Farjado leaned back to look at her. "We'll see Inca ruins, an ancient civilization of Indian heretics, savages who were conquered by the first Spanish to arrive."

"Perhaps these people would have fared better without the influence of Spain."

"Dangerous talk."

She shrugged. "I know nothing about politics. That I leave to my husband. Did the Spanish fleet bring any materials, silk or satin?"

He settled in the seat and smiled. "Ah, you would like a new dress!"

"Of course—or is that also dangerous to discuss?"

He laughed. "Hardly. Nothing is dangerous today. It's a beautiful summer day and I'm with a lovely woman."

"Gracias." And while she smiled and talked, she wondered where Josh was. She felt as if a net were drawing closer around them. Could they escape Chile without harm?

When the carriage halted, the general helped her step down onto a dusty lane beside the low, rolling foothills of the Andes.

"This way," he directed, taking her arm, while his driver remained behind with the carriage. They climbed through high grass up a steep incline dotted by *alerce* trees. On a level area they walked through crumbling stone ruins, granite partitions for rooms long overgrown by vines and wildflowers. Lianna remembered Madryn's proud man-

ner and wondered if the maid was descended from the
people who had once lived in these ruins. People who had
lost everything to the *conquistadores*.

They finally halted in the shade of a tree. The only
sound was the sigh of the wind across the hill. Lianna
touched the bright blossom of a red fuchsia that twined
through a tree. "You wonder what the people were like
who lived here. What they did and how they felt."

"I can tell you what *I* think and feel," he said huskily.
"Lita, you're a beautiful, desirable woman." He reached
for her and Lianna rested her hands on his arms.

"Sir—"

"You cannot give me a good reason to stop." His black
eyes burned as he said, "That husband of yours has all but
abandoned you. I find you infinitely more fascinating than
an estate or a deck of cards." He lifted her hand and
turned it to kiss her wrist, then raised his head to pin her
with his gaze. "Admit it. You're bored to death in that
house."

"You're an astute man. How I wish this conversation
had transpired before the fleet sailed from Valparaiso."

His brows arched questioningly. "What do you mean?
The fleet is still in the harbor."

"It hasn't sailed?" Her heart began to pound. Josh had
hidden the fact of the fleet's presence from her!

"No." He reached out to caress her shoulder. "But I
won't escort you to Valparaiso nor allow you to go."

"Why?"

"I regret with all my heart that I must deny you
anything, but why should I send you away? That's the last
thing I want." His voice hardened. "Also, you're married
to a *marqués* who is immensely wealthy and holds great
power. What you're asking could cost me everything."
General Farjado slipped his arms around her waist, drawing her to him. "But I will help you forget your loneliness."

"No," she answered, her mind still on Josh.

"Don't be foolish! Why shouldn't you have happiness?"
He leaned forward to kiss her cheek. "He does as he
wants. He has a Creole mistress—"

Her attention was snatched up violently. "It's a lie!"

"Would you like to meet Luisa Otero?" he asked cynically.

Lianna sucked in her breath swiftly. "No!" Josh had deceived her about the fleet. He had admitted kissing another. Now the general calmly announced Josh had a mistress. Captain Raven had forced a union on her that would end bitterly. He risked her life daily. All her grievances rose like a cloud of dust caught in a swirling wind, but the news of a mistress hurt like a knife wound. She asked, "What would happen to a person found untrue to Spain?"

Imperceptibly General Farjado straightened and his eyes narrowed. "Such a person would most likely be exiled." The sunlight dappled his swarthy skin. He asked softly, "Is Don Cristóbal disloyal?"

Lianna looked into his black eyes. The acceptance of the fact that Josh had a Creole mistress stung more than she cared to admit, but never would she cause Josh to go to prison or be harmed. As she stared at the general, she realized all she wanted to do was to erase the burning memory of Josh's kisses, to stop the aching need she felt for him.

General Farjado was a handsome, worldly man. She tilted her head to regard him from beneath thick lashes. His lips were fuller than Josh's. If his kisses could stir her as much as Josh's, then it was not just Josh Raven that held special magic for her. General Farjado's eyes narrowed as she stared at him.

"My husband is a loyal subject," she whispered.

His arms tightened around her and he leaned down to kiss her. With desperation Lianna wrapped her slender arms around his neck. He crushed the breath from her lungs and leaned back against a tree to fit her to his length while he kissed her.

She felt nothing except revulsion. His hand pulled free her fichu, caressing her throat, moving to the neck of her dress. Lianna pushed forcefully; her breath came in gasps. "I've made a mistake!" she gasped.

"No, Lita, come here," he murmured as he tightened his arm around her.

She struggled, her heart pounding. "No! Give me time to think!"

"You want this; your body trembles for caresses . . ." He held her in an iron grip; his mouth stopped her protests as he kissed her savagely. Desperation mushroomed in Lianna and she struggled, finally breaking free, only to be yanked back into his embrace. Anger already raged within her because of the news about a mistress; now it deepened over the general's brutal use of force, and without pausing to think, Lianna slapped him.

The sound of her palm on his cheek was loud in the silent countryside. His eyes narrowed and his lips thinned.

Suddenly her rage vanished as she realized she had made an enemy. "*Perdón!* I lost my head. I'm sorry." She retrieved the fallen fichu.

"You wanted me to kiss you," he said angrily. "I saw it in your eyes."

"I was carried away by the moment."

"You'll regret the slap." His tone was harsh as he said, "Someday you'll be mine."

"I'm wed to another. I forgot myself momentarily. It won't happen again."

She rushed down the hill, ignoring the weeds catching and snagging the billowing skirt of her dress. She was frightened of what he might make of her question about loyalty to Spain. If General Farjado and those in power were as evil as Josh had said, she didn't want to give him any weapon to use against Josh. Suddenly she came to her senses and slowed. She turned to look over her shoulder.

General Farjado walked toward her, his black eyes fiery. Her heart pounded loudly in her ears, but not from fright. There was no question that she was deeply, irrevocably in love with Josh! Only his kisses could inflame her.

In the carriage she was silent while General Farjado watched her, a brooding look on his features. She tried to talk to him, but his answers were clipped.

As soon as they reached her house, she touched his arm. "Thank you . . ."

He took her hand tightly in his grasp, crushing her fingers until she gasped. "Sir!"

"Doña Lita, I do not like being slapped."

She felt a knot of fear form in the pit of her stomach. Desperately she kept her voice light and took a chance. "General, perhaps it was myself that I was angry with." She leaned forward to brush his lips lightly.

He drew in his breath and looked at her intently. "If we weren't in front of your house—"

"But we are. We'll have tomorrow. You caused me to lose control over my emotions, and it upset me. I'm sorry."

For the first time since they had left the hillside, he smiled thinly, his black eyes burning into her. "Perhaps you can make amends. We'll ride tomorrow."

"*Sí,*" she answered, loathing the thought of another ride with him, knowing that he would demand her kisses, but she was afraid to cross him. He leaned forward and brushed her cheek with a kiss.

"Sir!"

"Call me Ramón, *mi amor.* Wait, I'll help you out."

"No! Please, I need to be alone."

He smiled and kissed her fingers, his tongue flicking over them until her skin crawled with distaste. "Of course. Until tomorrow, Lita *mía.* You're a passionate woman." His hand drifted across her breasts. "Perhaps I can be enticed to forget the slap . . ."

"I hope you can," she said. "*Adiós.*" She climbed out of his carriage and hurried upstairs to her room and closed the door. She sat by the window and tried to calm herself, but her worries grew.

She had made an enemy of General Farjado—unless she gave him her kisses freely tomorrow. And if she did, would he demand more? She laced her fingers together tightly, her blood running cold. How foolishly she had acted, but she had been driven beyond reason by her need of and love for Josh. Luisa Otero. His mistress. The knowledge hurt more than she would have believed possible.

Nervous over the day's happenings, she rose and paced the floor. She was in danger from General Farjado and dreaded the carriage ride tomorrow. How could she refuse his demands? From his actions in the carriage, she knew he would want more of her than mere kisses.

How she wished she could take back her question about loyalty to Spain! And now there was the worry of Quita, who had the power and wealth to hire someone to eliminate the threat to her own well-being.

Lianna continued to pace restlessly, looking time and again for some sign of Josh.

Within sight of land about two miles north of the docks at Valparaiso, a ship lay at anchor. Captain Edwin Stafford stood on deck, his feet braced while a breeze tangled his golden hair. He took no notice of the wind, his brooding gaze resting on land in the distance while he watched a ship row out to meet him. Lianna was so close now. Soon the only thing to stand between him and all he had ever wanted would be Josh Raven. A smile curled one corner of Edwin's mouth. He relished the moment he could run a rapier right through Joshua Raven's heart!

Hopefully, he could do it before the revolution started. If so, he could get Lianna and both of them could safely sail home to England. It had been months since Edwin's ship had stopped at a port and he felt the need for a woman tear at him. He wanted Lianna and he didn't want to wait!

The longboat came aside and a man climbed swiftly up the ladder to step over the rail. He bounded forward, offering his hand.

"Timothy Paddington, Captain Stafford. Welcome to Chile."

"Thank you. Call me Edwin, sir. We'll work closely together."

"Are we glad you're here! I hear you've brought arms and supplies."

"Yes. Come below to my cabin. We'll have lunch and talk. How about a brandy first?"

"Excellent! Fine ship you have here."

"Thank you, sir—"

"No, it's Timothy. As you said, we'll work together. How's England?"

Edwin curbed his impatience with the man's questions,

trying to show interest in the details of the revolution, quickly gleaning facts he wanted to know—Joshua Raven was alive and well. As was his beautiful wife. There were no children. The revolt of the patriots could commence at any time because Chile's summer would be the most opportune time for a battle.

Edwin listened and learned and finally asked his own questons. After lunch he leaned back in his chair, watching Timothy Paddington as he said casually, "I have a peculiar question."

"Ask away," Timothy said with good cheer, taking another sip of brandy.

"I have an old enemy here, a Spaniard, an enemy from sailing days. If I wanted to have him brought to my ship without anyone knowing his whereabouts, could I pay someone to do this?"

"Of course! Get your men to perform the task. Or if it's a very private matter, I can give you the names of two or three fellows. Ask at the Paloma Cantina for Ovidio Gonzales or Hector Ortiz. Both of them would do it for you and keep their mouths closed."

Edwin smiled. "Thank you. I have an old score to settle and the man would never answer a challenge. No, more than likely, if he gets wind I'm here, he'll flee or try to do me in some dark night," Edwin lied, embellishing his remarks while he committed the two names to memory. He would like to face Josh Raven right here on his ship. And if Lianna were here also, they could sail as soon as Raven was dead.

"You'll be coming to stay at my house a week from tonight," Timothy said, and Edwin shifted his attention back to the slender man seated opposite him. "I'll hide you. It's unfortunate you don't speak Spanish—then we could pass you off as a Spanish nobleman."

"Regretfully, my Spanish is exceedingly limited."

"Well, it won't matter. We'll whisk you away to join the patriots in the mountains if it looks as if your help will be needed there. In the meantime, we hope the Spanish won't have an inkling of what is about to transpire."

Edwin smiled, raising his glass in a toast. "To secrecy—
and to success."

Timothy smiled and leaned forward to touch glasses as
he nodded agreement. "We're so glad to have you," he
repeated. "You don't know how badly we need help."

"You don't know how badly I've wanted to get here."

Timothy's eyebrows arched and he grinned. "I understand you and your men are mercenaries."

"We are, and we relish a good fight."

Timothy laughed. "By George, you're a breath of fresh
air. Tell me more about London. Stuffy old Quimby is
paying you! I'll bet it's breaking his heart to miss the
fight. He loves odd ports in the world. On your way here,
did you stop at Belém?"

Edwin settled back in his chair, stretching out his long
legs while he talked, his mind half on the conversation,
half on memories of Lianna.

After two more brandies he waved a cigar at Timothy
and said, "I've heard about your prowess with the sword.
I've been taking lessons from Monsieur Toussaint in London. Would you have time to give me a little practice
against a real swordsman?"

Timothy laughed and exhaled a stream of gray smoke.
"Of course! One mustn't get rusty." He stood up and
peeled off his coat while Edwin crossed the cabin to open
a cabinet. "Select the rapier you want."

Timothy's smile vanished as he picked up first one and
then another. "These are magnificent weapons! The very
finest!" He looked up at Edwin and smiled. "You learned
your lessons well, I suspect. I'm glad we are not in
earnest."

Edwin laughed. "You won't say that minutes from
now. I'm a novice."

Within minutes Edwin knew he could win in a challenge
with Timothy Paddington, and satisfied with the knowledge, he deliberately made a feint at a bad moment.
Timothy dodged, lunged, and swept Edwin's rapier from
his hands.

Edwin bowed and smiled. "Thank you. I've learned
quite a bit."

Timothy smiled back. "Yes, and I think you just let me win," he said softly. "I'm doubly glad we're friends."

Edwin retrieved the rapier. "Let's have another brandy and then I'll show you the weapons you can take to the patriots."

Late that night in Santiago, Lianna sat in the darkened library with only one small oil lamp aglow while she tried to read. She gazed at a book, not seeing the words, her thoughts adrift when she heard the clatter of boots in the hall. Her heart jumped, then raced in eagerness. She heard Josh's voice as he told Fletcher good night.

Lianna hurried to the door to find Josh headed for the stairs, striped coat in hand, his shirt open at the throat, his cravat undone. His walk was that of a man of power and assurance. His detachment made him able to deal with risk, and she guessed before she spoke that he wouldn't share her fear over the events of the day.

"Don Cristóbal."

His green gaze appraised her, lowering slowly over her embroidered white robe. Her hair was caught behind her neck, tied loosely in a pink ribbon. As he looked at her languidly, she wanted to walk into his arms.

"*Buenas noches,*" he said, and motioned. "Come up-stairs with me. I'm weary."

"Where've you been?"

He looked mildly amused as he replied, "Playing monte, a Spanish game of chance. I've been with Governor Marcheno and your charming friend General Farjado."

"Don't call him that!"

Josh looked down at her, his brows arching. "Ah, something happened while I was gone. I wondered. the general has been casting speculative looks my way all evening."

They entered his room and he closed the door.

"Josh—"

"Wait, Lianna," he commanded, and walked through his room and hers, checking to make sure they were alone and the doors closed. He pulled off his cravat and dropped it, and suddenly she could remember clearly their wedding

night, when Josh had dropped off clothing bit by bit until
he stood naked before her, desiring her. He casually unfastened the top of his shirt, then paused as he looked
intently at her. He crossed the room and tilted her chin up.

One dark eyebrow arched. She could not resist looking
at his lips and thinking of his kisses. Fighting for control,
to hide her feelings from him, she asked breathlessly,
"What happened between you and the general tonight?"

"Lower your voice," he cautioned, "or you'll have us
all in prison." He walked away to pour a glass of brandy.
He raised the bottle. "Would you care for brandy, Lianna?"
There was a note of pain in his voice.

"No, thank you." The light flowed softly across his
profile and made him look younger and more vulnerable
than ever before. His brow was furrowed and his hand had
a tremor.

"So finally something has been too large for you to
overcome," she said softly, wondering if he had given his
love totally to Luisa Otero. "I would like to see the thing
or person who has succeeded in getting the better of you."

"You wouldn't want to see what I've just witnessed."

Lianna tilted her head to ask, "And what merry place
have you been spending the evening?" The words that had
plagued her all day, words she had intended to avoid
saying, came swiftly. "With your mistress, Luisa Otero?"

Fires blazed in the depths of his eyes. "Luisa isn't my
mistress. I wish she were, so I could—" He snapped his
mouth closed. "I've been at the prison."

She was stunned and confused by his answer, and her
heart jumped with his denial that Luisa wasn't his mistress!

"That isn't what I was told."

He set down his brandy, reaching her swiftly. His
fingers bit into her flesh. "Who told you? General Farjado?
Damn the man! Did he also kiss you?"

Lianna's eyes narrowed, and she faced Josh squarely.
"Yes."

He grasped her shoulders in a vise like iron. "Did you
let him? Did you enjoy his kisses?"

In spite of the pain, anger caused her to defy him.

"That is none of your . . ." Her answer died; never had she seen such rage. Her own anger vaporized into terror.

"Answer me!" His blazing eyes bore through her, compelling the truth.

"No."

His breath expelled in a hiss, and he dropped his hands, turning abruptly to walk to the mantelpiece and lean against it with his back to her.

Lianna stared at him, unable to avoid asking, "Why? Would it have mattered to you if I had said yes?"

His head raised slowly as he turned to face her. Hatred filled each word. "The man is unspeakable. If you had liked his kiss . . ."

She felt shaken and couldn't keep from prompting, "If I had?"

"I think I could slit your lovely throat," he answered in such simplicity that her veins turned to ice.

"Why do you hate him so?"

The silent rage was replaced by anguish, and Josh doubled his fist. "General Farjado is inhuman. Tonight I was taken by Governor Marcheno to see the interrogation of the political prisoners. I saw Farjado at work. He is a fiend straight from hell." Josh thumped the mantel. "I could do nothing . . . nothing."

"What had these prisoners done?" she asked woodenly, her fears mushrooming.

"Who knows? They may have done nothing more than raise the ire of the governor or the general or some other loyalist who is unscrupulous and in power. The prisoners may have been growing too strong, too big a threat to someone. Some of the loyalists are despots who rule according to their own whim, and they are a long way from Spain and its rule. The prisoners have no recourse, no one to turn to with their pleas against such power."

"How dreadful," she murmured, realizing how precarious a position they held and what damage she might have done earlier in the day. "Josh, there's something I need to tell you. I went for a carriage ride today with the general." Reluctantly she told him about the afternoon. How she wished she could take back the day, relive each moment and tell General Farjado she wouldn't go with him. She shook, feeling an ominous invisible threat of disaster looming in the shadows like a hulking beast ready to devour them. "I'm afraid I've done something wrong."

"Tell me. Perhaps I can help," Josh said gently.

"Today when we were at the ruins—" She bit her lip, dreading to admit to him what she'd done.

"What happened?"

"I asked General Farjado if one is severely punished for being disloyal to Spain."

"Oh, damn, Lianna."

"I'm sorry. I didn't realize how dangerous it could be to ask. I asked him to take me to the Spanish fleet in Valparaiso. It hasn't sailed yet." There was only a flicker in Josh's eyes to indicate any change in his feelings.

"What did he say?"

"He refused, saying you are a *marqués* and too powerful for him to attempt anything like that, that he wouldn't anyway because he didn't want me to leave Santiago. then I asked him about disloyalty."

"And what did he answer to that question?"

"He said it would mean only being sent home to Spain."

"Damn the lying man!"

"Josh, he asked me if you were disloyal."

Green eyes rested on her in an impassive, unfathomable stare. Then a faint smile lifted one corner of his mouth, causing creases to deepen in his cheeks. "So," he said softly, "at last you had the chance to carry out your threat, to betray me. What did you answer?"

"I told him that you were a loyal subject."

"And missed your chance for betrayal?"

"I wouldn't betray you."

"Thank you for that much. We'll go soon."

"That wasn't all." She had his full attention as she told him about the meeting with Quita. "I know she was terrified and angry to find us here."

He finished the brandy in his glass and said, "Under the circumstances, I think we should go."

"Now? Leave at night?" Panic made her shiver. If Josh would drop everything and leave suddenly, what she had revealed to the general must have been catastrophic and placed their lives in great jeopardy. "Surely we can wait to pack."

He shrugged. "I feel the same as I do at sea when a squall approaches. There are too many indications of trouble."

"And I've caused it. I'm sorry."

"It's not all your fault. Several things are working together. I don't want to stay and risk our lives."

"I'm sorry. I let General Farjado goad me into it."

"Goad you into it?" the derisive gleam returned. "How was that?"

She hated Josh's sardonic drawl. "He told me about Luisa Otero."

"She isn't my mistress, Lianna. He lied to you. Not that I wasn't tempted, but something stood in my way."

Lianna's heart skipped, then began beating twice as rapidly. If *she* stood in his way . . . "Josh, who stood in your way?"

He smiled coldly. "Why bother to ask? You, of course. We are always at cross-purposes, you and I. We'd better go quickly. I'll ring for Fletcher and tell him. He'll handle the servants." He removed a brace of pistols from the desk. "That explains much about tonight."

"What does it have to do with tonight?" she said, wanting to pursue the remark he had made about cross-purposes.

"There was no reason to take me to view the prisoners. I tried to avoid it, but the governor was persistent. General Farjado was in charge; now I suspect he did it deliberately to impress on me what power they have and what they can inflict."

"It still gives them no reason to arrest you."

"A man as ruthless and powerful as the general can find a way, but it is little Quita who worries me. We're a threat to her existence. She stands to lose too much by letting us live. She can easily hire assassins."

"Quita?"

"Lianna, she stands to lose everything." He moved around the desk toward her. "We're no longer safe here.

I'll go to the mountains to join the patriots. Simms can take you to *El Feroz*.'' He tugged the bell-pull to summon a servant. ''And not only is there Quita causing us trouble, Farjado wants you. Any charge he can trump up will do. Any charge—or simply make you admit my disloyalty.''

''I wouldn't.''

''You're very brave, but no one can withstand the things I've witnessed tonight. You'd admit gladly to anything they asked. I would also. There's not a man alive who could resist such barbaric treatment as that beast Farjado can inflict.''

''I can't go like this. We're leaving everything behind.''

''That's exactly what you did when you boarded *El Feroz* and exchanged places with Quita.'' He frowned and said harshly, ''But before I sail from Chile, I'll come back to Santiago to hunt down the Count of Marcheno and cut him to ribbons!''

''You'd risk your life over an old hatred and for revenge!'' For a moment her fear was diminished by regret. A knock sounded and they both turned to look at the door.

''Come in,'' Josh said in a casual tone. When the door opened to admit a maid, he commanded, ''Would you send the butler in?''

''*Sí.*'' Maria nodded and left.

''Get your cloak, Lianna. Change as quickly as possible.'' Josh removed his shirt, baring his chest in the warm glow of candlelight, and despite the urgency of danger, Lianna couldn't move. She ached to touch him, drinking in the sight to keep forever in her memory.

''Hurry,'' he said, his eyes narrowed as he watched her.

''Of course.'' She paused. ''I did something terrible to you. I betrayed you after all.''

His voice was low as he said, ''Not knowingly.''

''I'm sorry, Josh.''

''It doesn't matter. Forget it, Lianna. I've done things to you I shouldn't have. Get ready,'' he said, turning as Fletcher appeared.

Thinking about Josh's words, Lianna left the two men. She dressed in the boy's clothing she had worn before. Her gaze swept the room and she selected two things to drop into her pocket: the diamond necklace from Josh and the wilted gardenia from the ball.

When she rejoined Josh, a cloak covered his dark clothing. He wore gloves, a sword belt, and pistols tucked into his waistband. His gaze swept over her. "Let's go quickly."

He took her arm, started toward the door, but suddenly stopped. With his finger on his lips he motioned her to silence.

Lianna held her breath, watching him move stealthily to the door. He yanked it open.

27

Juanita straightened, her eyes opening wide. *"Dios!"* she gasped, and turned to run.

Josh stepped forward, caught her around the waist, his hand clamping over her mouth. Swiftly he carried her back into the room. "Close the door," he commanded.

Before Lianna could close it, Fletcher appeared. "Spanish soldiers are coming down the street. Simms has gone to warn the others. I have horses ready in back."

"Can you and the men escape?" Josh asked.·

"Yes."

"Go, and take Lianna! Ride for the mountains, for Pablo's. Leave me a horse, and I'll follow."

"You won't get away!" Juanita snapped. "General Farjado knows your traitorous intentions! I've reported everything I've seen and heard to him."

Josh swore softly, glancing at Fletcher. "Go!" While he tied and gagged Juanita, Lianna left with Fletcher.

They ran along the corridor, but on the stairs she stopped. "Go ahead, Fletcher. I'll come with Josh."

"Dammit, that isn't—"

"Go ahead. He may need help."

As he turned and ran across the courtyard, she raced back toward the house.

Josh plunged down the stairs to meet her. "Lianna! You should have gone with Fletcher." Holding Lianna's arm, he was crossing the courtyard when they heard pounding at the front door.

"Run," Josh commanded. When they stepped outside, Lianna turned for the stables, but suddenly a Spanish soldier stepped in front of them.

Silver glinted in Josh's hand as he whipped out a dagger. The soldier's cry was cut short in a gasp. Josh plunged the knife down, and the soldier dropped to the ground.

"This way." Josh lifted her to the top of the high wall that surrounded the house. He climbed up swiftly, then dropped into the saddle of a waiting horse. He swung Lianna down into the saddle of the second horse.

"Now, Lianna, stay close. Ride!"

She urged the horse forward. The bay's legs stretched out as they raced down the street. While Josh led the way, his horse pounding across a yard, then leaping a fence, Lianna followed. Her mount gathered himself, soaring over the fence, landing and galloping after Josh until they rode from town into an open field.

The wind rushed against Lianna, whipping her hair from her face while they raced across the flat land under a bright, full moon.

Josh rode on ahead, horse and man as one, his hat pulled low over his eyes, his broad shoulders outlined against the gray night sky. Above the sound of the horses' hooves a shot rang out and fright gripped Lianna. When she glanced over her shoulder, her panic increased.

The moon shone clearly on horses and soldiers coming after them. Ahead stretched a vastness of plain before they would reach the mountains. It was flat, open land which offered no protection, no cover until they reached the mountains. The race would be to the swiftest.

In the empty night, the sound of the horses carried; their pursuers rode relentlessly after them. As they raced, Lianna could feel her bay strain with effort. Lather formed and blew back against her, flecks of white on her dark breeches. She regretted pushing the horse, yet she had to or they would be prisoners of the Spanish.

Josh's horse was holding up with greater ease; the distance between the two of them was slowly widening. She cast another glance over her shoulder. The soldiers had fanned out, six of them spread in a line as they galloped in pursuit. It would be only a matter of time until her horse could no longer keep up the deadly pace.

The pace slowed and the soldiers gained. And finally the terrain changed. The ground began to swell and fall; mesquite and acacia trees had to be skirted. Lianna looked back. The distance between her horse and the Spaniards had narrowed, while the length between her horse and Josh's had widened.

What would happen to them if they were caught? Josh's remarks about the torture of prisoners couldn't be forgotten. She looked at his broad back and her heart constricted painfully. She had betrayed him as surely as if she had told General Farjado every detail of their lives.

A sob was snatched by the wind, Lianna unaware that she had made a sound, oblivious of hot tears that streaked her face.

The soldiers gained. A cloud of dust rose behind them and hovered in the air. Suddenly Josh reined his horse, slowing to fall back beside her. He leaned close, yelling to her. "We can't outride them. Our horses will soon drop. We'll divide. You take the mountains."

"No," Lianna cried, realizing that he would sacrifice himself to save her.

As they galloped side by side, Josh continued calling instructions above the thunder of the horses. "Ride to the left. In that direction, up the mountain, you'll find an adobe hut. A boy, Pablo, is there. You must reach him and tell him I've been taken prisoner."

Lianna clutched the reins tightly, a wave of dizziness striking her. Josh—a prisoner of the Spaniards! She cried out, "No! You can't! You know how they hate you!"

"Lianna," he shouted, "listen to me! You must get to Pablo! Fletcher may be with him."

With a burst of energy, Josh's horse lengthened its stride and raced ahead, the brown mane flowing, Josh's cloak fluttering. He wheeled the horse to the right, then turned in the saddle and waved. His cry was muffled by the noise of hooves and wind, but she knew what he wanted.

She tugged the reins and her mount veered to the northeast. The landscape was rougher; occasional huge boulders lay on the ground.

Racing southward along the base of the foothills, Josh led the soldiers away.

As Lianna gazed down at the lone figure riding ahead of the soldiers, the tightness in her throat made breathing difficult. She sobbed with agony for Josh until another concern loomed. Two, then three horsemen separated from the soldiers and reversed direction, coming after her while the others pursued Josh.

She had to reach Pablo. The possibility of Josh at the mercy of General Farjado and Governor Marcheno made her ill. Lianna urged her horse forward.

The land sloped upward in a steep incline which forced her to slow, but also caused her pursuers more difficulty. Below them, on the plain, Josh was no longer in sight. Only a cloud of dust indicated where the riders were.

Behind her she could see three silhouettes of Spanish soldiers moving steadily after her. Ahead, she scanned the wooded mountian slope for an adobe hut.

There appeared to be nothing higher on the slope except mesquite, acacia, rocks, and boulders. She debated changing course—but which direction? To the left or to the right? Either way she might ride farther from the hut and miss it.

Every passing moment could mean the difference between survival and death for Josh. A large angular shape, white in the moon's brightness, caught her attention. She guided the horse through a rushing mountain stream glistening with water from melted snow. An adobe hut loomed before her, and desperately she called, "Pablo! Pablo!"

A small figure clad in dark cotton pants and shirt emerged from around a corner. The boy led a saddled horse. The moon shone fully on him as Lianna approached, and she reined her horse. "Please, Pablo, ride for help! The Marqués de Aveiro, Captain Raven, has been taken prisoner. Please go!"

"*Por Dios!*" the boy exclaimed. "*Sí*. I will ride like the wind. His men are ahead. Come, *señora*," he said as he vaulted into the hand-tooled saddle.

"No. Three soldiers are coming. My horse is ready to drop. You'll stand a better chance of getting help if you go alone. Find an Englishman named Fletcher. Tell him Josh is a prisoner. Go now. I'll lead the soldiers away."

She could hear horses approaching while they talked.

For an instant the boy looked at her; then he turned his horse. The silvery moonlight shone brightly on the slight figure astride a black horse.

He disappeared around a corner of the hut. Lianna turned her horse in the opposite direction and flicked the reins.

The pause to talk with Pablo had given the soldiers an advantage. They had narrowed the distance. Glancing down the slope, she saw the riders divide, two after her, one riding toward the hut.

Upward she climbed, with the grim knowledge that it was only a matter of minutes until she would be a prisoner, but every second she could give Pablo would mean a chance for the word to be passed along about Josh's capture. With the boy rode their only hope for survival. Her horse slowed; its sides heaved from the strain.

"Doña Lita!"

She stiffened when she heard the call, recognizing General Farjado's voice. The memory of his savage kiss was a nightmare coming true. She had no illusions what lay ahead with her capture. Grimly she climbed, urging the horse to one last burst of strength.

They headed for a cluster of boulders. Lianna dismounted and scrambled up the rocks, tearing the skin off her fingers in her rush to escape.

She heard horses, then a man's heavy breathing behind her. Spurs jingled and boots scraped on the boulders.

"Doña Lita, your flight is useless. Save us time. We have your husband."

Josh captured! Lianna closed her eyes and swayed.

Behind her she heard the general. "Come here!"

Desperately she reached up to try to climb higher over

the rough boulders. Hard arms closed around her waist like
chains and yanked her off her feet. General Farjado spun
her around to face him.

Lianna struggled momentarily. He raised his hand and
slapped her. The stinging blow snapped her head back, her
hat tumbled off, and dark curls fell free as she cried out.

"Now we're even," he said. His fingers bit into her
shoulders as he called to his men, "I have the woman!"

She looked up into a face bathed in moonlight. He ran
his finger down her cheek, along her throat, then placed
his hand over her breast. "Now you are mine."

"No!"

He squeezed his fingers into her flesh and she gasped
with pain. "Yes. Come, mount up and we'll return to
Santiago. You may watch what we do with your husband."

"Please"—Lianna felt as if she would faint—"let him
live and I'll do whatever you want."

Farjado's fingers wound in her hair and yanked her face
up. "Perhaps we can bargain after all."

He pulled her along until they reached a soldier who
waited with her horse. She climbed into the saddle, stonily
watching General Farjado mount and take the reins to her
horse.

"If you oppose me or try to escape, the torture will go
harder on your husband." He turned and led the way, the
soldiers moving into line behind Lianna's horse.

They descended slowly, all need for hurry gone. When
they passed the adobe hut, Lianna cast one brief glance in
its direction.

The moon shone on the simple structure, giving it beauty
in the night that it wouldn't hold under the harsh, revealing
sun.

No one stirred near it, and Lianna prayed that Pablo
would get help. She felt numb and cold, racked with fear
for Josh. And she began to understand his terrible hatred
of the Count of Marcheno. If they tortured Josh, she would
live with hate the rest of her life, just as Josh had!

They rode lower, through the acacia and mesquite, the
horses picking their way carefully down the mountain. The

discovery that Josh was a prisoner was agonizing torment. Was he already at the prison? Would her body be tempting enough to bargain with Farjado for Josh?

Suddenly a man emerged from thick brush. In one swift, fluid motion he came up to snatch General Farjado off his horse, and both men rolled to the ground.

28

A horse reared, pawing the air. Two more men rushed out from behind the mesquite. A Spanish soldier drew his pistol. A shot rang out.

In an instant Lianna recognized broad shoulders and an angry profile. Josh was free! She grasped the reins, trying to wheel her horse out of the way. Fletcher's golden hair was easily detectable in the darkness.

"Cabrón!" General Farjado gasped, jumping to his feet to slam a fist against Josh's jaw, sending him sprawling. With an ugly swish of metal, Farjado drew his sword.

Lianna gazed on helplessly, unable to interfere. Farjado lunged, his blade slicing the air. Josh dodged, drew a pistol from his waistband, cocked it, and fired. The general slumped to the ground.

Fletcher's sword glinted, and another Spanish soldier crumpled and fell. The third leapt on a horse and urged it down the mountainside, lying on the animal's neck.

Josh raised his pistol and fired, but the Spaniard plunged down the slope unharmed. Josh turned and swung up into the saddle behind Lianna. The other two mounted the remaining horses.

"Will Simms take her to *El Feroz*?" Fletcher asked.

"We can't risk it. Spanish soldiers will be after us."

"She can't go with us," Fletcher argued, as if Lianna weren't present.

"There's no choice. I killed a Spanish general. Soldiers

will be all over this mountain tonight. We need to ride as quickly as possible.''

As Josh took the lead, he said, ''We have a rendezvous in the mountains, where we'll get supplies, fresh horses, and clothing. Pablo went ahead to tell them we're coming.''

''I thought you were taken prisoner,'' she said.

''I almost was. Fletcher and Drake joined me while I was fighting the soldiers. We overpowered them, then Pablo found us and I knew we had to save you.'' He leaned down close to her ear. ''Are you hurt?''

''No.'' She wanted to run her hands over him, to reassure herself he was with her, unhurt and free! She clung to him tightly.

''We're safe now, Lianna, but we have to ride. They'll be after us soon.''

During their steady climb, as they gained altitude, the wind increased. It whipped against Lianna, flinging long black tendrils of her hair across Josh's shoulder. She turned to look ahead, and the sight weakened her limbs to jelly.

The Andes *cordillera* lay around them, the lower slopes dark where they were covered with mesquite and chaparral, the high jagged peaks bathed in moonlight, snow sparkling with the glitter of millions of diamonds. Wind scooped up snow and flung it into the air in sprays of white off the nearest peaks. The suggestion that an army of men, animals, and weapons would cross such a barrier was absurd, a deadly venture.

''No army can cross this!'' she cried, the wind snatching away her words.

''We have to try,'' Josh yelled.

The horses picked their way over the mountain, then began the descent, winding down to a valley. They rode through a grove of pines, then lower, out of the wind to a mountain stream that rushed with silvery brilliance, splashing and gurgling across rocks as it tumbled down the slope.

''We'll follow the stream,'' Josh said. ''We'll lose the soldiers here.''

Within the hour, Lianna was hungry and tired, her hands numb with cold. Ahead, spirals of smoke rose from three adobe houses. Lianna was heartily glad to think about stopping, but she suspected that in a few hours, at dawn, she would be riding with Simms for the coast and *El Feroz*. And she wondered if Josh would survive the coming conflict, if she would ever see him again.

They crossed another stream, then rode along the valley toward the adobe houses. Patches of yellow light spilled from the windows, while the stream caught silvery glints of moonlight. A gentle wind rustled the leaves of willows along the stream, creating an illusion of peace.

"You think we're safe from the soldiers here?"

"I think we will be tonight. Tomorrow at dawn, we'll leave."

And she knew the unspoken words. He would join San Martín, and he would leave her behind. Lianna ran her fingers across Josh's hand, feeling the ridges of veins and tendons. She wanted to beg him to ride with her to the ship. The patriots had failed each time they had tried to gain independence. The mountain trek seemed a deadly, foolhardy venture destined to fail before the fighting ever began.

The door to the largest adobe house opened and a man holding a musket stepped outside.

"Hold your fire! Josh Raven here!"

The man called to someone inside the house, then more men came through the door. Within minutes Josh lifted Lianna down and they entered a brightly lit house with a fire roaring in the fireplace. After the ride in the night air, the smell of meat and beans simmering made her mouth water. Josh took her arm to lead her to a house next door.

"You may freshen up, then join us to eat. I'll go back with the men."

With a rush of cold air, he was gone. She turned to look at the small, primitive house. A fire blazed in the stone hearth; the furniture was made of rough logs laced together into chairs, a table, and a bed made from a hide stretched and lashed to a wooden frame. Guanaco hides and a bright red comfort were piled on top, red curtains covered the windows, and gray wolf hides covered the stone floor. Light from lanterns flickered, adding a rosy glow to the room. It looked like paradise after the hard climb on the *cordillera* and the hours before when she had expected to spend her days in prison, or worse, with General Farjado.

She shivered, remembering 'he battle, the chase; then hunger stirred her to move. Water was heated in a pot near the fire and a tin tub stood in a shadowy corner. Lianna poured a scant amount in the tub to bathe, relishing the bath, but moving swiftly so she could join the men to eat.

After she had dressed, she heard a rap on the door.

Ducking his head to get through the door, Josh stepped inside. "Ready to eat?"

"I could eat something live, I'm so famished."

"I'll clean up quickly." He crossed the cabin to touch the water in the tub.

Startled, she realized he intended to bathe. "There's more water heating," she said, and turned her back, sitting down in front of the fire. While she warmed her feet, she became conscious of every sound he made.

She heard Josh pull off each boot; she heard his clothing rustle and drop. Water splashed and she knew he was in the tub. And it was impossible to fight the images that rose in her mind, the all-too-clear pictures of his body.

She heard him splashing and clenched her fists, burning with desire, fighting the urge to turn and go to him.

"I talked with Collo, one of the patriots," he said. "Tomorrow we'll ride ahead to join the army. You'll stay behind with Simms. When Santiago falls, I'll send word or come get you."

She sat in silence, fighting her own battle.

"I'm hurrying. The meat is ready and smells delicious. Lianna, would you please bring the kettle of warm water? I'll rinse off with it."

She drew in her breath, and reluctantly picked up the kettle. She kept her gaze focused on it, fighting the impulse to look at him, hating the raging need she felt.

His strong hands reached out to take it. He slanted her a look. "Mind pouring it over me?"

She wanted to fling it at his head. When he asked, she glanced up, and her sweeping gaze took in his glistening wet shoulders, rivulets of water running across his chest, the dark hairs twisted and matted wetly, the muscles beneath more fully revealed. His knees were bent, his strong arms resting on the sides of the tin tub.

"You can manage, Josh!" She handed him the kettle so swiftly that it almost fell. Josh caught it, and Lianna went to stand near the fire.

"Ah, Lianna, women are so damned difficult to understand. You're angry because I asked for a kettle of water. Now, what harm was there in my request?"

She burned with embarrassment, wanting to tell him he was teasing her beyond endurance.

"Maidenly modesty?" he persisted, and she heard the laughter in his voice.

"Will you hurry!" she snapped. "I'm famished."

He chuckled. "Do I hear fires crackling in your voice?"

"Of course not!"

"Any chance of a back scrub from you?"

"No! Great grief, you can be difficult!"

"*I'm* difficult?" he asked innocently.

"No, you're marvelous company! You're teasing me and you know it!"

He laughed. "Come on, Lianna, let me hear you laugh."

"You're not stirring my amusement with your remarks. I don't feel like laughing."

"And what do you feel?" he asked in a husky drawl that changed the atmosphere at once.

She drew a deep breath and turned to look at him. "You know the sight of you makes me want you!" she said swiftly, her words tumbling out in a rush. "I love you."

"If I change my life," he said bitterly, all humor gone from his voice.

She turned her back. "It's an impasse, Josh. I can't live with you going into battles constantly."

"I'll be ready in a minute," he said gruffly. Great splashing sounded behind her, then clothing rustled. Listening to him dress, she bore the agony of more mental images.

Finally he said, "I'm done."

She turned around. He stood with his hands on his hips,

white shirt open at the throat, breeches snug on his thighs, his booted feet spread apart slightly.

His gaze was stormy and unsettling, and she felt torn between love for him and hatred for the life he lived. "Can we go?" she asked quickly. "I'm hungry." But all need to eat had gone with the sight of him.

"Of course." He placed her coat around her shoulders. Did his hands linger? Or was it her imagination? His coat was made of sheepskin with matted curls, giving his shoulders even greater breadth.

Silently they went out. When they stepped into the cool night, Lianna saw a man mount a horse and ride around a bend of the creek, where he was hidden by tall willows.

"Someone's leaving?"

"He's going to stand watch, merely a precaution. The loyalists will be inflamed over their general. We don't want to be taken by surprise."

She shivered and pulled the coat tighter, watching where the lone figure had disappeared into the shadows.

Inside the house, Josh introduced her to the patriots, then left her talking to one while he moved to a corner to talk to two men. She caught him watching her once and wondered what had happened. His brow was furrowed in a frown and he looked angry.

Josh listened to the patriots, returning to sit down across the table from Lianna. They had a meal of *maté*, a green tea, served in gourds and sucked through a tube called a *bombilla*. Also, flagons of wine, pale white tortillas, and roasted corn sat on the long table. There was a pot of meat and beans, which was ladled out by a stocky bearded patriot named Collo. Lianna met Pablo and thanked him. His large brown eyes were warm as he flashed a smile and said, "Sí, Señora Raven."

All the time Lianna ate, Josh was aware of her. He could remember her words in Santiago, her statements that she no longer loved Edwin Stafford. Could he believe her? Collo had ridden swiftly from Santiago only an hour ahead of Josh, and just before dinner Collo had told him that an English mercenary had joined them, dropping anchor off Valparaiso—Captain Edwin Stafford.

Torment gnawed at Josh over whether to tell Lianna or not. He held only a tenuous thread of her love, because she demanded he give up the sea—and he had nothing else. Yet, did he want to tell her Edwin had sailed to Chile and given his pledge to support the patriots' cause for her?

What a fool he was over her, Josh thought. He didn't want to tell her about Stafford, yet he couldn't give up his life at sea for her either. Farming was foreign to him after all these years; the sea was his life, but without Lianna it looked incredibly empty.

As he drank the *maté*, he wondered too about Stafford. A captain—he was damned young to be in command, whether he was a mercenary or not. He watched Lianna, brooding over the latest turn of events. The man had to have sharp wits if he could go from groomsman to captain that swiftly. She hadn't fallen in love with a simple country lad.

Josh ate heartily, consuming wine with a vengeance. Lianna wondered why, but then dismissed it, as he showed no sign of becoming foxed. The men made their plans, deciding that at dawn they would leave.

Lianna wanted to go while Josh was occupied. She stood up and said, "I'm tired. I'll say good night."

Instantly Josh was on his feet. "I'll see you to the house." He caught up a sheepskin coat and came around the table to take her arm while the men politely told her good night.

They stepped out into the cold and hurried next door. Nagging worries over their future, his safety, were replaced by the intimacy of the moment. Her heartbeat speeded when he dropped the latch in place.

"I'll be safe. Go back and make your plans with your men." She pulled off her coat swiftly so he wouldn't touch her.

With a cynical smile he walked past her, his spurs jingling slightly. "The fire has died down. I'll build it again." He shrugged out of his coat and knelt to place more logs on the glowing orange embers and gray ash.

His features, highlighted by the fire, were marred by a bruise on his cheek that had turned dark blue. His tight

breeches molded to his legs, pulling tautly over his muscles, and longing tore at her. At dawn they would part. At
dawn . . . Would it be forever?

He poked the logs, sending a spray of red embers
dancing up the chimney. Then a tongue of flame curled
over the brown logs, and the corner of one blackened,
catching fire.

Josh turned, and at his unwavering gaze a tongue of
flame curled within her. She couldn't breathe or move or
speak. Her heart thudded in her ears and her gaze was
pulled as if by an invisible force, drawn inexorably down
over his open-throated shirt, the white pleats lying on his
tanned skin, short curls of chest hair revealed in the neckline. Her gaze lowered over his narrow hips, then jerked
upward as she exhaled swiftly, her cheeks flaming.

He crossed the room. She tried to look anywhere except
at him. "Josh, the men are waiting . . ."

"What's the matter with your voice, Lianna?" he asked
huskily, unable to go or to resist moving closer to her,
holding back the words she might want to hear about
Edwin.

She looked down at the floor, then at the fire roaring in
the grate. "My voice . . ." The words came out a whisper. She tried again. "My voice is fine."

"Ah, what a little liar you've become," he teased, his
blood heating when he saw the reaction she was having to
him.

She closed her eyes. "We are at a hopeless impasse,
Josh. I don't want a future with a pirate—and you won't
change."

He raised her chin. Lianna squeezed her eyes more
tightly closed. She felt as if she stood on the brink of one
of the ridges they had ridden along tonight, as if she were
poised beside a fatal, breathtaking drop, buffeted by the
winds of passion. . . .

Her hands wanted to reach out, to touch him. Her
breasts felt heavy, needing his caresses. Her lips felt swollen,
and to her very soul she burned with an ache that only Josh
could assuage. He would ride out of her life tomorrow,
taking all her love.

"Josh," she whispered, then bit her lip. How close she had come to pleading desperately with him to change his life for her. Tears stung. She wanted this man's love as she had never wanted anyone's.

"Look at me!" he commanded.

Her eyes flew open at the harshness of his words, and she saw the stormy tempest in his eyes.

"Look at me, Lianna. Don't close your eyes." His fingers tangled her hair and caught it up to pull it over his face while he breathed raggedly. "How sweet you smell." He dropped the strands and looked down at her. "Lianna, I want to say I'll give up everything for you, but I don't know any other life! I can't give up the sea." He grimaced as if in pain. "And I wonder if you really know what your heart wants. I gave you so little choice."

Tears stung her eyes and she fought them back. "Don't torment me. Go! go fight your battle!"

He drew a deep breath. "Lianna, Edwin is in Valparaiso."

————•••◆▶•••————

29

Lianna's eyes widened as she stared at him and frowned. "Edwin?"

"Dammit, yes! He's waiting to take you home to England."

"How do you know?"

"I learned from Collo," Josh said bitterly, feeling as if she had already forgotten him. He turned abruptly, and slamming the cabin door, left her alone.

"Josh!" She ran and opened the door, but he was already walking away. Calling to him again, she started out after him, but froze when a man rode out of the shadows and began speaking to him. She waited a moment, then, shivering with cold, returned to her cabin, where she sat by the fire, trying to fathom why Edwin would be in Santiago. Dawn would come soon enough, she told herself. Dawn, and farewell.

Later, in the darkness, Lianna's eyes opened as a shot echoed across the valley.

"Soldiers!" a man yelled as more shouts accompanied the sound of horses' hooves.

Pulling on her boyish clothing, Lianna swiftly pinned her hair up and put on her boots. As she drew on gloves, Josh arrived.

"Good, you're ready! Here, Collo sent this to you," he said, holding out a vicuña coat and a flat black hat. "You'll need the coat in the mountains. And put this in your waistband." He handed her a pistol. When she fumbled with it, he took it, tucking it against her waist so that the muzzle angled away from her.

"Captain!" Someone pounded on the door. She recognized Fletcher's voice. "Spanish soldiers are coming down the mountain. Collo, two of his men, and I will hold them off while you and the others go."

"I'll stay with you."

"No. Your wife needs you—go."

They ran to the shed, where a man saddled horses for Simms, Josh, Lianna, Pablo, and four men. Mounting the horses, they rode swiftly, galloping along the stream while shots rang out behind.

As they raced, gunfire echoed through the valley. Then suddenly all was quiet. Lianna glanced at Josh's furrowed brow and realized he was worried about Fletcher and the others.

Josh turned when they heard hoofbeats; then Fletcher, Collo, and Pérez rode around a bend into sight. Pérez was slumped in the saddle, a dark red stain showing through his coat.

Josh and the others halted until Fletcher reached them.

"Juan was killed."

"Damn!" Josh muttered bitterly. "Pérez, how badly are you hurt?"

"It's my shoulder," he answered. "I'm all right. Soldiers aren't far behind."

"Let me wrap your wound," Josh said.

"No. Let's ride while we can. We'll have to go south to reach a pass, then turn north to Mendoza."

Collo rode ahead. Josh turned his horse, and they continued. Soon they left the valley and began the ascent, occasionally glimpsing the Spanish soldiers trailing behind them.

Josh wheeled his horse around to ride beside Pérez only once, but quickly fell back to join Lianna. "Are you all right?" he asked as he reached out to squeeze her arm.

"Yes," she said over the sound of hoofbeats. "Will we stop tonight?"

"If we lose the soldiers."

"Do you know how many are following?"

"I've counted about a dozen."

"Pérez looks as if he may fall out of the saddle."

Josh watched him a moment, then reached over again to pat her hand before flicking the reins and riding ahead.

As they traveled over increasingly steep and uneven ground, Pérez groaned, causing Josh to turn and gallop back.

Lianna saw Pérez slump in the saddle and start to slide just as Josh leapt off his horse and caught him. "I'll wrap his wound," he said, lowering the man to the ground. "All of you continue, I'll catch up."

"I'll help you," Lianna said, dismounting. For the next quarter of an hour they worked swiftly to get the wound bound and Pérez on horseback again.

Days later, when they rode into Mendoza, a town on a high plain, the streets were still strewn with flowers, and blue-and-white flags waved because of the celebration of the departure of the Army of the Andes. But an eerie tension prevailed. San Martín, Bernardo O'Higgins, their Army of the Andes—all the able-bodied males—had left a day before Josh and Lianna's arrival.

Lianna could sense Josh's impatience despite his attempts to appear composed. Collo had relatives and made arrangements for Lianna and Pablo to stay with a family while Josh prepared to leave to catch up with San Martín.

It took a day before they had secured four pack mules, food, and scanty equipment. Josh, Fletcher, and the others left at dawn, but Lianna waited half an hour before she followed, leaving a note of thanks to the family who had given her shelter.

Tugging her hat down over her head, she wrapped a red woolen shawl around her shoulders, then galloped away from Mendoza toward the sheer eastern wall of the Andes. Within an hour she caught sight of the men riding ahead of her. And it took only a few more minutes before she recognized the figure that turned around and headed back in her direction.

Raising her chin, determined to go with Josh across the mountains, Lianna braced herself for his anger as she watched him approach. He sat straight and tall on a sorrel stallion, the sheepskin coat making the width of his shoulders enormous. A few feet away he halted. "What the hell are you doing here?"

"I'm coming with you," she answered calmly, hoping her breathless voice didn't reveal her apprehension.

"You can't fight in a war! Go back to Mendoza."

"I'll stay behind when the fighting begins. There'll be some place I can wait."

He swore. "You can't cross the mountains with us. The trail won't be anything like the one we followed to Mendoza. There won't be any riding through valleys on charted paths. We have to cross this . . ." He swept his arm out and she glanced at the *cordillera*, its peaks obscured by clouds but its treacherous cliffs quite visible.

"If I don't go, you'll have to come back to Mendoza. It could be a year or more," Lianna protested.

His horse pranced and snorted, pawing the ground as if sensing his master's anger. Josh's brows narrowed and his expression was as formidable as the *cordillera*. "You're in haste to get to the ship, to get back to your precious Edwin!"

She drew in her breath sharply. "I am not rushing back to Edwin," she said firmly. "But I don't want to wait in Mendoza."

"Turn back, Lianna."

"I have a right to come," she said raising her chin. "If you don't come back for me, no one will."

"You mean if I'm ki—"

"Don't say it!" She reached out swiftly to touch his lips.

He frowned, looking at her while she yanked her hand away. "Don't say things like that!" she said. "I'll take care of myself."

"Look, Lianna—"

"You're losing time arguing. I'll follow. There's no way to stop me unless you take me back to Mendoza yourself."

"San Martín will send me back with you! He won't allow a woman."

"He doesn't need to know. At a distance, my appearance is deceptive, and I'll trail at the end. No one except those with us now will know there's a woman present."

"I can send Fletcher with you."

"You need every man you have," she countered, meeting each argument he presented.

"I'll have to carry you across those peaks!"

"No, you won't. I won't be a burden," she promised.

"I can't take the time to fight with you. We don't have the equipment to cross the mountains. We need to catch up with San Martín."

"Then why are we standing here?"

Josh whirled his horse around and rode away. After the first startled second, Lianna shook the reins and urged her horse after him. When they reached the others, she rode behind the cluster of men, who merely nodded or murmured a brief greeting. Josh, however, didn't glance her way again.

As they climbed steadily, winding up the mountain on a rough and narrow trail, she felt Josh's smoldering anger. Not once since he had turned to ride away had he looked back to see if she were following.

Chilling thoughts tormented her. She knew that when they fought their way back to Santiago, Josh would kill the Count of Marcheno. Josh's hatred, his deadly thirst for revenge, would always stand between them. Could she fully accept a man who would take another's life cold-bloodedly? And of course there was Edwin. He waited for her, but she would have to tell him about her love for Josh. Gradually they reached a terrifying height. Lianna closed her eyes as the horses slowly walked along a ledge beside a great abyss. She could only concentrate on steadying her horse now.

The wind howled and whistled across the vast space, while great Andean condors with their black wings spread soared and dipped between the peaks, hovering, as if waiting for a rider or horse to slip over the ridge and tumble hundreds of feet below. Above them on the mountains, snow drifted and patches of ice glistened in the sunlight. Lianna clung to the horse and kept her eyes on

Josh's squared shoulders. Twice, when they followed a hazardous trail along a winding, narrow ledge, he turned to gaze impassively at her. She tried to meet his cool stare with one equally composed.

Late in the day they reached a slab of rock where there was barely room for the horses on a sloping ledge that was only a few feet wide. To their left was a straight wall of rock, to their right a drop hundreds of feet to snow-covered rocks. While wind howled and lashed them, Lianna leaned forward over the horse's neck and clung tightly, closing her eyes. Her horse stumbled. She gasped as a hoof struck a rock and sent it plummeting over the side. She watched it tumble down the mountain, ricocheting off slabs of granite, then barreling down the sharp incline. As they slowly wound up the mountain, the sheer rock beside them changed to a snow-covered slope, while the ledge remained as narrow as before. Several times Josh glanced at her.

Ahead, Fletcher's horse whinnied, the sound echoing across the ridge. Within seconds there was a sharp crack from above, then a rumbling began. Snow and ice broke loose and cascaded down, gaining speed. "Go!" Josh yelled.

Lianna gasped as she looked up at an avalanche rushing toward her.

"Lianna!"

Snow pelted Lianna, small chunks and sprays of fine flakes, while she urged her horse forward, feeling it lengthen its stride.

She squeezed her eyes shut, terrified as snow struck her. She tried to keep from thinking about the open space to her right, but her palms were damp inside her gloves and she trembled when she felt the horse give a lunge forward.

Lianna opened her eyes to see the narrow ledge fan out to a safer width. The men had halted to look back.

Behind, tons of rock and snow slid downward with the roar of continual booming thunder. When it stopped, Lianna let out her breath, shivering as she looked at the place they had just crossed. The ledge she had ridden on was gone;

only a slope of mountainside buried beneath glistening snow was left.

Without a word, the men turned to ride ahead, leaving Lianna and Josh. He sat quietly, watching her with a strange smile hovering on his features. "You haven't lost your bravery."

"I was terrified."

"So was everyone else."

"Even you?"

"Of course." He grinned and flicked his reins, moving his horse beside hers. His hat brim tilted low and almost hid his eyes. "I'll always admire you, Lianna. Sometimes I want to shake you, but I still admire you."

"Am I supposed to say thank you?" she questioned, suddenly aware that the others had continued across the mountain and were lost to view. The wind blew with an eerie moan and whipped over them in cold gusts, blowing sprays of snow against them.

"Look, we're on top of the world."

She surveyed the panoramic view around them—jagged peaks, low clouds, blinding snow, and the sun an orange ball of fire about to disappear behind peaks to the west. But her gaze returned to Josh's brilliant green eyes, whose golden flecks sparkled.

He swung a leg over his horse and dropped to the ground. Pushing his hat to the back of his head, he took the reins from her hands and dropped them. "Get down, Lianna."

Despite the icy blasts of wind, Lianna felt a warm flush stain her cheeks. She looked into his determined eyes and hesitated.

"I said come down here."

"How well you wear arrogance, Josh! We'll lose the others . . ."

When he reached up and pulled her down, her pounding heart drowned out the howl of the wind. His arms banded around her. "This is a special place, a special moment. We'll be part of history." With each word his voice grew thicker, until its raspy sound soothed her nerves. "We'll always remember this."

He leaned down; his lips touched hers briefly, and a wild need burst between them. The force of the avalanche she had witnessed paled when compared with the sweeping passion that now filled her. She clung to his broad shoulders as if she could hold him forever. She wanted him desperately—and loved him completely.

While the wind buffeted them, its wintry blasts unfelt, Josh held her to him. He wanted to push her down in the snow and take her there, to make her accept his life and stay with him no matter what he did. He shouldn't have allowed her to journey with them, yet this morning, against all wisdom, he had yielded.

He groaned deeply but the sound was muffled by their eager kisses. He knew she mistook his agony for passion. Time and again he wanted to tell her he would give up the sea and anything else she asked if she would remain his wife, but he couldn't. He kissed her hungrily, wanting to run his fingers through her hair, feel her warmtth pressed to him.

When he moved his lips away and gazed at her, their ragged breathing filled the silence. Snowflakes drifted down, swirling lightly. She lifted her chin in a way that wrenched his heart. What went through her mind? "You're in my blood," he whispered. "I don't think I'll ever be free . . ."

"You know I love you, Josh."

"Yet you won't be my wife unless I settle down. You want to tame me. I can't live that way, Lianna."

Lianna winced and turned to look for her horse. Why wouldn't he give up pirating if he loved her? Was it his compelling need to possess everything around him? Or pure lust? She asked, "Josh, why do you have a lion's head on so many belongings?"

A strange look of hurt surfaced, then quickly vanished. "I had nothing for so long. I suppose I wanted to feel that some things in the world are absolutely mine."

She looked at him intently, seeing more than she had ever seen before, realizing they both had had so little love in their lives. And she was about to toss aside her one great love because he wouldn't meet her demands. She frowned, feeling the wind lash her as her thoughts raged over the problem. Some of Josh would be better than none, but when they returned to Santiago, could she live with his deliberate slaying of Quita's husband?

His face was a dark scowl as he swung her into the saddle. "We have to catch up with the others."

As he mounted swiftly and rode ahead, she looked at his broad back, his hat tilted back on his head. If he pulled her down again to take her, she would not resist him! She reined the horse and glanced back at the spot where they had just stood and kissed. It was the top of the world, a place where few would ever travel, kisses she would always remember, a moment swept by tides of passion that had changed her because she had reached a decision—she wanted her pirate husband under any circumstances!

Catching up with the men, Josh rode ahead as Lianna rode behind in silence. She grew colder by the hour, but lost in her thoughts, she was barely aware of it. All her life she had yearned for love, discovering it first in Edwin, and then fully in Josh.

Perhaps if she stopped seeking, and merely gave herself totally to Josh, who had grown up in a household as barren of love as her own—perhaps someday he would abandon his wild, dangerous way of life. And whether he did or not, she would have his love and she could offer hers in return.

Lost in thought, she disregarded the snowflakes that pelted her face. She was his wife, she loved him—and she intended to stay with him forever!

As if he sensed her thoughts, Josh wheeled his horse around and rode back to her. "Are you all right?"

Nodding, she wrapped the warm woolen shawl around her neck and over the lower part of her face. She was suddenly heated by her determination to yield to Josh's wishes, to return his love regardless of whether he went to sea or stayed by her side. And as for the Count of Marcheno—her mind was a blank. She would try to persuade Josh to forget his revenge; beyond that she refused to speculate. Josh rode ahead quietly, and she stared at his back. Tonight she intended to tell him of her love!

The chill began to penetrate her clothing, until she

ached for a warm fire and shelter. When they found a gentle slope, Josh called a halt.

Nearby, a sheer rock wall thrust up out of the mountain, forming a small cave with a ledge jutting out a few feet in front. Josh and Fletcher climbed over the rocks, disappearing inside the cave. Within minutes they came down to join the others.

"You'll sleep up there in the shelter, Lianna," Josh said, pointing to the cave. "It's not large enough for all of us."

While the men pitched the tents and built a fire from sticks and firewood carried by one of the mules, Lianna began to work alongside Collo, acutely conscious of Josh's presence. When she saw Fletcher crawl inside a tent and he didn't reappear, she asked Josh aboout him.

"He has *soroche*, mountain sickness. If you feel ill, tell me." He grinned. "The cure may be worse than the illness."

"What's that?"

"Garlic and onions. Fletcher's chewing on them—which, thank heaven, neither you nor I have needed yet."

As he walked away, she went back to helping cook ground *charqui*, jerked beef, peppers, and cornmeal, which they boiled in iron pots. When they sat down to eat in a circle around a roaring fire, Fletcher, whose normally tan skin was ashy gray, joined them but ate little. While they ate, Josh said, "In Mendoza, I talked to Agustín Padilla, one of San Martín's men who was too ill to go. We should catch up with them tomorrow, because we can travel faster."

"Did Padilla tell you the plans?" Fletcher asked.

"Yes." Josh picked up a stick and drew a long line in the snow. "Here are the Andes. General Juan de Las Heras will take a division and the heavy artillery and go through Uspallata Pass." He drew another line at a right angle to the first.

"General Miguel Salas, San Martín, and O'Higgins, with two divisions, will go farther north."

As Josh etched a third groove in the snow, Lianna looked at his head bent over the lines. Orange flames highlighted his cheekbones and wide forehead. Dark lashes fringed his cheeks as he looked down. What a complicated man he was—charming yet sensual, kind yet bent on revenge. Could he be bound by an emotion stronger than hate?

His green eyes shifted to hers, and she blushed. He paused, frowning slightly as he focused on her. He had the most unsettling way of discerning her thoughts. She looked down at her hands, and Josh went on with his explanation.

"San Martín, O'Higgins, and Salas will take this route, Paso de Los Patos. San Martín has his squadron of grenadiers."

"*Dios!*" Collo said. "The highest points in the *cordillera*."

"How can they get over the two highest, least-traveled passes?" Fletcher asked. "We had a damned difficult time today on lower peaks."

"Only time will determine if it's possible," Josh said quietly. "They've copied the Incas' methods and have made rope bridges. Fray Beltrán, who's now an artillery commander, has made fifty thousand horseshoes for horses and mules from the pampas. Just as we're doing, they're carrying everything—fodder, grain, firewood, blankets, twenty-five thousand pounds of jerked beef, hundreds of swords, cannon, two thousand cannonballs, salt, corn."

"With that many men and animals, we should catch up with them soon," Collo said.

"I hope we'll be with them tomorrow," Josh replied.

"I pray this time we succeed in gaining independence," Collo said as he flung another small log on the fire. "We've tried before and failed. Chile should be free."

"Freedom is a valuable thing," Josh said, and Lianna turned to look into eyes which reflected dancing orange flames from the fire. "Come, Lianna," he said as he stood, "I'll see you to bed. We rise early in the morning."

Her heart thudded in anticipation, and she moved eagerly away from the fire.

Gathering an armload of firewood and handing Lianna a torch to carry, Josh led the way, their boots crunching as they left the men and climbed the rocks up to the cave.

Once inside, Josh stacked the wood carefully and ignited it with the torch he took from her hands.

"I brought hides up earlier."

She stepped into a space that was large enough for the two of them and spread the soft brown guanaco hides which lay on the smooth rock floor of the cave.

Outside the mouth of the cave, the wood began to catch and burn, crackling in the silence. Its fiery blaze created a screen of privacy and gave a rosy glow to the inside of the cave.

But the warmth from the fire was not what heated Lianna's blood. She pulled off her boots and looked up as Josh ducked his head and entered. He stood a few feet away, his long legs planted apart, his hat pushed to the back of his head with brown locks of hair escaping. The air between them was tense, filled with unspoken words.

"I'll join the men now. This may be our last night before we reach the army."

"Josh, when the battles are over, can you ever forget the Marchenos?"

"I've explained my feelings to you. It's a constant hurt. I owe revenge to Phillip, to Terrence, to all those men."

She shook her head. "If it were the other way around, would you want Phillip to sacrifice everything to take another's life? Quita carries their baby."

He drew a sharp breath, but the hardness of his jaw was proof of his resolve. "I can't help what eats on my soul!"

"No matter how steeped in hate you are . . ." She paused and held her breath. "I love you and I want to remain your wife whether you're a pirate or not."

He inhaled deeply and his chest expanded. "And what about Edwin Stafford?"

She pulled off her hat and shook her head, her hair tumbling down. "I don't love Edwin. I love only you."

"I shouldn't have forced you into marriage, Lianna. You may be too young to know what you want. And I've crossed swords once with Edwin over you. I imagine we'll cross swords again."

She hadn't thought of Edwin fighting Josh for her, and she knew Edwin wouldn't, once she told him of her love for Josh. She pulled off her coat and reached up to untie the laces of her shirt. When she pushed the neck open, Josh drew in his breath.

The fire outlined Josh's frame; his shadow loomed gigantic on the walls of rock. Desire flamed in the depths of his eyes.

"You said Luisa wasn't your mistress. Why not?"

His chest expanded and each word came out with effort. "You came between us each time I was with her."

Relief and joy were as solid as the rocks of the cave. Watching him, she tugged her shirt down over one shoulder, baring her creamy flesh. A blush heated her cheeks, yet it was the only way she could give to him totally. He waited. She could see his chest rise and fall rapidly, then grow rigid as she slipped off the other shoulder of the shirt and dropped it around her waist.

The crackling fire faded to nothing, dwindled by the roaring in Josh's ears. Her words pounded in him: "I love you." Had she truly forgotten Edwin Stafford? Josh wanted to take her, and to keep her forever, to believe her without question. He stood, feeling the hot surge in his loins as she pushed off the shirt, then slipped away her cambric chemise.

He clenched his fists with restraint as desire burned in him. Then, remembering her shyness, he began to comprehend the depth of her actions as she slowly undressed before him, her blue eyes never leaving his. Lianna began to unfasten her breeches. With each garment that fell away came the clear message of the love she wanted to give. And Josh felt as if he were finally becoming whole, finding all he needed and all he had longed for through the years. She was lovely, the only woman he wanted, and she had known so little love in her life, he wanted to make it all up to her.

Moving forward, coming to stand before her, his fingers reaching out to finish the task, his breath ragged, he looked into her eyes. "You're sure?" he asked hoarsely.

Standing on tiptoe, Lianna raised her mouth and met his lips, trying to show him that she loved him without qualification.

His coat fell open, and she reached up to push his hat

off his head—to run her fingers in his hair and drink in the taste, the smell, the feel of the man whom she loved. Love which she wanted to bestow until he was bound by it.

He caught her hair in his fist, twisting it so that she had to look up at him. His voice was a growl as he demanded, "What are you after? Why do you want to save Marcheno? He means nothing to you."

"No, he doesn't. But you do."

"Ah, Lianna!" he cried, releasing doubts and surrendering to her with a harsh cry. Then he lowered his head and his mouth covered hers, his tongue penetrated her lips, his body demanded all.

No heady wine had ever sent her senses reeling as much as Josh's kisses and his touch. She was blinded by white-hot desire, deafened by the roaring of heated blood pounding in her veins, but beyond that she was consumed with the need to pour out her love to him.

With trembling fingers Lianna untied the laces to his shirt and tugged it free from his breeches; then she slipped her hands beneath the white cambric to touch his flesh. This physical need linked to one that went much deeper—to the soul.

Josh leaned back to look down at her bare breasts, which longed for his touch. Lianna closed her eyes and tilted her head back, kneading his back with her fingers, letting her hands drift over the slope of his firm buttocks.

Gasping, he bent down to circle a taut nipple with his hot tongue, to make her cry out and ache with longing while she swayed and clung to his powerful shoulders.

Her hands went to the fastenings on his breeches, and his fingers closed over hers. "Lianna," he whispered, catching her hands up in his, to kiss her fingertips. He started to unfasten his breeches and she pushed away his hands.

"No, love, let me."

His muscles tightened while he stood still for a few more seconds; then with a groan he crushed her to his hardness, his mouth meeting hers in an almost savage desperation.

He swung her into his arms, lowering her to the furry

hides, then knelt over her, his manhood throbbing while he devoured her in a burning gaze.

She lay tumbled on the thick golden hides, her ivory skin pale in contrast to the golden hides, her black hair fanned beneath her head with locks spilling over her shoulders, her enormous blue eyes framed by thick black lashes. She moved her hips sensuously and naturally. She had a slender grace to her limbs that he loved, yet there was a sensuality to her full, lush breasts and her deep enjoyment of bodily pleasures that made him want to prolong their touching.

He closed his eyes, dropping down to pull her to him. "I want to give you everything, love. All the happiness possible . . ."

She locked her arms around his narrow waist and held him close while she turned to kiss his salty flesh that smelled faintly of leather.

Josh shifted. "You're in my blood, Lianna! I'm ensnared . . ." he whispered. He cupped her breast in his rough hand, her warm flesh filling his grasp as his thumb flicked over her nipple. "I love you."

Josh was fire and warmth to her. She locked her fingers in his hair, pulling his mouth to her breast, giving her eager flesh to his kisses.

"I love you," he whispered again and again. His head roamed lower, his moist tongue touching her intimately as she gasped with pleasure.

Love and desire wove through her like threads binding her together until they were one cloth. Lianna's fingers touched his legs, gliding upward to caress him and make him groan with need.

Spreading her pale, slender legs, Josh moved between them, pausing to watch her as she clung to his shoulders, whispering, "I want you so badly . . . forever."

When her hips came up to meet him, he thrust into her soft depths and she gasped wildly. And this time she tried as desperately to give to him, moving her hips to meet his deep thrusts until her senses spun and thought was gone.

How long he had waited! How many nights he had dreamed of this! Josh watched her until he too was lost to the wild surging passion that consumed them, hearing her soft cry dimly above the pounding of his heart.

"Lianna!" he gasped hoarsely.

He moved urgently, feeling whole. In a burst of ecstasy, he shuddered with release as her hips rose to welcome the gift of himself which he offered her.

Lianna stirred when during the night, she felt his arms tighten around her, and in the morning she opened her eyes to meet his gaze.

"It's time to ride. It's dawn, and the men are ready," he said, reaching down and pulling her to him. In the tense silence he kissed her in a hard, hungry way that took her breath.

Within the hour they were saddled and riding across the mountain, and later that morning they caught sight of José de San Martín's Army of the Andes.

"Look!" Josh halted and stretched out his long arm, pointing ahead.

Lianna and the others stopped. In the distance, on another mountain, a line of blue-and-red uniforms wound for miles against the snowy slopes. Lianna's pulse quickened at the sight. Hundreds of mounted men, soldiers on foot, then pack mules inched their way slowly upward toward a peak covered by gray clouds.

"There's the hope of Chile and freedom from Spanish tyranny," Josh said. "Let's join them."

Moving at a dangerous pace, Josh led them along frozen ground, across a raging river, and over rough terrain. They reached the trailing end of the army by late afternoon.

Josh slowed to ride beside Lianna. "I'm going ahead to tell San Martín we're here." He grinned suddenly. "I won't introduce you until we're out of the mountains."

She smiled in return. "I don't mind."

"Keep your hat on, love. Don't let that long black hair fall down." With a wink, he turned his horse to ride forward to talk a moment with first Fletcher, then Collo. She watched him leave, his hat pulled low as he passed the long line of mules and vanished from view. All day, since they had left the cave, she had been aware of his gaze following her. Occasionally she turned to catch him studying her; he would shift and look away, but each time her breath caught. The night had been both renewal and discovery. In giving without reserve, she had found rapture. She ached to touch him, to lie in his arms again.

The rest of the day she watched for his return, and disappointment became as nagging as the cold. That night Fletcher helped Lianna pitch a tent. She ate with soldiers, keeping close to Fletcher's side and finally crawling into the tent alone, seeing no more of Josh.

During the night she awoke to find hard arms closing around her, and Josh pulled her to him.

"Josh?"

"Shh. I didn't intend to wake you. I've been with San Martín and Bernardo. Go back to sleep. Tomorrow will be bad."

In spite of the layers of clothing between them, Lianna felt every touch as if it were branded on her naked flesh. She nestled against him and kissed his throat beneath his beard.

"You're so sure of everything," she said sleepily, almost to herself.

"Not everything, Lianna," he answered, surprising her that he had heard her statement.

Unable to resist, she moved her hand over his thighs. His voice was a rumble. "Lianna?"

She shifted, moving so she could raise up to kiss him, and in seconds he turned her beneath him while he showered her with kisses. "You'll freeze without clothes, even in this sleeping bag."

"I don't care," she whispered, tugging frantically at his shirt. She wanted him more than she had ever wanted anything before.

Later that night, his deep voice was a rumble in her ear as she lay on his chest. In drowsy tones he said, "I saw Rinaldo Sepulveda."

"Rinaldo!"

"Aye, remember he fled to the mountains to join the patriots."

"Does he know . . . ?"

"That you're here?" Josh laughed. "Yes, your secret is safe with him. He told me one in turn."

She waited, and when he was silent, she propped herself up to look at him. Josh ran his fingers through her hair. "Rinaldo and Madryn were secretly wed the night before they left Santiago. Only their parents and his brothers know. One of his brothers, Lucas, is with General Salas."

"I'm so glad they're wed!" she said, settling against his chest, thinking of Madryn and her happiness. Long after Josh had fallen into an exhausted sleep, Lianna lay awake in his arms, her flesh tingling as she remembered their lovemaking. She awoke in daylight to find Fletcher shaking her.

"Get up, Lianna. We need to saddle the horses. Josh has gone up front with the generals."

After eating quickly, Lianna mounted the horse Fletcher had ready. When the terrain permitted it, Fletcher and she rode forward, passing the long line during the day, moving ahead of the mules and provisions.

Days ran together as they climbed higher across the mountains, and there were few moments alone with Josh. After the first few days, he returned to ride close in front of her. Rinaldo came with him, greeting Lianna with joy and laughter lighting his eyes.

"If I had known, I would have brought Madryn along. How I miss her."

"You'll soon be with her," Josh said.

Rinaldo grinned and shrugged. "We have a secret, but by the time we're out of these mountains, our secret will no longer be something to hide. We expect a child."

"How wonderful!" Lianna exclaimed, hugging him as his brown cheeks flushed and his grin widened. Josh and Fletcher congratulated him, Josh clapping his hand firmly on Rinaldo's shoulder. "Take care, *compadre*. Get back to that pretty wife of yours."

"I intend to, sir."

They moved into line, and after that Josh and Rinaldo and Fletcher rode near Lianna. Each day the march was slower and more dangerous. The first time they reached one of the yawning chasms that had to be bridged, the line waited long hours while a rope bridge was secured in the rocks and finally anchored on the other side.

Lianna held her breath when she crossed, the bridge swaying in the air far above a river rushing through a rocky gorge.

Later, they encountered a ledge so narrow that it looked impossible. One by one, they began to file across, horses hugging the mountain as they traversed the ledge. Ahead, Rinaldo's mount moved cautiously, following a long line of soldiers. Behind him, Josh came just as cautiously, Lianna trying to follow and ignore the fright that made her head swim.

Suddenly there was a resounding bang above them, one Lianna had heard before.

"Get back, Lianna!" Josh roared, and jumped off his horse, squeezing between it and the mountain.

She looked up to see a wall of snow crashing toward her.

30

Josh pulled Lianna off her horse as the animal whinnied and started to rear. Its feet slipped and it plunged over the ridge. Lianna screamed, snatching at the bridle, her fingers catching the leather. Josh yanked her to him, knocking the breath from her lungs as the bridle tore out of her hands and her horse went down the mountain.

Ahead, Rinaldo flung himself off his horse.

"Jump! Jump, Rinaldo!" Josh cried while Lianna screamed.

Rinaldo lurched toward them as white snow cascaded over him, sweeping him down, his hands grasping at air and snow while his scream was swallowed up by the roar of the avalanche.

Blackness swamped Lianna as she stared at Rinaldo tumbling hundreds of feet below. Her head was jerked around and Josh crushed her against his chest. "Don't look," he snapped. "He's gone."

The line of animals and men backed up, while ahead, the army disappeared from view in a blinding torrent of snow.

Tons of rock and snow thundered in front of Lianna only a few feet away while Josh held her tightly. She clung to him as if he were the one solid thing in the world.

She felt hysterics threaten. She wanted to scream and cry, to turn and run from sliding snow and the terrifying drop inches in front of her. And the thought of Madryn's deep love for Rinaldo tore at her heart with the sharpness of a knife.

Gradually the snow stopped moving and silence descended, broken by horses whinnying, shouts from the men who were on the other side of the snowslide, the jingle of harness of the horses behind them. Josh turned slightly, waving his hand.

"Get back! Move those animals down the mountain!" he shouted to the men behind him. While they gradually inched back the way they had come, Josh led Lianna back to safety, then took charge.

"We'll have to cut through the ice and snow to get to the others. Fletcher, Collo! I need some more men."

Lianna sat down, shaken and weak as hot tears began to flow. Josh pulled her into his arms, holding her tightly.

"Josh, they loved each other so much, and they have a baby coming!"

"I know, Lianna," he said gruffly, clinging to her tightly. She looked up at him and saw him wipe away tears as he gazed at her solemnly.

"How do I know when it'll be you? Please, let's leave this country and go home! I love you and I don't want to lose you because of a cause that will mean nothing to us a year from now!"

He held her tightly against his chest. "Lianna, how I wish I could take you and go, but we're caught in this. I have to see it through."

His voice was filled with agony and she clung to him, unable to resist the sobs that came as she thought of Rinaldo. "Josh, she loved him so much!"

"I know," he said softly, holding her until she finally quieted.

How long they stood with their arms wrapped around each other, she didn't know, but finally Josh moved away a fraction, keeping his arm around her shoulders and holding her close as Fletcher spoke to him.

"Sorry, Josh, but we need you to get a bridge over the expanse that fell."

"I'll be back," he said, looking into her eyes, and for once she felt as if she could tell what he was thinking as he squeezed her hand. His eyes were filled with sadness, but also his gaze lingered as if the love between them had just become deeper and more important because it was threatened by danger. He kissed her cheek and left. Watching him square his shoulders as he strode away, she sat down, breathing the cold air deeply while she fought nausea. Numbly she watched Josh and the others climb back onto the narrow ledge and begin to work their way across, digging a path through the snow to reach the others, working on a precarious slope of loose rocks and snow that could give way at any moment. Suddenly she turned her back; she couldn't watch him, feeling fear chill her more than the ice and snow.

Rinaldo was gone; her horse was gone; how many men had been swept to their deaths? How close she and Josh had come! If he hadn't dismounted and pulled her down, they too would be gone.

She put her head between her knees, fighting another wave of nausea while worries plagued her. Would the army cross the Andes? Or would they be lost or trapped in the snowy peaks?

Hours later, after eating, they mounted new horses to cross the ledge again. Lianna stared straight ahead at Josh's back, not once looking below at the new slope of snow that had taken Rinaldo and so many others with it.

Days ran together as they fought danger and dizzying heights, finally to come out of the mountains twenty days after they left Mendoza.

They came down to the warm Chilean valley in the summertime, to Chacabuco, where the Spanish were waiting.

Josh pitched a tent on a grassy slope in the shade of a tree. He took Lianna to it, lifting her off her horse. "We're going to meet the Spanish, and there will be fighting. Lianna, you're a damned stubborn woman, but you're to stay out of the fighting."

"Don't worry, Josh. I want no part of it," she answered solemnly. She fought the urge to plead with him not to go. She could see the glitter in his eyes, and knew he relished the conflict. "You're still a bloodthirsty pirate!"

"I've waited a hell of a long time for this."

"Go, then, and kill all the people you can!" She entered the tent, a mixture of emotions churning in her until she was sick. She didn't want to watch him ride to war. She hated his eagerness to fight, and she feared for his life.

For a long moment Josh stared at her back. She deserved better than he was giving her, yet years of habits couldn't be changed instantly. He dropped his hand to his gunbelt and left her, swinging into the saddle to ride away without looking back, and within minutes his attention was taken by the battle.

The sound of gunfire had already commenced, and Lianna stood in the cool shade of the tent listening to the deep boom of cannon. They had crossed the Andes in an impossible trek, yet perhaps even graver danger lay ahead. And how long before Josh would return? If the Spanish won and he were taken prisoner, she knew what the penalty would be for treachery.

Nausea that had threatened overwhelmed her. Lianna rushed outside behind the tent and leaned over, retching. She straightened as a chill struck her. Every morning lately, she had been sick. And she finally acknowledged the fact that she was carrying Josh's child. She gazed up at green leaves rustling overhead, and beyond them a blue sky, while her spirits soared with joy.

Tears stung her eyes as she said a silent prayer of gratitude. To this child she would give all the love in her power to give. She clutched her middle in a fierce determination that she would have this baby. For a moment she was tempted to tell Josh, then thought better of it. Not until the battle was over and they had settled their future. And with thoughts of the future came thoughts of Edwin. She wondered where Edwin was at the moment, and fears rose as she realized she had to get to him before he encountered Josh. She had to tell Edwin that it was Josh, and only Josh, she loved.

Before the day was over she saw a broad-shouldered hatless rider approach. Sunlight glinted on his brown hair. His dark beard and mustache, the spurs on his dusty boots, made him look more ruthless than ever, yet her heart leapt with joy and relief at the sight of him. Dust and ragged clothing couldn't hide the tempered leanness of a body that was vital and strong.

A small bloodstain darkened his collar, and a cut ran across Josh's temple, but his eyes gleamed with triumph. He leaned over, jubilantly scooping her up on his horse before him. "We did it, Lianna!"

"Did what? What's happened? You're hurt."

He laughed and kissed her swiftly, then leaned back. "The Spanish are fleeing for Valparaiso. Chacabuco has fallen!"

"So quickly?"

"Yes, in only hours! The last few soldiers are still fighting it out, but it'll all be over before sundown. San Martín and Bernardo will ride for Santiago!"

"It's impossible!" Relief filled her and she clung to him, smelling the acrid odor of gunpowder in his clothing. Josh had survived the trek, the battle!

"Because of the false rumors, the Spanish were expecting the battle to come far to the south. They had their strength in the wrong places. Now, all this part of Chile is free! The Spaniards have fled or yielded. They were devastated by our appearance out of the mountains!"

"Thank goodness."

"Josh!"

They both turned to see a man riding a horse. He raised his pistol and fired it skyward, giving a whoop. "I'll buy you a hot rum in London a year from now!"

Josh laughed. "And then I'll buy you one!"

The man galloped away and Lianna smiled at Josh. "So you won him over. That was Lord Paddington, wasn't it?"

"Yes. It's a start. I have some friends in London."

"I've gotten to know Celeste Brenthaven well, Josh. You'll have two staunch friends there."

He smiled. "*We'll* have, Lianna. It's we—I want to give you everything."

"I don't need everything, Josh," she said, thinking of the new baby, of the uncertainties that lay ahead.

As if it had called them to mind, he said, "Now we'll go. We're riding to Santiago."

She heard the unspoken words and said them aloud: "You intend to find the Marchenos."

"Yes. The long wait is almost over."

"Josh—"

"Lianna, I know what I have to do." He turned his horse. Suddenly he grinned. "Come on. I'm going to give some generals the shock of their lives when they discover a woman has crossed the Andes with them!"

Josh introduced her first to José de San Martín, pulling her hat off her head to let the long black hair down. The general's dark eyes widened and his breath went out in a hiss as he bowed over her hand, then listened in amazement to Josh's revelation.

While Josh talked, she studied the man who had liberated so many from tyrannical rule. He looked ashen and ill, his color was pale, yet his dark eyes reflected his intelligence and his jaw was set in determination. Long sideburns graced his cheeks and bushy brows accented his eyes above a prominent nose.

Finally he smiled. "Mrs. Raven, a soldier in my Army of the Andes!" He turned to a grenadier. "Carlos, a flag, please."

The soldier vanished inside a tent, then emerged with a flag in his hands which he gave to San Martín, who handed it to Lianna. She looked at the square of blue and white. An emblem of the sun, above clasped hands holding a liberty cap, was encircled with a laurel wreath.

"Keep this for your children," San Martín said. "You have a remarkable husband, and I'm indebted to him for his help."

Lianna blushed and glanced into eyes that met hers like a touch of emerald fire. "Thank you, sir. I will treasure it and keep it."

"Now, we go to Santiago," Josh said. "We return to my ship and to England."

San Martín laid his hand on Josh's shoulder. He paused to turn his head and cough, then said, "*Gracias*, Josh."

They parted and Josh took Lianna's arm, lifting her

easily onto his horse before he mounted behind her. They had ridden only a few minutes when Fletcher met them, his features set and grim as he kept his gaze on Josh, never once glancing at Lianna.

"There's a Captain Edwin Stafford searching for you."

"Where is he?"

"I don't know where you can find him. I just know he's here, and he's looking for you and your wife."

Lianna gripped the saddle, suddenly aware Josh's life might be in danger from Edwin unless she had an opportunity to talk to him first.

"I'm here—he can come find me," Josh said lightly, and urged the horse forward, turning as soon as they were alone to look at Lianna. "Edwin's here—do you want to go to him?"

"Of course not." She shook her head. "I told you, I love you, but I should tell Edwin. I owe him that."

Josh stood in the saddle and leaned over to pull her up against him and kiss her passionately. When he released her he smiled. "I hope you know your heart fully, but I won't ask again. Let's find O'Higgins and be on our way. Stafford will have to hunt us down."

Unable to locate Bernardo O'Higgins, Josh, Fletcher, Simms, and Lianna rode toward Santiago.

She looked back over her shoulder, aware Edwin was somewhere close at hand, searching for her. Again she prayed she would find him first and tell him of her love for Josh. Along with her fears over Edwin, as they approached Santiago, another fear surfaced. Josh would take his revenge on the Count of Marcheno—and leave Quita a widow unless Armando was the survivor.

When the two-day ride was over, they found the town in celebration. The Spanish officers and soldiers had fled, and the patriots were overjoyed and welcomed the Army of the Andes. Along with the army, Josh and Lianna rode into town, past Santa Lucia Hill, along the boulevard by the Maipo River to the Plaza de Armas and the *cabildo*. Bells tolled steadily and the red-and-yellows flags of Spain were gone, replaced by the blue-and-white flags of independence.

They gathered with a crowd in front of the *cabildo*, where San Martín was offered rule as supreme director of Chile. When he declined, a chant began: "O'Higgins! O'Higgins!"

"Our part is done here," Josh said. "I need to see Madryn," he stated, but Lianna knew the unspoken words. He also intended to hunt down the Marchenos.

As Josh, Lianna, Fletcher, and Simms left the crowd and wound through the city, they heard someone shout, "Captain Raven!"

Josh reined and turned. "It's Lucas Sepulveda, Rinaldo's younger brother!"

Lianna halted as Lucas rode up to shake Josh's hand. "*Viva la libertad!* I've been with General Salas."

"*Viva la libertad!*" Josh answered.

"Come home. Madryn will want to see you. Where's Rinaldo? I can't find him."

"I'm sorry," Josh said quietly.

Lucas' eyes widened as he stared at Josh. "What happened?" he asked, his smile vanishing. "I thought the Spaniards gave up without a fight."

"They did. Rinaldo went down in an avalanche as we were coming over the Andes. I'm sorry," Josh repeated, and put his hand on Lucas' shoulder.

Lucas bowed his head, turning his horse. After a moment he looked at Josh as he wiped away his tears. "Will you come see Madryn?"

"Of course." They rode with him to a small adobe house where Lucas climbed down as stiffly as an aged man and called to his family. Lianna braced for Madryn to receive the news about Rinaldo. Josh helped Lianna down and kept his arm around her waist, holding her close. She was glad for his strength and presence. When Madryn appeared in the door, a smile lighted her features. "*Señora!*" She saw Lucas and her smile faded.

"Rinaldo?" she whispered as he walked to her to put his arms around her and talk softly to her.

Lianna felt tears come, and Josh pulled her against his chest to hold her.

Lucas's parents came out and learned the news, and the

next hour became a blur of pain to Lianna. Sadness enveloped them all as relatives learned and the news slowly spread to friends.

Lianna was hugged by Rinaldo's mother, her hand shaken by his father. They had met the night Lianna had left Simms to lead them to Josh's ship, and a sad welcome was given to Josh and Lianna, as well as to Fletcher and Simms.

As neighbors began to congregate in the small house, Lianna saw Josh talking quietly to Madryn; then he pulled her into his arms and held her while she cried.

Tears dampened Lianna's cheeks, and she knotted her fists, hating war and battles and fighting. She crossed the patio and waited until Madryn came to talk to her. A new spurt of tears came to Madryn's eyes as she moved to hug Lianna.

While Josh went inside the house, Madryn smiled faintly. "*Señora*, I will have Rinaldo's child. At least I'll have a part of him."

"I know. Rinaldo told me."

"I pray it is a handsome boy like his father." Madryn looked at Lianna. "And you also will bear one!" she whispered.

Lianna stared at her in shock. "You guessed!" She looked down. "I don't look different . . ."

Madryn smiled, a smile tinged with sadness. "Not there—it's in your eyes."

Lianna smiled, then sobered. "Captain Raven doesn't know yet."

"Ah, men," Madryn said as if she were a hundred years old. "I won't give away your secret." They were both silent a moment; then Madryn asked, "Do you want a boy or a girl?"

"All I hope is that this baby has Josh's green eyes."

Madryn wiped her eyes. "Rinaldo said he wanted a girl, and I want a boy just like . . ." She broke off to cry, and Lianna patted her shoulder helplessly, knowing there was nothing she could say or do to help.

Later, Madryn took Lianna's hand to lead her to a bedroom, where she opened a chest and picked up a soft white-and-blue blanket.

"I made this for my baby, but I want you to have it for yours. You'll remember me and Rinaldo when you use it."

Lianna took the fleecy blanket and held it to her heart. "Oh, Madryn, it's lovely, and I'll always treasure it!"

Someone rapped on the door. "Lianna," Josh said, "we must go."

Lianna stood up, folding the blanket and looking around helplessly. "I don't want Josh to see this now."

"Put it in your blouse." Madryn watched as Lianna tucked it into her shirt near her waist, before reaching to retrieve the pistol she had removed from her waistband when she arrived.

"You wear a gun?"

"I did when we came over the Andes, and now I think nothing of it. I'll return it to Josh soon and wear dresses again."

The two women looked at each other, and Lianna knew she was parting with one of the closest friends she'd ever had. She reached out to hug Madryn. "I'll pray for you and the baby. I'm so sorry." Tears stung her eyes as she turned swiftly to open the door to face Josh's observant gaze. He leaned against the wall opposite the door, still dressed in a dusty, torn white shirt and black breeches, his sword belt holding a cutlass fastened around his narrow hips. He straightened to take Lianna's arm. "Ready?"

"Yes," she answered, handing the pistol to him. "I'm through with this."

With an arch of his brow, he accepted the pistol and thrust it into his waistband. He pulled Madryn into his arms to hold her a moment while she cried softly against his chest.

"He was very brave. You can tell your child that his father fought to liberate Chile."

"I would rather have him here with me," Madryn cried as Josh stroked her hair.

"I know," he said softly.

Madryn stood on tiptoe to kiss Josh's cheek. "Thank you. You're a wonderful man."

To Lianna's amazement, Josh blushed. "It's nothing, Madryn. It'll be of no use to me."

Lianna was lost, wondering what they were talking about. Madryn turned to take Lianna's hand while still holding Josh's, and put their hands together. "Always," she whispered, "be thankful you have each other."

A new wave of tears threatened, but Lianna knew if she cried it wouldn't help Madryn. Josh gazed at her solemnly while he said, "I will, Madryn," and Lianna wanted to throw her arms around him and hold him close.

Madryn moved away. She nodded and said, *"Adíos,"* then closed the bedroom door. Josh took Lianna's arm, and they told the family farewell.

By now, word had spread and more friends had arrived, so the house was full as they stepped outside.

Lucas caught up with them to shake Josh's hand. "Sir, how can I thank you enough!"

"Don't say another word. The land, the money—let it go for Madryn and the child. They deserve it."

"You're a generous man."

Josh said, "I'm sorry about your loss."

They mounted their horses, and Lianna moved close beside his. "You gave them land?"

He stared straight ahead. "It was nothing, Lianna. I won land and money gambling when I posed as the *marqués,* but it's mine. It's a small gift."

"Oh, Josh, it's a wonderful gift!" She squeezed his hand and he reached across the space to hug her.

She turned her head against his shoulder, unable to keep from crying again over Rinaldo. "Josh, I hate it!"

"I know, Lianna," he said grimly.

After a moment she straightened and rode beside him. Her eyes scanned the crowd, constantly watching for Edwin. She had to talk to him before Josh and he had a confrontation.

When they arrived home, accompanied by Simms and Fletcher, they found the house deserted, the doors standing open.

"Josh!" Fletcher whispered. They turned to see a man slipping out of the shadows across the street. He mounted a horse to ride away swiftly, heading toward the road for Valparaiso and the coast.

"It is no concern of ours." Josh shrugged, but Lianna had looked into the man's dark eyes that seemed to carry a silent threat, and she had a foreboding of evil.

Inside the house there was an eerie silence except for a fountain splashing in the courtyard. Their voices had a hollow echo when they spoke. Josh unbuckled his cutlass and placed it on a table, then turned to his men.

"Fletcher, you and Simms divide. See if you can learn if the others have started back to *El Feroz* or where they are."

"Aye, captain," Simms answered.

"Also, Simms, will you see if the carriage is still here. If it is, Lianna can ride in it to Valparaiso."

"Aye, sir."

While they talked, Lianna glanced upstairs and longed for a hot tub and a dress. Her hand slipped around her waist to the bulge beneath the left side of her shirt, the blanket, which was warm against her skin. Her attention shifted as Josh returned from the *zaguán*, where he had walked with Simms. His spurs clanked on the marble floor, and he faced her with his hands on his hips.

"I'm going to the Governor's Palace. I'll come back and get you."

"Josh, please don't," she said. "Hasn't there been enough bloodshed?"

He frowned. "You plead for the Marchenos after what they would have done to you?"

Suddenly a deep voice cut into their conversation. "I'll save you both the trouble." With a long-handled pistol pointed at Josh, Francisco Marcheno stepped out of the library doorway to face them.

31

Lianna gasped while Josh stood quietly, looking cool and relaxed, as if it were a social call. "So, you waited for us?"

"Actually, I've been hiding here. I didn't expect you back. Armando, his wife, and Salina are riding for Valparaiso now."

"Let her go," Josh said, jerking his head in Lianna's direction. "She's as Spanish as you are, and a loyalist."

While she looked into Francisco's dark eyes, Josh continued, "She's Quita Bencaria, a maid from Spain."

"You're lying!"

"You heard our conversation before you made your presence known. She's been my mistress, nothing more."

Francisco's brow furrowed; Lianna wanted to fling herself into Josh's arms, to plead with Marcheno, anything! After all this time, all the dangers, to face death now, when they were ready to sail and she was with child, was unbearable.

"I did hear your conversation." He glanced at Lianna.

In casual tones Josh said, "Let her live. Take her to Spain with you or the soldiers will imprison her here." He looked at Lianna. "See, I'll repay your passion with generosity. Your life lies in my hands."

"Not in yours, *señor*," Francisco said dryly.

"Then shoot the Spanish wench, but she's one of your own," Josh said as if he cared nothing.

Francisco motioned with his gun. "Get away from him."

Lianna felt icy, yet her mind raced for an opportunity to stop Francisco. She moved away from Josh toward the table where he had so casually laid his cutlass earlier. She knew nothing about using a cutlass, but Josh was quick. If she could give him any chance, he would make the most of it.

"Sir, can I go to Spain with you?" Lianna said as she edged toward the table.

Francisco watched Josh, who moved impatiently. "Stand still! You fooled us all, Don Cristóbal—or do you care to tell me your English name?"

"Joshua Raven."

"The name Raven . . ." He shrugged. "How disappointed I am that I can't take you back to Spain."

Lianna reached down, her fingers closing over the hilt of the cutlass. With all her strength she yanked it up and flung the weapon at Francisco.

Silver glinted, flying through the air in a high arc. It caught Marcheno's attention, and he whirled to face it. He squeezed the trigger and there was a deafening blast.

The blade sliced downward to sink into Marcheno's chest. As it struck, Josh leapt at him, and the two men crashed to the floor. Suddenly Francisco went limp. Josh sat poised above him, grasping the pistol he had wrenched from Francisco's hand; then slowly he stood up.

Closing her eyes, Lianna swayed, feeling ill. Josh came to put his arm around her shoulders.

"I killed him!" she whispered, stunned at what had happened.

"And if you hadn't, I would be dead. You just saved my life."

Someone swore softly, and they turned to see Fletcher standing in the doorway. "Where did he come from?"

"He was hiding in the house," Josh said.

"The carriage is in front," Fletcher said, glancing at Lianna. He turned and left them alone.

She shook violently. "I want to go. Now. I don't want to change clothes, to go upstairs. I can't bear to look at him, Josh."

"We'll go."

She heard the grimness in his tone and looked up to see a flinty expression on his features as he gazed down the hall toward the outside.

"You want to catch Armando and Quita," she whispered. And of all the disasters in their venture, this seemed the worst—the cold-blooded culmination of Josh's hatred.

"Yes. They haven't sailed. They can't be far ahead, because they expected Francisco. Come on, Lianna. At last I'll confront the Count of Marcheno." He took her arm and they left. Outside, they found the carriage ready, Simms and Fletcher waiting.

"As far as we can find out, your other men have gone to Valparaiso to the ship," Fletcher said.

"Good. Fletcher, let me have your sword."

While Fletcher unbuckled the belt and Josh fastened it around his hips, he said, "Lianna, you may have the carriage. I'll ride ahead."

She knew the unspoken words. He wanted to be free to look for the Marcheno coach, to find Don Armando. Lianna climbed inside and sank down on the seat, sitting stiffly, her mind refusing to think about what lay ahead.

The day had darkened, with storm clouds boiling overhead, hiding the sun, yet the air was cloying and hot. In spite of the heat, Lianna was chilled, shocked at the death of Francisco, dreading what might happen in the next hours, and wondering where Edwin was. She gazed out the window and remembered their arrival so long ago, recalling Josh picking sunflowers and his teasing words. She prayed that the count and Quita would be on the coast, on board a Spanish ship, out of Josh's reach.

She was stunned by events. The victory of the patriots had been overshadowed by other happenings that were more personal: Rinaldo's death, Edwin so close at hand, Josh's private war.

Hours later the coach speeded up and Lianna leaned out to see a cloud of dust on the road, a black coach lumbering ahead, and Josh galloping after it.

Her fears became reality as she watched, bouncing with each jolt of the carriage. She heard the pistol shot and saw Josh fire into the air. The coach lurched to a halt and he

leaned forward to yank the door open, then backed his
horse away with his gun drawn. Leaning out the window
with wind and dust whipping her face, Lianna watched
him jump from the saddle and draw a sword.

The distance between them narrowed; then her carriage
halted. The moment it stopped, she flung open the door.
Fletcher barred her way. "Don't try to stop him!" he
snapped.

"Get out of my way, Fletcher."

"He's waited years for this moment. You can't imagine
what they did to twenty-four people."

Lianna stepped back, slammed the door shut in his face,
and rushed out the opposite door. She ran toward the
Marcheno coach while Fletcher rushed around the front of
the carriage to stop her.

Josh held a sword pointed at Count Armando's throat.
Quita had stepped out, and Francisco's wife, Salina, stood
beside the carriage. Dressed in a blue silk dress with
diamonds and rubies around her neck, Quita was pale as
she glanced at Lianna. *"Por Dios!"*

Armando called Josh a foul name. He moved his hand
slightly and his heavy ruby ring glinted. Lianna glanced at
it and saw the serpent's head. When Armando moved, Josh
pressed harder with his sword, pricking the skin and drawing blood.

Armando shouted, *"Cabrón!* My brother will avenge
us— "

"Your brother is dead."

Armando gasped, and Salina slumped to the ground in a
faint. Quita closed her eyes, then opened them, looking at
Lianna. *"Por favor, Quita, Madre de Dios, por favor . . ."*

"Get out of my way, Fletcher," Lianna demanded flatly,
looking into angry gray eyes that narrowed. Suddenly his
expression changed. He stepped aside, and she rushed to
Josh. "Let them go, Josh!"

"How did my brother die?" Marcheno asked.

"By a sword thrust," Josh said, ignoring Lianna. Josh's
sword tip moved higher on Marcheno's throat. "Get away,
Lianna."

"Lianna!" Armando snapped, and Quita paled, dropping to her knees to raise her hands. *"Por favor,* please, captain, let us go . . . let us go."

Lianna clutched Josh's arm. "Stop it" she cried.

Quita sobbed, a high, wailing sound as she rocked back and forth, her skirts lying in the dust, her hands over her face. Marcheno's face blanched.

"Por Dios, por favor . . ." he said, "leave my wife—"

"How much mercy did you show Phillip?" Josh thundered. "Get back," he said to Lianna.

"You can't do this!" she cried. "You can't murder them coldly, willfully!"

"They've done worse! He would have had you arrested, tortured, handed over to Farjado—"

"That's their burden. Don't become like them!" Hot tears streaked her face as she pulled at an arm like iron. She felt desperate to stop him. Josh's body was straight as a ramrod as he held the sword pressed against the count.

"Get away, Lianna. You won't want to watch." Josh ground out the words with an ominous softness.

"No! Let them go! All my childhood I lived without love. You've given your life to hate, Josh. Don't throw away love. Don't become a murderer! It will be on your conscience forever!"

"I've murdered before."

"You've only killed in self-defense," Lianna argued. "As you did in the fight with Farjado. It would have been your life otherwise. This is different. This is hate."

"Dammit!" Josh's hand shook. "When I remember Phillip and what this beast did—"

"Stop clinging to that memory," she begged. "It's on his conscience. Don't have his death, hers, their unborn child's, on yours! None of it will bring back your brother." She shook with sobs. "There has been so little love in our lives . . . so little. Please . . ."

"Fletcher!" Josh bellowed. "Get her out of here!"

Fletcher's arms wound around her, picking her up. As Lianna screamed, Fletcher's hold tightened. Everything swam, and she couldn't get her breath.

Fletcher called to Simms to start the carriage as he held Lianna tightly pressed to him.

Suddenly she knew it was useless to fight. She went limp with sobs. As the carriage lumbered along, Fletcher eased her onto the seat and sat facing her quietly while she cried. He stared at her while the wind whistled around them. "You have hysterics over Josh's violence, yet you murdered Francisco Marcheno without a qualm."

"Because it would've meant Josh's life if I hadn't."

"You care for you husband that much!" After a moment he said quietly, "I think I've misjudged you."

Lianna looked into Fletcher's eyes and for the first time felt as if all animosity were gone, yet the moment was of little consequence. Lianna wept with a sense of absolute loss.

At port in Valparaiso, *El Feroz* looked majestic riding at anchor in the bay. The English colors flew abovedecks, along with a blue flag bearing a golden lion. Men were busy getting ready to sail. Beyond it were two more ships flying the Union Jack. Lianna hurried up the gangplank and followed Fletcher to the captain's quarters. He held his silence when he noticed a man watching them. The man leaned against a barrel on the wharf, then straightened and hurried in the direction of a small boat.

"Fletcher!" Lianna whispered.

"I saw him. It's the same man who watched us in Santiago," he said grimly.

"Why would someone watch us now?"

"I don't know." He took her arm to go below, and opened the door to the captain's cabin. "This is yours."

When she saw the familiar surroundings, Lianna's heart lurched. "Thank you," she whispered as he closed the door and left.

All she could think of was Josh holding his sword against Marcheno's throat. Would he kill Quita and Salina as well? An ache in her chest was unbearable and she felt as if something inside her were dying a little too. As she sat still in the silence of the cabin, she realized it was also a beginning. She placed her hand on her abdomen and thought about the child, praying it was healthy and would have Josh's eyes. She pulled the tiny blanket out and rubbed its softness against her cheek, then dropped it in a chair.

She had few possessions, almost as little as she'd brought aboard from Portsmouth. There were four treasures to keep: a faded, wilted gardenia from the ball; the flag of Chile; the diamond necklace from Josh; and the baby blanket.

She crossed the cabin to the washstand to bathe her face. In a few minutes Fletcher sent a steward with hot water and Lianna bathed, glad to change from the dusty clothing into a dress. She wore a blue muslin, tying her hair behind her head with a ribbon. She stood turning the gold wedding band on her finger, her tie to Josh; and now there was a more binding tie, their baby.

Would Josh appear with the Marchenos' blood on his hands? She dropped into a chair and placed her head in her hands.

Suddenly there was a scuffle outside and the cabin door banged open.

Fletcher came stumbling into the room, propelled by a man who stepped in behind him, holding a saber at Fletcher's throat.

"Edwin!" Lianna was stunned to face him.

"Lianna, I mean no harm to anyone, but they wouldn't let me come aboard to see you."

She stared at him, unable to think or to answer.

"She's wed to another," Fletcher said.

"Fletcher, please leave us alone," Lianna said, knowing she would now have to tell Edwin about her love for Josh.

Fletcher said, "I think I should protect Josh's interests—" The saber tip prodded sharply, bringing a prick of blood that darkened Fletcher's white shirt.

"Shut your mouth!" Edwin snapped. "And do as she asked."

"Edwin, please don't hurt him!"

"Burford!"

A burly sailor appeared. Edwin nodded. "Get him out of the way so the lady and I can talk."

"Don't do this!" Fletcher said to Lianna. "If you—"

The sailor swung a club, striking Fletcher on the side of the head. Lianna gasped as he crumpled to the floor. The sailor caught him beneath the arms to pull him out.

"Edwin, how you've changed!" She stared at him in shock, wondering how much she really knew him.

"He'll come around in minutes. Lianna, my ship is docked only yards away. Come aboard and let's talk."

She stared at him in indecision, wanting to blurt out that she loved only Josh, yet knowing it would be a cruel way to break the news. "Edwin, Josh will be along shortly. We can talk here."

"I don't want to have to keep clubbing his men on the head." He smiled. "Lianna, please. I've sailed around the world for you. Can't you come talk for an hour?"

"Of course," she said, feeling guilty but dreading the hour.

His smile broadened. "Ah, Lianna, we have so much to discuss." He took her arm to go up the gangway. Topside, each of Josh's men was guarded by Edwin's men. Edwin and Lianna hurried down the gangplank to a longboat, and within minutes she was whisked down to the captain's quarters on Edwin's two-masted schooner, the *Eagle*. The ship was smaller than *El Feroz*, the captain's quarters cramped. While she heard men pour onto the ship, Lianna stared at the man she knew so well, yet hardly knew at all. Edwin had changed, hardened. A scar cut a jagged path across his cheek, and his shoulders were broader, more filled out. He was tall, broad-chested, dressed in an elegant white shirt and blue breeches, yet the gray eyes gazing at her were so familiar. He held her hands, holding her away from him while he smiled. "How beautiful you are!"

"Thank you. And you're more handsome than ever."

He smiled as he motioned her to a chair and moved to a table to pour two glasses of brandy. "It seems forever, Lianna."

She said, "Now you're a captain! How did you get your own ship?"

He crossed to hand her a glass of amber liquid, holding his out. "To the most beautiful woman on earth."

She laughed. "Thank you, but that's ridiculous!" She touched her glass against his, hearing a faint clink; then she took a drink. The brandy was bitter, a flame going down while she sat back and watched Edwin move to a chair. "I didn't return home after you left. I signed on a ship."

She gazed at him in surprise. Edwin sat back in the chair looking relaxed and composed, and again she realized how vastly they had both changed. "You didn't know anything about sailing."

He smiled. "No, but neither have many men before me. I couldn't go back to the farm. At the time, I had a notion of finding you."

She blushed and knotted her fingers together. "I'm sorry."

"Don't be, Lianna. I'm glad. I couldn't have achieved this if I'd returned home to work."

"That doesn't explain how you became captain," she said, and waved her hand. "How did you get your own vessel?"

"We were sailing back to England when we were attacked by pirates. We were caught in a storm with a crippled ship." While he talked, Lianna realized Edwin was as busy assessing her as she was him. And she wondered if his conclusions were as startling to him as hers. He had been an awkward, bumbling youth, but now he was poised. He looked as hard and fit as the seamen on *El Feroz*.

El Feroz . . . Green eyes with golden flecks came like mist drifting down from the sky, to envelop her in a fog that shut out the world.

Edwin was talking. With an effort she tried to force her thoughts to his words. The cabin was warm and she ran her fingers across her brow.

". . . when the fight was finished, there were only some twenty of us on my ship who had survived, and the others were less fit to captain than I was. Suddenly I had my own ship."

While he talked, Lianna turned to glance out the window again. He continued, "We returned to England, where

I was hired by Lord Quimby as a mercenary to carry weapons to Chile.''

"I was afraid Josh had harmed you that day the ships crossed paths."

Edwin laughed. "No, he merely chased me off the ship. I heard your father died. I'm sorry."

"Thank you," she answered perfunctorily, her thoughts on Josh. Edwin's voice seemed to recede as he talked, and she felt faint, wondering if her pregnancy were causing her head to swim.

"To old memories, Lianna," Edwin said gently, and held out his glass.

Without thinking, she touched his glass again and drank, closing her eyes momentarily. It felt as if the ship were moving. "Edwin . . ."

He crossed to her, placing his hands on her shoulders. "Are you ready to go back to England?" he asked, his gaze searching her face.

Lianna looked up into gray eyes and saw only green. She listened to Edwin and heard only Josh's husky voice. Josh's image filled her mind.

Edwin swore, startling her. "You love him, don't you?"

"Yes. I'm sorry. That's why I came to talk to you and explain. We were so young, Edwin. You told me I was a child, and you were right."

"No!"

"I'm sorry," she said again. "You know I wouldn't deliberately hurt you."

"I heard you scream that day, Lianna. You didn't love him then."

"No. maybe not. I don't know what I felt then, because I was shocked to see you and I wanted to talk to you. I was afraid Josh might kill you."

He moved to pull her to her feet. "I love you more than ever," he said softly. "You're all I've dreamed about since we parted in Portsmouth."

"Edwin, I can't stop what I feel," she whispered. "I love Josh."

"The day we fought the Spanish ship, he admitted to me the marriage was forced. You didn't love him then, and he hasn't given you a chance to see whom you truly love. Give me a chance, Lianna.''

"I can't! I love Josh deeply. Edwin, I'm sorry," she repeated, feeling dizzy. "I don't feel well. I should go back," she murmured, swaying. His arms steadied her. "It feels as if the ship is moving," she said with a rising panic.

"Careful, Lianna. Come here." He led her to his bed. "Lie down a moment."

She couldn't argue with him, feeling as if she might topple over in a faint. She sank down and lay back, closing her eyes. "We're not moving, are we?" she asked, having difficulty forming the words. She wanted to get up and insist she be taken back to *El Feroz*, but it took too much effort.

"Childhood is over, Lianna. We've both grown up, but I know what I want as much now as I did when we were in England."

"I don't know how you found me," she murmured.

"I had someone watching your house in Santiago. I got word when you returned."

"I'm deeply in love with my husband."

"Give me a chance, Lianna! Just a chance. Once we loved each other—I don't think you truly know what you want!"

His voice shook with emotion. She couldn't comprehend the depth of his feeling—and she didn't share it. Each moment that passed, she felt torn. Her heart was elsewhere, and nothing could change her. She wanted to ask Edwin to take her back to *El Feroz*, but words wouldn't come.

"I want you, Lianna, and now I'm not a simple grooms-man." His voice deepened. "I know what I want and I intend to have it."

His arms slipped around her as he lifted her up, moving to sit beside her.

"No," she whispered, wanting to push against him but unable to do so. She remembered the bitter taste of the brandy and looked at him. She was on the wrong ship, in the arms of the wrong man, and she knew without a doubt

there was no way she could make any kind of life with
Edwin, but she couldn't stop him. She felt boneless and
dizzy. "The brandy . . ."

"I'm going to get my chance, Lianna. It has been
denied to me by fate too long." He pulled her to him to
kiss her, and she couldn't fight him or stop him or feel
anything. She wanted to scream at him to stop and take her
back. It seemed impossible Edwin would take her against
her wishes, yet she knew how much he had changed and
hardened.

Edwin bent his head to kiss her again, trying to force a
response. And while he kissed her, he could feel the
movement of the ship beneath him as it gathered speed and
put out to sea.

He fought the urge to peel away Lianna's clothes and
claim her body. Time enough later.

Now he'd win her love. They had a long voyage and he
knew from years past how to please her; he knew what
women liked in bed. Lianna had been forced into the
marriage with Josh Raven, and then, with time, she had
come to love him, but it could work the other way also.
With time and absence and childhood memories in Edwin's favor, he could make her forget Josh Raven. And
now that they had put out to sea, she would have to accept
her fate. He would have the voyage to win her over—and
he could delay their landing in England until he did win
her over!

What a shock she would receive when she reached
England and discovered the extent of her father's wealth,
wealth that would belong to Edwin Stafford! His! He
forced his thoughts back to the present and whispered,
"I'll never let you go, Lianna."

He ran his hand along her cheek, watching the effort she
made to open her eyes. "Take . . . me back . . ." She
murmured the words in a slurred voice. Her lashes fluttered. "Josh . . ."

Edwin couldn't resist. He lowered his head to kiss the
soft fullness of her breast, his hand touching her, stroking
to stir a response.

"No! Josh . . ." she said, her hand fluttering in the air, the protest a mere whisper.

"You'll be mine and you'll want to be mine by your own choice," Edwin said. "I know you, Lianna, and I'm no longer a simple farm lad."

"No," she whispered again. Her head spun, and a wave of blackness engulfed her.

He felt her go limp in his arms and laid her back on the bed. His body was hot with desire, and he was tempted to possess her now, yet his ardor cooled as he thought about her being unconscious. He wanted a response from her; he wanted her to know when she was his.

He ran his hand over her body, feeling the softness, the curve of her hip, slipping his hand beneath her skirt to touch her legs. "You'll be mine soon enough," he said, smiling as his hand moved higher beneath her skirts, taking liberties that he had dreamed of many nights. He moved away abruptly, knowing he should go above. She would stir soon enough and then it would take all his wits to placate her.

32

Josh held the sword at the throat of Don Armando while Quita wailed and mumbled prayers. The carriage with Lianna started up and gained speed, rushing down the road away from them, but her words floated in the air, running through Josh's mind. "... *so little love in our lives* ... *don't throw away love* ..."

The only barrier left between them was his own hatred and revenge. He glanced at the coach receding in the distance, then at the trio in front of him, and his thoughts churned.

He knew if he plunged the sword into the count, he might lose Lianna forever—he would lose the best part of his life. Lianna loved him and gave her love whether he was a pirate or not.

What did she have to do with this evil man sweating before him? In truth, he had to answer: Nothing! He didn't want revenge to cost him love. He lowered the sword. "God deliver justice to you. Get in your carriage and go."

Marcheno's eyes narrowed; then he moved swiftly. "Get in, Lianna."

"Marcheno."

Josh's cold voice stopped the man instantly. It was on the tip of Josh's tongue to reveal Quita's identity. He looked into her big dark eyes, watched her bloodless lips move in prayer, and realized she was part of the reason he had Lianna.

"Go," he repeated.

Marcheno picked up Salina, and the three climbed into their carriage. Within seconds it rocked down the road as the horses ran at full tilt.

And slowly, steadily, Josh felt a weight like an anchor lift from his shoulders. Nothing stood between him and his love for Lianna! Nothing!

No longer would hatred lie between him and the woman he loved. And his blood heated at the thought of crushing her in his arms, of seeing her look at him with love in her eyes.

"Lianna!" He cried her name and laughed aloud as he threw his arms in the air, looking at clouds sweeping across the blue sky. He leapt on his horse and urged it forward. Tonight they would sail for England and he would hold her in his arms, hold her close as he had that night high in the mountains in a rocky cave. Images made his loins ache and his breath halt. He gave the horse freedom to gallop, the wind tearing at his face as he shouted, "Lianna!"

He drove the horse as fast as possible, but the time seemed to drag. When he finally reached the dock at Valparaiso, he flung himself off his mount and raced up the gangplank of *El Feroz*. His heart thudded and he was breathless from more than his run as he reached his cabin.

Behind him Fletcher called, "Josh!"

"Later, Fletcher. Set sail for England!" He flung open the door and stepped into the cabin.

One glance showed it was empty, and he turned to face Fletcher, who stood behind him.

Fletcher's cheek was blue with a bruise, his lip was swollen, a cut ran across his forehead, and he scowled murderously.

The first icy touch of disaster rocked him. "What happened? Where is she?"

"Edwin Stafford came aboard with his men. She left with him."

Josh felt as if he had turned to glass and was shattering into a million tiny fragments. Never had he truly loved a woman before, and never had he truly lost as much. He closed his eyes and swayed, clenching his fists until his arms ached. He wanted to be dead, to do anything to avoid the pain that tore at his insides.

Hot tears stung his eyes. He had lost her forever, through his own damn-foolery. He opened his eyes and saw Fletcher had turned his back and was standing a few feet away.

Josh's voice was a croak, sounding distant to his ears as he asked, "Did she go willingly?"

Fletcher nodded without looking at Josh. "Yes, sir. She did. Stafford had his own ship; his men prevented us from interfering while she left with him. They've sailed."

Josh was consumed with fiery pain. He had lost the one thing in life he wanted with his whole heart. He had lost her forever. She was with the man she loved. For the first time in his life he felt totally defeated. And the hurt engulfed him in waves.

"Set sail, Fletcher. We go north. We'll sail around the world. Let's be gone from this place."

"Aye, sir. There are storm clouds to the south. Perhaps we can outrun them." Fletcher's boots clattered on the ladder, then faded.

Woodenly Josh closed the door, torturing himself with memories, staring at the bunk where Lianna had lain in his arms.

He leaned against the door, lost in his thoughts, unaware of the commotion abovedecks as they set sail, of the rise and fall of *El Feroz* as she put out to open sea.

Josh was mired in memories, of Lianna's lips, her arms, her sweet laughter. How she had grown and changed, risking her life for Madryn, making the grueling trek over the mountains. Risking all by giving her love to him freely.

He wanted to go home to England, to give her everything she wanted, to pamper and love her and see her eyes light with happiness.

He swore and ran his hands through his hair.

And remembered her fingers twining in his hair . . . her pink-and-ivory body writhing in passion, her gasps of love . . . her words, "I love you."

She couldn't love Edwin Stafford! He straightened and his thoughts began to clear, to see everything from her view. She thought he had murdered the Marchenos, and maybe her feelings were in a turmoil. She might have wanted to tell Edwin that she no longer loved him. Suddenly Josh could think of logical reasons why she might have gone with Edwin—yet why would she sail with him? And he thought about Edwin, any man who had gone from a groom to captain of his own ship was bound to be ruthless, clever, and persuasive.

Josh's heart began to pound. He would get her back! She was still his wife and he wanted his chance to tell her he had let the Marchenos go unharmed. How could she have cried so much when she pleaded for the Marchenos if she hadn't loved him deeply? He remembered the night in the cave, her ardent lovemaking—she couldn't love Edwin Stafford and have made love to him as she had that night! He had to see her face-to-face and have her tell him she wanted to be with Edwin.

Clinging to a thread of hope, his blood thundering in his veins, he whirled to open the door and race up the hatchway. The first mate stood beside the helmsman, giving commands. In long strides, his breathing constricted by his urgency, Josh reached them.

"Helmsman, put about."

Fletcher spun around to look at him.

"We're going after her. She's still my wife. I have to hear her make the choice. Overtake that damned *Eagle!*"

"Sir, look south," Fletcher said grimly. "We'll be riding into a squall."

"So be it. Go with full speed."

"Aye, captain."

Josh ran below to change clothing. He felt intoxicated with purpose. She had to love him! He could feel it to the marrow of his bones. And how much he loved her! He would take a lifetime to show her.

He crossed the cabin, and as he did, for the first time he noticed something crumpled in the chair. She had left something behind. He picked up a soft blue-and-white woolen square of material, so tiny. Turning it in his hands, he puzzled over it. Why would Lianna have a bit of knitting? It was finished, yet too small for warmth, for anything except . . .

His chest constricted violently. "Lianna!" He crushed the woolen blanket to his chest, then flung it down and raced abovedecks to take the wheel himself.

Lianna stirred and sat up. Her head pounded and she was disoriented, trying to think, to remember. She swung her feet to the deck; her mouth was dry and she held her head in her hands a moment. Memory returned and she gasped, crying out, "No!"

She stood up, but dizziness struck her and she had to sit down again. She stood up slowly this time, clinging to the bunk, feeling the deep rise and fall of a ship in stormy waters.

The door to the cabin opened and Edwin entered. He stopped, seeing her awake, and then he came inside and closed the door behind him.

"Lianna—"

"How could you! You put something in the brandy." She wanted to scream and shout at him, but her head swam and words were an effort; her mouth felt dry, as if filled with cotton.

"Forgive me," he said, crossing to sit near her. "I just want some time with you. When we reach England, if you still love him, I'll let you go."

"I love him! I want to be with Josh now!"

"Listen for a moment." He leaned closer, his fingers laced together and elbows resting on his knees. "Fate separated us when we were on the brink of realizing our love. You didn't love Captain Raven then, nor when you married him. He told me he forced you into the union. I love you, Lianna, and at one point in time you loved me. Give me a chance—just for the length of the voyage. I promise once we reach England, I'll return you to him if that's what you want."

She hurt badly and all she wanted was her husband. "Please take me back. Please . . ."

"I beg you, give us this chance!"

She blinked, feeling tears rise as she gripped Edwin's

hands to plead with desperation, "Please take me back to him before he thinks I've chosen willingly to sail with you!"

"He took you by force and you didn't like him, much less love him. If I take you by force now, how do I know but what you'll love me—I'm the man who has known you since we were babes. We've laughed together, played together . . . my kiss was your first, and at the time you liked it. Give me this chance, Lianna. If I hadn't been poor, you would be my wife now, and we would have a blissful union."

His eyes became red, and she felt torn with conflicting emotions. She regretted what had happened, she regretted that Edwin still wanted her, but she loved Josh with every ounce of her being, every breath.

"Edwin, I've changed," she said. It was an effort to get out the words. "I love Josh, truly love him for eternity. I'm sorry for the pain I've caused you, but you're a very handsome man. You're young and captain of your own ship—the world is filled with lovely women who would adore you."

"I only want one," he said, looking at her intently. "Please, Lianna, give me this voyage."

"I can't. Don't you see, it's as if you're tearing my heart out. I love Josh."

They stared at each other and she realized Edwin was as hard and ruthless as Josh and the Count of Marcheno. She saw her answer in his eyes.

"I won't ever change," she said.

"I think you will."

"How can you expect me to love you when you treat me this way!"

"He was worse and you think you love him!"

"He wasn't!"

"He took you. Don't tell me you willingly fell into his bed when you sailed from Portsmouth!"

She blushed, not wanting a discussion with Edwin about her intimate moments with Josh. She looked down. "Please let me go."

"I'll promise not to take you to bed until you want me."

"Edwin, please don't do this! I beg you to reconsider." She began to cry, feeling helpless and unable to control her emotions. Her head throbbed violently and she felt queasy, unable to cope with all that was happening.

He leaned closer, his voice quiet as he said, "I'm sorry for the manner I've done this, but I saw no other choice. I love you with all my heart—more than Captain Raven ever could. The man's a pirate, Lianna. Is that what you want, to wait at home for a pirate who is an outcast in his own land?"

"I love him."

"And later, if you had children, they too would be outcasts, left alone with you while he sailed around the world."

"Nothing you say can change my mind."

"I'm sorry, but I think you'll change. If not, you'll have my deep apologies when we reach England."

He stood up to go. "You should eat soon; we're sailing into a violent storm."

"Edwin—"

He turned back to face her.

"You must take me back. I'm expecting his child."

Edwin blanched and his jaw firmed in anger over Lianna's announcement. "It won't matter, if you love me," he said stiffly.

"It matters, I see it in your eyes."

"No!" He crossed the room to her to stroke her cheek. "There's enough love for you and a child. It will be my child, Lianna. We'll both love it," he said quietly, but his thoughts were seething. She would bear the man's whelp. A child! He hadn't counted on that, but it shouldn't matter. There was sufficient money to hire nannies and governesses and he would be free to do as he pleased. "If you love me, this child will have both parents. You know what it means to go without a father's love, and Captain Raven's first love is the sea."

"I can't help what's wise—I love him!"

He stroked her throat. "You'll change once you near England." His fingers drifted to her shoulder. He felt her stiffen and removed his hand swiftly.

"Don't draw away from me. I'll wait, Lianna. Don't fear me." He *would* wait, for a time. Soon enough she would grow hungry for a man's touch, and she would be more vulnerable. He thought of Molly, and the thought of Molly's lush body, her lusty needs, made him hard with desire. Swiftly he turned his thoughts to sailing. He walked toward the door and said, "This is your cabin for the voyage."

"No!" She stood up to stop him from leaving, but her head spun and she had to cling to the bunk while Edwin closed the door behind him.

After the door had closed, she stood quietly staring at it until finally she felt able to get a cloak and go abovedeck.

Lianna stood at the rail watching the high waves and empty horizon. A chill wind whipped across the deck, pulling her long black hair free of pins and twirling it across her cheeks.

An arm dropped across her shoulders and Edwin said, "Come below. It grows chilly. A squall is rising."

"I can't bear to sit in a cabin." She turned to face him. "This is so futile. When we parted, we both were children. We didn't know what we wanted."

"I did, Lianna. And I wasn't a child. A child doesn't gain captaincy of his own ship within the time I have. A child—I had known women since I was fifteen! I know what I want. I love you and I always will and I think in a month's time you'll love me in return."

"Never! I'd fling myself into the sea if I thought I'd never see Josh again."

"And destroy his child?" he said with a sardonic smile.

She felt a hot flush rise to her cheeks. "No, I want this child. But I want my husband desperately. Edwin, Papa is dead. When I get home I'll inherit everything." She tilted her head to study him. "If I gave it all to you, you'd have wealth and you could find a desirable woman who would truly love you. If I did that, would you take me back to Josh now?"

The question hung in the air while Edwin's mind raced wildly over the possibilities. It was on the tip of his tongue to say yes. He didn't want Lianna and Raven's child. He wanted everything else, because she was right: there were ample women who could make him happy. But wisdom cautioned him—she might go back on her promise. And even if she didn't, Josh Raven would force her to do so. Edwin had tried to learn everything possible about Raven when he had been in London. He knew that Josh had been disinherited and made his livelihood as a privateer, a pirate. With a child, Raven would be a total fool if he let Lianna give away her inheritance, and Edwin knew enough about Josh to know he wasn't a fool. Josh also was a sea captain with a wide reputation for his seamanship, and there were few fools who survived at sea.

Lianna's wide blue eyes looked up hopefully. How he wished with all his being he could make the exchange with her and get her off his hands, but he knew he would come out with nothing.

"Lianna, can't you understand—it's you, not your inheritance I want," he lied, wishing there were some way to ensure the bargain but knowing there wasn't.

She turned away to cling to the rail, and he felt bitter disappointment that he couldn't have given her what she wanted—and received from her what he wanted. He left her to see about the ship, watching her from the poop deck. Wind whipped her hair and cloak, and he frowned. He didn't want her to become ill. If she died, he would lose everything. He frowned, rocking on his heels.

The sky changed from blue to gray while clouds boiled on the horizon. The sky and water blended in a charcoal gray to the southeast, and jagged lightning streaked the sky. After a time, Edwin reappeared at her side.

"Lianna, get below. We're in for a real blow."

Before she could answer, a seaman called, "Sails! Northeasterly!"

At an angle to the storm clouds loomed white sails. Edwin's eyes narrowed and he called for a sailor to bring a telescope. He raised it to his eyes. "Someone is coming after us swiftly."

Lianna's heart began drumming and she held her breath. Her fingers shook as she reached up. "May I look?"

Edwin frowned, handing her the telescope. "It's a frigate.'' His voice faded as Lianna held the telescope to her eyes and peered intently at the sails. She couldn't make out the colors in the distance, but her heart pounded wildly. Suppose . . .

Edwin raised an eyebrow and looked through the glass again. ''The damned storm grows worse with each second. We have to outrun it.''

''Oh, Edwin, turn back. You're sailing into the teeth of the storm.''

''If we wait, it could be a pirate ship. One of the Spaniards.''

''It could be Josh.''

''You're seeing what you want to see. We have to go swiftly before the storm's fury sets in.'' Raising his voice, he called an order, and within seconds the *Eagle* ran faster, cutting through choppy water with a swift rise and fall.

Lianna raised the glass and looked again, still unable to make out the colors. Her heart jumped when she saw the ship was slowly gaining on them. Edwin patted her shoulder. ''Lianna, go below before you get the ague in this wind.''

Her throat burned as if she had swallowed a chunk of hot coal. Those sails resembled *El Feroz*—yet how many other frigates under full sail would look exactly the same?

Edwin left her to join the helmsman. Lowering his voice, he commanded, ''Put in toward shore as we go south.''

The man's eyes widened. ''Sir, this is a rocky coastline.''

''Helmsman!''

''Aye, sir.''

''Run as close as you dare until I tell you to change course sou'westerly again.''

''Aye, captain.''

Edwin Stafford turned to look at the sails following him. ''I'll win this time, Raven. I'll win everything.''

''Captain?'' the helmsman asked.

''Nothing. Hold your course.''

''Aye, sir.''

Within minutes the sky darkened more, the waves rose

higher, causing the ship to roll. Lianna clung to the rail, watching the white sails grow larger. Cold drops of rain began to pelt her. She raised the glass to look as sheets of rain drifted across the sea. Great white sails dimmed and blurred into gray—white sails and a blue-and-gold flag.

Aboard *El Feroz*, Josh Raven let the helmsman take the wheel, while he stood with his feet braced apart to ride with each pitch and roll of the ship. He raised the telescope to his eyes. "Dammit! I know that's them. Look, Fletcher, see if it's his flag."

Fletcher took the scope, raised it, and in a second handed it back. "Aye, it's the *Eagle*. And a damned bad storm we're sailing into."

"It won't be the first." Josh looked through the telescope again. "We'll overtake the ship in two hours. It doesn't have the speed of *El Feroz*."

"They're changing course, sir. They're headed south-easterly—toward land."

"Damm! Doesn't the fool know this coast! It's rocky and dangerous. Change our course to follow."

"Captain—"

"If they drop anchor, I don't want to sail past them. Nothing can stop me. Fletcher, the woman I love is on that ship. And my babe."

Fletcher's head snapped around, and suddenly he grinned. "Glory be! Josh Raven a father. A damned good one you'll be, too!" Fletcher's grin widened. "Glory, a child! That's good news!"

Josh raised his eyebrows. "I thought you didn't approve of my lady."

Fletcher flushed, his burnished skin becoming flaming red. "Aye, sir, I didn't when we sailed from England. But I do now. She's a fine woman, sir."

Josh felt warmth fill him, because he knew Fletcher didn't give his praise lightly. At some time Lianna had earned Fletcher's grudging admiration.

Fletcher turned to stride to one of the men, and within seconds all the men on shipboard were grinning—and working as hard as they could to help their captain reach his goal.

They lost sight of the *Eagle* as sheets of rain lashed *El Feroz*. Grimly Josh fought the wild sea, hauling on the wheel, clinging to it when waves battered him. "Lianna!" he called hoarsely.

Fletcher clung to a lifeline and shouted, "What's the fool doing?"

Josh peered into the storm. "He's doing it deliberately!" Josh realized Edwin Stafford was running close to shore for only one reason. He shouted, "Change course, mate!" He tugged on the wheel in desperation.

Suddenly an outcropping of land and rock, jutting miles out to sea from the mainland, rose before them. Frantically Josh fought the waves, but the wind caught *El Feroz* in all its fury and smashed it against the rocks.

The sound of splintering wood was loud; a great shuddering ripple coursed through the ship, throwing men off balance as they slipped into the sea.

Josh gave one wild cry of futility; then a wave smashed down, slamming him into unconsciousness as his head hit the deck.

Aboard the *Eagle*, Lianna clung to the rail until hard fingers grasped her shoulders to turn her around. Edwin lifted her off her feet.

"I know it's *El Feroz*! I know it!"

"Shh, Lianna. It doesn't matter now. We're separated by a storm. The wind carries us south."

"Edwin!" she screamed as she watched the ship turn in a crazy angle and dip down out of sight, waves washing over it. Then it was seen no more. "Josh!"

"My God," Edwin gasped, feeling a swift surge of joy. His plan had worked! *El Feroz* had gone down against the rocky shore! Now there would be no rival to stand in his way! He fought a grin as he turned Lianna to him, scooping her up to carry her below while she sobbed wildly.

He poured a brandy and dropped something into it, swirling it as he crossed to thrust it into her hands. "Drink this."

She took it and drank, distraught and, to his relief, not
thinking that he might have drugged her again. He knew
she didn't want him to touch her or comfort her so he
moved away, securing the cabin as the storm's fury increased. In minutes Lianna turned to him.

"You gave me something . . ." she said, her words
slurred. "I don't know you . . ."

He moved to take her arm, holding her steady as she clung
to a bulkhead. "You've had a shock. You need rest and
that's the easiest way. I'm sorry, Lianna, for your loss."

Tears welled up and she cried; her knees buckled and he
caught her, holding her in his arms until her eyes closed.

She would get ague easily if she didn't get warmed. He
undressed her swiftly, flinging down the wet clothes until
she lay naked on the bunk. He felt a swift stir of desire as
he looked at her. She was beautiful, with a tiny waist and
lush, full breasts. He ran his hand over her, feeling her
cold flesh, and crossed the room to a chest to produce a
heavy nightshirt. He slipped it on her, getting her into bed
and beneath the blankets. He tucked them in tightly so she
wouldn't roll out with the tossing of the ship.

The squall became a gale, and Lianna became ill. For
days she was sick, the rough sea adding to her misery.

They sailed back the way she had come with Josh, and
each day became more difficult and lonely. Edwin seemed
subdued and left her alone for the first half of the voyage;
then gradually he began to appear at her side more and
more often until they reached a point of being politely civil
with each other, but beyond that Lianna could not go.

She reached England in October, in time for the birth of
her child, a black-haired, green-eyed boy whom she named
Phillip.

When Lianna entered the parlor, the skirt of her pale
yellow batiste dress swirled slightly with each step. As she
entered a dark, high-ceilinged room with plain mahogany
furniture, Edwin rose to his feet. Lianna held out her
hands and turned her cheek for his kiss.

She noticed how handsome Edwin looked with his elegant blue woolen coat and trousers. His golden hair was

pale from days at sea, his skin burnished like teak. She had gradually grown more civil to him, but there was still a stiff formality between them.

She sat down facing Edwin, who moved his chair closer. "I have an appointment soon. There's so much business to take care of in selling the *Eagle*'s cargo."

"I hope you're getting good prices."

"They're excellent. And as soon as Dr. Quenten says you can go out, I'll take you for a ride in my new carriage."

"I hope it's soon," she said with a lack of interest. "Lord Raven, Josh's father, wants to see me," she said. "I don't know whether to see him or refuse."

"You might as well see him and find out what he wants," Edwin said, wondering about the latest turn of events.

"I suspect he wants to see his grandson, and I'm not sure he deserves to."

"Let the past alone, Lianna. Hatred serves no good purpose."

She looked up sharply, and he frowned. "You still hate me over your loss."

She shook her head and turned away. "I know you meant no harm to Josh. I'm sorry, Edwin. It's still hard for me to accept."

"And you still hope," he said bitterly.

"I can't stop hoping," she said. "I'll send word that I'll see the duke."

Five days later she faced the man who had caused Josh so much misery. The duke was intimidating from the moment he swept into the living room. The family resemblance in Lord Raven's green eyes and the shape of his jaw and cheekbones was so strong it made her hurt to look at him. How she wished it were Josh! Extremely handsome, the duke had thick white hair, and his size was formidable. She wondered how Josh had ever defied such a giant of a man. As his cold eyes seemd to bore through her, she wanted to take a step back away from him, but she refused to do so. She smiled and waved her hand. "Won't you be seated?"

He dropped his cloak negligently on the sofa and sat down beside it. "You're my daughter-in-law."

"I didn't think I was, since you've disinherited Josh and refused to claim any kinship."

He smiled. "You're not afraid of me. I expected you to be."

"No, I'm not afraid. Perhaps I should be; I know a great deal about you."

He frowned and leaned forward. "I came to see my grandson. I've heard he's named Phillip."

She had debated over and over whether to allow him to see Phillip or not, but suddenly she wanted him to see Josh's child. She rose and tugged on the bell-pull, having left instructions earlier. In moments there was a faint rap at the closed door. Lianna crossed the room and opened the door to take the baby in her arms.

Phillip gazed at her with wide green eyes, tugging at the lace on her dress. She carried him across the room. "Your grandson, your grace."

She put the child in his arms and moved away slightly.

"He looks like a Raven. He's a fine one," he said, and she wanted to cry out and ask why he was so proud of this baby, yet had treated his own firstborn so dreadfully. "Look at him smile," the duke went on.

"I don't know if he smiles or if it's just a twitch of muscles," she said.

"He's smiling at me," Lord Raven said proudly. "Look at that. I'm your grandfather, Phillip."

Lianna was stunned to hear him talk to the baby in tones that changed rapidly from proud to wistful. He stood up and carried Phillip up and down the room.

"Ah, he looks bright and healthy! Phillip's namesake. Too bad you didn't know Phillip."

She received another shock, wondering why the duke was so certain she hadn't known Phillip. He glanced at her and smiled. "I see the surprise in your eyes. I've learned about you. You're from Wiltshire and you married Joshua in Spain."

"Josh went to Chile to fight because you caused him to

be unaccepted in London,'' she said, the words tumbling out rapidly.

The duke scowled. ''I wondered why he chose to get involved in the conflict, but I never understood his actions.'' He looked down at the baby in his arms. Phillip was tugging loose the duke's cravat, trying to chew on the ends of white silk. Lord Raven chuckled. ''Acts starved. This one won't be unaccepted in London. Indeed not!'' He handed Phillip back to Lianna. ''He's a fine boy. Thank you for allowing me to visit.''

''Come anytime you'd like.''

''Thank you. I'll do that. He's a fine baby.''

He picked up his cloak and left. Lianna followed him into the hall while a butler opened the door.

In an hour Edwin appeared, wanting to know about the visit. Early the next morning Lianna was summoned downstairs to find a large wooden crate had been delivered for Master Phillip Raven.

The servants pried open the crate, and Lianna picked up a card with the duke's name. Inside the crate was a wooden rocking horse for Phillip. When she showed it to Edwin later, he ran his hand across the glistening wood.

''The old devil must be softening with the years. He has a soft spot for his grandson.''

''Too bad he didn't have one for his own son.''

''Maybe he has regrets,'' Edwin said solemnly, and she looked up.

He moved closer, waving his hands helplessly. ''I'm sorry. I did you a great injustice, Lianna, but I was so blinded by love— ''

''Don't apologize, Edwin. We can't undo the past.''

''I still love you,'' he said huskily, and she drew a sharp breath, moving away from him swiftly.

''I'm sorry. My heart is elsewhere.''

Edwin paced the solicitor's office and swore. ''*El Feroz* was smashed in a storm. And you can't find out if there were survivors?''

''Sorry, sir. No. The Chilean coast is remote.''

''Dammit, now she may be a widow and free to wed again.''

"Right, but it will take time to have him declared legally dead. Quite a good deal of time."

"I can't wait!" Edwin wheeled and struck the top of the desk with his palm.

"Matters of the heart tend to make one impatient—"

"Heart!"

"Ah, Mrs. Raven inherited quite a sizable estate. Which you handle, since she has been shut in at home awaiting the birth of her child."

Edwin drummed his fingers on the desk. Raven had to be tough to have survived at sea, so it was even possible the man had survived the shipwreck.

Devon Tarpley continued, "I hope her health is better now."

"She's still weak. It was a long delivery. If she requests the annulment, can we start procedures?"

"Yes, I can try. She should write a letter stating her reasons, that she was forced into marriage against her will . . ."

Edwin rubbed his jaw impatiently. How could he get Lianna to request an annulment? He squared his shoulders and said, "You'll have the letter this afternoon if possible. What time should I return?"

"Isn't that hasty when she has just been through the throes of childbirth?"

"No. We know what we want."

"How's three o'clock this afternoon?"

"Fine. I'll be here with a letter from Mrs. Raven."

Edwin ran through several plans on his drive home, rejecting first one idea and then another, finally deciding on a course of action. His jaw firmed and he took a deep breath, turning his horse around toward Lianna's.

Within minutes after they were seated in the front parlor, she noticed his frown and asked, "What's wrong? You look concerned."

"Problems of first one sort and then another," Edwin said tersely, and stood up to walk to the windows and stare outside. She wondered about his business, knowing he had taken up lodgings in London and sent his ship out under his second in command while he remained behind to be with her.

She wondered what could bring such a shuttered look to Edwin's face. "My father's estate is impoverished—is that what concerns you?"

Edwin faced her, shaking his head. "No, Lianna. Your father's estate is ample for your needs."

"Thank you for handling all the details. I couldn't have before Phillip's birth, and I still don't have the inclination to do it."

"I'm happy to do it. It's only right and natural."

"If that isn't what disturbs you, what causes your scowl?"

"I don't know whether to tell you or not."

"Edwin!" She stared at him in surprise, thinking it was something to do with him, not her. "For heaven's sake, what's wrong?"

He frowned, a muscle working in his jaw. "This will come as a terrible shock, but Josh Raven is in London."

The room spun briefly and Lianna felt faint. "When did he get here?" she asked, and her voice seemed to come from a great distance.

"While I was in Portsmouth seeing about my ship."

Her eyes widened. "He's been here . . ."

"For over a month," Edwin lied. "I met with him this morning."

Suddenly she knew why Edwin was solemn. Her feeling of foreboding deepened. She wanted to hear what he had to say, and she wanted to stop him at the same time. "And?" she prompted.

"Lianna, I don't know how to say this."

She looked down at her hands clenched in her lap and fought tears. After all this time, she had hoped and prayed that it had been *El Feroz* pursuing the *Eagle* into the storm, that Josh might have survived and come after her. And time and again she had told herself how foolish it was to hope that he could have survived a shipwreck, yet each night she prayed for his safe return. And now . . .

"He doesn't want to see you—or Phillip," Edwin said quietly.

"I can't believe it!" She clenched her hands while her

heart seemed to stop beating. She hurt, a long, aching pain that started in her heart, and she wondered if she would ever be free of it again. "I have to hear him say it," she said, unable to believe Edwin, momentarily wondering if it were some of his deceit again, yet what would he gain? She wouldn't have known about Josh if Edwin had kept quiet.

"Lianna," he said gently, "he sent a messenger to me to meet him. I have no idea where he resides, and he leaves this afternoon for his new ship. He wants to be free."

"I have to hear him say it," she insisted, feeling that Edwin had to be lying. Josh couldn't have changed so much.

"I'm not lying to you!" he snapped.

"I can't believe Josh doesn't want to see his son."

"Perhaps he thinks it's my son."

She drew her breath. "You let him think that—"

"No! I told him the baby was his, but he knew nothing about it when you parted, so he has his doubts now. And he doesn't want to see you."

"I have to see him."

"And have him hurt you anew?" Edwin rubbed his hand over his jaw. "I didn't want to tell you, but there's a woman in his life, Lady Wellman. They plan to wed if you'll set him free."

"Josh, marry . . . ?" With her mind reeling as if from an invisible blow, she stared beyond Edwin, forgetting his presence. Dimly she heard him add, "Lady Wellman is enormously wealthy, Lianna. She can give Josh the acceptance in society he never had."

Lianna put her face in her hands and wept silently while Edwin waited. He gave her his handkerchief. "You must be brave. He wants you to write a letter asking for an annulment. As much as I've wanted the same thing, Lianna, I can't ask you to write now, when you've received such a shock."

"I still would like to see him."

"Lianna, he's a sailor who has known many women. And Lady Wellman can do everything for him," Edwin added reasonably. He tilted her chin upward. "If you don't believe me, I can take you to Lady Wellman and have her tell you yourself."

Lianna looked into Edwin's unwavering eyes and knew the last thing she wanted to hear was another woman tell her she had Josh's love and Lianna no longer did. And she knew Josh would move heaven and earth to be accepted in London. "No, I don't want to see her."

He sat down beside her, taking her hand in his. "You owe this letter to Phillip. It may take months, even years to get an annulment. Start now, because I can be a father to Phillip. Don't wait until you have to explain to your son why his father denied him, why he hated him."

A wave of emotion rocked her and she clenched her teeth. She didn't want Edwin to be father to Phillip! It was Josh, only him. The pain was all-consuming, hurting as badly as when she had been at sea and thought Josh might have perished.

"Be brave, Lianna. You've been so brave in the past. Do this for Phillip."

"All right."

Edwin summoned a butler to fetch a quill and paper and he dictated to her while she tried to see the paper through a blur of tears.

As soon as the letter was done, Edwin whisked it away and pulled her to her feet. "I have an appointment. I must go. Damn Josh Raven. I'll make you forget him, Lianna." He kissed her lightly and left, closing the door while she sank down and cried. She moved to the window. Josh was in London. He was alive—and would marry another. Of all the pain she had suffered, this seemed the worst. For a moment bitter hatred rose toward Edwin for his treachery in whisking her off *El Feroz*, but her anger faded as dull hopelessness—a burden of loss—overwhelmed her.

"Josh, I love you," she whispered as her tears fell.

Two weeks later Lord Raven came to call, his arms loaded with presents for Phillip. Lianna smiled as she ushered him into the nursery. "You'll spoil him terribly."

"It will do the child good!" He picked up Phillip and

swung him in the air, then lowered him to the floor to place a box in front of him. Lord Raven dropped down on the floor and began to untie the ribbon for Phillip. Lianna sank down on the floor, pulling Phillip onto her lap.

"The years have a way of changing a man," Lord Raven said. "I miss Phillip."

Lianna looked up sharply into green eyes. "I was harsh on Josh. Perhaps we were too much alike. We grated on each other's nerves."

"If you get a chance, I wish you would tell him," she said, thinking of Josh, who had just been in London. She started to tell Lord Raven, but then held back. He and Josh had never gotten along. He loved Phillip and she would leave things alone.

"I don't think I could tell him." He pulled a set of wooden soldiers out of the box, neatly stacking them in rows in front of Phillip, who picked one up and began to chew on it. Lianna took it from Phillip as the duke said, "But I can make amends. I don't want Phillip to be an outcast. I've changed my will. Josh will inherit, and in turn, Phillip will inherit everything I possess."

Lianna drew a breath, momentarily closing her eyes, thinking swiftly that if Josh knew, perhaps he wouldn't be as interested in marrying a wealthy woman. It was on the tip of her tongue to tell Lord Raven that Josh had been in London, but she realized if he learned Josh was marrying someone else and ignoring his son, he might disinherit Josh after all. She brushed a thin lock of Phillip's soft hair and was quiet except to say, "Thank you."

The duke's face flushed and he stood up suddenly. "I must be on my way. You can open the other boxes for him. Give me Phillip for one last hug."

He held out his hands and she handed Phillip up to him. He carried him around the room, talking softly to him, then returned him to Lianna and left abruptly.

When Edwin stopped an hour later on his way to Portsmouth to see about one of her father's ships, she told him the news of the duke's change of heart.

Edwin's jaw dropped, and he stared at her. "Phillip will

inherit the Duke of Cathmoor's estate someday! Great God in heaven, do you know how much he'll own?''

"Remember, Josh will have it first," she said flatly.

"Yes, but he's sailed away, and with the kind of life he lives, his days are numbered," Edwin said quietly. "Lianna, I'll be gone for almost a month. May I kiss you good-bye?''

She wanted to say no, but Edwin had been good to her and Josh was gone forever. She nodded and he walked over to her, a cynical smile on his face.

"You want to refuse. I won't push myself on you. Good-bye, love," he said softly, and bent to kiss her cheek.

Lianna turned so her lips brushed his. Edwin drew his breath and wrapped his arms around her. "I've waited and waited," he said hoarsely, and kissed her deeply.

She wrapped her arms around his neck, then stepped away when he released her. As soon as the door closed behind him, she wiped her mouth with her hand and began to cry. "Josh . . .''

During the next month Lord Raven's visits stopped. Lianna decided he had gone on a journey or back to his farm, and dismissed it from her mind until Edwin came rushing in one day.

His eyes glittered and she could hear the excitement in his voice. "Lianna, I just learned that Lord Raven is dead.''

"Oh, no!" She felt regret and sadness, because she had come to like him in spite of the cruelty she knew he had inflicted on Josh. He had another side to him, one he had shown to Phillip. "I'm sorry." She sat down on the sofa and ran her fingers over her brow.

"Good Lord, don't tell me you cared for him! His reputation is of a man as mean as the devil himself!''

"He wasn't to us!" she snapped, and saw Edwin frown. "I'm sorry, Edwin. He had moments of kindness and he showed that part of himself to me and to Phillip.''

"That he did," Edwin said more calmly.

"He looked as strong as ever the last time he was here," she said. "What happened?''

"They don't know who did it, but someone found his body on his estate with a shot through his heart."

"Oh, no!" She closed her eyes, hating the violence in life.

"Lianna, you really do care about him!"

"Yes. He loved Phillip."

"You have a tender heart." He paced the room, then stopped in front of her. "Come join me, and we'll ride in my carriage. It's a decent day today. It will do you good to get out of the house."

"I have to check on Phillip."

"Betsy's with Phillip. Come along, Lianna. Don't brood over the duke." Reluctantly she let Edwin take her arm.

Four months later, in March, Edwin was again in the office of Devon Tarpley. "I summoned you at once," Tarpley said. "Joshua Raven is in London."

33

"The devil!"

"He's here to claim his inheritance, and word has it he intends to refurbish his father's house or build a new one."

Clenching his fists, Edwin swore bitterly. He wanted to put his fist through Devon Tarpley's calm face, but it wouldn't aid his cause. "Why isn't this marriage dissolved?"

"It takes time for these matters, and it complicated things when it looked as if he had been drowned at sea."

Edwin's mind raced. "How long has he been back?"

"I sent word at once, and you were away in Portsm—"

"Dammit, how long?"

"A week today."

"A week. And he hasn't made an effort to contact Lianna."

"Strangely enough, he's going by another name. If you hadn't asked me to watch for his arrival, I never would've caught this. He's going by Brougher. Mr. Joshua Brougher."

Edwin's thoughts raced. Why hadn't Raven tried to see Lianna? Was he really eager to end their marriage? Lianna had sworn that Josh Raven had known nothing of the child. It wouldn't take long for him to learn. The damned annulment procedure took forever.

"Could you find out if he's asked for an annulment?"

"I went personally to call on his solicitor. He doesn't want an annulment."

"Dammit to hell!" Edwin shouted, and shook his fist.

He shouldn't have gone to Portsmouth to see Molly, but the long months had built fires in him. Lianna's figure had returned, and she had become a very desirable woman again. If he was to remain patient with Lianna, he needed Molly to satiate his appetite.

He leaned over the desk, his voice a hiss. "Get that marriage annulled!"

"The Church can't be rushed. These things take time."

"Do it!" Edwin stormed out and slammed the door behind him. He paused on the street, watching carriages moving in front of him. His own waited a few feet away. The handsome pair of bays had cost him dearly. Thank heaven he had been paid well by Lord Quimby, giving him funds to stay with Lianna. With the baby, she had been too occupied to take an interest in legal matters, willingly following his suggestion to turn them over to him. Someday she would make a good wife—in all ways but one. He pretended not to notice how she stiffened slightly if he touched her. That too would change in time.

Joshua Raven had survived! The man was tough, and the Church was slow to act. Edwin climbed into his carriage and took the reins, his eyes narrowing thoughtfully. If Raven met with an accident, Lianna would someday get over him. And Phillip would inherit. The child would own the world . . . and if Edwin married Lianna, he would be legal guardian of it all.

He mulled over the notion. Too bad Raven had survived the wreck of his ship. But if he met with a fateful accident at home . . . Edwin clamped his lips together and turned his carriage in the direction of the river. He knew where to go to find the men he wanted, and this time he would get proof that Raven was dead—he would ask them to cut off his ears and bring them to him.

While Edwin Stafford rode past the gin shops and the chandleries of London, in another solicitor's office a conversation on a similar topic was taking place. In fawn-colored trousers, Josh Raven stretched his long legs and listened to a solicitor report on the progress of the annulment of his marriage to Lianna Melton.

For the thousandth time he reminded himself he would have to go carefully. Lianna had left with Edwin freely— her own choice. She had sought the annulment—again, her choice. He clenched his fist. All his life, he had fought for what he wanted; he would fight for Lianna and his son. A son! What a thrill he had felt when Markham said, "She has a boy." His throat tightened and ached. He should have been at her side for the birth.

The tormenting thought that she might now love Edwin deeply, he refused to accept. He listened to his solicitor's droning voice. Finally Hiram Harkham stopped reading a report aloud and looked up.

"Block it," Joshua said quietly. "I don't care how you do it, but stop the proceedings."

"I can't do that! This is a decision of the Church—"

"You can write a letter explaining that the father doesn't want the annulment, that she thought I was dead, that there is a child now. Do whatever you can. I want time. Give me every minute possible."

"Do you realize how much time has passed?"

"I nearly drowned! I just arrived in London last week."

"She wrote this letter last November. The annulment could have already been granted, and word may even now be on the way."

Joshua leaned forward. "If you receive word it's granted, notify me at once, whether it's midnight or dawn."

"Of course. Edwin Stafford has been pushing for it with all the means at his disposal."

"I don't give a damn what Edwin Stafford is pushing for. Get a letter off today, saying that the situation has changed."

"Very well. Now, as to your father's estate, I have a document for you to sign."

Joshua swiftly read the paper spread before him, still amazed that his father had changed his will. Josh wondered what had brought about the change of heart. After all this time, he suspected that all doors would open to him now. He signed and asked, "What about the fund for Fletcher Chance?"

"All deposited and ready, first payment to be made in three days."

"Right." Joshua stood up, extending his hand. "Let me know if there are any developments."

"Yes, your grace."

How strange the title sounded to his ears. He had inherited his father's title, his house, his lands, his wealth. And it would all mean nothing if he didn't have Lianna.

His mouth curved in a smile. "Just call me Mr. Brougher. I prefer to keep my arrival quiet for another few days."

"Yes, your . . . Mr. Brougher."

Outside, as Joshua mounted his new chestnut stallion, he thought about the costume party held by a childhood friend, the Duke of Haydon, only two weeks away. Josh's pulse jumped because he had heard the guest list, and Lianna would be there. No mask could hide her identity from him.

His thoughts were so befuddled with memories of Lianna that he didn't see the broad-shouldered young man who rode out of the shadows. Sunlight made spun gold of his hair as he turned his horse directly into Josh's path, then rode beside him.

"Daydreaming, Josh?"

Josh laughed. "I suppose. Fletcher, a week more and you go to sea. I'll miss you terribly."

"Instead of me, you have another."

"No, not yet."

"I didn't mean Lianna," Fletcher said softly. "You're being followed."

Careful not to turn and look, Josh stared ahead down the broad lane as they rode past the park. "I hadn't noticed. Are you sure?"

"You wouldn't notice an elephant tagging after you. Your thoughts are in a foggy haze over Lianna," Fletcher said dryly.

"True enough, friend. Fletcher, I have a son!"

"Great saints in heaven! I'm glad!" Fletcher clasped Josh's shoulder and squeezed tightly.

"I don't know any more than that. I pray he isn't named Edwin!"

"A son—that's grand."

Josh's thoughts shifted back to their previous discussion. "Who's following me?"

"Two men. They're big enough to be stevedores. And armed to the teeth."

Josh digested this bit of information in silence. He felt a sudden flare of elation. If Edwin Stafford were having him followed—and there was no one else except Edwin to care—he must pose a threat. Perhaps Lianna was not so in love with Edwin as she had hoped to be! He said, "I won't underestimate Edwin Stafford a second time. Fletcher, ride back to my solicitor's office. I want a full check on Stafford and on Lianna's inheritance."

"If I go, you'll be alone."

"In the middle of London on a sunny day! Go."

Fletcher laughed and wheeled his horse around. Half an hour later, Josh stopped at another office to talk with the architect who would work on a new house. Josh couldn't bear to live in the gloomy manor with so many terrible memories from childhood. He would have a new house built for Lianna.

He clenched his fists thinking of her. He wanted to storm her damned house and take her in his arms and kiss away every protest, but he had done that the first time and she had hated him for it. This time he would hold his impatience in check and try to win her love back.

Josh sat across the desk from Henry Rathborne as they studied drawings of the new Raven House. "I want a wing built to the west, a sunroom here, to run the length of the south side." Josh sketched what he wanted, his tan fingers moving with surety.

"It will cost dearly."

Green eyes settled on Rathborne. "Cost is no problem. Time is. How long will this take?"

Henry Rathborne mulled the question. What a plum the duke was giving him! Raven House would be talked about for decades as an architectural feat!

"A year."

The Duke of Cathmoor shook his head. "No," he said

flatly. "I want it done in months. Two months. Funds are no problem. If you can't—"

Henry Rathborne was experienced enough to recognize finality. He said hastily, "Three months. I'll have it done."

"Excellent! Start today."

"Yes, your grace."

Josh held up his hand. " 'Mr. Brougher' for now. For a few days longer. If the neighbors inquire, or the villagers ask, tell them a Mr. Brougher owns it and will settle there when it's finished."

"Yes, Mr. Brougher," Henry Rathborne answered, thinking the man was as eccentric as he was rich. Little did that matter as long as he paid his bills. And judging from the fine cut of his clothes, Mr. Brougher could well afford all that he asked.

Josh stood up to go, glancing at the wide arched window. "Dark is setting in. We've been long at this. Sorry if you're late to dine."

"No. I have dinner much later, and I'm excited over this opportunity. I hope the new Raven House is all we both want."

"Fine. When will you visit the site?"

"Ten in the morning."

"I'll ride with you and we can go over everything again."

"Good."

Josh bade him farewell and left, stepping out into an evening grown dark with fog. Mist rose from the river and swirled over the streets, leaving a dampness on the skin, blurring the outlines of buildings. With the horse's hooves ringing on the cobblestones, Josh rode down a darkened lane to his London house, where he ate alone. Food had lost its appeal and the hours when he was alone were torment. He ran his hand across the small scar on his temple. It was a miracle that he and Fletcher had survived the shipwreck. He hadn't come this far to lose Lianna now. And a son! He hoped the boy had blue eyes and black hair. If only the annulment could be held up for a while . . .

At midnight he lay in bed unable to sleep, staring into

the darkness, when he heard a steady knocking downstairs at the door.

It couldn't be Fletcher, who had a key. Fletcher was out wenching and drinking. A cold sweat broke out as Josh remembered his instructions to his solicitor to wake him at any hour of the night if he heard the annulment had been granted.

Hastily Josh tossed back the covers, snatched up his breeches.

As another series of taps sounded, he opened the door. A hooded man stood in the darkness. Instantly all of Josh's caution flared to life, and he doubled his fist.

"What is it?"

"A message," a hoarse voice said. "Mrs. Raven wants to meet you. Come in an hour to the Brass Bell Tavern."

"Aye, I'll be there. Tell her—"

A hand waved. "She'll meet you." The messenger slipped into the foggy night and vanished.

His heart pounded and he raced up the stairs, then paused, his eyes narrowing. Could it be a trick? He remembered the two men who had followed him. But he had to go. If Lianna was there and he didn't go . . .

Setting his jaw, he dressed rapidly, all in black, placing a knife in his boot, tucking a loaded pistol in his belt. His hands shook in his eagerness. Lianna, Lianna . . . how badly he wanted her. He took the stairs two at a time in jubilant strides. Lianna!

He rode to the Brass Bell Tavern, which was near the docks on the Thames. With a cloying dampness, the gray fog swirled and enveloped him, while on the river a ship's horn gave a forlorn blast. In spite of the weather and the hour, nothing could dampen Josh's spirits. He listened carefully, trying to be sure he wasn't being followed. At the tavern, lights glowed in yellow shafts through the window. He dismounted and tethered his horse, then entered.

A fire roared in the grate and three men sat at a table nearby. The tavernkeeper, a man with a full, bushy red beard, looked up as Josh entered.

Cautiously Josh went to a table and called to the tavernkeeper for mulled rum. Facing the door, Josh sat with his back to a wall and wished once more that Fletcher had been home. His spirits began to plummet. He couldn't imagine Lianna in such a place. It wouldn't be safe for her unless she brought servants and waited in her carriage. And if it was a trick, he was alone.

Pulling his hat lower, he cast surreptitious glances at the men. One had the hilt of a dagger protruding from the top of his boot; another's coarse woolen coat bulged as if the butt of a pistol were tucked into the waistband beneath it. With dark eyes, one looked impassively at him, then away. Josh set his jaw grimly. It might be a trap—set to waylay him on his route home. He sipped the rum and waited, his patience growing shorter, disappointment swamping him. Again he had to curb the urge to fling himself on his horse and pound to Lianna's house, demanding to see her.

The door opened and a small wiry man stepped inside. His dark eyes came to rest on Josh; then he strolled to Josh's table.

" 'Evenin', sir."

"It's a damp night."

The man leaned across the table. "Josh Raven?"

"Aye."

"Hinton here. The lady waits in her carriage. Follow me."

Josh stood up, tossed coins on the table, and followed the man out the door. Every muscle tensed, and he peered into the empty foggy street. He whipped out his pistol and jabbed it against Hinton's back.

"Mate! I'm a messenger for the lady. Damn, get that out of my ribs!"

"As soon as I see the lady, I will."

"Mr. Raven, I can't—"

Josh prodded harder. "Take me to her."

"This way," Hinton said.

They turned the corner down a narrow alley beside the tavern. As they wound along narrow, fog-shrouded streets, Josh's anger and impatience rose. They turned another corner. Suddenly, from behind, there was a footstep. Josh started to turn, but something cracked against his head with a blinding pain, almost buckling his knees.

Hinton spun around, snatching at the pistol. Josh pulled the trigger. Along with the blast from the pistol, a cry shattered the night, and Hinton crumpled in the street.

As he fell, two burly men jumped on Josh from behind, smashing him down on the slimy cobbles.

Fists pummeled him, a booted foot kicked his ribs, and pain exploded in his side. He grabbed a foot and pulled, sending an attacker crashing, but another slammed his foot down on Josh's wrist and ground his heel.

Josh's blood ran cold as he heard one of the men say, "Cut him. Get his ear."

He rolled, flinging off the man, coming to his feet. One jumped him from behind while the other struck a staggering blow on the side of his head with a club.

He went down again, fighting his attackers. Something slashed down his face, and white-hot pain followed. Dimly he heard hoarse yells, running feet. Hands slipped away, and he fell forward on his face, lying in a pool that was warm and wet. Feet pounded the cobblestones and faded, then grew louder again. Voices came and receded in waves. A man said, "Two dead!"

"This one has a hole in his middle the size of my fist."

"Go through his pockets. Poor bloke's dead now. We'll toss him in the river."

"Lud! This one's alive! He's cut to pieces, bleedin' like a headless chicken." Hands turned Josh. He wanted to open his eyes, but the effort was too great.

"Let's get him home to Mandy. She'll take care of him. Look at the size of those shoulders—like a pugilist's."

"Let's leave him. He's probably a thief. Dressed all in black."

"Look here at this watch. It's worth a fortune."

"Probably stolen."

"We'll take him home."

"I say leave him."

While they argued, Josh struggled to tell them where to take him, but no sound would come. Pain racked him and he hurt in a dozen different places.

"Someone may come back and finish the job."

"Lookee here at the blunt. Dead bloke has a guinea."

"Let's haul him to the river, then we'll come back for this one."

Footsteps scuffled, faded. Josh was conscious of hands lifting him roughly. Pain tore at him, worse than before, enveloping him in blackness as he lost consciousness.

Two days later, Edwin Stafford was summoned to his solicitor's office because an annulment had been granted dissolving the marriage of Lianna Melton to Joshua Raven.

Lianna stood at the window watching Edwin come up the steps to the front door. Sunlight glinted on his pale golden hair, heightening the contrast between his champagne-colored coat and trousers and his dark, burnished skin.

Her grasp tightened around the baby in her arms. Phillip's wide green eyes were the same as his father's. Her throat burned, and she wondered if she would love Josh Raven forever.

Reluctantly she handed Phillip to Betsy. "Captain Stafford is here. I just saw him come up the walk."

"Good. You don't see enough people. You should renew your acquaintances with your friends."

"Betsy, you're a love! In another week I'm going to my first party since Phillip's birth. And then my dearest childhood friend and her husband are returning to London from Paris. Melissa will have me in a social whirl that will make you scold me to stay home."

"I don't believe it. You've seen no one, save this baby, the servants, the duke, and Captain Stafford."

"Betsy, look at Phillip's long lashes. He smiles even in his sleep."

"He's a beautiful baby, Mrs. Raven. And his mother is too pretty to waste away in this house."

"Thank you, Betsy," Lianna said laughingly.

She went down to join Edwin in the library. He turned to greet her, kissing her cheek, then holding her at arm's length to look at her.

"How beautiful you look in blue!"

"Thank you, Edwin. Phillip's still awake. Would you like a peek at him?"

"This time, I shall have to decline the offer. I'll look at his mother instead."

"My, you sound excited," she said, hiding her disappointment that Edwin wasn't more interested in Phillip. "Did you sell more of your ship's cargo for a glorious sum?"

Edwin slipped an arm around her waist and drew her to him. Instinctively Lianna placed her hands against his chest to prevent his drawing her too close.

His voice became husky. "The annulment has been granted."

She closed her eyes and drew a deep breath, feeling a sharp pain cut into her as one of the last ties to Josh was severed.

"Lianna, marry me." Edwin's mouth came down upon hers, and she tried to respond to his urgent kiss. She finally broke away.

"Edwin, I can't help the way I feel. Give me time—"

"No, it would be a mistake. You have to pick up your life and go on. Marry me within the week, Lianna. Give Phillip a father."

"This week? Edwin, I can't!"

"Yes, you can."

"It's too soon. I don't—"

"How much pain will you let Josh Raven inflict on you? When you were delirious at sea, you told me about his cold-blooded killing of the Marchenos. He has denied his son and you." His voice changed and became flat. "I need you, Lianna. I love you. I made a mistake by not running away with you long ago, but I was young and ignorant and too poor."

"My father would have hunted us down and sent you to prison."

"I want you to marry me."

She gazed into Edwin's dark gray eyes and felt something wither. She owed it to Edwin to marry him, but she didn't love him. Agitated by his proposal, she moved away. "Give me a month."

"No. I've waited, I've fought battles, I've sailed around
the world for you. Lianna, don't deny me. I'll be a good
father to Phillip."

A week! She clenched her fists. She didn't love Edwin
and she wondered if she ever could. His hands dropped on
her shoulders and he stood behind her, his breath fanning
lightly over her neck, and she felt nothing except regret
and kindness, no wild tingles, no fiery clamoring to turn
into his arms.

"Lianna, marry me. Phillip needs me. I'll take care of
you."

"Edwin, you should wed someone who loves you
deeply."

"No! Shh . . . I've always wanted you. How I love
you, Lianna!" He kissed her neck and whispered, "Marry
me—I promise I won't rush you. I'll wait until you come
to my bed."

She turned around. "Edwin, let's wait and not rush—"

"Shh, I want you. Only you. Marry me in a week."

"I just can't." She felt trapped, yet what he said was
true. He had been so good to her. Phillip needed a father.
Josh Raven hadn't wanted to see her or his son when he
had been in London after Phillip's birth. She raised her
face. "Three weeks from today."

Exultation flared in his eyes so brightly that she felt
guilty. "Oh, Edwin, I'm not sure we're doing the right
thing."

"Of course we are! Three weeks. I will post the
announcement."

He crushed her to him and kissed her with fiery passion
and she returned it, but it took an effort. When he left, she
went to the window to watch him walk away, but tears
made everything blur.

Fletcher Chance crept up the stairs and fell across the
bed. He turned to gaze at the spinning ceiling. Where the
hell had Josh gone? All week his architect had been looking for him. The solicitor wanted him to sign more papers
about his inheritance. A bookkeeper had come to apply for
work.

Fletcher heard pounding on the door downstairs. With a groan he heaved himself to his feet and went to answer, wondering who would call at such an early hour in the morning. He opened the door to face a stranger.

"Mr. Brougher?"

"He's not in."

"I have an urgent message for him from Mr. Markham."

"His solicitor?" Fletcher sobered slightly. "I can't find him. Mr. Markham sent word yesterday about the papers he needs to sign."

"This is another matter. Is a Mr. Chance here?"

"I'm Fletcher Chance."

"I'm to inform Mr. Raven or you that the annulment has been granted."

As Fletcher swore, the man's brows arched, and he stepped back. "That's all, sir."

"Here." Fletcher handed him some coins and closed the door. He was sobering quickly now. Something had happened to Josh. He remembered the two burly men who had been following him.

Fletcher ran upstairs, ignoring his pounding head as he reached for his shirt. Something terrible must have happened to Josh to keep him from home. And now the marriage was dissolved. Lianna Melton Raven was free to marry again.

Several days later Fletcher stood on the wharf impatiently watching sailors come and go until he spotted one that he knew.

"Lyon Murdock!"

A thick-set man with a barrel chest and a full black beard turned. His face split in a grin and he reached Fletcher quickly to pump his hand.

"Damn, haven't seen you, Chance, for years! A pup you were."

"Murdock, you old sea dog! How's it go? Did you just get in?"

"A week ago. We sail again in a fortnight."

"Want to earn a golden guinea for a few hours' work?"

"Aye, anytime. You've struck fortune?"

"It's my captain's. Josh Raven of *El Feroz*."

"Rumor had it that it sank in a storm."

"It did, but a few of us survived. He's missing, Murdock. I want London combed for him. I have to find him. Will you help for a day?"

"For you and Captain Raven—he's a good man—I'll give you two days. No nights!" He laughed.

"I'll be here this time each day to pay. If you find him or any whisper about him, tell the tavernkeeper at the Brass Bell. That's the last place he was seen."

"Aye, that I will."

Fletcher watched the man stride away and frowned. He'd combed the taverns and finally learned that a man who fitted Josh's description had waited in the Brass Bell, then left with another man. Josh Raven seemed to have vanished off the face of the earth. And a murdered man had turned up, a small thin man shot through the middle, not far from the Brass Bell the night Josh had disappeared.

Impatiently Fletcher shifted his weight, clamping his jaws together. The marriage announcement of Lianna and Edwin had been posted. They were to wed within two weeks.

He had to admit he hoped Josh could win Lianna back. He'd grown to like and admire her, and he knew how much Josh loved her. Something he would have deemed impossible before the journey to Chile. Thoughts of Lianna had been what drove Josh to fight for survival after their terrible wreck at sea.

And now the son—Josh would be the best of fathers. If he had the chance. He would be crazed if he found he had come so close, only to have her wed Edwin Stafford now. Damn—what could have happened to Josh?

Fletcher swung around and hurried up the lane to the Brass Bell again. He waited until he could talk to the tavernkeeper, Ned. The man polished a glass as he came to stand across the bar.

"Any word about him?" Fletcher asked.

"No. But there have been two in here asking questions."

"What kind of questions?"

Ned shrugged, his bushy brows arching. "His description. Had I heard of him or seen him or had anyone asking about him.''

"What did you tell them?'' Fletcher asked grimly.

"You paid me dearly. I said no I hadn't seen the man, didn't remember him, and hadn't had a question about him.''

"Good!'' Fletcher reached beneath his cloak, produced a pigskin pouch, and withdrew several guineas. Ned's brown eyes glittered and his hand quickly covered the coins Fletcher placed on the bar.

"What did the men look like?''

"Sailors, stevedores—big and brawny. But they'd been in a bit of a fight. Banged up and bruised, they were.''

"Then he must have escaped, else they wouldn't be searching for him. I have to find him before they do.'' Fletcher let out his breath. "I'll be back.'' He stopped outside the tavern, looking up and down the street. Where was Josh Raven?

Josh moved and groaned. He ached from head to toe. He had to get away from Chile, back to Lianna. He tried to call her name as he saw her look at him with laughing blue eyes.

"Now, lie still, dearie.''

Cool hands touched his face and he felt something wet on his brow. His eyes flickered open and everything spun; then a face appeared over him.

"Lianna!''

"No, dearie. My name's Mandy. Don't talk. Lie still. You've been hurt.''

He had to get to Lianna. To get home to England. He tried to rise, but he couldn't raise his head from the pillow.

"Lianna . . . '' he gasped.

"We'll try a little broth soon. Lie back and close your eyes.''

"How's he doing?'' a man's voice asked.

"He's burning up with fever.''

"They really messed up his face.''

"He's a handsome one, all right.''

"With a cut from hair to jaw?''

"He'll heal."

"Mandy, come here and quit fussing over the stranger."

She giggled and the sound made Josh stir. He groaned and fought to get up, but his body wouldn't obey. He had to get home to Lianna, but he couldn't move his legs.

Days and nights blurred, and Josh had no idea of time when he was conscious. Then one night he opened his eyes and his head seemed clear. He remembered what had happened to him.

He had to get home. He struggled to sit up, and looked around a small house. Across the room from him was an iron bed with rumpled covers hiding someone from view. A snore came from the bed.

Josh threw back the covers and searched for clothing. A man's breeches lay over a chair. He stepped into them, finding them too large in the middle, too short in the leg, but he fastened them on.

When his head swam, he sat down. He hurt all over and had to fight a wave of nausea, but, grimly determined, he dressed in the ill-fitting clothing, then tiptoed out of the house, trying to get his bearings in the strange place.

The street revolved slowly, and he reached out to cling to a wall until he righted. Where the hell was he? He staggered down a lane, hiding in dark shadows when he heard people approach.

He would be at the mercy of footpads, since he had no more strength than a bowl of Yorkshire pudding. The air was tainted with the odor of fish and stagnant water. He wandered toward the smell and finally spotted masts above the rooftops, outlined darkly against a gray night sky. The river! He had his bearings, and turned another corner.

It seemed to take hours and hours. He passed out once, then came to, lying on his face in the street. As he neared his house, he prayed Fletcher would be home. He saw his house and lurched toward the door.

A man moved out of the shadows toward him.

"Fletcher! Thank goodness . . ." He peered closer. "You're not Fletcher—"

Hands reached out to grasp him roughly.

Josh summoned all the strength he had to resist. He jerked away and shoved the man.

"Come on, mate. You can't fight me. This time we finish the job. This time we get your ears so we can claim the money."

Josh backed away as another man stepped out of the shadows. He felt like crying out in frustration and helplessness. He had struggled all night to get home, survived the beating they had given him, only to have them overpower him on his own doorstep.

He backed up until he reached the wall, and watched helplessly as they began to close in like wolves. Moonlight glinted on the silver blade of a dagger.

"I told you we'd get him if we watched his house! I knew he wasn't dead."

Josh shifted, his foot kicked a stone. He swooped down to pick it up, and as they lunged, he threw it through his own window.

He fought like a wild man, but he was too weak to hold them off. He sank to his knees.

"Hold him down!"

Suddenly there were shouts, then the hands dropped him and he sprawled on the cobbles.

"Get him inside, quickly."

"Fletcher . . ." He lost consciousness, drifting into a blessed oblivion.

Edwin held the husky baby in the air, the sleeves to his champagne-colored broadcloth coat pulling tautly. Frilly white lace cuffs fell back over his sleeves as he said, "Little Phillip is in good form tonight."

"Up rather late, I'd say," Lianna said while she beamed with love. She smoothed the blue silk skirt across her narrow waist, thankful her figure had returned to almost the same proportions as before Phillip's birth. She said, "Betsy, he's yours."

"You'll be spoiling him right well, Captain Stafford," the stout nurse said, sounding as pleased as Lianna.

"Absolutely rotten!" Edwin said sternly, and Lianna had to bite back a smile. He handed over the baby and turned to drop a blue velvet cape across Lianna's shoulders.

"To the ball, m'dear."

" 'Night, Betsy," Lianna said, and took Edwin's arm as they emerged into the upstairs hallway with its gleaming oak floors. As they started down the broad stairway, Lianna said, "Edwin, this is a costume ball—it's hardly fair to go as Lord Nelson and dress so handsomely."

"I have a mask and this is quite fair. And look at you—Marie Antoinette, your dark hair hidden with powder. It will make me sneeze."

She laughed, relaxing as they entered Edwin's coach. When they were seated, he said, "How good it is to see you smile."

"I'm looking forward to this, my first ball in so long." For one fleeting second she had almost said "since the governor's ball in Chile," but she caught herself in time. She tried to keep all memories tucked away, securely under control, trying as time passed to forget everything.

The horses trotted past St. Paul's Cathedral and Lianna glanced at the dome; within minutes she looked out at the bastions of the Tower of London—familiar sights that should have made her feel at home, but didn't. Only one person could make a place home to her.

The hoofbeats of the horses on the cobblestones were loud in the early-spring air. When they halted at the Duke of Haydon's house, it was ablaze with lights, music from violins carrying outside. Edwin handed their capes to a butler, and they were announced. They chatted with their host and hostess and various guests, eventually making their way to the ballroom, where Edwin turned to take her into his arms for a waltz.

She let her mind go blank while she enjoyed the music and the dancing. They whirled in a circle and she missed a step. Across the room a man with burnished brown hair and broad shoulders, dressed as Henry VIII, stood with his back to her. She felt her heart thud against her ribs; then he turned and her breathing resumed. She looked up to find Edwin frowning at her.

"Your new horses are beautiful," she said. "I can't wait to ride again."

He relaxed and smiled. "I shall buy you a grand horse. Remember how we used to race? And you would win."

She laughed. "I thought you always let me."

He smiled. "I did. Every time."

They turned and she watched a tall man in a wolf costume enter the ballroom. His long-legged stride was like Josh's.

"Dammit, Lianna, do you see him in every man in the room?"

"I'm sorry. It's the first time I've been out, Edwin."

She glanced at the man in the wolf costume again and he turned, revealing a wisp of blond hair at the back of his head. Edwin's arm tightened, pulling her roughly to him. His voice was hoarse. "I'll make you forget him."

"Edwin, don't be angry. Please."

He smiled, but it was frosty, and Lianna was glad when the dance ended and Edwin became engaged in conversation with their host. He kept his arm lightly around her waist until the duke asked, "Mrs. Raven, would you mind if I steal Captain Stafford a few minutes? I have ship plans drawn up and I've heard the captain is quite knowledgeable about the type ship needed to haul rum and spices from the islands."

"Of course." She walked away, fanning herself. With the hundreds of candles and the dancers, the room was warm. She strolled toward the open doors to the terrace. As she neared the doors, she stopped dead.

Just outside, in the shadows on the terrace, sat a man watching her. One leg swung negligently, one hand was on his knee. He wore a devil's mask that covered his features. Below the mask, he was dressed in a black coat, snowy white shirt with lace at the cuffs, and black trousers. She shook her head slightly. She did see Josh Raven in every tall dark-haired man! If he were here, he wouldn't be sitting in the shadows on the terrace. He would be the center of attention among the dancers.

She stepped outside, welcoming the cool, and was compelled to glance at the man. The devil mask was appropriate, she thought, because of the calculating way he openly watched her. His eyes were in shadow, but she knew he followed her path as she stepped outside. She had to pass him. Lifting her chin, she walked past, trying to ignore the tingling she felt from being watched.

A hand reached out and closed around her wrist, and every nerve in Lianna sprang to life.

"Lianna," came a husky voice.

34

She turned, her breath halting, her pulse racing as she fought an insane urge to fling herself into his arms.

"Josh!"

He sat holding her wrist, waiting. Finally he said, "You're going to marry Edwin."

"Yes." She wanted to cry out that it was because he had rejected her, refused to see Phillip, and because he had turned his back on both of them.

She narrowed her eyes and looked intently at him. It was impossible to see his eyes while he wore the damnable mask. Perhaps it was better that way. If she looked into his eyes, she might do something terribly foolish.

"I thought you would be in there dancing," she said, unaware of the words. She trembled as if chilled.

"No. I've been waiting for you."

"Why?"

"I wanted to see you." He turned her palm up and raised the mask a few inches. She knew he intended to kiss her hand, and she knew she should jerk free of his grasp, but she stood still and watched him. The moment his lips touched her palm, she closed her eyes and relished the warmth that spread through her. Not all of Edwin's passionate kisses could do what one brush of Josh's lips on her palm did.

He raised his head. "Do you love Edwin?"

She felt as if he had slapped her. He had cruelly refused to see her when Phillip was born, yet when her wedding to Edwin was announced, he showed up. Was he trying to prove he still held her heart, even though he didn't really want her?

"Answer me, Lianna. Do you truly love Edwin?"

Her heart pounded wildly, and she fought emotions that warred within her. She wanted to grasp his hands and pour out her love for him, yet he didn't want it. She hated him for wielding his power over her so arrogantly. In the dark, without looking into eyes that could probe to her soul, she could lie.

"Yes."

"Look at me. And don't lie to me," he commanded.

She wanted to protest, to say it wasn't a lie. But she only raised her head as he shifted slightly. Light from the ballroom fell over the mask, over emerald eyes that continued to stare at her.

"I want to hear you say it in truth."

She couldn't. She couldn't say anything. She ached to feel Josh's arms around her. How she wanted him to hold her!

"So you don't love him!"

"I'm going to wed him in three days."

"Why, when there's no love?"

"I recall being told marriage could be very good without love."

"Ah, you have developed claws, Lianna."

"Only to survive. I use your own words."

"I want to see you tomorrow."

"No! There was a time—but now I'm betrothed to a man who adores me."

"What time can I call?"

"You can't! Not now, when I'm to marry Edwin this Friday."

"You owe me that much."

"How can you say such a thing when you . . . ?"

"When I what?"

"It's of no importance now. I can't—"

"Oh, yes, you can. I'll break down the damned door if you don't agree to a time. And I don't want Edwin present."

She felt giddy. There was a wild current coursing in her.

And he was the dearest person on earth to her. "Oh, Josh, why didn't you come!"

"I'm here now, Lianna. Here to stay! Ten o'clock in the morning."

His hand brushed her throat like a stick of fire while his husky voice enveloped her in its warmth. "Ten o'clock tomorrow."

"Lianna!" Edwin called from the doorway.

She rushed to him before he discovered Josh's presence. Her shoulder blades burned and she fought the urge to turn around and glance back at Josh. When she stepped into the light, she could no longer resist looking around. The terrace was empty. Why hadn't Josh joined the other guests? And why did he want to see her now, when it was so close to her wedding?

"Who was the man you were talking to?"

"One of the guests. He had on a mask."

"He didn't tell you his name?"

"No, Edwin, he didn't."

"You tremble."

"It was cold on the terrace."

"A dance will banish your chill. Come, Lianna." She stepped into his arms, and it took a great effort to follow Edwin's conversation because she was thinking of another man and another place.

Outside, Josh slumped in the carriage across from Fletcher, who signaled to the driver to start home.

"I'll see her at ten tomorrow."

"Here, take a drink of brandy. There's blood on your coat."

"Damn. Shoulder hurts like hell."

"Take off your coat, let me look at that wound. You shouldn't have stepped out of bed."

Josh tried to pull off his coat, but when he raised his arm, pain shot across his shoulders, and he swore. Fletcher scooted onto the seat beside him. "Here, I'll do it." He eased the coat down, swearing at the sight of a blood-drenched shirt. "I knew you should stay home!"

"I had to go. There's so little time left."

"Did you have a chance to tell her what that swine has done?"

"No."

"You didn't want to tell her?" Shock filled Fletcher's voice.

"Not yet."

"Why in blue hell not! You shouldn't be out on the street. If they waylay our carriage, jump you anytime you're out of the house, you won't survive another beating. Right now you couldn't defend yourself against a small lad."

Josh gasped with pain as Fletcher doubled up his coat and applied it to the wound to stanch the flow of blood.

"You want her to wed him without knowing what he's caused?" Fletcher persisted.

"No! She'll learn the truth soon enough," Josh ground out through clenched teeth. "But I want her to stop the wedding to Stafford for one reason only—because she loves me."

"I can't believe my ears! Josh Raven—smitten by love until his wits have fled."

"Dammit, Fletcher, I may not be sorry to see you go next week."

Fletcher laughed. "No, you won't be, because I postponed the sailing. I told my men that we won't sail for another week."

"You can't stay because of me," Josh said, clasping his hand on Fletcher's shoulder. He felt a lump rise in his throat, that Fletcher would care enough to stay with him.

"You've always claimed me as your brother—and that's what a brother is for," Fletcher answered in a husky voice. His tone returned to normal as he added, "Besides, I have to stay and see to it that you're not sliced into shreds. And to refuse to tell Lianna the truth about Stafford— perhaps they clubbed your brains into pulp."

"Not quite," Josh answered, laughing. "Ouch! It hurts to laugh, and my head swims."

"Raven, I hired four more men today to guard your house—and you."

Josh laughed, then bit it off as pain struck again. "I'll have a king's army traveling with me."

"If you don't, you'll not survive. I saw men lurking about the street today. Stafford is ruthless. And for Lord's sake, tell Lianna so she knows what sort of man she's dealing with."

"I want her to love me above and beyond all else, Fletcher. Something you will someday understand."

"When my brains have dried up! Zounds! How'll you explain your face?"

"Footpads jumped me."

"She didn't see you tonight?"

"No, because of the mask."

"It'll be a shock."

"I know," Josh answered grimly.

"And that won't stand in the way of your lady's love. There's more to her than an empty-headed flower who wants only a handsome man."

Josh laughed. "I wasn't handsome to start with. Now—"

"Now you're wounded. The cuts will heal and the scars may not be terrible. And she won't be put off by the sight of you."

" 'Pon my soul, Fletch, I do believe you heartily approve of my ex-wife!"

"I do. I pray you win her back."

"Thanks. Thanks for everything, my brother. But now . . . I can't stop my head from spinning, and the carriage grows unbearably . . ." His words faded as he slumped in the seat. He would have fallen had Fletcher not reached out to catch him.

Deep into the night, while Josh slept fitfully, three people stood awake in the darkness gazing out their windows. Fletcher shifted the curtain slightly, his eyes narrowing as he watched a figure emerge from the shadows and move closer to the house. The man faded back into darkness, hiding in the black shadows of an oak. Fletcher's fist clenched. Damn! Why hadn't Raven told her about the danger, about Edwin's treachery?

At the same time, Edwin Stafford gazed out and punched the wall with his fist. Raven had more lives than a cat! He should be dead now. How had he slipped past the men and attended the ball? How had he been strong enough to go? Evidently Raven hadn't guessed the reason for his injuries. Or if he knew, he hadn't told Lianna. The fool wouldn't get another chance. He wouldn't see her again until after the wedding! Edwin hoped he had made that clear to the men watching both houses.

In yet another darkened bedroom, Lianna gazed at the cloud-streaked sky, aware that Josh was somewhere in London. He would arrive at ten tomorrow morning. Excitement filled her, though she also felt guilty at her deception. She looked at the diamond that glittered on her finger, then opened her other hand to stare at the simple gold band Josh had placed on her finger in Spain. Closing her fist, she held it to her heart.

The next morning Lianna changed dresses three times, finally deciding on a blue muslin with a high neck and long sleeves. Her hair was shining, fastened loosely at the back of her head, long tresses flowing down her back. Little Phillip had been fed and bathed, and she debated whether to take him downstairs with her or not. Should she ask Josh if he wanted to see his son? She handed the baby to Betsy. "I must go downstairs now."

"Mr. Raven arrives soon. We'll be ready if he wants to see Phillip," Betsy said, a note of curiosity in her voice.

Lianna twisted a wispy black curl and Phillip laughed, making her smile. She kissed his cheek and went to wait in the parlor.

She stood at the window gazing at the street, waiting for Josh's carriage. Behind her a light tap sounded and her butler appeared, his face pale. "Mr. Brougher is here to see you. He said you were expecting him."

For an instant she was startled; then her heart jumped as she remembered Josh's full name. "Show him in, Charles."

"Yes, ma'am."

She tried to hide her shock when Josh entered the room. He wore a black hat pulled low over his eyes, a long black cape with a steeped collar, the points meeting his hat brim.

His face was hidden from sight and his walk was not Josh's long purposeful stride, but a halting limp.

"Thank you, Charles," she said, and waited while he closed the double oak doors.

"Good morning, Lianna."

A flash of warmth stirred her blood. "Where's your carriage? Why the cape, Josh?"

"I didn't want Edwin to know that I'm here."

"How could he?" She forgot her question as he crossed the room to the window to stand with his back to her. He removed his hat, revealing his thick brown hair. "You limp, Josh. What's happened?" she asked in an unsteady voice.

While he unfastened the cape, he said, "I was set upon by footpads and my face is cut badly. I didn't want to shock or frighten you."

She started toward him, stopping short before she reached him. "You won't frighten me. Turn around."

She steeled herself, but it took all her will to keep from crying out. On the left side of his face a jagged cut ran from hairline to jaw. Another went across the bridge of his nose. Another along his right cheek and jaw. A small one on his temple. She clamped her lips together, shut her eyes, and struggled to resist the compelling urge to throw her arms around his neck.

Holding his breath, Josh watched emotions flicker in her face, and his heart leapt at what he saw—until she closed her eyes. Was she repulsed by the sight of him?

He couldn't curb his need to touch her. How he loved her! He had dreamed of her for so long now that he had to reach out and take her hand.

Lianna looked down at her slender fingers encased in his large strong hand. He drew her closer and his touch was alchemy. It transformed her completely, reminding her of all their shared moments. She couldn't blank them out; she wanted Josh Raven too much.

She reached up, drawing her fingers over his cheek. "I'm sorry you were hurt."

"The cuts will heal with time. They're nothing but

surface wounds. It is wounds of the heart that last," he said huskily, and watched her eyes widen.

Lianna couldn't speak; she trembled slightly and drank in the sight of him.

"I love you, Lianna."

She saw the confirmation of his words in his eyes. Lianna had dreamed of hearing Josh say those words for so long, it was hard to realize she hadn't imagined them.

He waited while the silence stretched into minutes. Words rose to her lips, but she held them back. She was betrothed to another, and Josh had had almost a year to come forward and announce his love. Did he say it simply to prevent her from marrying Edwin—or to try to claim Phillip?

"Say it, Lianna," he whispered. "I see it in your eyes. Tell me."

She almost did, but her reasoning plagued her. She pulled her hand free and walked away from him, turning to the window to escape his probing eyes. She knew he would delve mercilessly into her mind and soul if she gave him the chance.

"I love you," she whispered, against her better judgment.

Suddenly his arms were around her, and he pulled her tightly against him. When he flinched, she stepped back. "Are you hurt elsewhere?" she asked.

"Dammit, yes. I want to hold you, but my shoulder has a cut. Come here." He turned her so that she nestled against his side. When he tilted her face upward, it seemed that her heart ceased to beat as she looked into his eyes. She realized he wanted her, but she had to know why he had waited so long to reveal his feelings.

"Josh, why now, after all this time?"

His lips touched hers and she moaned with pleasure, seeking his with an agonizing need. His mouth met hers, and their passion was all-consuming. Tongues touched, reuniting hearts that pounded wildly. His kiss deepened into a savage hunger which she eagerly met.

Josh ignored the pain that burned in his shoulder and the aching wound in his leg as he crushed Lianna in his arms joyfully. Desire throbbed in him and it was an effort to hold back, to take her sweet kisses and nothing more. While he curved his arm around her narrow waist, he couldn't stop his fingers from moving to cradle her head, twirling the silken strands of her hair.

"When may I see my son?"

"Now," she answered, her pulse jumping at his words. *My son.* "He's in the nursery."

"Will I frighten him?" Josh motioned to his face and Lianna shook her head.

"No. Of course not, he's only a baby."

When they reached the nursery, Betsy stood up from the rocker and picked up Phillip. "Here's Mum. Ah, the wee one is anxious." For the first time Betsy saw Josh Raven as he followed Lianna into the room. Her eyes widened as she stared at him.

"This is Betsy, who has been so good to Phillip." Lianna blushed as she said the baby's name. Every move, every word, proclaimed the love that had once been between them. She took the warm baby. "Betsy, this is Captain Raven."

"How'd you do, sir."

"'Morning, Betsy," Josh said, but his gaze was fastened on the child in Lianna's arms, and suddenly she felt a tightness in her throat.

Betsy left the room, and Lianna couldn't remember what was said to her. When the door closed, leaving them alone, Lianna looked at Josh. He moved closer, gazing down at the baby in her arms.

"Phillip?" His voice was husky as he asked.

She held out the baby. "Phillip Rinaldo Brougher Raven."

Josh took the child as naturally as if he had been holding babies all his life. The young boy reached up to catch a bit of his father's pleated cravat, cooing as he pulled it free, cheerfully tugging it loose.

"Phillip Rinaldo. How grand!"

Lianna stared at Josh intently, shocked to see his eyes moisten with unshed tears. Her heart felt as if it were wrenched in two. What if Josh loved his son? What if he loved her—and she had pledged to marry Edwin?

Josh turned his back, walking away and talking softly to Phillip, who gurgled and explored his father's throat and jaw with his tiny fingers.

How right it seemed to have Josh here! Everything blurred as Lianna had to fight back tears.

Abruptly Josh turned. "Why isn't he named for Edwin?"

She drew a deep breath, remembering how angry Edwin had looked when she had told him the baby's name. And she had countered by asking if he wouldn't have his own son named after him.

She couldn't answer Josh in an even tone, for her voice was deep and breathless. "He wasn't here, and all I could think of was that he's yours, Josh. I named him for you, for your brother."

He came back and Phillip held out his hands to Lianna, who took him, acutely aware of her hands brushing against Josh's. Phillip nestled down against her shoulder, and Josh put his arms lightly around both of them, smiling at them. Everything he did was both wonderful and painful. She loved the way he was looking at her, yet she knew she shouldn't.

He sobered and asked, "Was it a difficult delivery?"

"They said for the firstborn it was not unusual."

"Wasn't Edwin here?"

"No, he was in Portsmouth."

"Who was with you?"

"I had a midwife and Dr. Quenten."

His eyes changed to a dark green. "I'm sorry I wasn't here," he said roughly.

"I am too," she said, wanting to tell him how she had cried and cried for him. She remembered how badly it had hurt the next month when Edwin had told her Josh was in London and didn't want to see her or Phillip. She turned abruptly.

"Betsy!"

Betsy entered immediately, and Lianna returned Phillip to her. She asked Josh, "Shall we go downstairs now?"

Josh took her arm and they left. As they descended the curving stairs to the front hall, Lianna received a shock. She looked down into Edwin's upturned face.

Behind him the butler said, "Mr. Stafford just arrived, ma'am."

Murderous rage flared in Edwin's gray eyes, then was swiftly banked. His voice was cold when he said, "I didn't realize you had a guest, Lianna. I didn't see a carriage in front."

Josh's hand tightened on her waist and he wanted to jam his fist down Edwin Stafford's throat! He forced a smile to his lips. "I came another way. And I'll leave now."

Edwin's eyebrows arched. "It looks as if you had the worst of a swordfight."

"I'm here in spite of it. Perhaps something my opponent didn't intend," Josh said lightly, and enjoyed Edwin's flush.

"Beware, sir, next time they may be more accurate in their thrusts."

"Good advice. Next time, I'll watch that I'm not jumped from behind."

They reached the bottom of the steps and Edwin came forward swiftly to take Lianna's arm and pull her to his side. There was no opportunity for Josh to ask to see her again. He set his jaw and turned his attention fully to her. "Will you see me to the back door?"

She started forward, but Edwin detained her. "Charles!" he called.

The butler stepped forward. "Yes, Captain Stafford?"

"Will you show Mr. Raven out through the back?"

"Yes, sir."

Josh was incensed. It took every ounce of his self-control to remain calm and detached, to force his voice to a normal tone. "Thank you. Good day, Lianna, Captain Stafford."

"Josh—"

"Come, Lianna. Charles is capable of showing your guest the door." Edwin propelled her toward the library, closing the door behind them while Josh followed Charles. He left through a gate in the back wall, climbed into the waiting carriage, and was soon down the lane.

"Damn!" Raven swore a string of oaths while Fletcher sat quietly waiting. "I'd like to run him through."

"You're lucky they didn't run us through. He has two men watching her house. You slipped past them neatly when you went in." Fletcher looked out the window. "Did you tell her anything?"

Josh grinned. "Aye, that I love her. And I saw my son. He's named Phillip!"

Fletcher let out his breath. "Phillip! I begin to see why you're grinning from ear to ear."

"Phillip Rinaldo Brougher Raven is a beautiful baby. He has her black hair, his eyes are green, and he smiled at me! Fletcher, you should see him. His fingers are perfect and he has a dimple."

Fletcher laughed. "My, you sound like the proud father!" He quickly became solemn and said, "If you didn't tell her what a scoundrel Stafford is, then does she still plan to wed Friday? And your son will belong to another."

"Never," Josh said coldly.

"Then you'd better warn her. You have two days left."

"There'll be no ceremony between Lianna and Edwin Stafford. If I can't do anything else, we'll carry her off the day of the wedding!"

Fletcher groaned. "And have her hate you for using force again! Tell her about him!"

"I will, in time, if it's necessary, but I don't think it will be. She doesn't love him."

"Then why wait?"

Raven laughed. "I've already told you that I want her to love me, not return to me because Stafford is wicked."

"And in the meantime, while you wait to talk it over with her, Edwin Stafford slits your throat!" Fletcher snapped.

"I almost wish he'd try that instead of sending his hired men," Josh said coldly. "I'll go see her tonight. I don't think it will be necessary to discuss Stafford."

"I think your brains were dashed upon the rocky Chilean coast."

"You won't help me?"

"Of course I'll help. I'd like a chance at Stafford myself."

Josh laughed. "Don't call me bloodthirsty!" They rode in silence for a time, then Josh clenched his fists. "I hate to think of her with him right now. I wish these wounds would hurry and heal.''

Lianna crossed the room and sat in a wing chair by the fire while Edwin closed the library doors and faced her.

"Did you invite him to come?"

"No." She turned the diamond and watched it glitter. Then slowly she slipped it off.

Edwin's fingers closed around hers and he pushed the ring back in place while he knelt before her. "Don't, Lianna."

"Edwin, I can't wed you." She pulled the ring off swiftly.

"After all he has done, you'll go running back to him?"

"He has actually been so very good to me," she whispered, remembering his husky voice declaring that he loved her.

"Dammit! I've risked everything for you, and now he just walks in and takes it."

She stiffened and felt racked with pain. "Edwin, you're strong and handsome, you own a ship—"

"It means nothing if I don't have you!" He stood up and pulled her up into his arms. "Lianna, don't leave me! I'll be good to you. I'll love Phillip. I'll love his Spanish heritage as much as his English. You've given me your pledge. Promise me you won't see Raven again."

She closed her eyes in agony. "I can't!"

"Yes, you can. You've promised to become my wife. Can you ignore that he refused to see you or Phillip when you needed him?"

"Edwin, please!"

"You'll throw everything we have aside, and then, when he leaves you to sail, to take a mistress, to ignore his son . . .''

She felt tears course down her cheeks.

"Put my ring back on your finger, Lianna. If you don't, you'll shed tears forever over him." He pulled her to him. "You've promised me."

"Edwin, I have to think things over. I must ask you to go."

He stiffened, then crushed her in his arms and kissed her roughly on the mouth. She could only remember how sweetly it had felt to have Josh's fingers brush hers. She struggled away from Edwin, wanting to be free. But his grip tightened and he kissed her bruisingly.

"Edwin, stop!" She gasped for breath and touched her sore lip. How could Edwin love her so deeply when she felt nothing for him save fond childhood memories? Her eyes opened, and she wondered if there was another reason for Edwin's love . . .

Edwin released her, his gray eyes darkened to slate. "I won't let you go. I won't let him hurt you again." He held her arm tightly. "Get your cloak and come with me for a carriage ride. I won't leave you alone here to think about him."

Desperate to avoid going with Edwin, she said, "I have a dressmaker's appointment for my wedding dress."

"Then come to dinner with me tonight."

"Edwin, give me time to think!"

"Dinner tonight, Lianna. Promise me."

"Very well."

With one more embrace, Edwin left. As soon as he was gone, Lianna hurried upstairs to bathe and dress in a pale gray woolen dress. An hour later, she sat in the office of her solicitor.

"Mr. Drayton, I want to go over the figures of my inheritance from my father."

"Of course," he said, peering through rimless spectacles at the papers before him. "Mr. Stafford has all the facts at his disposal, and he's handled everything quite well. Perhaps you would like to summon him, since he has made the decisions for you to date—"

"Mr. Drayton, may I see what I've inherited?"

"Of course." He opened a drawer, rummaged in it to produce a stack of papers tied in a band. He unfastened it and turned one for her to view.

"Now, you've inherited the house in London. Your father owned two ships—a three-masted schooner and a main-topsail schooner. Both are presently at sea, but the

Lexington will dock shortly." Lianna scanned the list, already knowing about the schooners and the house.

Mr. Drayton turned to another page. "Your father had his last cargo stored in a warehouse. This you gave your permission for Mr. Stafford to handle. He sold it for you at a tidy sum. You'll see the figures here."

She scanned the list, satisfied that Edwin had driven a good bargain.

"Now, money on hand which is currently in the bank. Here is the list, because your father kept sums in the bank in Liverpool, where his ships dock, as well as here in London. Mr. Stafford, I'm sure, has informed you of all this. You inherited the sum of three hundred thousand pounds."

Lianna's mind reeled. She felt as if she had stepped off the edge of a mountain and slammed to earth hundreds of feet below. "Three hundred thousand pounds!"

"You didn't know?" Mr. Drayton frowned and peered intently at her, his blue eyes filled with curiosity.

"No. I left everything to Captain Stafford."

"I presumed he had reported everything. You signed the papers."

"I was ill, then bore a child and hadn't recovered when I signed them. He simply showed me where to sign and I left everything else to him."

"Good Lord!" His narrow jaw dropped. "Let me get you a glass of water. You look as if you might faint."

"I won't faint," she said so emphatically that he sat back down in his seat.

"Mr. Stafford said it was all right to keep these funds in the banks where your father had them—that does meet with your approval, doesn't it?"

She stared out the window, barely cognizant that the solicitor was talking. Three hundred thousand pounds! In addition to ships and the house and the farm, the land. The first thought that struck her was how frugal her father had been. How few enjoyments in life he'd had.

"Mrs. Raven, are you all right?"

"Yes, just surprised."

"I'll get that water." He left in a rush, as if thankful to escape her presence.

Edwin had known the enormous sum she was worth and had never mentioned it. For the first time, Lianna began to wonder if Edwin was the same docile childhood friend she had known when she was young. He had always said that to survive at sea, one had to be tough. To become captain of his own vessel so swiftly would mean he had to be ruthless.

A glass of water was thrust into her hands. She drank, her thoughts formulating swiftly.

"If I become Captain Stafford's wife, this would become his property," she said.

"That's correct, but that should be no problem, as you have trusted him to take care of everything for you. And he has done so admirably well."

She stood up. "I'll be going home. Thank you, Mr. Drayton. I'd rather you kept this visit between the two of us."

"Of course, Mrs. Raven. Whatever you say."

Lianna stepped outside. As she walked to her carriage, she glanced at a man standing in the shadows near the door. He turned away, pulling his hat down over his eyes. She shivered, feeling suddenly cold from looking into impassive blue eyes. She climbed into her carriage and looked back to see the man mount a horse and turn in the opposite direction.

Why had Edwin kept the sum from her? Was it a simple oversight? Or was that the reason he wanted so desperately to wed her when he knew she didn't love him? At last she faced the question squarely. She looked down at her lap at the glittering diamond. She remembered Josh's visit, his kiss, his declaration of love. She loved him. Whatever he had done, in spite of all the differences between them, she loved him and she would not wed Edwin Stafford. Could Edwin have lied to her about Josh planning to wed Lady Wellman? Could he have lied to her about many things?

She slipped the diamond from her finger, dropping it into her reticule.

And when she did, her heart soared. She had to find Josh. How insurmountable were their differences?

The nagging awareness of the Marchenos' death reminded her that barriers still lay between them, but she would not marry Edwin this Friday, and she wanted Josh to know it.

She had known Edwin so long, yet so little. And in comparison, Josh so briefly, yet he had bound her heart forever.

Where did Josh live? How could she find him? A cold notion tore at her—how soon would he return to *El Feroz* and sail out of her life? She would find Josh and worry about the questions later. Right now, she had to tell Edwin.

Edwin paced the floor of his parlor. "The man has more lives than two cats!"

A burly man stood waiting, running his hands down his baggy woolen breeches. He shuffled his muddy boots. "He's surrounded by an army now. We can't get to him. He slips in and out of that house at night or goes out the roof and through the one next door."

"I want him out of my way." Edwin ground out the words. He looked up. "Fletcher Chance. Everywhere he goes, Chance is with him. Does Chance go out alone?"

"The yellow-haired man? Aye. He has a ship in dock—"

"Take Chance on my ship. Leave a trail so Raven will know where he is and where to follow."

"You want him to know?"

"That's right."

"We kill the yellow-haired—"

"No! Take him so Raven will follow. Just give me time. Tomorrow is all that I ask. Get them to sea. I don't give a damn what happens then." He smiled. "The money I offered for Raven is still there if you kill him." Edwin's pulse raced, and he felt like grinning. He would beat Joshua Raven yet! He went to a desk to withdraw a box. Opening it, he counted out golden guineas. Each coin clinked loudly in the silent room. Edwin dropped them into a bag and turned to hold it out.

"You keep Captain Raven away from London for twenty-four hours—until this time tomorrow—and I will pay you again as much."

"Damn! We'll do it!"

"You kill him—and I have to know that he is dead—and I'll triple the sum."

"Aye, sir! Aye, right away!"

The man pulled a black cap on his head, then paused. "The yellow-haired one?"

Edwin shrugged. "Do what you want. I have no interest in him."

"Aye, sir. He's strong and healthy. We can sell him in the islands."

"Groley, don't fail this time," Edwin said. "You might not ever sail again if you do."

"Aye, sir." The door closed quietly behind him.

Edwin walked to the window to gaze outside, clenching his jaw until it ached. Lianna had been to see Drayton. Now she would know her wealth. It might not matter. Women were woolen-headed on such matters. And tonight . . . He drew a deep breath, his muscles relaxing. After tonight, she would do exactly as he demanded. Too long, he had been patient, waiting, courting her. Tonight the waiting was over. And once they were married, he would be good to her. Tonight was something that had to be. He had tried to win her with patience. Now he would do so with force. And once she was Mrs. Edwin Stafford, there was little Josh Raven could do.

Lianna went upstairs and changed into a pale blue velvet dress. She secured pins in her hair on top of her head, then left for Edwin's.

He met her in the hall and led her into the parlor. She entered a room more elegant than her home. A fire burned warmly on the grate.

Edwin, dressed in a chocolate-brown coat and trousers, came forward to take her cold hands and turn them up to kiss. "How lovely you look!"

"Thank you. Edwin, I want to talk to you before we have dinner. It's urgent."

He smiled. "You sound concerned. Wait while I tell Morgan to hold dinner."

Edwin left and she went to stand in front of the fire. She

looked at the gold velvet chairs, the gilt furniture. Edwin had a ship, he had sold his cargo well. Had she misjudged him? Even if she had, it didn't matter. Never again would she consider anyone except Josh Raven.

She dreaded the next hour, but Edwin had to be told, his ring returned, and she was determined to see it through tonight.

Edwin entered the room and closed the doors, shutting them into an intimacy she didn't welcome. The heavy gold draperies were drawn, the oil lamps burned low. She lifted her chin. Edwin smiled and turned to lock the door.

The first inkling of alarm rose within her. She ignored it because her concentration was on the task ahead.

"So, you went to see Drayton today?"

Shocked that he knew, she nodded, then remembered the man who had watched her leave the solicitor's office.

"Edwin, why didn't you tell me the amount of my inheritance?"

He shrugged, pocketing the key to the door as he came to her. "You were ill—you trusted me with everything. It's all there, Lianna. I didn't rob you of a farthing."

"I'm sorry." She flushed, embarrassed at his stinging comment. "I was just shocked to learn the sum. I was surprised that you hadn't mentioned it once, but I know it's all there."

His mouth curved in a sardonic smile, and he took her hands in his. Her fists were doubled, holding the ring. His brows arched as she turned her hands up. She opened her fist, revealing his ring.

"Edwin," she said firmly, "I have to return your ring. I can't marry you."

He smiled. Lianna stared at him in shock as he looked at her with satisfaction.

"No, Lianna, you won't return it," he said softly.

35

Josh went down the hall and stopped in the open door of Fletcher's room.

Fletcher pulled on sea boots and stood up. "I'm going to the *Challenge*. I'll be back in an hour."

"Good. Tonight I want to see Lianna—unless Stafford is with her. If he is, I'll wait."

"Josh, every time I see my ship . . ." Fletcher's voice trailed off and he swallowed hard.

"I'm glad you like it. You've earned it, Fletch."

"No, I—"

"You should have shared in everything. Our father . . ."

"You've been so damned generous."

"Off with you now, and get back here on time."

"Aye, that I will."

Josh turned away, thankful Fletcher had his own ship. It gave him great pleasure to spend money on Fletcher, to give him a ship and a stipend for life. Josh knew that Fletcher would sail as soon as Josh had wed Lianna and was no longer in danger from Stafford. Josh sat down at his desk to look at papers he needed to return to Hiram Markham.

He pulled off his shirt and summoned his valet to ready a tub.

While Josh bathed, he thought of Lianna's blue eyes as she had watched him with Phillip. His son! What a marvel the baby was! Josh laughed aloud. He couldn't wait to hold him again. And he couldn't wait to hold Lianna. She didn't love Edwin Stafford. Whatever held her back, it wasn't love for Stafford.

Suddenly he tossed aside the washcloth and stood up, splashing water over the sides of the tub. He reached for a towel. He wouldn't wait until late tonight to see her! He would summon Fletcher and go now.

"Pritchard!" he shouted to his servant. "Have my horse saddled immediately!" He would dress, take two of the men, and ride to the quay to get Fletcher.

Within half an hour, Josh, Simms, and Drake approached the tall masts of the *Challenge*, Fletcher's new frigate. Dressed in black boots, trousers, and coat, with a snowy white shirt, Josh rode eagerly along the quay. Torches burned along the dock, lighting it, making it easy to see men moving on the ship. His gaze swept the area, looking for the frigate he had purchased for Fletcher. His brows drew together as he saw it ready to sail, the gangplank being raised.

"What the devil! They're sailing!"

Without waiting for the others, Josh urged his horse forward and dashed to the edge of the dock to shout to a sailor in the waist. "I want to speak to Captain Chance."

"They've taken Captain Chance!"

"Who?" Raven shouted, muttering, "What in blue blazes . . ." A cold knot of fear formed in the pit of his stomach.

The sailor, a man who had served with Josh, motioned with a wave of his hand as he yelled, "Two men came on board and asked to see the captain. He climbed into a carriage with them, and the next thing, I saw them carry him aboard their ship. We'll go after him."

Josh peeled off his coat as Simms caught up. "Toss a rope. I'll go with you."

"What's happening?" Simms asked.

"They've taken Fletcher." He flung down his coat while instructions were yelled aboard ship. "Simms, watch Lianna's house. Stafford's done this to keep me away from her."

"Aye, sir."

"If you can talk to her, tell her someone has taken Fletcher."

A rope was tossed, uncoiling in an arc while Simms swore. Josh cut across his words sharply. "Here, you and Drake hold this rope while I get aboard the ship."

"Aye."

He turned to the stocky sailor. "Simms, don't let her wed Stafford, if you have to draw a sword to stop them!"

"Aye, sir. I'll do my best."

Drake and Simms held the rope tautly, while Josh wrapped his hands and feet around it.

"Hurry, sir. We can't hold long because the ship is moving."

"Aye. I'll swim for it if necessary." Hand over hand, Josh scrambled quickly along the rope, up toward the side of the ship. His arms began to ache from the pull; in seconds he felt the rope slacken and knew Simms and Drake could no longer hold it.

It fell free and he put out his feet as he swung to the side of the ship, then pulled himself up the rope. Hands reached down to help him on board.

"Thank God you're here," the first mate said. "The command is yours. You can still see the sails as it leaves the harbor," Brompton added.

"The name of the ship?"

"The *Eagle*, sir."

"Where's the damned ship?"

"There, see? We can catch them."

Josh saw the white sails in the distance, and rage made him shake. "Aye, we will catch them. Get this under way."

"Aye, sir!"

Josh cursed in a steady stream of words that made a sailor nearby look at him sharply, then move away. Whatever trick Edwin Stafford was up to now would fail! This time, Josh would not be wrecked on a stormy coast. And if the man dared to harm Fletcher, Josh would get revenge! He saw Drake and Simms riding away. Angrily he strode down the deck and shouted orders to the helmsman.

36

Edwin slipped his arms around Lianna's waist and pulled her to him.

"Edwin, don't," she said, feeling a wariness grow. She wriggled free and handed him the diamond ring. "I'm sorry."

He dropped it into his pocket and smiled. "And tomorrow, how compromised will you be when you've spent the night here with only me? The servants are gone."

His gray eyes glittered with triumph, and his voice held a harsh note beneath the calm. She backed away a step, glancing at the locked doors. "Don't do something foolish. You can't gain anything by it."

"Isn't it intriguing? He took you by force and later wanted to wed. I wanted to wed—and later took you by force."

"No, he didn't take me by force, and I never said as much." She backed up another step, realizing how alone they were, how helpless she would be against his strength. "For so long, I thought you were the one person who loved me . . ."

He shrugged out of his coat and placed it over a chair. "As a boy, I did. What I said to you on the dock at Portsmouth, I meant. You were my childhood friend—and I was a stableboy, ignorant, young. We were both children." His voice dropped. "I told you that you were everything I had ever dreamed of—your home, your possessions, you."

For a moment her rising fear was buffered by sadness. "You envied what I had? What happened, Edwin? What made you so hard?"

His mouth curled in a crooked smile, and his voice was cynical. "Poverty, watching you sail away while I could do nothing." He pulled his shirt free of his trousers, and her panic returned. "You were angry with Josh Raven, Lianna, for murdering his archenemy, the Count of Marcheno, yet on the high seas life is cheap, and only the strong and ruthless survive. How did you think I could have become captain and owner of my own ship so quickly?"

"You said your ship was wrecked and there were few survivors." She backed around the sofa, putting it between her and Edwin. He dropped his shirt, revealing a chest fully as broad as Josh's, rippling with muscles, a strength she would be defenseless against.

"There were few survivors—and I eliminated the captain and another crewman. In a storm it's easy to get washed overboard."

"Edwin, I don't know you at all," she whispered, appalled by his confession.

"No one can be sure about another except himself," he snapped. "Who can be certain of anyone else on this earth?" His voice changed, dropping to a coaxing tone. "There's no hope if you try to run or fight me. We're here alone, you can't escape. You can't match my strength."

"Don't, for your sake as well as mine!"

"Save your pity. I'll make you mine—as I should have on board ship."

"Edwin, all those years . . . as children we were friends, but now you are so cruel," she said, staring at him in shock.

"There's no reward for kindness, Lianna, and you now have a great fortune. We were friends, and when you get over your pain and anger, we will be again. I know you as well as I know myself. I'll please you once we are wed."

"I won't marry you. Edwin, you have changed so much . . ."

"The first time I slit a man's throat, I was sick to death myself. The second time, I could stand it. The thir—"

"Edwin!"

"Life at sea is violent. Your precious Joshua is no fainthearted man. He's as ruthless as they come. I'll give you a chance, Lianna. I don't want to hurt you unnecessarily. Go with me right now to a priest. We can be wed, and you'll save yourself pain."

"No, I won't marry you."

"We'll see, Lianna. I know you value your life because of Phillip." He came closer and she moved away warily, wanting to look for a weapon, yet scared to take her eyes from him. His bulging manhood proclaimed his desire and he moved with ease that told how sure he was of his conquest.

"I'll hate you forever."

"I don't give a damn. If you don't acquiesce, I will make it so painful and degrading that you'll do whatever I ask," he said flatly.

"Josh will kill you."

"I'd welcome a battle with him. The last fight was on his ship, surrounded by his men."

"And did they aid him in his fight?" She sneered, knowing full well the captain would be left to fight his own battle if possible.

Edwin's face flushed. "I was new to the sea and hadn't learned to use a sword properly. I have now, and I would like another chance at him."

"When did you learn the size of Father's estate?"

"When I returned to London to outfit my ship and sell my cargo."

"So that's why you came to find me."

"Yes. It wasn't true love, as I said. Women are in every port, and so far, Lianna, you're too cold to heat a man's blood properly."

"Then let me go!"

"No. I've waited and come this close to fortune. And now, with Phillip standing to inherit—as his guardian, I'll have wealth beyond my wildest dreams. I've already spoken for a new ship. By dawn, Lianna, you'll consent to wed."

"No! Edwin, don't!" She looked around frantically for a weapon, saw the poker, and ran toward the hearth.

He barely made a sound as he sprang over the sofa, landed lightly on his feet, and grabbed her, spinning her around into his arms. Edwin crushed her in his arms, his mouth came down savagely on hers, kissing her, bruising her lips until they bled. He released her so suddenly she staggered backward.

"Take off that dress, Lianna, or I'll rip it off."

"Edwin, I feel so confused . . . Perhaps . . . Kiss me first," she breathed softly, and held out her arms.

She saw the flare of surprise in his expression; then he growled, "So, you like it rough, eh?" He laughed. "And all this time I thought I had to be so cautious. Come here, wench."

Lianna smiled and walked to him, throwing her arms around his neck.

She stood on tiptoe to kiss Edwin. His hand yanked the pins from her hair and it tumbled down as she ran her fingers over his chest, raking her nails across his flesh while she rained kisses on him. His fingers fumbled at the buttons of her dress and she felt it fall from her shoulders. While his fingers roamed freely over her full breasts, she ground her hips against his and trailed her hand over his buttocks while she kissed him passionately.

He groaned softly. "What a tigress you are! If I had known!"

Lianna twisted closer against him, reaching back with one hand, her fingers closing around the poker. If she missed, if Edwin stopped her, his fury would know no bounds. And in a few minutes all her chances for freedom would be gone.

Suddenly, with all the strength she had, she broke free and swung the poker, locking both hands around it as it came down.

Edwin's eyes flew open. "Damn, Li—"

The poker crashed down on his skull with a sickening thud as he lunged for her, his hands locking on her waist, sending them both crashing to the floor.

He fell on her, pinning her down, and her heart pounded in fear. He lay, a deadweight on top of her, blood pouring from the wound in his head.

Lianna struggled to push him aside, pulling her dress up over her shoulders. She yanked on his coat, anything to cover her. Frantically she searched the pockets for the key, then decided Edwin might have lied. There might be servants waiting in the hall.

Swiftly she extinguished the lamps, thrust aside the drapes, and unfastened the locks on a window to open the casement. She dropped outside and ran for her life.

When she reached home, she slipped in through the back gate. She knocked on the door, hearing the lock turn. It swung open and a maid peered out.

"Let me in, Marie."

The maid gasped. "Mercy! Mrs. Raven!"

Lianna stepped inside, her pounding heart beginning to return to normal.

"Thank goodness I'm home. Is Phillip all right?"

"Phillip's fine. But you?" Her round eyes were filled with fear and her jaw hung open as she stared at Lianna.

"I'm all right now. Ready a hot tub, please. I want nothing more than to bathe. And tell Upton to refuse entrance to Captain Stafford. No one is to enter this house tonight with the exception of Mr. Brougher."

"Yes, ma'am," Marie said, and left to do as she was told.

Lianna went into the nursery to look at Phillip. Betsy lay asleep, snoring softly in her room with the door open between them. Lianna touched the sleeping baby to reassure herself that he was safe, then tiptoed out.

When she bathed, she scrubbed as if to wash away the distasteful memory of Edwin's touch. How much he had changed since childhood! Along with anger over the difficulties he had caused her was sadness over the discovery of the man he really was.

It was impossible to sleep and she left one small lamp burning while she lay staring into space, the swift-changing events swirling in her mind. Where was Josh and why hadn't he returned to see her? Had Edwin harmed him?

Looking down, she saw she had clenched the covers into knots. Slowly she released them and thought about the morning.

The next day, Lianna dressed, summoned Betsy to get Phillip ready, and shortly, over the protests of her closest servants, she was in a gig on a journey to Cathmoor Manor. She left strict instructions behind: Upton was to try to discover how badly she had injured Edwin. No one was to relate to Edwin Stafford her whereabouts.

She received instructions how to get to the manor from a curious apothecary in the village. He polished the glass counter while he peered at her through spectacles.

"Ma'am, a Mr. Brougher has taken over the property—to everyone's relief in these parts."

"Does Mr. Brougher stay there?"

"No, ma'am. Word has it he's going to build a new house. No one stays in the old house."

"How can I find Cathmoor?"

He craned his neck to look past her. "You're a lady alone? You and the baby?"

"Yes."

He leaned closer, smoothing his long black beard while he talked. "Don't go, ma'am. I don't know what prompted you to want to see Cathmoor Manor, but don't take the baby or yourself near it."

"You said no one lives in it."

His voice dropped to a whisper. "The old duke's ghost haunts it." The man's voice gave Lianna a chill, and she tightened her arms around Phillip. Determination outweighed all else, and she persisted, asking him, "You've seen the ghost?"

"Ma'am, did you know the duke?" He looked at Phillip and she was thankful Phillip lay sleeping and didn't have his wide green eyes, so like Josh's and the duke's, revealed.

"I've met him."

"Hmpf." He arched his eyebrows and looked at Phillip. "He was a mean one, a real devil. Killed off his wife—"

"You mean murder?"

"No, ma'am. Made her life such a hell, she just ran away. Left two sons that he was a tyrant to until they got old enough to run away."

The chill Lianna had felt before intensified in an aching hurt. Josh had told her how cruel his father had been; she had seen the scars on his back, but the flat, calm statement of the apothecary added to the picture of how terrible Josh's childhood had been.

"Had a bastard son and daughter by Drusilla Chance."

"There was a daughter?"

"The old duke ran her down with his own carriage. She got in the way. He just went right on. Tossed some coins out the window."

Lianna gasped without realizing it until he nodded. She thought of the duke holding Phillip and wondered if time had changed him, if he'd had regrets or guilt.

"Y'see? The duke had three women in the village—two of them mothers of his bastard children. One hanged herself. Another disappeared from the village one night. Never seen again. The mother of the boy lost her mind. Someone came and fetched him to a family in London, and someone pays a nurse to care for her. Sends her a pension, but she doesn't know anything. Don't go up there. No one will. Someone finally put a ball right through his black heart. They hauled the duke's body out of there and laid it to rest and left the house just as it was. You don't want to take a baby there."

"I'll just look at the outside, if you'll tell me how to find it."

"I think you'll regret it."

Lianna wondered if she would have to give up and go elsewhere for directions, but he continued, "Take this lane. You'll see one branching to the north. It has stone pillars, and the lane that goes to the house is overgrown with brambles. Doubt if you can get the carriage down it anyway."

"Thank you. Mr. Brougher doesn't stay around these parts?"

"No, ma'am. Heard he's a ship's captain and strong as an ox. Won't help if he meets a ghost, but he doesn't intend to live in the house, I'm sure."

"Thank you."

"You take care, ma'am. It's no place to go."

"I'll remember." She left, climbing into the small open carriage to take the reins. While she had been inside, the sky had become overcast with dark clouds. Thunder rumbled in the distance.

Betsy and Upton had been scandalized that she would take Phillip and go alone without a driver. They were afraid of Edwin's interference, afraid for her to travel alone. As if to seek reassurance from something harmless and normal, she glanced down at the picnic basket.

When the road became shadowed by spreading branches of trees and the only sound was her gig, she was tempted to turn around and go back to London, yet she felt she had to see where Josh had spent his childhood; maybe she would understand better his hardness. And something deep within her made her want to take Phillip. It was a link to his past too, even though he was too small to know.

Edwin bound by greed, Josh by hatred. She looked at Phillip, whose eyes were open now, and was fiercely determined he would have love, so much love. He stirred, opening his eyes, and she talked to him while she drove the gig.

She would have passed the lane, except for the stone pillars. The path was overgrown with weeds, but the bushes were low, and she urged the horse along it. Even though spring had come to England, beneath the overgrown branches it was dark and cool.

Shortly she glimpsed Cathmoor through the trees, the house gone to ruin. Birds flitted through a broken upstairs window. The front door swung on rusty hinges; the emptiness and silence were bleak and desolate. Once more, she almost turned the carriage toward London, but she felt compelled to see where Josh had lived.

Clutching Phillip tightly in her arms, she picked her way through the brambles to the front door. It creaked as she pushed it open and entered.

The house looked as if it had remained untouched since the duke had died. A rat scurried across the floor, disappearing beneath the great staircase that wound to the second floor. Along with statues, pots with long-dead plants lined the hall. She went into the salon and stood quietly. Beneath the wear of time was a bleakness. Her home had been sparsely furnished, with little beauty, but this held furniture that was large and dark, oppressive in appearance. She looked over the mantelpiece and gasped, then went closer.

A picture ran from the mantel to the high ceiling, and at first she had thought it was Josh; then she noticed the differences. She moved closer and looked at the duke at a young age; his face bore similarities to Josh and Fletcher, to green eyes and thick brown hair, to the prominent cheekbones of both sons.

Phillip stirred, and she held him tighter, holding her skirts up as she moved on. Rats scurried across the long banquet table in the dining hall. She could see where a pistol had been fired at the wall. Silver flagons were overturned on the table and dusty plates still rested there. The creak of the front door grated on her nerves and she wanted to go, but she had to see Josh's room. Reluctantly she clung to the banister and climbed the steps, carefully avoiding a spot where rotting wood left a hole.

At the head of the stairs she paused, trying to decide which door to open. Wind banged a shutter and she jumped. Stiffening her shoulders, she crossed the hall and entered a small bedroom. There was a narrow bed, a washstand, and nothing else. It was devoid of anything, and she wondered if it had been occupied. She remember Josh's answer when she had asked him about the lion's head on his belongings—and he had answered that he had owned nothing for so many years.

She tried another and found the same. A bed, a washstand, nothing more. She entered another room and knew she was in the duke's room.

A bed, canopied with heavy velvet that was brown with dust, stood at one end of the room. There were chairs and a fireplace. A woman's dress lay on the floor. She moved around the room, looking at the possessions: a snuffbox, a brace of pistols, a yellowed shirt on the floor, a pair of worn boots. She glanced at a corner of the room and froze.

A long rawhide whip rested against the wall, its leather darkened. She wondered how many lashings had been inflicted on Josh and Phillip. She turned, hurrying to look at other rooms, opening doors to find the same desolation, until she opened the door on a room where a woman's dresses were strewn about. The bed was canopied, and the room held chairs and a desk. The two barren rooms had to belong to Josh and Phillip. Her heart ached for Josh and she could finally imagine him as a child, growing up with such a father, becoming so hard that he couldn't love or recognize love when it came to him.

"Oh, Josh!" she cried softly, aching because of the terrible childhood he'd had.

Suddenly she had to get out and away. She started down the steps and stopped dead as she looked down at the foot of the stairs.

37

―――――•――••――•――――――

Josh stood below. Dressed in a leather riding coat, high brown boots, and brown trousers, he held out his arms.

Clutching Phillip, she descended the stairs. Green eyes held hers, their silent message unmistakable. She came down the last steps, walking into Josh's open arms. As he banded them around her, she closed her eyes. At last she was pressed to his heart, where she had longed to be.

He held her carefully, so he wouldn't crush Phillip. "Lianna," he said hoarsely.

"I had to see where you lived when you were a child."

"I love you more than my life, more than anything."

Tears burned her eyes. "I had to see where you grew up, what . . ."

"And so you did."

"I'm sorry."

"It's all past now, as is your childhood." He scooped her up and headed for the door. "Let's get out of here."

He swung her into the carriage. "I'll be right back."

"It's going to rain." Thunder rumbled loudly and Josh looked skyward. "A spring shower. I'll be only a minute."

He went inside. Lianna wondered if there was something he wanted to keep. Why would he return to Cathmoor now, after all this time?

He came out in long strides and tied his horse to the carriage before they left. She looked at his horse, lathered from a hard ride.

"Josh, your horse . . ."

"I came as swiftly as possible. Edwin Stafford had Fletcher taken aboard the *Eagle* yesterday."

"Oh, no! More of Edwin's treachery."

"Otherwise I would have seen you last night."

"Is Fletcher safe?"

"Aye." Josh laughed. "He slipped free in the night. We gave chase, and he jumped from their ship. We fished him from the water and raced for home. I went to your house as soon as I could." He looked down. "Phillip still sleeps. Our talk won't wake him?"

"He can sleep through a gale."

"My little sailor." Josh brushed the baby's cheek, then squeezed Lianna's shoulders.

"I'll show you where we'll live."

Her heart jumped at his words. It was settled in his mind and in hers, even though they hadn't talked it over. She rested her hand on his knee.

"I love you—and you already know it."

"But I want to hear you say it over and over forever. I knew when Upton told me you had driven to Cathmoor Manor. It would take love and courage to enter that ghastly place."

"Josh, did Edwin cause your wounds?"

"He has tried everything in his power to keep me from you."

She closed her eyes in pain. "I'm sorry, so sorry! I knew when I went with him, as soon as I was on his ship, I knew I had made a mistake. He asked me to come talk to him and then he gave me brandy with something in it that caused me to lose consciousness."

Josh turned in the seat to stare at her while he swore bitterly. "Fletcher said you left of your own free will."

"I'd intended to go only for a brief time."

"I tried to catch up with you."

"I saw the sails. Oh, Josh!"

A drop of rain struck her and Josh slowed the gig to pull off his coat. "Here, hold this over your head and above Phillip."

Josh glanced over his shoulder and she looked back,

then stiffened in shock. "Josh . . ." She watched a tongue of flame curl out of an open upper window.

"Aye, it's long past due. When the timbers burn, the stones will fall. That great roof will come tumbling down because the Horsham slabs of stone are heavy. I'll have this land cleared and give this plot away to a family wronged by my father."

His voice became rough. "It gives me great pleasure to spend my father's money on people he treated cruelly."

"I hope, as time goes by, I hear that tone in your voice less and less. Josh, your father came regularly to see Phillip."

"I can't believe it!" He stared at her, amazement in his eyes.

"He did. He was so proud of Phillip."

"So that's why he changed his will. I wondered what had brought it about."

"Maybe he began to regret some of the past."

"I doubt if he would have changed toward me."

"He said the two of you were too much alike." She watched him, soft locks of brown hair curling over his forehead, his face covered with healing cuts he'd suffered because of Edwin, and she ached to be in his arms again. She touched his knee, catching his fingers in hers.

He smiled at her. "Let's be gone from here. Ah!" Phillip stirred, and Josh reached down to scoop him into his arms. "Lianna, take the reins and let me have a word with my son."

They huddled together, Josh holding the coat with one hand, Lianna holding part of the coat with the other.

When they reached the road, she looked back to see a spiral of black smoke billowing upward. A light rain fell, but not sufficient to stop the roaring fire that sent flames dancing skyward.

"This is a large estate," Josh said. "I'm building a new house on the opposite end of the land from here, as far from this as possible."

"And my farm, Josh? What about it?"

"We'll do whatever you want." Holding Phillip, Josh took the reins, halting the carriage beneath a tall tree to wait until the rain stopped. He shifted Phillip and placed his arm around Lianna's shoulders.

"Lianna, there's a vicar down the road. This child needs a father, ma'am. Will you marry me?"

Her heart slammed against her ribs. She gazed into shining eyes filled with love and felt like laughing and crying and throwing her arms around him at once. "Yes!"

"Even if I'm a jackanapes pirate and a—"

"Josh Raven! Don't remind me what I said. I hoped you would forget."

"Never. I'm getting soaked. Let's go."

They were wed with Josh holding Phillip. When he reached for her finger, Lianna produced her gold wedding band. For an instant Josh looked startled, then slipped it on her finger. Next he reached into his pocket to withdraw a gold band set with a sparkling diamond, which he slipped on beside the plain band.

His free arm circled her waist and he leaned down to kiss her lightly, whispering, "Now you are mine, Lianna, truly and forever."

Outside, the rain had stopped, the sun peeping out from behind gray clouds, and a rainbow arched across the sky. She glanced to the west and saw no sign of smoke.

"Josh, it's beautiful out!"

"We'll go home." How marvelous the words sounded! Only one dark worry nagged. She thought of Josh's temper, his need for revenge—what would happen when she told him about Edwin? She couldn't bear more bloodshed.

In the carriage, Phillip cooed, patting chubby fingers on Josh's knee. "Look at his smile, Lianna! It's yours."

She laughed, dabbing at Phillip's chin. "I do hope I don't drool down my front. Josh, he's so sweet." Talk centered on Phillip as they rode home, and nothing was said about their future. By the time they had reached Lianna's front door, the sun had dipped below the horizon and the evening was chilly. Lianna gathered her skirts, but Josh's hand closed on her arm.

"Wait here, love." He jumped down, carrying Phillip in his arms. He went inside for a few moments, then returned to climb into the carriage.

As they started down the street, she scooted close beside him. "I had forgotten how arrogant you can be. Where are we going?"

"Home." The word sent a thrill coursing in her. She looked down at her plain blue woolen dress. The hem was dusty from the old manor.

"Josh, I should have changed. Look how dusty this dress is."

He laughed. "Lianna, your dress is of little interest!"

His words in a husky voice kindled flames that heated her. He slowed the carriage and handed the reins to a lackey, then jumped down and lifted Lianna out of the carriage to carry her inside his house.

She gazed at a house filled with plants, French cherrywood furniture covered in pale blue velvet. A butler took Josh's coat and she heard him turn to talk softly to the servant.

"Pritchard, this is Mrs. Raven." He lowered his voice. "You have tonight off, and will you inform the others the same?"

"Yes, your grace."

Lianna glanced at her husband, thinking about his title. Josh was a duke. It meant nothing. What was important was the love she felt. His cuts were healing, but he would always have scars. In spite of the wounds, he looked handsome enough to take her breath. She wanted to be in his arms, to kiss him.

It seemed like eternity before the butler left, Josh took her arm, and together they went upstairs to his large bedroom. Remembering the terrible empty room at Cathmoor, she gazed around at an enormous room with a fire burning in the fireplace, a large bed covered with a fluffy blue comforter, oil paintings on the walls, and a blue velvet chair.

"This is beautiful. You like blue."

"The color of your eyes."

"Oh, Josh!"

He closed the door behind them and his voice dropped to a husky rasp. "How long I've waited . . . Come here, love."

And all the things she had intended to talk over with

him, to ask him about and to tell him, went out of her mind. She was lost to smoldering eyes that set her afire. He crushed her to him and his mouth came down to kiss her hard, to discover again her sweetness while she returned the kiss hungrily.

"Lianna, I couldn't have survived the wreck if I hadn't been driven to get back to you . . ."

Dimly she heard his words; then they penetrated and she became fully aware of them. She pulled away a fraction.

"I thought I saw your ship go down. Josh, can we forget . . ."

He raised his eyelids, looked dazed from her kisses, then straightened and frowned. His voice became harsh. "That damnable Stafford tricked me. Like a fool, I followed him into the rocky shoreline and *El Feroz* was torn to shreds."

For the first time, the extent of Edwin's treachery dawned on her. "Josh, when did you arrive in England?"

"In early March."

"Oh, Josh!"

He frowned. "Why the shock, Lianna? That damnable Edwin has done something."

"It's over." She shook her head. "I thought I knew Edwin, but he has changed . . ."

"He grew into a man, Lianna. You knew him as a child. Are you the same?"

"No."

He smiled. "You have the same blue eyes, but inside, we've all changed." While he talked, his fingers rested on her collarbone and he toyed with the fastenings on her dress. The slightest touch was a burning caress, and her attention began to drift from his words. His voice became husky as he said, "Take your hair down, love."

She smiled into eyes darkening with passion.

"Thank you, Lianna, for changes you wrought in me."

It took seconds for his words to register in her mind. She blinked, focusing on him. "What changes?"

"I let the Marchenos go unharmed."

"Josh!" His hands steadied her, closing firmly on her

waist. She wrapped her arms around his neck, gazing at him in shock. "Thank heaven!"

He tilted her chin up, his gaze lowering to her mouth, making her lips tingle as he drew closer. His lips brushed fleetingly, but she felt as if something had slammed into her middle, taking all her breath. Her lips parted and she stood on tiptoe as he crushed her in his arms and kissed her passionately with all the hunger that had built up for so long.

Lianna returned it fully, her heart pounding in hammer-blows as her fingers trembled and eagerly tugged at his clothing. Josh shifted her, loosening buttons, then he raised his head to look at her as he pushed the dress off her shoulders.

"Josh, how I've dreamed about you! I consented to marry Edwin because—"

"Forget it. I know you love me, and I know how unscrupulous Stafford has been. Shh, no more . . ."

He slipped off her chemise and his gaze lowered, taking in the sight of her, making her tremble for his touch.

Lianna pushed away his clothing, gazing eagerly at his muscles and lean body. She ran her fingers across his chest, down over his flat stomach, and heard his swift intake of breath.

He scooped her into his arms to carry her to the bed, and placed her down carefully, then stood over her, look-ing down.

"You have filled my dreams and now you're here. I won't sail again. I'm here, Lianna, to stay."

She held out her arms, her heart beating wildly. "Come here, love."

He caught her hand, turning it to kiss her palm. His voice was as breathless as her own. "First, Lianna, let me show you how much I love you . . . how very much I love every inch of you." He moved to touch her foot, to stroke her ankle, to kiss her lightly, watching her all the while.

As his kisses moved higher with slow deliberation, she felt as if she was being consumed by flames. She couldn't lie still, but moved her hips, wound her fingers in his hair, stroked his shoulders, his strong neck. His tongue flicked hotly, seeking intimately, driving her to cry out for him until she sat up swiftly and pushed his shoulders to the bed, to turn above him. Her dark hair mingled with the short locks on his chest as she stroked and touched a body she had dreamed about countless nights.

Finally he moved over her, still watching her hungrily. Lianna's legs held him closer as he slowly filled her and waited, poised. "I love you," he whispered.

She gasped, raising her hips to his, impaled by his manhood, seeking and, as he moved, so swiftly finding the rising ecstasy that banished the world. Together they moved, thrust meeting thrust as they renewed their love. Josh's harsh cry mingled with Lianna's gasp. His release drove her to rapture, to her own release.

Josh lowered his weight, crushing her into the feather mattress as he clung to her and showered her with kisses, with murmurs of love.

Finally he turned on his side, pulling her close as he stroked her cheek and pushed damp tendrils of hair from her face while they continued whispering endearments to each other. They each had unspoken vows they longed to voice.

"Josh . . ." She paused, dreading to tell him, yet knowing she must explain. "Within a month after Phillip's birth, Edwin came one afternoon with news."

Josh shifted, propping his head on his hand.

"He said you were in London and refused to see me or Phillip, that you wanted nothing—"

"Damn the lying bastard!" He ground out the words, and a vein throbbed in his temple as his face darkened in a flush. "Lianna, I won't, but I could kill Edwin Stafford with joy."

"I think I might have," she whispered.

Josh's gaze returned to her. "I had something in mind a little stronger than a broken heart," he said dryly.

She touched a lock of brown hair that tumbled over his forehead. "So did I, Josh. I struck him over the head with a poker last night. When I left his house, he was lying on the floor in a pool of blood, unconscious, and I sent Charles—"

She stopped as Josh fell back on the bed with a whoop of laughter. He held his sides and rocked with glee.

She sat up, annoyed, yet feeling mirth bubble up in spite of her conscience. "It isn't a cause for laughter if your wife goes to prison for murder!"

"Lianna! Damn, I chose well! I hope you split his head in two! How I wish I could have peeked in the window."

"Joshua Raven! Stop that scandalous laughter!"

He sobered, firmed his lips, looked at her with his green eyes dancing like devils.

"Not another laugh from you. I didn't intend to slay him!"

Josh swallowed hard and closed his eyes.

"You'd better hold it in, your grace! Not one laugh more!"

He gazed at her solemnly, but she saw the corners of his mouth twitch. "So, while I tried to protect myself with an army of men, my sweet little wife downs the scoundrel with a poker!" His brows arched. "What forced you to take such action?"

"I told him I wouldn't marry him and he was determined that I would. He intended . . ." She blushed.

Josh's merriment faded instantly. He caught her chin. "Did he hurt you?" His gaze was searching.

"No!"

"Now I would like to find him and give him another blow."

"Yesterday after you left, I went to see my solicitor. I let Edwin handle all my affairs because I was too ill—"

Josh swore and pulled her to him. "I should have been with you, dammit!"

She returned his hug and sat up again, stroking his chest as she talked. "I went to see my solicitor. My family always lived in such a frugal manner. My father hated to spend a shilling." She turned a lock of his dark hair around her finger, continually having to touch him, as if to make sure he was truly there. "I knew my father owned two ships and our house. Edwin sold one cargo for a good sum. I inherited three hundred thousand pounds—and that, not me, is what Edwin wanted."

Josh touched her chin. "When did you stop loving him?" he asked huskily.

"I don't think I ever loved Edwin. When we parted in Portsmouth, I realized he cared. He was the first person to care for me, but he cared for my possessions really. I loved you long ago, but there were differences, and your anger . . ."

Josh's arms enveloped her and he pulled her down on top of him, crushing her tightly. His voice was rough as he stroked her head. "Neither of us had love. I didn't know how to recognize it when it came. I didn't know . . ."

"And I, Josh, didn't know how to give it—not until we were in the mountains. I saw that I had spent my life trying to get love—my father's, Edwin's, yours—when all I needed was to give it."

"You'll have it now," he said, his voice dropping to a rumble. "Lianna, how much love you shall have! All that's within my power to give."

Her throat burned as she clung to him until she felt his chest shake with laughter.

She sat up and looked at him. "You're thinking of poor Edwin again."

"_Poor_ Edwin—never poor. The man is a devil, but how I would have enjoyed the sight of you bashing the rascal with a poker!"

"I see I shall have to do something to make you forget Edwin!" She trailed her fingers across his stomach.

"Edwin falling to the floor from your blow . . ."

Her hand drifted to his thigh.

"Lianna."

She looked up.

"The next time, I'll be with you for the birth of our child."

A week later, they stood on the quay, Josh holding Phillip as they both waved. Sunlight made a golden halo of Fletcher's hair as he waved back from the deck of the _Challenge_.

Lianna linked her arm through Josh's and leaned close.

"How beautiful his ship is. And how thankful I am that you're not on it!"

Josh turned to her, his expression alight with love. "Sail away from you? Not ever." A twinkle developed. "Nor will I take you on another voyage—at least not soon."

"If I was a bad companion, it was your fault."

"I'll admit that you're right."

She laughed. "Well, perhaps not all your fault."

Phillip batted his hand against Josh's chest and they looked down. Josh stroked the baby's cheek. "I was frightened I'd come home and discover you had named him Edwin."

"Come home? You knew before—"

"You left something behind."

"The blanket Madryn gave me. I knew it was gone. You knew all that time . . ."

"Aye. It still makes me want to find Edwin and finish the job."

"Thank goodness he lived!"

"He's sailed from England. It proved too much of a disgrace to be laughed at for almost getting killed by an angry woman with a poker."

"No one knows that but the three of us."

Josh's eyes twinkled. "You might be surprised, Lianna, how news spreads in London."

"Josh Raven!" She blushed. "You spread that around . . ."

He laughed. "It was a sweet revenge, if a damned mild one! Ah, Lianna, how I love to see you blush."

She laughed. "That's a strange thing to enjoy."

"Your pink cheeks are pretty." He glanced at the frigate, moving fast now. His voice lowered. "Your blush is fetching, but what I like to see most of all is your blue eyes darken with love as they do when I kiss you."

She felt her cheeks grow warmer.

"Josh, someone will hear you."

"No one except you, but shall we go where there's sure to be no danger of being overheard, where I can kiss you and hold you?"

He swung her into his arms while she clutched Phillip tightly. "Josh, people will stare."

"Let's go home, where we can be alone," he said huskily. "We have a honeymoon to plan."

About the Author

Sara Orwig is a native Oklahoman who has had many novels published in more than a dozen languages. She is married to the man she met at Oklahoma State University and is the mother of three children. Except for a few unforgettable years as an English teacher, she has been writing full-time. An avid reader, Sara Orwig loves history, acrylic painting, swimming, and traveling with her husband.